The Escape Artist

Other Books by Judith Katz

Running Fiercely Toward A High Thin Sound

THE ESCAPE ARTIST

A NOVEL BY JUDITH KATZ

Firebrand
Books
Ithaca, New York

This is a work of fiction.

Parts of this book have appeared in earlier versions in the *Evergreen Chronicles,* the *Green Mountain Review,* and *Tasting Life Twice* (Avon).

Book and cover design by Nightwood

Printed in the United States on acid-free paper by McNaughton & Gunn

10 9 8 7 6 5 4 3 2 1

Library of Congress Cataloging-in-Publication Data

Katz, Judith, 1951—
    The escape artist : a novel / by Judith Katz.
        p.   cm.
    ISBN 1-56341-085-0 (acid-free paper). —ISBN 1-56341-084-2 (pbk. : acid-free paper)
        1. Jewish women—Argentina—Buenos Aires—Fiction. 2. Lesbians— Argentina—Buenos Aires—Fiction. I. Title.
    PS3561.A757E83   1997
    813'.54—dc21   97-2934
                                                            CIP

Acknowledgments

I WANT TO THANK my writing group, the Berthas—Barrie Jean Borich, Lynette D'Amico, Ellen Lansky, Susan Rothbaum, and Morgan GrayceWillow—as well as Frieda Gardner, Sarah Jacobus, Joanna Kadi, and Robin Schribman for their careful reading and generous feedback during the course of this adventure. Sima Rabinowitz helped with several unwieldy foreign phrases, and Linnea Stenson advised on several unwieldy magic tricks. Susan Denelsbeck, Mary François Rockcastle, and Lynette D'Amico offered beyond-the-call-of-duty technical and architectural advice as I built this tale into a novel. Janet Aalfs, Victoria A. Brownworth, Ann Follett, Deborah Keenan, Roseann Lloyd, and Emma Missouri, along with all listed above, have given consistent support, love, and cheerleading throughout this process. Elissa Raffa, with whom I shared a life and a home during five of the years I worked on this story, read it carefully and listened honestly.

Florence and Lester Katz, the Bush Foundation, the National Endowment for the Arts, and the Minnesota State Arts Board provided financial support during the writing of this book. The Cottages at Hedgebrook supplied shelter, solitude, community, and three meals a day for six essential weeks in the spring of 1995.

In 1994, the Asociación Mutual Israelita Argentina, which housed, among other things, the Buenos Aires YIVO archive—a repository of Jewish culture and history—was blown up by terrorists. I was fortunate to be able to use that now-disappeared archive to further my research on this book in 1992. I also did research at the YIVO archive in New York City and the Lesbian Herstory Archives in Brooklyn. In addition to the photos and articles I found

To the memory of my grandmothers,
Sarah Lizabitzky
and
Anna M. Katz,
Olehen ha shalom

and to my sweet friend, Esther Izbitzky,
may she rest, at last, in peace

...Show me what's under the counter,
Show me what's under your skin,
Show me the way to get out
And I'll show you the way to get in.

Muriel Rukeyser, *Houdini*

PART ONE

Transatlantic Wedding Trick
(1913)

I

SWEET HANKUS! I saw a magic act in Warsaw once. I was sixteen years old—it seems a long time ago. My best friend Tamar and I were searching the marketplace for my father, it was late, and I had a message for him from home. Well, by the time we got to his bookstall it was all closed up, tight as a drum, and we couldn't find him anywhere. The rest of the marketplace wasn't exactly dead. Other stalls were open, and there were still plenty of people milling about. Close by, a handful of women bargained with vendors for the last rotten fish of the day while half a dozen Russian soldiers in sharp creased uniforms stood around smoking cigarettes and laughing at absolutely nothing. The vendors kept arguing when we walked past, but the soldiers whistled. We giggled because they embarrassed us. When we didn't stop to admire their big guns, though, they spat at us: "Jews!"

Tamar's thin shoulders went up around her ears. Mine did too, but I couldn't resist the urge to turn around to those soldiers and stick out my tongue. One of them raised his hammy fist at us; the others held him back. In my heart of hearts I prayed that his comrades wouldn't let him strangle a young girl in broad daylight. Still, one never knew: he was, after all, a soldier, and we were, after all, in Warsaw. Suddenly, I became terrified. I grabbed Tamar's hand and we ran to join the small crowd that was gathered in the center of the square.

What they were watching, what Tamar and I watched too, was a man eating fire. He was remarkable, Hankus! In his satin vest and pantaloons he sucked in huge gulps of flame and then breathed them out again in a steady stream. But remarkable as that fire eater was, he was nothing compared to the magician who followed.

When he stepped forth and swirled about in his sorcerer's cape, when he spun in a circle with his tall silk hat, those stupid soldiers with their quick fists and bad tempers disappeared from my mind as quickly as they'd frozen my heart. For what a magician he was!

He snapped his long fingers and gold coins spilled out the tips; he shook a crimson scarf and it turned into roses. He pulled a rabbit from his top hat and a dove from his own gleeful mouth. Then he clapped his hands and a tall woman with brassy blonde hair in a skinny blue gown appeared. He bowed to her like a gentleman, lifted her up with one hand, and laid her into a splendidly painted wooden box.

Tamar and I stood with our mouths wide open while the magician proffered a snaggle-toothed saw and waved it in the air. We held our breath as he proceeded to saw the beautiful box and the woman inside it in half. The woman screamed as the saw went back and forth across what was by now her belly, but to me it sounded fake. Then the magician pulled the two brightly colored box halves apart and she screamed again. That time it sounded a little more real. He tickled the feet of her sliced-in-two bottom and the top part of her laughed. He kissed her laughing mouth and her split-off toes curled. Then he pushed the two halves of the crated woman together and spun them around. A minute later he opened the box with great flourish and up she stood, all put together exactly the right way. I never forgot that for the rest of my life. It's a lucky thing, too.

Tamar and I couldn't stop talking as we walked home. "How do you think she got back in one piece?" I burst out.

"It's a trick," answered Tamar flatly. She snapped her fingers over a *groszy* and tried to make it disappear.

"I know it's a trick, but could you do it?"

"The woman's part or the man's?" she asked, a wicked glint in her eye.

"The woman's part is harder," I said. "Think of it. You have to act like you're enjoying yourself even when you're cut off from your own head. All the man has to do is wave a wand around and say some silly words."

I could smell spring in the breeze that blew up from the Vistula. It was still a little chilly, but the trees were budding. I watched Tamar's red hair blow in that breeze; I also watched her lovely mouth. I wondered if I were to cut her in half whether that mouth would keep smiling mischievously, and if she screamed whether her scream would be anguished or false. Then I wondered what would happen if she were the magician and I were the one cut in two, and a little thrill went all the way through me.

"It can't be that hard," said Tamar. One last time she snapped her fingers. To our great satisfaction, the *groszy* was gone.

"Let's try it." My eyes flashed. "You be the woman."

"No, you," Tamar whispered, and she leaned over and kissed me right on the mouth in the middle of Grzybowski Street! "Catch me!" she shouted, and took off toward home.

It made my heart beat unbelievably hard to chase her, yet I chased her fast as I could. Her wondrous red hair blowing back in the breeze pulled me toward her, and the taste of her dazzling lips on my own. You have those same lips, Hankus. When I look at you now, when I saw you for the first time all those years ago, I thought of Tamar. Yes, I said to myself, Hankus Lubarsky has the same dangerous mouth as Tamar. She may be alive still, and maybe she isn't. Maybe that speedy kiss she gave me on Grzybowski Street was the last Tamar ever bestowed on a woman, maybe it was one of many. I never kept track of her after I left Warsaw. For the longest time after I was taken—until I met you—I thought only of myself. I couldn't imagine life in Warsaw after I was stolen from it. If I imagined such a life I was certain I would die of a broken heart.

But at that moment I didn't think about exile, although my fate had been sealed that same afternoon. I thought about soldiers and also magicians and Tamar's thick red hair and her lips on my own. I wanted her to kiss me again on the mouth as that magician had done his divided assistant. I wanted her to linger, though, to kiss me slowly and take all the time in the world. I wanted to catch her, take her up in my arms, and let her whisper love into my hungry ears.

When we got to our building I caught up with Tamar at last. "Abracadabra!" she shouted, and ran into her flat. I crept up the last flight to mine.

I heard my father's voice then, and another man's, laughing and chatting at the dining room table. I overheard them when, still flushed from my adventures, I came in the back door. "You know," the stranger said, his voice like honey, "my sister is a great fancier of books."

"I had a feeling from the first moment I saw you that you hailed from a family of quality," answered my father. "In the morning, after *shul,* come with me to my stall and I will show you all the rare books I have for sale. Perhaps you can bring something back for your sister—something Polish to remind her of home!" My father, who was a reluctant salesman at best, sounded so enthusiastic about showing this man his goods that I wondered if he'd been drinking.

The man laughed, though not warmly. "Oh, I'll find her something." His Yiddish was Warsaw, but rolled into it was something else I couldn't recognize, a different juiciness. I'd never heard an accent like that before.

"Who's talking to Papa?"

My mother looked up from the soup she was stirring. "Some foreigner he met in *shul* this morning. His name is Goldenberg. I sent you out looking for Papa an hour ago. Where have you been?"

"You found him yourself, so what does it matter?" I poked my head into the dining room. Back then, Goldenberg's sorry life hadn't caught up with him yet, and he was a handsome man. Even I, with my heart set only on Tamar, could see that. But right away something about him rubbed me wrong. "What's he doing here?"

"You're awfully fresh. Your father met him this morning at *shul,* and now they're having a cup of tea together, and in a minute, they're leaving for evening prayers."

Since my grandmother's death, my father had become the kind of man who went to synagogue morning and night. Always he used to go on the *Shabbes* and holidays, but now, with his dear mother suddenly in heaven, he became even more pious. He went whenever he could to say *kaddish.* I wanted to go with him, but it wasn't allowed.

I craned my neck to see again into the other room. My mother poked me on the shoulder, handed me an onion and a kitchen knife, and said, "You'll get to talk to him yourself tomorrow. He's coming for dinner."

I shivered.

"He's coming to meet *you*," continued my mother.

"But why?"

"Because he's rich and single and lonesome, Sofia. Enough is enough, now chop."

That night I dreamed I was in a circus act. I had my back to a beautiful fire-red wall with yellow flames painted around the edges; my hands were tied tight by my sides. My mother appeared in her good black dress and a sparkling white apron. She wore a giant satin turban on her head with a pink ostrich feather stuck on the front. She looked absurd. She clapped her hands and out came my father, who wore a tuxedo and shiny gold cufflinks. His feet were bare. He carried an armload of kitchen knives that he passed to my mother, handles up; I wondered how he did it without cutting himself. Suddenly, there was a drumroll and a spotlight on me. My mother threw her first knife. It spun through the air and landed with a *thunk* just above my right shoulder. The second knife landed just above my left. Then she threw two at once. They whizzed toward me in slow motion, it seemed, one to the side of each of my ears. My father blindfolded her, spun her around in a circle three times, and pointed her in my direction. "Hah!" shouted my mother as she threw the remaining knives at me all at once. I held my breath and my heart was in my mouth as the knives came down *thunk, thunk, thunk* all around me. Then my mother whipped off her blindfold and both parents bowed. I was stuck to the board. Nobody helped. My parents were carried aloft by the crowd.

I woke in a sweat, my poor heart pounded, my throat was tight and completely dry. I imagined Tamar in my small bed beside me with her head on my neck. I cried.

The next day after school I came directly home as my mother ordered, for our dinner guest was coming and there was much to do. I braided the dough that my mother mixed up for the *challah*. I baked the honey cake all on my own. I chopped carrots and onions for our thin chicken soup. I set the table with newly polished silver. Once the kitchen and dining room were ready, it was time to prepare myself. I put on the good navy blue dress my mother set out for me. It was one of those scratchy woolen affairs with a tight sailor collar we young girls were forced to wear at the time. I rolled on my one pair of black stockings and shoved my feet into the black shoes I wore only on the most special occasions. They pinched and I hated them, but what could I do? They were the best I had.

My mother pushed me down onto a hard wooden chair; she dragged a brush through my hair one hundred times and tied it back with a blue bow. She took a cake of rouge from her bureau drawer and rubbed her thumb in it, then she roughly brushed that thumb across my cheeks and over my lips. She shook her head. "No matter how hard I try, I'll never make you look a lady. Go down and see if Tamar can help."

I trudged down the steps one at a time to Tamar's flat. I was embarrassed for her to see me with lipstick; I felt like a clown and Tamar looked perfect just plain. I found her with her sister at the kitchen table slicing beets and carrots. Her mother was in the other room polishing the candlesticks. "You look nice," Tamar said. I couldn't tell what she was thinking behind her eyes. "Did they dress you up like that to meet your father's new friend?"

I nodded my head sadly.

"It must be serious, to put all that stuff on your face."

"Watch out," her sister took her beet-red fingers and pointed them at Tamar, "or I'll do it to you."

"Just try it." Tamar picked up her own beet and aimed it at her sister.

I wanted to take one of the thick slices and make Tamar's lips red as mine. Instead I asked, "What do you mean, *serious?*"

"He might want to marry you." She took a big bite from her carrot. "That's what they want sometimes when they go with your father to *shul*."

"I'd die first."

"Tell your parents no," she advised. Then she swallowed her carrot and kissed me good-bye.

Back in those days, Tutsik Goldenberg didn't look like a weasel; he looked like a man. But a weasel he was and a slick one, too. I told you before he was handsome enough, but that wasn't the first thing anyone noticed. First people noticed how clean he was, how he shimmered, they thought, from cleanliness. For his modern western clothes were spotless, his white teeth sparkled, and underneath his fingernails there was never a speck of dirt. Tutsik Goldenberg's shoes glistened; they carried, it seemed, none of the dust that burdened other men. And always, in those bygone days, a gleaming white handkerchief sat in Tutsik Goldenberg's breast pocket, plumped and ready to dab a tearful eye—his or anyone else's.

Yes, everyone thought he glittered only from cleanliness until they realized that Tutsik Goldenberg glittered also from the diamonds he wore: on the stickpin that held his silk tie in place, the dazzling cufflinks that stuck out from his pressed linen jacket, the fat gold rings that jumped from the pinkies of both his well-manicured hands.

How could it be, some wondered, that a man so clean and not at all hard to look at could seem so oily on closer view? Surely it wasn't the pomade he used only lightly to work his mass of curly hair into place, or the tiny bit of imported cologne he sprayed about himself like rich gentile men sometimes did. And it certainly wasn't the well-blocked derby that he wore at a slight angle tilting to the left, nor the slim short cigars he smoked—but rarely, at least in Europe, in the company of ladies.

Back then, Tutsik Goldenberg always comported himself like a gentleman. No, it wasn't until he opened his mouth that a clever person realized what an eel Tutsik Goldenberg was. Yes, so slippery was he that some people sensed trouble vaguely and patted their wallets unconsciously just after Tutsik Goldenberg left the room. People felt a certain chill, an iciness in the presence of Tutsik Goldenberg that caused them to pull their scarves tightly about them, for almost always a shudder went down the spine as Tutsik Goldenberg passed by.

But it wasn't wallets Tutsik Goldenberg stole; if a man dropped a *gulden* or a few *kopecks* fell from a pocket, Tutsik Goldenberg was the first to pick them up and hand them back. If he won at craps, it was usually on the up and up. He didn't cheat that way, although with pinochle it was another matter entirely. Tutsik Goldenberg *did* carry a knife and a set of brass knuckles, although he rarely showed these among refined people; he paid all debts incurred in Europe on time and with interest.

No, by all outward appearances, Tutsik Goldenberg was an honest man. But a person had a feeling after eating *Shabbes* dinner in his company, or smoking one of his fancy cigars, that Tutsik Goldenberg was up to no good. Yet no one in any of the tiny synagogues where he appeared on *Shabbes* eve during the European spring months could put a finger on it. And, of course, after he left a table and the father of the house felt for his wallet, and the wallet was still there—often fatter than before—everyone thought they were imagining things. For Tutsik Goldenberg was a rich young man, and he had come to pray in their humble synagogue and eat at their meager table on Friday night. Best of all, even on the *Shabbes,* he had offered the father of the house the sweetest deal.

Jewish men in the cities, big and small, of Poland and Russia, Hungary and Lithuania, fell over themselves to be the first to invite Tutsik Goldenberg home for *Shabbes* dinner. He had his pick of perfectly cooked chickens and *cholent* potatoes. More importantly, he had his pick of any of their daughters. For Tutsik Goldenberg was a modern Jew who looked to all like a high-class salesman. One thing bothered the fathers, though: if he was a salesman, where were his cases?

"Ah," Goldenberg would say, but only to the fathers, as he sat at the tables well laid by their silent wives, "I'm in the export business."

The fathers scratched their beards and nodded approval. They signaled the daughters to bring forth the good brandy. "And what do you export?" the fathers always asked, pouring the brandy themselves for their fancy stranger.

"Diamonds and other fine jewels," Goldenberg told them in earnest.

"If you are an exporter of diamonds and other fine jewels, *Reb* Goldenberg, pardon my ignorance, but what could possibly bring you to our little *shul?* We are honest working men, but practically paupers. If you knew what this chicken cost me—"

"Ah," Goldenberg would say, looking sadly into the eyes of that father, "I'm a rich man but I am a lonely man and thirty years old. I am looking in your little *shul* for a fine and wholesome wife to make the best part of my life complete."

"A *Jewish* wife?" the father of the house asked, just to be certain, for Goldenberg as a modern Jew wore no beard and might wish not to be encumbered by the weight of a woman's piety.

"A Jewish wife," the still boyish Goldenberg concurred. "I have tried all the usual routes, the matchmakers and *shadchens,* I've met rich daughters from here to Chernigov (or Kovno or Plock), but all anyone is interested in is filling their own pockets. Ah, my friend, my host, if you only knew how my heart aches for a good Jewish wife...."

And with that the father's eyes always twinkled and his mind worked fast. "Have you met my Rachel? My Merl? My little Sofia?" the father asked, then added quickly, "Of course, her dowry is quite small—"

To which Tutsik Goldenberg, each and every time, lifted his bejeweled hand and stopped the father right there. "A dowry? My good man, I have told you already, money means nothing to me. But can your Racheleh cook? Does Merl sew? Will Sofia follow the Jewish laws to make me a happy man, in the kitchen and in the bedroom? For I have been lonely, lo, these many years, and what I truly desire is the companionship of a Jewish daughter, righteous and pure."

"This daughter is a saint among women," the father always quickly confirmed. "The *challah* you ate tonight, this is a *challah* that she braided into a bird with her own dainty hands—my wife only stood and watched. The chicken soup that passed your lips? Her own creation. And as to the *challah* cover, the tablecloth, the napkin on your lap, my daughter finished these with her own dainty hands. Look, *Reb* Goldenberg, look here *Pan* Salesman, Mr. Broker in diamonds and other fine jewels—my daughter is a feast among women. You have only to gaze upon her luscious cherry of a mouth, her delicious green eyes, the rise of her delectable breasts to see what a fine wife she will be."

True enough, no matter how exaggerated a father's claims to his daughter's household abilities, that young woman of the house where Tutsik Goldenberg was treated like an honored *Shabbes* guest was always *zaftig,* flirtatious, and well under twenty. By the time brandy glasses were emptied and the dinner dishes cleared, wedding arrangements were practically made.

And this was no accident. For before Tutsik Goldenberg made his way to the Western Wall of any synagogue in Slutsk, Brody, Tarnopol, or Minsk, before he took a seat at the table of a down-and-out but upright citizen of Lodz or Lublin, Belz or Warsaw, Tutsik Goldenberg had done his homework.

He came into a town on Monday and got himself a room in a respectable inn as far from where the Jews lived as possible. He spent the next three days quietly shopping and watching the goods. He sat in kosher bakeries and bars with a Yiddish newspaper in front of his face as the customers came and went, so busy with their own daily business they hardly noticed him. He listened to the people talk about themselves and their neighbors; when he wanted to know more about a particular young woman, he sprung for a sandwich or a glass of schnapps. By Thursday afternoon he understood the lay of the land. He figured out what tasty dish belonged on which table, so to speak, so that by Friday night, when he presented himself to the *shammes* for a synagogue seat, he knew exactly which generous father he was about to take advantage of.

Dinner over, marriage contract all but signed, Tutsik Goldenberg always ended his first evening with his would-be in-laws the same way. "Imagine it, *Reb* Ansky, *Reb* Mordkhe, (in my case) *Reb* Teitelbaum. Here I have traveled all this way, for how many months, in search of just the woman who would make me happy. Me, a man who does business in South America, Constantinople, and all of Europe. And where do I find my love and my heart? Just here, in Chudnov, in Praga, in Kotsk, only miles from my little hometown. Ah, God has surely blessed me tonight." And even the most *frum* father of the most beloved bride-to-be—the soon-to-be *shver* of Tutsik Goldenberg, importer/exporter of diamonds and other fine jewels— was sorely tempted to break the Sabbath law and smoke one of his prospective *aidim*'s fine cigars. For he was soon to be a happy man, a rich man—by association and because of the bride price Tutsik Goldenberg had generously offered to pay. No dowry necessary. No, none at all! For hadn't Tutsik Goldenberg been searching his life long for a perfect wife, and hadn't he found her, his own beloved, here at this very table, in this very home?

This was the web he caught me in, that Tutsik Goldenberg, with his clean fingernails and his diamond-covered hands. Yes, I was daughter at the table on that particular April night, just one week before *Pesach*. It was my *challah* cover that the father of the house was showing off to his honored guest at this *Shabbes* dinner; my hair brushed one hundred strokes; my meager chicken cooked to a turn; the rise of my lovely bosom and painted red lips. The glittering Goldenberg never once looked at me or my mother. His entire dinner was spent staring straight into my father's eyes, joking with him, telling him stories of his life in faraway Argentina (for that is where we soon learned he came from), as if we, the women of the house, were invisible and his food and drink, the same food and drink my father was bragging about, appeared by magic.

He made me terribly uncomfortable. While I was used to being brushed aside by my father from time to time, in light of his more spiritual pursuits, and while my mother was often abrupt with me and tended to order me about, I was not at all used to being looked past in the way that Tutsik Goldenberg was looking past me now. In the kitchen, where we piled plates with chicken and potatoes, my mother whispered, "What a wonderful, good-looking young man—"

"Young?" I was incredulous. "He's thirty years old!"

"That's not very old at all." My mother handed me a sprig of parsley to put on the plates. "Play your cards right and he'll make us all happy."

I turned my nose up. What I wanted to do was spit into Tutsik Goldenberg's food. "He's an old man," I muttered, "a cold fish." I borrowed a phrase of Tamar's. To strengthen my case I pulled my lips up and down like a perch.

My mother grabbed my rouged face roughly in one hand and held her serving spoon up above me like a club. "Cold fish or not, this *young* man is offering us the chance of a lifetime. Go give him his dinner, and when you do, smile."

It didn't seem to bother her at all that my father was so obviously fascinated with Tutsik Goldenberg, he looked not only past me but past my mother as well, and only into our dinner guest's lively eyes.

After that interminable, tasteless meal, the men retreated to my father's study. I was relieved and was just about to slip out the door and down to Tamar's flat when my father called my name. "*Sofia*," he shouted, which was very unlike him, "come bring *Reb* Goldenberg some brandy!"

I pretended I didn't hear him and continued to make for the door, but my mother tapped me on the shoulder and handed me the silver tray, "Go now," she said sternly.

"But he's detestable," I whispered.

"He's rich," she said firmly, "and very attractive." She straightened my bow and pinched my cheeks for color. "I'm telling you, smile when you look at him if you know what's good for us all."

I gripped the silver tray with both hands. My shoes pinched as I walked. The men were poring over a huge leather book, the collected works of Shakespeare translated to Yiddish. Tutsik Goldenberg was fingering the pages carefully as if they were cash. Oh, why didn't I pretend to trip and spill the brandy everywhere?

"Ah, Sofia, sweet daughter. Set the brandy down," my father told me when he looked up.

"Now turn around." It was Tutsik Goldenberg who said this to me, sneering, "And show me your stuff."

I first looked at my father, then at my mother. She stood behind me with a plate full of honey cake. They looked at each other helplessly. My father turned to Goldenberg.

"I'm not sure, *Reb* Goldenberg, we understand your meaning."

Tutsik Goldenberg pulled himself up and shut the Shakespeare with a little pat. He cleared his throat and adjusted his rings. "You'll pardon me, *Reb* Teitelbaum, but the night has made me merry. I've overstepped my bounds—I find your daughter so captivating. She intoxicates me and I become, you must forgive me, impertinent."

"Not at all," my mother said suddenly. "*Reb* Goldenberg meant this as a compliment," my mother told my father, "I'm certain."

For the first time all evening Goldenberg seemed to see my mother. He stood and took her hand, looked right into her eyes. "*Chavereth* Teitelbaum is not mistaken. It was a compliment from the heart of my giddiness." He looked sheepishly at my father. "*Reb* Teitelbaum will find it in his heart to forgive me this Sabbath eve?"

"Of course he will," chimed my mother.

Goldenberg dropped my mother's hand and put his arm around my father's shoulders. "*Reb* Teitelbaum, consider the *mitzvah*. Me, a lonely man, successful in business but with no one to share it, and suddenly, through the virtue of your generous hospitality, a miracle! No, *Reb* Teitelbaum, this is a a double *mitzvah*. It happened on *Shabbes*—God will remember your goodness, and I will remember your goodness, mark my words."

My father shrugged. Then he slapped himself on the cheek and smiled. "These modern times, I don't want to seem prudish, *Reb* Goldenberg, but you understand a father's concern—"

Tutsik Goldenberg put a repentant hand to his heart. "What is more sacred?" he said, almost sadly. "My apologies, *Reb* Teitelbaum, my heart." He caught my eye, and I don't know if my parents saw it, but I know for a fact he winked. It sent a shiver down my spine.

Then it was my father who spoke. "You know, *Reb* Goldenberg, we shouldn't be making such arrangements on a Friday night, but times being as they are..."

Tutsik Goldenberg looked at my father with profound disbelief. "*Reb* Teitelbaum, do my ears deceive me? In spite of my incredible rudeness you are willing still to grant me my only wish?"

My father shrugged and nodded his head.

"There *is* a God!," Goldenberg burst out, "a God of loving kindness! And *Chaver* Yakov Teitelbaum, his messenger is you!"

There was much back slapping and more drinking. Even my mother partook. Myself, I retreated to the dark of my parents' room and stared out the window. I could hear the men mumbling and laughing. Then my father roared my name. "Sofia! Sofia! *Reb* Goldenberg is leaving us for tonight. Come bid him good-bye."

I didn't budge. My father kept calling me. Then my mother appeared in the doorway. "Just because he was rude doesn't mean you have to be. Besides," she hissed, "he *apologized*. Now go to him and say good night and do it with respect."

I could not move. My mother pulled me by the arm and dragged me to the dining room.

Goldenberg was once again adjusting one of his diamond rings. My father was agitated, full of false cheer when I appeared. "Ah, here she is, *Reb* Goldenberg. Our blushing bride...Sofia, please, say good night to your fiancé. You're engaged to be married." Then he looked nervously at Tutsik Goldenberg, who looked up from his ring and smiled.

"What? Engaged to him? That's what this was all about from the start?" My mother slapped me then and there.

"Now it is I must apologize to you, *Reb* Goldenberg," my father practically bowed, "the shock of good news. My daughter is usually the most compliant of girls—"

Goldenberg got up from the table and, for the first time all evening, really looked at me, looked me up and down with a sly smile. He took the hand I held over my stinging cheek. "Don't think about it twice, *Reb* Teitelbaum. I like a girl with a little spirit. I am only surprised that a girl so lovely as your daughter has not been snatched up much sooner." Then he kissed my hand but looked straight at my father. A horrible shudder ran through me.

In his custom, Tutsik Goldenberg took his leave of our table and disappeared from us for several weeks. A note came to my father by messenger the very next day. Sudden business troubles had developed and he was leaving for Odessa on the first train after *Shabbes*. He hoped the enclosed money would make a start for my trousseau. He would pay the balance of the bride price at their next meeting, which he hoped would not be too far in the future, perhaps a week or two after *Pesach*. In the meantime, again many thanks for the fine dinner, how honored he felt to be a future member of the Teitelbaum family, so sorry he could not be there to say his thanks in person, with much respect, etc. etc., Tutsik Goldenberg.

I was greatly relieved that he was gone. Even as my mother began to sew my wedding dress and my father began to arrange with the rabbi, I hoped against hope that Tutsik Goldenberg would never return.

Tamar and I spent hours alternately laughing (imagine it—the idea that I should be married!) and weeping. For Argentina was on the completely other side of the world, further than New York and with upside-down seasons, so that when it was snowing on Tamar here in Warsaw it would be sunny and warm on me. "I want to get married someday," I said, "but Tamar, that man is a monster. You should see the way he looks at me!" And also, I thought, the way he does not.

"Maybe he won't come back," Tamar offered. "I've heard of that, they make all kinds of promises and then they never show up again."

"But he paid my father money. I saw it. And my mother has already started sewing a wedding dress."

"Well, then," Tamar shrugged, "there's not much we can do."

Of course Tutsik Goldenberg did come back, three *Shabbes* evenings later, on the arm of my father, the two of them slapping each other on the back like old drinking pals. "Bayla! Sofia! Our diamond seller is back, our son-in-law! Set another place at the table, our bridegroom has returned!"

My mother quickly sent me out to the dining room to greet them. "We'll have no repeat performance of the last time," she warned. "He's our honored guest and your husband-to-be."

"All you care about is the money," I muttered.

My mother raised her hand to me again, then put it down. "No, no, Sofia. What I care about is you."

I went out to greet my father and my so-called fiancé, even curtsied to him and, against all instincts, offered my hand. Tutsik Goldenberg kissed it briefly, a cold, sandpaper kiss, then stood back to examine me with his hands on his hips as if I were a piece of livestock. This time my father pretended he didn't notice. "Oh, she's sweeter than I remembered her. She'll do quite nicely. *Froy* Bayla," Goldenberg looked at my father though he'd addressed my mother, "I'm starving. What can you give this poor *lantsman* to eat?"

At dinner, Goldenberg referred to my parents as *shviger* and *shver* and to me as his future treasure, but not one word was said about an actual wedding. Finally, when my mother and I left the table for cake and brandy, my father meekly approached the issue. "*Reb* Goldenberg, dear—"

"*Shver* Teitelbaum?"

"The summer is fast approaching. I've announced our lovely Sofia's fortunate engagement to you, and now all of Warsaw wants to know—"

"Ah, the balance of the bride price. *Shver* Teitelbaum, I'll bring it myself first thing Sunday morning."

"Bride price, nothing, *Reb* Goldenberg. I may be a poor man, but I'm an excellent judge of character and I know you're good for the money. What I want to know, what the town wants to know is—"

"When's the wedding?" My mother put the cake plate down in front of Tutsik Goldenberg with a thud.

"Yes, well...the wedding." Tutsik Goldenberg adjusted his diamond cufflinks and looked blankly at my mother. He turned to my father and said, "*Reb* Teitelbaum, you are a scholar and a man of business. Out of nowhere, with an empty pocketbook, you provide for your family each *Shabbes* with a little chicken, a few potatoes, an onion, some salt—"

"Yes, well," my father began.

Goldenberg continued without hearing. "I am a man of business only. My studies are as scant as the food on this table. But as a man of commerce, I can turn a little chicken and some honey cake into fat geese and fabulous strudels. I can snap my fingers and bring gold and chocolate to your table, yes, even to this sad little table in the middle of Warsaw. On Sunday morning, *Reb* Goldenberg, you will be a rich man. But in order to make you rich, I must deprive you of a very great pleasure. As you know, three weeks ago I was called away to Odessa for a business emergency. That emergency now requires that I take myself back to the home office before winter settles in. The home office is in Buenos Aires, and winter there commences in June." Tutsik Goldenberg took my hand into his own. He held his face in my direction but his eyes settled on my mother. "I will pay you our agreed upon bride price on Sunday, but on Monday I must come and get our little Sofia and take her with me to Argentina."

"Without a wedding?" My mother's mouth hung open. "I won't hear of it!"

Tutsik Goldenberg let go of my hand and sat back in his seat. "*Froy* Teitelbaum, then you mean to tell me the arrangement is off?"

My father stood up and cleared his throat gently. "I'm certain, *Reb* Goldenberg, she means no such thing. But please understand her concern, which, as Sofia's father, is my concern as well. If you don't intend to marry our beloved daughter here in Warsaw, *Reb* Goldenberg, where do you intend to do it?"

"Why, on the ship, *Reb* Teitelbaum. There is a rabbi on the ship. It will be wedding and honeymoon all in one. My only regret is that you will not be there to give the bride away. And as for Sofia, she has quite a life ahead of her in Argentina. I have an apartment on Talcahuano Street that is the envy of the entire Jewish community. I will provide her with servants, pamper her with sweets. She will have little to do all day but lie about like a lady."

"Couldn't we arrange to have our rabbi perform the ceremony here, tomorrow evening?" My mother was frantic.

"I'm afraid that's impossible, *Froy* Teitelbaum. I have a thousand loose ends to tie up."

"And well you should," my father shook his head sadly, "well you should. A man who can turn honey cake into chocolate must certainly take care of his own business and make room for more."

"But to prove to you, my future *mechutonim*, that I am a man of my word, let me show you what I am forbidden to give our cherished Sofia on this Sabbath eve." With a flourish that rivaled my marketplace magician, Tutsik Goldenberg reached into his pocket and brought out a velvet box. He opened it, and even I was dazzled by the diamond ring within. "This is the first thing I will give your precious daughter as our ship sails away to our blessed life in the new world. Mark my word, *Shver* Teitelbaum, you won't be sorry. And as for our darling Sofia," he touched my cheek with an unyielding finger, "life as she knows it will never be the same."

2

EVERYTHING MOVED IN A HURRY NOW, for suddenly, after his long absence, I was destined to leave Warsaw with my horrible groom in only three days. True to his word, Tutsik Goldenberg delivered his cursed dowry money on Sunday, although he met my father in a Jewish tavern and they did their dealings there. My father came home that evening as he rarely did, with whiskey on his breath and glassy eyes. He looked sorrowfully at my mother and me as we sat sewing up the hem of my wedding dress, that dress neither one of them would see me wear. There were tears in my father's eyes as he flung his arms around me and held me so close I could hardly breathe. "Forgive me, *neshomeleh*, blood of my blood, soul of my soul." He dropped a handful of gold coins on the table before us. "It's for you, my sweetest darling." How sadly he whispered, "You must believe we do this all for you."

You may think, as I did at the time, that my parents sold me off from greed alone, but they did not. Both had lived in Warsaw all their lives. They knew by heart every tale of every *shtetl* that had been burned to the ground by drunk Cossacks and drunk Polish peasants. They had memorized all the rapes of all their cousins and cousins' daughters, and cousins' daughters' cousins in Chelm and Kielce and places between. They could sing, like folk songs, the burnings of synagogues and the Torahs within them in every small town up and down the Vistula, with special wailing for each beheading and disemboweling, for each defecation on holy ground. My parents were naive in the face of fast-talking young dandies like Tutsik Goldenberg, but in the ways of Polish life for Jews—no, absolutely not, they were no fools. To them, Tutsik Goldenberg was a miraculous ticket for their daughter's safe passage. I'd laugh about it now, Hankus, if it wasn't so sad.

We didn't know exactly what kind of clothes to pack for life in Argentina, and Goldenberg, when my mother had asked him, was vague. "You shouldn't worry, *Chavereth* Teitelbaum, about such small things as wardrobe. When she comes to my home on Talcahuano Street, as is my job, I will provide." And so we packed up a paltry trousseau—some new cotton underclothes and one of my mother's refurbished old dresses, thrown into a threadbare carpetbag. My mother carefully wrapped the wedding dress in brown paper and tied it in a cardboard box. I didn't know why I needed it, especially since I was to be married in the captain's quarters on a ship, not under a *chupeh* in a synagogue as my parents had wanted. But my mother, God bless her, insisted. "No Jewish girl should be married without the proper dress and veil! Swear to me, Sofia, that you will wear it on your wedding day, no matter what!"

I swore, but I was sorry I promised. On Yom Kippur nights even all these years after, God always knows just how sorry I am.

On the Monday evening I was to depart, Tamar and her mother and sister came to bid me good-bye. Tamar and I stood with our arms around each other. She drew her radiant hair back from her face and whispered, "You must write to me about all your adventures." Then she pulled away and said solemnly, "I forbid you to cry."

Goldenberg arrived at seven exactly in a rented *droshky* complete with a seedy-looking driver and a dappled horse who had seen better days. He patted my father heartily on the back. "Well, *Reb* Teitelbaum, we're almost *shver* and *aidim* now. It's nearly official!"

"Yes, *nearly* official," my mother piped in, "but not until the knot is tied in the eyes of God."

"Certainly not," answered Goldenberg, whose own eyes, I noticed, were wandering ever so slightly over Tamar, and not just her fiery hair, either. He caught himself when I did and looked in my mother's direction, yet past her. "Mark my words, lovely *Chavereth* Teitelbaum, not a hair on this innocent girl's head will be touched until we have become as one in the captain's quarters."

"I certainly hope that's the case, *Reb* Goldenberg."

My father was obviously embarrassed. He cleared his throat and said softly, "Bayla, *Reb* Goldenberg has proved true to his word in all cases until now. I see no reason to mistrust him."

My mother shook her head and looked for sympathy from Tamar's mother, who sadly shrugged. Tamar and her sister rolled their eyes.

"*Froy* Teitelbaum, what can I do to convince you that the virtue of your sweetest Sofia is safe? Does it help to know that I firmly believe it best to taste the fruit when it is ready to be eaten and not one moment before?" Goldenberg pinched my mother on the cheek and winked. My mother blushed and looked away. "Besides," he continued, "we'll be joined on the train by my lovely Aunt Sara, who has been so kind as to act as our chaperone all the way to Hamburg." With that he glanced at his pocket watch. "And the train, as you know, waits for no one." He handed my carpetbag and the cardboard box in which my dress was packed to the driver, who Goldenberg called Dov Hirsh. "Come along, little flower, it's time we must go."

"Not so fast," said my mother, and I thought that finally she had come to her senses and I was to be saved. Instead, she held out a small bundle wrapped in blue silk. "If I am to be deprived of the pleasure of seeing you under the *chupeh,* at least allow me to give you these now."

I took the gift and pulled back the silk wrapping. There were my grandmother's candlesticks. "Thank you," I uttered. And then I *did* cry.

The men shook hands, Tamar hugged me, my mother with great tears kissed me good-bye. Then she handed Goldenberg our lunch basket. By the time that sorry-looking horse began to trot away, everyone but Tutsik Goldenberg's driver was crying. When I waved for the last time, Tamar wouldn't meet my eyes.

Tutsik Goldenberg's demeanor changed entirely once he'd waved my family good-bye. Where he had been laughing and chatty with my father, he became sullen and silent with me. And what did I think, trapped in a carriage with a man I detested, who spoke not one word, who looked only straight ahead of him, and never at me? I was frightened and felt horribly betrayed. I was certain my parents had done this to punish me, for what awful deed I had no idea. "It's for your own good," my mother's voice echoed in my head, but I didn't believe it. No, not for a minute.

Even wrapped as I was in a blanket, the *droshky* ride was dismal and cold. Darkness had descended on Warsaw, and even the Satski Gardens with their fabulous fountains all lit up did nothing to lift my spirits. We passed churches and statues, but when we drove past the train depot my sorrow turned to pure terror and Tutsik Goldenberg showed his true self.

"*Reb* Goldenberg, I'm confused, sir, for isn't that the train station there?"

He poked the driver, Hirsh, in the back with his walking stick. The *droshky* sped up and Tutsik smiled.

As we passed out of the city I thought it best to jump out of the carriage, but if I did, what would become of my candlesticks, my wedding gown? How would I find my way home? "*Reb* Goldenberg, I beg of you—how will we get to Hamburg if not on that train? Where will we meet your *Tante* Sara?"

"Let me worry about that, Sofia. Yes, let your groom worry about that." Tutsik folded his hands and sat very still. The *droshky* sped into the dark. I could hear the horse *clop-clop* on the road, but I saw not one thing as we flew through the night.

I was too frightened to sleep and try as I might, I couldn't get my captor to talk. As a last resort I offered him food from my basket. He waved it away.

Finally we came to another town which I later learned was Plock. By now I was not only terrified but ready to face my fate. I was certain that this man Goldenberg, my practical joke of a fiancé, had paid my father hundreds of *zloty* for the privilege of killing me in the dark of night in this faraway place.

"Get out," he spat when at last the *droshky* stopped in front of a small hotel. "Hirsh!" he called to the driver, "get her bags. See her to her room and I'll meet you in the bar downstairs." He handed my basket to Hirsh. "There's a kosher treat or two in there, smells pretty good. Have it all if you want it."

"That's mine," I cried weakly.

"I don't care," replied Goldenberg. "Ask me, young lady, if I care."

Hirsh looped the basket over one arm, then took my carpetbag and threw it into the lobby before him. I clutched my wedding dress and candlesticks to me for dear life and followed the driver in. Hirsh pulled the desk clerk to him by his necktie, a frail old fellow with big yellow teeth, and whispered something in his ear. The clerk glanced over Hirsh's shoulder at me, then looked at the roll of *zloty* in Hirsh's hand and rang a bell on the counter. A boy, not much older than me, in a grey suit with a brimless cap which sat on his head at an angle, wearing a pair of dirty white gloves, looked me over and sneered. He took my bag and headed for the stairs. Hirsh pulled a chicken leg out of the basket and, to my surprise, handed it back to me. I clutched it to me with my other parcels and the bellhop made no effort to take it away.

"Well?" snarled Hirsh. He was a big fellow, bigger than Goldenberg, in a tight suit that left his shirt cuffs hanging. While Goldenberg was the height of fashion, Hirsh looked like he was pushed into hand-me-downs. He wore an English-style bowler on his head, that he kept shoving back with a scrawny, grimy thumb.

I looked at him with wide eyes. My heart beat impossibly fast. I'd no idea what he wanted me to do.

"Don't just stand there, dear. Follow the boy up to your room. I got an appointment with your hubby-to-be, so you're on your own for the evening. We're taking the 4:00 A.M. train to Hamburg. You better get your beauty rest while you can." He looked dangerously at the bellhop, who was eyeing me from head to foot. "And you, boy, these goods are paid for in full. If they become damaged in shipping, you'll compensate for it with your head." Hirsh flicked his wrist and an evil-looking razor opened almost out of nowhere. "Am I understood?"

The boy held his breath and nodded.

"All right then," Hirsh said, and walked out the door.

I stared from the bellboy to the desk clerk. I was frozen where I stood.

"Just follow Janusz," the desk clerk sighed. He was so busy counting out Hirsh's *zloty* he didn't even look up.

I had never been inside a hotel before, just stared at the stately ones in

Warsaw from the outside. This one you never would have known was a hotel except for the sign out front. It had no columns or fancy revolving doors. Worse, it smelled like a barn. Janusz, the bellhop, climbed the stairs quickly, even carrying my carpetbag. It was all I could do to keep up with him, my basket and box slipping out of my grasp as he mounted those rickety stairs two, sometimes three at a time. Finally, when we reached the third floor, he took a sharp right, dropped my bag, and jiggled an old iron key into a stubborn lock. Then he kicked the door open and ushered me in. It was a dismal room that smelled of old cigars and schnapps, and even with the dim light from the hallway I could see the walls were filthy. There was a tiny bed with a sagging mattress stuffed with horse hair and hay, and a wobbly wooden chair with a table to match. An oil lamp sat on the table, unlit. A dirty window that faced into nowhere gave no clue as to where I was that night. I let my parcels fall to the floor.

"Chamber pot is under the bed," the bellhop said in the most matter-of-fact way. He looked into a cracked white pitcher and blew into the dusty drinking glass that sat on the windowsill. "Should be enough water to hold you 'til your boyfriend gets back." Then he lit the oil lamp and, without another word, walked out and slammed the door. The last I heard of him was the scraping of that old key in the lock. I ran to the door and pulled on the knob. I tried to open the window but it wouldn't budge, and I knew once and for all that I was not to have the fine life Tutsik Goldenberg promised my father. I banged at the door, I tugged at the window, and finally, I sank down on that pathetic bed and cried.

At length I fell asleep. I awoke with a stab to my heart as I remembered where I was, who had delivered me here. The walls of that little room flickered in the oil lamplight. I sat up, and on the wall before me I saw the strangest painting. It was a young woman, bundled in rags, head down, walking into a snow storm. Her shawl and kerchief blew back into the wind, her feet were bare, and on her back she carried a load of firewood. The woods looked so dismal and uninviting, I thought only of the danger awaiting her there. The more I looked at that sad cold girl, the more I thought, Sofia, that is you. *Release me*, I begged. *Oh God, please release me.* I banged on the window, threw myself at the door; the oil lamp flickered but nothing changed. Even thoughts of home didn't comfort me, and thoughts of my lost darling Tamar only made my tears more bitter.

Hours passed as I sat on that bed and stared at the painting. I ate some of the food my mother packed, but I wasn't so hungry. Then at last I was rescued, or so it felt, for just when I was certain my only salvation was to smash the lamp against the wall and burn that hotel down, a key sounded in the lock. The door opened and a woman stood before me grinning, a woman not much older than myself.

I say not much older than myself because she was slight, her countenance youthful, but the fact of the matter was that her eyes were hard and her jaw stuck out defiantly. She wore a black woolen dress that seemed many years too old for her—it was absurdly matronly—and sitting atop her head was a flat black straw hat. Behind her stood the bellhop, who yawned sleepily in the hall.

"I am Tutsik Goldenberg's *Tante* Sara," she said coolly in Yiddish. I understood the language but her accent had that same funny lilt Tutsik Goldenberg's did. "Give the boy your bags and let's go, there's a coach waiting."

"Where is *Reb* Goldenberg?" I scrambled to collect my belongings. It was beyond my imagination how such a young woman could be Goldenberg's aunt.

"My nephew has asked me to inform you that he has important business here in Plock," *Tante* Sara said as the bellhop dragged my bag down the hall. "Unexpectedlike. So it's me alone who is to escort you to Hamburg. I'll watch over you as if you were my own niece and see to your every need. Tutsik will meet us in a few days time in Hamburg, where we will board the ship for Buenos Aires and, God willing, you will make the lovely bride your mother, God bless her, intended you to be."

"You're coming to Buenos Aires too?" Had I imagined that Tutsik told us she was staying in Hamburg?

"Why wouldn't I go there? That's where I live."

"I thought you lived in Europe, Ma'am."

"But only half the year." She winked.

So now there were two strange things. For one, this woman looked barely old enough to be Tutsik Goldenberg's sister, let alone his aunt; for the other, why would a person live in Poland during one winter then go to South America for the next? I was far too frightened to ask for explanations.

When we got outside I saw that the *droshky* had been replaced by a fine-looking coach. I looked up at the driver's seat and, to my great relief, it wasn't Hirsh sitting there this time, but a proper driver. I was happy to be breathing real air at last. This small pleasure didn't last long, though, for as soon as the bellboy threw my bag atop the coach, *Tante* Sara pushed me into it and climbed in behind me. She adjusted her straw hat and pulled at the fingers of her gloves. "You don't mind, dear, if I have a little smoke?"

To my utter amazement, *Tante* Sara lit a tiny brown cigar right there in the carriage and began to puff away. I had never seen a woman smoke before, never mind a Jewish woman, never mind a Jewish woman who was supposed to be my fiancé's aunt. In spite of my terror I found this absolutely thrilling; I couldn't take my eyes off her.

"What are you staring at?" She looked me in the eye then, as she puffed her cigar, and although I was frightened out of my wits (or perhaps because I was), I had never been so taken by a woman in my life. True, Tamar made me want to kiss her, to be kissed. But this *Tante* Sara, I felt a sudden desire for her to eat me alive. I wished for her never to stop smoking that cigar, never to take her eyes from my own.

Knowing Sara as we know her now, Hankus, this might strike you as very strange. But then, to me, a young girl of sixteen, certain that death was just around the corner, she was the most magnificent person I had ever seen. She continued to hold my gaze until the coach stopped, just a few minutes later—for me, much too soon.

A porter pulled the door open and *Tante* Sara tossed her smoldering cigar over his head onto the street below. "Let's get ourselves onto the train now and make our way to Hamburg. And we'll act like proper Jewish ladies, won't we. No smoking in public, and not a word of where we're going to anyone, eh?" She threw her head back and laughed.

At four in the morning, the depot was far from crowded. Yet it seemed there were people everywhere, awake, talking, reading newspapers. I had never traveled by train before, let alone in a first-class coach, which was more luxurious even than our little apartment in Warsaw: windows with lush velvet curtains drawn to show the beautiful Polish countryside, leather seats on either side big enough to hold three people. And here I was, going first to Germany, then on to the other side of the world, to a place about which I had hardly read in books, with a traveling companion who promised to be far more enjoyable than my sullen and standoffish husband-to-be.

For the briefest moment it stopped feeling like torture and seemed just the tiniest bit like an actual adventure. I started a letter to Tamar in my head.

"Now, listen," *Tante* Sara told me, as I tucked away my box and candlesticks in the rack above our seats, "if you play your cards right, who knows, Hamburg is an impressive city. If you behave all the way there, maybe I can get that no-good nephew of mine to take us to one of those fancy restaurants."

"Even a little café would be terribly exciting," I said, for I had lived my whole life on the edges of Warsaw and I was about to be married to a cold fish of a man. If it was offered, wasn't it my right to see a bit of the world before the door clanged shut on all possibility?

We rode alone in our fancy car until Poznan, my misery temporarily abated, when we were joined by two well-dressed older women who wore matching felt hats and carried umbrellas. *Tante* Sara sized them up and smiled in the calculating way I have seen her smile many times since. Her "nephew" Tutsik smiled at my family the same way during those *Shabbes* dinners. The two ladies pursed their lips and nodded to us in unison. I studied their faces and found that in fact they were not at all identical. The one directly across from me looked at us only out of the corner of her eye, and the one across from *Tante* Sara seemed to look only straight ahead.

The three of them exchanged pleasantries in Yiddish, but I was afraid to say anything. The one who looked from side to side asked, "And where do you travel to?"

"To Bremen," *Tante* Sara blurted, with a wide smile that was totally false. I was about to ask her what she was talking about when she patted my leg and then pinched me hard.

The sisters looked at each other and smiled. "We've a cousin in Bremen," offered the rounder of the two. She took out a pencil and a little piece of paper. "I'll write the address for you. Look her up when you get there. She's really quite dear."

"How pleasant." *Tante* Sara took out her change purse and presented me with a few *groszen*. "Find the conductor and have him bring your *Tante* Sara a glass of tea, will you darling?" She winked at the sisters. "I'm a little dry in the throat."

Who knows what she told the two sisters while I searched out her tea. When I returned they both looked at me with great sympathy, touched my chin with gloved fingertips, and made clucking noises like two fat hens. A conductor arrived and all four of us had tea, which we drank while the two sisters told us stories about Hamburg and Berlin. "Really, my dear, if you can get your *aunt*," she winked at *Tante* Sara, who put a quieting finger to her lips, "to postpone your trip to Bremen and take you to Frankfurt am Main, I am sure you would be in for the adventure of your life."

"Yes, yes," agreed her sister, "there are such museums, such fabulous cafés and theatres—are you sure you can't put off your trip for just a week?"

"You ladies seem not to understand." *Tante* Sara straightened her hat and sat up quite tall. "The specialist we seek out in Bremen is a busy man. If we were to go off and vacation in a place like Frankfurt am Main, beautiful as it may be, who knows when next we could get to see him, and little Sofia's condition might, *gottenieu,* worsen."

"Worsen?"

Tante Sara put her hands over my ears and shook her head sadly. "Perhaps, ladies, it is better to think of happier things."

Sara drained her tea glass and we rode along in silence together until the German border.

The train was stopped for half an hour while conductors and soldiers walked back and forth between the cars looking at papers and passports. I became extremely frightened, since I had neither, but to my great surprise and relief Sara produced both for each of us, although the German officer looked me carefully in the face and referred back to my papers often. *Tante* Sara was then asked the purpose of our stay in Germany. I was surprised again to hear her reply, "We are staying with my sister in Bremen, *Herr* Conductor. My young cousin is an orphan and quite ill. The poor dear requires constant care."

Often, when I am alone in the middle of the night, I wonder how my life would be different if I'd pulled myself away from Sara, had wiggled away when we stopped in Berlin and sought out those two sisters who had joined our compartment. True, I might have found myself in a similar situation. Who knew if they were benevolent ladies or of the same stock as Sara, or our old friends Perle Goldenberg and Red Ruthie? But I have heard of other women who spent their days saving the likes of me from the life I was embarking upon, and I wonder if perhaps those sisters might not have been women like that. In any case, it's no matter to me now.

At Berlin they departed. *Tante* Sara taught me to play pinochle, or else she dozed or I did, and in this way we passed the time until the train pulled into the station in Hamburg, which it turned out was our true destination. Sara took me to a small hotel near the terminal and deposited me in a single room. I asked her if she meant what she said before, that we might explore the sights of Hamburg.

"Did I say that? What kind of sights? They don't let the likes of you into neighborhood bars."

"Museums and cafés—"

"Did I say cafés? Yes, I imagine I did. You sit tight here and I'll see what I can do tomorrow."

The next day, fool that I was, I rose early and dressed. To my bitterest disappointment, when there finally was a knock on the door hours later, it was not *Tante* Sara at all, but a bellboy who brought me a breakfast of coffee and dry toast. He bowed to me when he served it, then clicked his heels and locked the door behind him.

I waited and paced the small room round and round, and still no one came. By one-thirty, when the hotel maid arrived with lunch, I was near tears. "Can you tell me where my Aunt Sara has gone?" I asked in Yiddish.

"Pardon, *Fräulein?*"

"Sara Goldenberg? Have you seen her?"

"Sara Goldenberg, *Fräulein?*" The rest of her answer was in a clipped, tight German, and I understood none of it.

"Must you lock me in?" I asked as she was leaving.

"*Fräulein?*"

"The door, must you lock it?"

"Certainly!" she said in German. She picked up my empty lunch things and left.

Dinner arrived in the same dismal manner, some salami on a hard roll and a bit of mustard delivered by a porter from the hotel. When he left he locked the door behind him, and I, increasingly despairing, sat on the bed fully dressed and wept. Where was Tutsik Goldenberg's Aunt Sara? Where was Tutsik Goldenberg? Where were my bags, and how could it be that I was here, trapped in a room in Hamburg, Germany, a city I had never seen, with no one to give me even the small pleasure of a breath of fresh air? And I was supposed to be marrying the man responsible!

It was after dark when someone knocked again. I had fallen asleep and it took me a few moments to remember where I was. Before I could fully come to my senses, the door burst open. There stood my groom, Tutsik Goldenberg, looking just as decked out and sparkling as ever, oiled and perfumed, tapping his cane impatiently and checking his watch. Beside him was a bellboy with a cart full of luggage, among it my carpetbag and wedding dress box, and once again, Hirsh. He looked shopworn compared to my fiancé. His bowler hat was dusty and sat oddly on his head.

"You must hurry now," Goldenberg said, "we've a boat to catch."

"But where is Sara?"

"Up to no good as usual," Hirsh snickered. "Do you come of your own volition or must we help you?"

"Where is *Tante* Sara? Where are my candlesticks?"

Hirsh looked at Tutsik Goldenberg and burst out laughing. "That's rich, a nice touch, Tutsik. *Tante* Sara."

Goldenberg slapped him across the face. The bellboy stepped back, and Hirsh immediately stopped laughing. "You'd best shut up, Hirsh, or next time you stay home with the women." To me he said in a sickening sweet voice, "My *Tante* Sara sends her apologies. She was taken quite ill this morning and was unable to meet you. I am sorry that I myself could not deliver the message sooner and show you a bit of this quaint city. As it stands now, my dear, we are due on the boat in twenty minutes, we sail at 1:00 A.M., and the captain has made a special arrangement to marry us at sea. You remember my driver and personal valet, Dov Hirsh. He will serve as our witness and my best man. Now, if you please, be quick about it and let us go. There is a carriage waiting outside."

"But isn't *Tante* Sara coming to Argentina?"

Tutsik took my arm and hurried me down the corridor. "Did she tell you that? Well, all plans are changed." He guided me down the stairs roughly. The porter and Hirsh followed.

"And am I to be married in the middle of the night?"

"But of course, my dear. The captain is Jewish. Practically a rabbi. He insists that if we are to spend the night together, the wedding must happen immediately. It's a formality, don't you see, so that we may share the same state room. When we get to Buenos Aires, then you'll see a wedding."

"You're telling me," Hirsh said, laughing.

"Hirsh, I warn you."

"No, really," Hirsh told me, "the weddings in Buenos Aires are the most glorious on earth."

3

MY PROMISED STATE ROOM was a tiny, stuffy cabin, and I was taken to it directly when we boarded the ship. By this time I had little strength (the meager meals I'd been served at the hotel offered no nourishment, the basket so lovingly packed by my mother was long gone), and I nearly fainted as we walked up the gangplank. Hirsh dumped me in the cabin and left me. An eternity later a steward in a clean white uniform brought me some food on a silver tray. He wore white gloves and lifted the silver covers which sat over each dish. Steam rose up from the plates, but I was too weak and tired to eat, too full of disappointment and confusion, and absolutely terrified. Where was my bag? Where was the box with the wedding dress I promised my mother I would wear? If I was to be married immediately, didn't I need to put it on? And what of those candlesticks, heavy and silver? Did *Tante* Sara make off with those? How on earth was I supposed to do it, sail off to a country halfway round the world, marry a man who never spoke to me, yes, how was I to do it all and live?

There was no sign here that I was really going to marry Tutsik

Goldenberg after all. No flowers from a loving suitor, no celebratory bottle of champagne. The cabin was barely furnished with a narrow bed, a little table, a pitcher of water and a towel laid out for me, and a chamber pot under the bed. There was an open steamer trunk set on end like a closet. A little round porthole was my only window to the world.

I poked at my food, then put the covers back on all the plates. I pulled at the cabin door, which, of course, was locked. I rummaged through the clothes in the trunk. None of them were mine—slips, boas, fancy lingerie, camisoles and brassieres, but my favorite dress, my own underclothes, were nowhere to be found. Exhausted, I threw myself on the narrow bed and tossed and turned until I fell to sleep. Once there I dreamed myself chained by the ankle to a red velvet fainting couch wearing no clothes at all. My beloved Tamar danced around me in a bridal gown exactly like the one I was to wear. Suddenly there was a loud bang, and Tutsik Goldenberg stood between us, himself naked but for a felt fedora. He waved a gun in the air wildly, then held it under my nose. "You are lucky tonight," he told me. He tossed the gun over his shoulder and laughed.

Sunlight poked through the tiny porthole when I awoke. A new tray with covered dishes and a little teapot sat atop the table. The chamber pot which I had used in the night was empty. To my great relief my wedding gown box and carpetbag were placed neatly atop the trunk. The candlesticks, I was certain, were gone for good. Again I tried the door, again it was locked. I knocked and pounded, but no one came. I could feel the boat moving. It terrified me. Furiously, I smashed the pitcher against the cabin door. Water flew everywhere. I sat on the bed and wept. When the steward came to take my breakfast dishes, I begged him in Yiddish to tell me where Tutsik Goldenberg was, but all he did was shrug and imply that he didn't understand. "Must you lock that door, Mister?" I asked him plaintively. This he seemed to understand perfectly, for he answered in stilted Polish, "It has been ordered, Miss." He turned sharply and left.

Who knows how many days and nights I lay trapped on the German ship *Viktorius* as it steamed across the Atlantic Ocean with a hold full of baggage and poverty-struck immigrants, and a passenger list, I learned later from Sara, that included the richest and finest European adventurers, businessmen, and socialites. While I languished in my prison, they spun above me, dancing in ballgowns to lovely music, my groom-to-be likely picking pockets all through the crowd. I could almost hear the hot saxophone and piano, the wine glasses clinking just above my head.

After what might have been two days, maybe three, I begged the steward to bring me *Pan* Goldenberg. He clicked his heels and left me, then returned a few minutes later, his arms full of magazines. With great ceremony he placed them before me on my little bed. "This isn't what I asked for..." I was deflated. "Please bring me *Pan* Goldenberg." I could barely hear myself.

The steward bowed and nodded. "But, Miss, be happy. I have brought you this." He opened his arms to the German magazines filled with photographs and drawings of women in fancy dresses; the newspaper, which was in Yiddish; and three magazines written in Spanish, containing nothing, it seemed, but drawings of thin, flat-chested women in fancy furs, or else pictures of women in no clothes at all. The Yiddish paper was three weeks old; its place of origin was New York City in the United States.

"But where is *Pan* Goldenberg?"

"Not available at this time, Miss." He clicked his heels together and walked toward the door.

"Look, Mister," I said, my voice full of tears, "could you bring me please a pencil and some paper? And I beg you—please find out when I can see Mr. Tutsik Goldenberg himself?"

"Very well, Miss," he said, and left me alone.

When he returned with my dinner, the steward brought with him a tray containing a sharpened pencil and five sheets of writing paper. To my surprise there also lay a packet of German cigarettes, a box of dainty wooden matches on which was written *"Viktorius,"* and a decanter of golden whiskey with a tiny glass. The steward filled the little glass and handed it to me.

"What is that?"

"Whiskey, Miss. The gentleman's orders."

"Pan Goldenberg?"

"Yes, Miss." He handed me the glass. "Drink up, Miss. I'm not to leave until you do."

I had taken schnapps before at my father's table, on the high holy days, and then only in sips. "Will *Pan* Goldenberg come see me soon?"

"This I do not know, Miss. *Salut*," he said stiffly. He stood and watched me, a bit agitated.

"I am to drink this all the way down?"

"If you please, Miss."

"But I am sixteen years old."

The steward looked at me quizzically. "You'll find it very good."

I looked at the glass and the whiskey, so golden, and the man in his short white jacket. I looked at the tiny hole in the wall that offered me no escape. The whiskey smelled both sweet and sharp. I took a sip; it burned my lips. I swallowed and coughed. The steward poured a half glass of water and handed it to me. I accepted it gratefully and drank it down. Little by little I felt resigned to my life in this cage. "What do they say in French novels, then?" I asked. *"À vôtre santé?"*

"À vôtre santé," Miss."

I raised my glass to him and finished the whole thing in a gulp. When this round of coughing subsided I felt warm and, for the first time since my travels began, calm. "Tell *Pan* Goldenberg thank you. Our wedding can begin anytime."

The steward looked again as if he did not understand. "Miss is quite comfortable now?"

"Oh, perfect," I said sadly.

He poured me another glass. "Very well then. I'll let *Pan* Goldenberg know that all is well."

As soon as I heard the door lock behind him, I stripped down to my slip, for I was too warm now, and dizzy, and interested in nothing. I toyed with a cigarette, lit it up, and with the first breath of smoke choked almost as hard as I had on the whiskey. But with each puff the smoking became easier. I watched myself in the porthole glass. This is how *Tante* Sara did it, then, with a tilt of the head and a wink of the eye, with the cigarette drooping from the corner of the lips. Here is how she holds it and here is how she puffs it and this is how she sips her whiskey, too.

I occupied myself in this way for some time. If I was to do nothing but live in a locked room, I might as well have some vices. That is what I believed my sweet Tamar would say. I made a mental note to ask the steward next for a box of chocolates such as I had read about in books. I smoked my cigarette until the stub nearly burned my fingers. Then I picked up the writing paper and composed this note in Yiddish:

My dear Parents,

I am distressed to inform you that the wedding you planned for me is a figment of our sorry imaginations. Instead of a joyous celebration, I am a prisoner on this steamer, although I do not know for what reason I am held. After going to such great lengths (and expense) to woo me, Reb Goldenberg has abandoned me completely, and I believe his promise to marry me was a hoax. Who knows why he paid you all of those zloty? I am doubtful that I will ever see the fair city of Buenos Aires, for I am certain I will rot in this cabin, whither and die. If he does not plan to marry me I cannot imagine what the "honorable" Tutsik Goldenberg plans to do with me.

Oh, woe am I! Rescue me if you can!

> *I remain,*
> *Your daughter,*
> *Sofia Teitelbaum*

I folded my letter three times and wrote upon it the address in Poland of my mother and father. I placed it on my untouched dinner tray with the intention of asking the steward to mail it at his earliest opportunity. I lit another cigarette, poured myself just a bit more whiskey (for which I seemed to develop a taste almost immediately), and attempted to decode the Spanish magazines.

I cannot tell you more about the hours that passed. I slept, woke, drank, slept again. Sometimes when I woke I looked at the newspaper and magazines, sometimes I peed into the pot, once or twice I ate some bites of food, two times I smoked a cigarette.

Then suddenly, in the midst of those furtive naps, the door to my cabin swung open with no knock preceding it, and at once I was surrounded by all three of them: *Tante* Sara, Dov Hirsh, and Tutsik Goldenberg. Each of them wore evening clothes, although Tutsik Goldenberg's were by far the fanciest. Sara looked bizarre, and in her new clothes it took me a moment to know her. Her frumpy dress was gone, and now her skinny frame was draped in a shiny, spangled blue sheath, whose bodice was cut low as underwear and hung straight down to just above her knees. On her head she no longer had her flat straw hat but wore instead a single blue feather that curled around her face. It made her look no softer, no less severe. Dov Hirsh appeared to be a cheaply rendered version of Tutsik Goldenberg—his dinner jacket sleeves a bit too short, his black tie slipping over just a hair to the side. While Goldenberg's hair was brushed and oiled neatly, Hirsh's hung down over his face.

The three of them together frightened me. There was a sinister gleam in each set of eyes. I sat up on one elbow. A strap of my slip hung down over my shoulder. "So," I said, trying to hide my sleepiness, "the time has come at last for our wedding."

Tante Sara laughed. "My God, Tutsik, she's drunk!"

"Of course she's drunk, I sent her a bottle of whiskey." Tutsik Goldenberg proceeded to take the fine gold and diamond rings off his fingers one by one. He handed them to Hirsh without taking his eyes from my face. "I see my darling bride-to-be has made short work of it."

"Well, yes, it's frightfully boring here otherwise."

Tutsik waved a piece of writing paper in front of my face. "But you have managed to entertain yourself, it seems, by writing pleasant letters home."

"I don't know what you're talking about," I answered. My breath caught in my throat.

"Fortunately, I have a particularly good relationship with your steward. He made sure I saw this before it was sent off in the mail boat tomorrow." Without changing his stance or his demeanor, Tutsik Goldenberg, mild-mannered purveyor of imported jewels, lifted his hand and hit me with the flat of it full across my cheek. My face reverberated. Sara turned her head and put a finger into her mouth. Dov Hirsh smiled.

"You are never to write another letter like this one, do you understand?" He hit me again. "Under any circumstances, to anyone." A third blow followed. "Now, luckily for you it is to my advantage to deliver you unmarked to our destination, which is indeed Buenos Aires." He snapped his immaculate fingers and Dov Hirsh dropped the rings into the palm of my groom-to-be's hand. One by one he replaced them. "I had hoped to avoid this, but for the rest of the journey, Sara will watch over you. I'd spell her with Hirsh, but he really can't be trusted. Pity, because of you she will miss the fairest part of the journey." He held my ill-fated letter over my head and lit it with a match. Then he opened the porthole and threw the flaming paper out to sea.

I said nothing, only looked to Sara, then Dov Hirsh, then looked away. "Have another drink. The captain is a good friend of mine. He makes sure my guests and I are provided with only the best. Now then, Hirsh and I will go back to the dining room and finish our dinner. Sara is going to spend the night. Hopefully you and I will not speak again until we reach Argentina's rich and beautiful shore." He held me by the chin. "Is there anything else you would like, dear bride?"

To spit in your face, I thought, but didn't say it. Really what I wanted more than anything was to be dead.

"Sara is an excellent pinochle player—it's rumored she's a sharp. Perhaps she'll teach you some of her fine tricks before the night is over." He touched his forehead and made as if to tip his hat. "*Buenas noches, Señorita.* Until we meet again."

We were alone together now, not in a coach, nor a compartment on a train, but here, in a tiny room aboard a boat steaming west. How I must have looked to her! My face smarting from Goldenberg's slaps, my eyes gleaming with tears. I covered myself as best I could, and still she stood before me, cold-eyed, her lips set in a smile that said to me nothing about happiness. She took her blue feather from around her face and kicked her shoes off.

She sat beside me on the bed. She leaned over me, touched my cheek with the same finger she shoved in her mouth when Goldenberg hit me, then drew it down over my lips, under my chin, traced my shoulders and the edge of my slip. Then without a word Sara kissed me, pushed my lips open with her tongue and sucked her way into me.

I was horrified and held my breath, did not move a muscle. Yet when she put both hands under my behind and pulled me to her, pushed my thighs apart and pressed her knee between my legs, some place inside of me felt a horrible thrill. She held me in this way for what seemed forever, kissing, holding, pressing. I was on fire and de- voured all at once.

She stood up and moved the straps of her beaded dress over her shoulders. It slipped to the floor and landed at her ankles in a glittery mound. And there she was, Tutsik Goldenberg's ersatz *Tante* Sara, naked before me. She leaned over and kissed me again, her breasts brushed my own. I squirmed to get away from her, and I gasped with strange pleasure. "Are you really Tutsik Goldenberg's aunt?" I whispered.

She burst out in a single laugh, then purred, "*Momentito.*" I lay completely still as she moved quickly to the cabin door and made certain it was locked. She came and lay beside me on the bed and kissed me once again.

Was it the whiskey? Was it the flat boredom of my captivity? Or had she tapped my most secret desire? How did I know what I was even meant to do? Somehow, I was brave then. I felt Sara's mouth on my own, I felt her hands on my breasts and behind, and soon my lips became greedy for hers and I was feverish and full of what I cannot tell you. I was swept away. Sara said nothing but certainly was not silent.

She knew far better than I how kissing was done and was much more expert at it than that wondrous Tamar. She knew how to make me move my fingers and hands to secret places without saying a word. She held me about the hips and waist, burrowed into me with her fingers and face, encouraged me to do the same to her. I was fearful but very wild. I was hungry and hot and dangerous. I had felt nothing like this in my entire life. Was this what Tamar wanted from me and I from her? It didn't matter now, for once tasting such a meal as this I would hunger for it the rest of my life.

How much time passed I never knew. When we stopped, Sara looked past me and suddenly sat up. She lit a cigarette and poured out two whiskeys. I tried to kiss her on the mouth again, but she wouldn't let me. Instead she handed me a glass. "Drink this," she commanded, and I obeyed.

I gulped down the whiskey. How it burned in my throat, how it opened up in the back of my head. I put down my glass and she poured me another. "You'll have no problem when we get to Talcahuano Street. Just do for Perle what you did for me. You'll have it soft until you turn twenty, yes, you'll have it soft. This I guarantee."

I didn't know what she was talking about, but I couldn't ask. I just looked at her as she sat beside me. Sara, whose eyes were dead, whose jaw was tight and set against everything, and yet who with just her hands, her mouth and tongue, had made me into a wild beast. Sara, with sallow skin and crooked teeth, stubby little fingers that looked nothing like the rest of her, who took long pulls of whiskey, not out of a glass but straight from the bottle. Who moments ago (was it only moments?) had me in her arms and at her mercy, took me at last from this tiny locked room into what village, what country, I had no idea. And now she said nothing, just stared past me to the porthole. "Not bad, little bride. No, not bad."

I dreamed again of my Polish home, my mother in a bride dress, me naked and laughing. She carried me on her shoulders down a muddy street, brought me house to house, knocked on every door. No one answered until the butcher's wife stood with her hands on her hips in the doorway. "You're late," she said, and *tsked.* "Late for the wedding, late for Tamar!"

"Too late for Tamar?" my mother asked.

"Too late for Tamar?" My own heart sank.

But there she stood, behind the butcher, my childhood neighbor, my girlhood friend, lovely Tamar. Tamar in her own wedding dress, her lush red hair flying about her every which way. And here another miracle occurred, another miracle of Tamar—who lived in the flat beneath mine and saw my soul, who sat beside me in history class, who looked over my shoulder in chemistry—sweetest Tamar, my childish love, who just one time bestowed on me a frantic kiss. Ah, Tamar, finally, in this dream, on this day, in a beautiful bride dress with hair that could burn, delivered at last by my own mother's hand, I picked her up from behind that butcher, took her into my own arms, and kissed her myself at last.

And I woke then with a horrible start, to the stuffy cabin and Sara's thin back. It was still and grey, I could barely breathe. I stared into the darkness and wept. I wept and I wondered if that wasn't why they did it: if my parents hadn't sold me out for a few *zloty* because somehow or other they knew that in my heart of hearts it was a woman I wanted.

Sweet Hankus, I never had her 'til you.

— 4 —

I DID NOT COME OFF THE SHIP AS OTHERS DID, to warm arms and comforting friends. I was wheeled off the boat, down the gangplank, in a wooden chair, bundled in blankets and shawls with an old straw hat such as Sara wore when first we met, in her *Tante* Sara disguise. It was she who did the pushing, no longer that hot, brittle Sara whose cold kisses kept me quiet the long rest of our journey, but *Tante* Sara, in those old same *Tante* Sara clothes. As she pushed she spoke to me in a birdlike, soothing Yiddish which I barely remember because I was drugged. They put something in my whiskey and something in the food and this mixed with the aftermath of Sara's long kisses guaranteed I wouldn't make trouble now. Who showed my papers, who carried my bags, I do not know. I was gone. All I remember is the *bumpity-bump* of the chair on the gangplank, a certain crush of people in all directions at once. Then the *bump bump bump* over cobblestones on our way to my new home.

I know now there were people on the docks that day looking out for the likes of me. Looking out for young women with men who smelled like Tutsik Goldenberg, or young girls with no one who were greeted by flashy aunts or uncles who looked like Dov Hirsh, with cruel-as-ice glints in their eyes. These watchers were from the Jewish Ladies Protection Society. They were making sure that ones such as me could be rescued from fates such as mine. But Perle Goldenberg and her brother Tutsik were wise to their kindness. Long ago they learned to take precautions. So here I was, no longer a drugged and terrified sixteen-year-old fresh from Warsaw, just off the boat. I was transformed into another *tante*, *Tante* Sofia, my lover Sara's decrepit old aunt. From Lodz, not Warsaw, an aunt not a mark, as old as a woman can be.

I've seen it since. I know how they worked it. Rolled me past those watchful Protection Society eyes, past those dear women with their notebooks and photographs of Red Ruthie and Madam Perle. They rolled me past the police who could care less, and the soldiers who I would one day service, until we were in the clear. Then they lifted me into a *droshky*, Sara jumped in beside me, and we were on our way to Talcahuano Street, my new home.

Was it raining? It was May, so maybe it was. It was likely damp and chill, but who remembers? Maybe it was a wonderful day, a rare winter thing in Buenos Aires. Yes, perhaps the sky was blue and clear and only a damp breeze blew down cobbled streets. It didn't matter, for after I was carted to my new home in Talcahuano Street I was trundled up a narrow flight of stairs and brought up to bed. I was allowed to sleep then, but for how many days I don't know. When I woke again it was indeed raining. I found myself in a satin camisole with Sara beside me on the bed. She was transformed, once again, in an open kimono, nothing underneath, smiling that joyless smile. She held a hollow gourd painted black, and a silver-tipped straw. "Drink this, my darling." She offered it with no warmth, but her eyes seemed just a bit softer. "Revive yourself, for soon our dear mistress is coming to call."

I sipped from the straw, although reluctantly. I knew that the drugs they gave me on the boat were in me still. But when Sara touched my cheek and kissed me on the neck I fell to her, in spite of myself. All she desired I would provide, anything she asked at all. And so I sipped from the silver straw, my first real taste of Argentina, in a locked room with slats for windows and a high ceiling and sad dreams to come.

"This is how we drink tea here in Argentina," said dead-faced Sara. She touched my cheek. My breath caught.

"But where am I drinking it?" I asked, in a horrible panic, "and where are my clothes?"

Sara shook her head and pulled away. "You're home little sister, dear cousin and niece. Welcome home now, dear auntie and lover. Madam Perle will appear in a minute or two and your life in this world will start over. But remember," she whispered, "Madam Perle may not look like one of those prim ladies who sits in the balcony at *shul* every chance she gets, but in truth, she is pious and sees herself as one of the righteous. No matter how you are tempted, do not, under any circumstances, take God's name—or Madam Perle's for that matter—in vain."

The door of my tiny room swung open and there before me, framed in that window of garish bordello light, stood the queen of Talcahuano Street, the woman now in charge of my fate, my new mother, Madam Perle.

Tutsik Goldenberg's sister was an astonishing beauty. Even in my stupor I could see this, and, indeed, it was nearly impossible to reconcile the way she looked at this moment with what Sara told me. She wore a fabulous green dressing gown over a black corselet, silk stockings, and open-toed satin slippers. Her luxurious black hair was piled atop her head, two heavy gold hoops dangled from her ears. Her face was painted. I had never seen such a face. Her lips were scarlet, there were thick black lines across her eyelids, and her lashes were long and lush. She wore rows of bracelets on each arm; when she moved her hands to speak they made a soothing jingle. Unlike her brother Tutsik, this woman, this Perle Goldenberg, exuded a remarkable, a breathtaking warmth. And yet, if one looked closely into those black eyes of hers, there was something of a madwoman there, something a person saw from time to time if she looked into the eyes of those women in the Warsaw marketplace who had a fish in one hand and a prayer book in the other.

She sat on the bed beside me. She smelled like lilacs and roses. She took my chin between her fingers and made soothing sounds. "How do you feel, sweet Sofia? Still a little groggy, eh?" She patted my cheek gently and cooed, "I'm so sorry about the drugs, darling. It's best to calm you down before you meet authorities. They can't ask you questions if you're asleep, and after such a long trip...well, who wants to be bothered." She gave my hand a little squeeze. "Sara here has shown you some of the ropes, I understand. There are a few more things you'll need to know before we can call it work, eh? Come to my rooms tomorrow when you're rested and I'll explain everything. Are you hungry, *neshomeleh?*"

In truth, I felt faint and famished but I was afraid to say.

"Oh, I am certain," Perle clucked over me like a mother hen, "I am certain you are starving after that long boat ride, and for a good Polish meal, I'll bet. The food on board ship is appalling, my dear. We'll have Marianna bring you up a lovely meal. Why just this minute she is cooking a delectable cabbage *borscht*. If word gets out, the entire Jewish community will be banging on our door for dinner. Yes, *borscht*, black bread, a little sour cream. You'll be back on your feet in no time. But that's not really where we want you, is it." She chuckled softly. Unlike Dov Hirsh's laughter it was clear to me that I was meant to be in on the joke, not the brunt of it. I wasn't sure why it was funny, but in spite of myself, I giggled too.

Sara whispered something in Spanish to Perle. "Ah," Madam Perle nodded her head and once again touched my face. "Sara tells me you have been concerned about your things—a valise, she tells me, and a cardboard box?"

"Yes, those, and a pair of silver candlesticks." It was the first I had spoken in a long while and my voice shook.

Perle looked at me sadly. "I'm afraid the candlesticks are nowhere to be found, my dear. But don't despair. The Sabbath is strictly observed in this house, and you may say the blessings over our candles every Friday night if you like. As to your other luggage, it's all right here in this room." She snapped her fingers and Sara put the wedding dress box in my lap.

"There," pronounced Madam Perle brightly, "just like Chanukah."

That is the moment my heart broke in Buenos Aires, once and for all. Was it the loss of the candlesticks, or the fact of my practical joke wedding dress? To this day I can't tell you. In spite of myself, I burst into tears.

"Oh, little *ziskeit.*" Perle took the box from me and slipped it under the bed. She touched my cheek, and I cried even louder. "Ah."

She leaned over and kissed me sweetly on the forehead. "I know what you're going through, Sofia. Sea travel always makes me melancholy, too. We'll leave you here to your dreams now," she crooned. "You must try, darling, not to be sad."

If I did have dreams that night, they were full of men with straight razors and women with knitting needles chasing me about the streets of Warsaw. I didn't have much time to remember them or think about their meaning, for I was summoned by Perle the very next day. Memories of my time with her were meant to occupy both my waking and sleeping life.

It was Sara who came to get me. She held out a blue silk wrapper. "Put this on. Courtesy of the house," she said flatly. "First we give you a bath, then you have an appointment with her Holiness, the boss." Sara sneered when she said this, and my heart stopped, but I followed her down the hall to a room with a big claw-foot tub which was already full of steaming, perfumed water. Sara took my robe and watched as I reluctantly stepped in. "Go ahead, Sofia, think of it this way—it's your own private *mikveh*. Then you go get blessed."

I sunk down and let the water play against my chin. I am sorry to say that after all the hotel rooms and my life on the ship, the bath water felt miraculous.

Sara handed me a huge round sponge and a bar of rose-colored soap. "Scrub yourself good, and don't get too comfy. Madam wants to see you in half an hour." She turned then and walked away.

I never had such a bath in my life, in that big long tub with water that came from a tap already hot. I splashed about and rubbed soap all over me, wonderful, flowery soap. I laughed and thought, This isn't so bad, a bath like this and a robe like that. Then Sara came back and rubbed me dry with a towel as big as I was, the way my mother used to when I was a little girl. I started to cry then, but I held the tears back. I didn't want anybody to know what a dope, what a baby, what a fool I was. How could my parents have let me go?

Once I was dried and perfumed, hair brushed and tied, Sara brought me at last to Perle's rooms down the hall. She knocked and a velvet voice said, "Come, darling." Sara nodded, and I walked in alone.

There were candles burning in Perle's room although it was three in the afternoon. Incense smoldered, as sweet, mysterious music spilled softly from a gramophone. Now, my room here had a bed that could easily hold two; Perle Goldenberg's bed could hold four. You've seen that bed, Hankus, you know it's true. Remember how it was made of oak, and those trumpeting cherubs carved into that enormous headboard? My first visit to Madam Perle at least a dozen pillows lay against that headboard, each covered with a satin case. Spread across the bed was a pink coverlet, and under this coverlet, propped up against those many pillows, sat a radiant Madam Perle.

She wore a robe that matched her sheets, and her hair was on top of her head in a swirl. She was reading a book by candlelight, sipping her tea through a straw. She put her book down, pushed back the covers, and said, "Come sweetheart, come sit by me."

Now you may wonder, with all the education Sara provided me on the good ship *Viktorius* as we steamed across the ocean, what was left for Madam Perle to teach. And it is true that thanks to icy Sara, by the time Perle invited me into her enormous bed I was already wise to some of the reluctant pleasures of my own body. But Madam Perle put me wise to the fact that my desire, or my *seeming* desire, could bring passion and yearning to others. She also did what Sara would never in a million centuries do: with each trick of my new trade, Madam Perle provided little homilies and fairy tales about how good these acts would get me in with God.

"I kiss you so."

She did, an exquisite kiss that pulled me into her, that melted me on the spot. Even as I tried to protest I moaned. "Ah, you're a natural, Sofia. In this line of work, your job is to do exactly as you've done—respond! Tell the truth—you felt that kiss, you liked it, isn't it so? But remember, dolly, as our very own Bible tells us, it is better by far to give than receive. Pleasure in this house is a job, dear, but done properly, it will bring you many blessings. Why, just listen to the men when you have them in the throes of ecstasy. Some will curse you, it's true, but most, when the job's well done, will call upon the lord above to bless you and keep you. And some, so satisfied, so transfixed by their pleasure, will even call out the lord God's name. Don't be shocked when this happens, and don't relinquish yourself to that ecstasy, either. Now"—she laid upon my lips a second most extraordinary kiss— "you like that. I can tell. But if you let go and relax too much, your life here will soon turn to hell. Respond if you must, but hold back your heart. Show feeling, but don't feel too much. When a man puts his fingers all over you, seem pliant, but don't give in to his touch. It's hard not to succumb to my caress. I'm irresistible, I know. But with men—it's easy, trust me. You'll see. Stay in control and you'll be in control, you'll be queen of the world. Look at me.

"When a man is panting and pushing, pumping on top of you and calling out to God, calling you his sweetest dear," she rolled her eyes back in her head and started writhing on the bed, "your job is to act as if he is the world's most marvelous lover, to call him by his first name, or better yet his private one, to melt under him, to make him think he is the world to you—and never to feel a thing."

On that cursed ship *Viktorius,* Sara brought out the *vildeh* in me, the wild animal. Here in the Talcahuano Street *shandhoiz,* Madam Perle went on to show me how to bring the *vildeh* out in others. She continued to lecture me on what customers would demand, and how they would demand it, drawing upon her vast experience. "You shall do as they ask, Sofia, for in spite of what dry old rabbis tell us, the Talmud prescribes pleasure, and pleasure you must provide! Think of yourself as an ancient handmaiden."

Madam Perle drew my horrified attention to a dazzling vial of golden oil. "They will ask you," she told me, as we lay in that enormous bed, "to anoint their precious *shvontzes,* and then order you to suck them off. Be sure to use only the oils we keep in the *shandhoiz,* nothing else. Sometimes these mangoes bring their own oil. It's frequently poison and makes the mouth swell shut. Take their vial, make as if you're using it, but distract them. Tell them what a sacred scepter that *shlang* of theirs is and then replace the oil with ours. If you have trouble putting that thing in your mouth, remember again, the Torah commands pleasure. You may find this particular form of it disgusting at first, but you get used to it after a while. They like you to swallow their semen. My advice in this case is to act like you've done it, then spit it out discreetly. Have you ever seen a man take his penis into his own hands and make himself come? I'm certain you have, for they do it on the streets of Warsaw all the time. It's a comical, pitiful sight. They become even more grotesque than they normally are. And those poor *shlubs* are spilling their seed! There's no hope for them in heaven. Just remember this and you'll always be in control. *Fashstais?"*

She passed me her *maté*. I took a sip, but my throat was tight from all this talk of sucking men. I swallowed finally; she smiled. She pinched my cheek, she touched my hair. "*Neshomeleh,* sweetheart...so much like I was at your age."

Then Perle handed me that vial of amber-colored liquid. "Put a drop here," she said, pointing to her lovely rouged nipple. I was terrified to touch her. "Just a drop on the finger." She tipped the bottle onto her own finger and held it under my nose. "Lovely, eh?" She rubbed the oil onto my nipple. I caught my breath. It was as if my breast were suddenly on fire, and yet it felt almost good. Madam Perle chuckled and kissed me on the top of my head. "Nice, isn't it?" She handed me the vial. "Now anoint me. Make me feel holy, too."

I did as I was told and placed a tiny amount on the tip of Perle's breast. She lay back and sighed luxuriously. "Wonderful, Sofia. Now drip the oil into the palms of your hands and hold it there until it warms. Just a few seconds. Rub your hands together lightly if you like...good...now spread the oil out across my belly and slowly work your hands down to my *peeric.*" She pointed to her vagina but did not touch herself. "Come ahead, I won't bite. Though if I do, it wouldn't be so bad."

I took a breath and gingerly rubbed the oil over Madam's soft, round belly, then down toward the line of her pubic hair, which was black and silky and, to my surprise—and I'll admit it, delight—woven into a tiny braid which was tied with a thin lavender ribbon just at its tip.

Madam whispered from deep in her throat, "Now stick your finger into me."

I held my breath and pushed my forefinger into her vagina, which was very wet and warm.

"Now quick," she murmured, at the edge of her breath, "take it away."

I pulled my finger out. Madam Perle groaned. She reached over and held my face in her hands. "You're a quick study, *hartseniu.* Oh, you'll do very nicely...now kiss me."

I cleared my throat and went for her lips. She stopped me with the palm of her hand. "I told you to kiss me and I meant it, but not on the mouth. Darling, kiss me down here."

In the days that followed, Madam Perle taught me much about the business of sexual pleasure and all things that accompanied it. She showed me how to smoke cigars and informed me which ones the great rabbis of Poland preferred. She explained which type of drinking alcohol was best in winter and which in summer, which ones the Talmud suggested, and which ones a woman could get away with sipping all day long.

Deftly she demonstrated the various tools of our whore trade. She showed me the many uses of the feather boa, the silk robe, the satin sheet and velvet quilt, and explained the possible religious implications of each. In the privacy of her rooms, Madam instructed me in the ways to employ a leather cock, how to tie a man down with silk scarves, demonstrated how I might ride him like a horse or offer my ass up to him like a dog. She taught me what great scholar enjoyed which implements and positions best.

Sometimes these lessons disgusted me, other times I was fascinated. Sara contended that Madam Perle made up these stories as she went along, but I'm not so certain.

There was a part of Madam's teachings—including the ways in which a lady must hold a blackjack to get best results when she wished to leave a gentleman knocked out cold; the fastest way to remove a wallet full of *pesos* from the vest pocket of a well-dressed dandy and put it back again, minus the *pesos;* the surest spot to place a knifeblade when you want an irritating gentleman to please leave you alone ("You'll trust me, Sofia, it ain't against the jugular")—that I found intriguing. "If he tries to beat you, if he flashes a razor, even if he has a gun, call out and Tutsik or Hirsh will come get him, for no man in this house is allowed to strike a woman." That was what I was told.

Good *morah* that she was, Perle sweetened my studious excellence with rewards: special delights for my pleasure only, demonstrations of her world renowned tricky dexterity with hands and tongue that included her ability to have fingers in three, four, or five places at once and still leave me begging for more.

But for me, her favors in bed and her peculiar interpretations of the Tanuch and the Talmud were the least of it. For the walls of Perle Goldenberg's bedroom were covered from floor to ceiling with books, many of which she found useful when instructing me in the art of my new vocation. Others had nothing to do with sex or God at all; they were simply wonderful stories. Madam Perle handed me Yiddish translations of French novels; read verses by the Greek poet Sappho out loud; lay beside me, belly down on the bed, and paged with me through picture books from Japan and Constantinople containing drawing upon drawing of women with legs spread and men with penises hard, dressed and naked, wrestling with each other in positions so complicated and so many that soon they engendered in me only boredom. There was also on those shelves a sorry reminder of home, for Tutsik Goldenberg had indeed purchased my father's leather-bound Shakespeare, and on my third day of lessons, how it startled me to see it by her bed. I said nothing and she said nothing, simply slipped the book under a pillow and motioned me, *Come ahead.*

In those earliest days when she called me to her, I did not know if I should enjoy her kisses, the feel of her tongue on my nipples and ass, all clearly designed to thrill me, or believe her when she said that God looked down and saw a *mitzvah* where I saw horrible pleasure. As if reading my mind, she'd whisper in that breathtaking way, "Be grateful, Sofia, this life is blessed and golden. Many look down upon us, but as I have told you many times, this profession is a gift from God. From the earliest days of the holy temple we women of pleasure have always been its guardians. Take this charge seriously, and your work here will be a journey of spirit that will bring you closer to heaven."

"Besides," Perle continued, "Tutsik has saved you from much worse fates."

For the first time since my ordeal began I almost laughed. Perle took my face between her fingers and was not gentle. "Would you rather be breaking your back in a sweatshop working for two or three pennies a day? Here you get the *Shabbes* off, good kosher meals, and are strongly encouraged to pray."

I didn't know what to answer. For at least in a sweatshop at the end of the day a person might leave and walk home in the open air. True, on Friday nights, Marianna brought me a most delicious portion of chicken, and a strange hush filled the whorehouse walls. I was pampered in a joyless way, though, with chocolates and fancy perfumes, and except for her books, and her promise of God, I was leery of pleasures in Perle Goldenberg's rooms.

There was a world alive in the Talcahuano Street house, but in those, my first weeks in Buenos Aires, I never saw it. I heard the customers come and go; once or twice I heard an argument and crockery smashing, or someone banging away on the piano. But did I ever sit in the downstairs parlor or have a meal at the dining room table with the others? No. My food was brought to me by Marianna, who also cooked it, and I ate while propped up in bed. Sara came once or twice into my room to make sure I wasn't dead, and the other girl, Rachel, poked her head in to get a look at me. I'd only the vaguest idea how their days and nights were spent; mine were spent either confined to my room or under the tutelage of Madam Perle. I'd seen nothing of Tutsik Goldenberg or Dov Hirsh. Occasionally, though, a male voice would ring up the stairs.

That was all about to change.

After three weeks of her guidance it appeared I was ready to do what Tutsik Goldenberg brought me here for. "There's a gentleman coming this evening," Perle said to me one afternoon as I was leaving her bed. "He's specifically requested you."

It was Sara who prepared me for my first night of work, with some help from Rachel. Just as my mother had made me up, had rouged my cheeks and tied back my hair to meet Tutsik Goldenberg that first night, so did these, my sisters in this horrid house, together work to make me beautiful. They applied lipstick and rouge, but also lined my eyes with paint and rubbed charcoal over my eyebrows. Rachel tied my hair up in a loose bun at the top of my head, and Sara showed me how to shake it out into a cascade. They squirted me with sweet-smelling perfume behind my ears and knees, between my breasts, and on my belly. They watched as I pulled a pair of silk stockings up over my chubby legs, then Sara tied them with garters. Finally, Rachel gave me my robe and a pair of matching satin mules. When I was decked out and painted to their satisfaction, Sara handed me a mirror. I nearly burst into tears at what I saw.

"No crying, you'll ruin our paint job," Sara said, and not kindly. "What are you blubbering about now? You're breathtaking."

That was Sara's opinion. She wanted me to look like a full-grown adult, and it was an awful disguise. In my opinion I looked ghoulish, like a vampire, a dead girl made up to appear alive. "Come," she whispered, "God awaits." Then she laughed and laughed.

I found myself nearly naked, on that night, in Madam Perle's chilly Talcahuano Street parlor, surrounded by Sara and Rachel and Tutsik Goldenberg and Dov Hirsh and three men I'd never in my life seen before, each with a brandy and a cigar. I sat perched in my silk robe and slippers on the edge of a brocaded chair. The men eyed and touched me. I held my breath tighter, though when Madam swept through she insisted I'd nothing to fear.

"No one will hurt you, you look like a rose. You're a queen, you're a princess, my dear."

A queen, I thought. Did I snicker? *A queen, that's just what I am. A Polish girl in an Argentine whorehouse. Just call me Sofia, queen of the damned.*

I did not feel beautiful or blessed. I felt obscene. Tutsik came up to me and pinched my thigh. I pulled back. "Uh-uh," he said to me, and raised his eyebrows. "Little bride, you've got to be a little more friendly than that. Didn't Perle tell you? The men like a spitfire, but they also take great pleasure in putting the fire out."

"Go to hell," I whispered.

He raised his fist for a second, then saw Perle staring at him and put his hand into his pocket. He went over and poured Dov Hirsh a fresh drink.

The customers terrified me; there was nothing holy here. I felt fingered and used up and filthy before the evening began. For these men, gentlemen and old country greenhorns both, came up to me and acted as if I were theirs. They blew in my ear, they tickled me under my chin. They rubbed my breasts through my robe and ran their fingers over my stockinged thighs. Those who didn't dare touch without paying did the same things with their rheumy eyes.

Just a few minutes later a man walked in and everything seemed to stop: the gramophone, the tinkling of glasses, even the johns shut up. He was an ordinary enough looking man to me. He was well-dressed in modern clothes, wore a little beard, and up close one saw he was slightly pockmarked. But I could tell from the way Madam Perle and her brother Tutsik practically genuflected when he came into the room that he was somebody special. "*Señor* Kahan," Madam grabbed him by the arm, "let me take your hat. Marianna!" Marianna took the hat from Madam. "What is your pleasure, *Señor?*"

"Vodka. Neat," the man said. He was older than my father, but not as old as I would see before my days in that cursed house were over.

"Then vodka neat you shall have, *Señor*. Will you take it now or shall Marianna bring it to you upstairs?"

"Well, it all depends," Kahan said, moving ever so slowly in my direction. It seemed at that moment as though all eyes were watching us. "I understand there's someone here who might be of particular interest..."

Madam Perle led him straight to me. "Marianna, *Señor* Kahan will take his vodka upstairs. Sofia, allow me to introduce *Señor* Zalman Kahan, cattle baron—"

"And lover," said he, as he took my hand into his own, "of young women."

I don't need to tell you I felt sick to my stomach. I must have blanched, for Madam Perle drew me aside. "Don't look so worried, *maideleh*. You know your job—passed all your tests. He likes you already, can't you tell?"

Señor Zalman waved at me discreetly across the room.

"Just relax, and let him be the boss. And a gentle boss he'll be. He likes to be the first man to put his penis in a girl. Someone has to do it, right? So if he'll pay us a few *pesos* extra for the privilege, why not?"

Indeed, I thought, I can think of many reasons why not. But it was time to get it over with. Kahan paid Madam Perle a handful of gold *pesos*. She counted them, handed him a token which he in turn, and with great ceremony, handed to me. I let him lead me upstairs by the hand. I wanted to cry. *Sofia, queen of the dead.* Oh yes, oh yes, that was me!

When we got to my room I wanted to throw myself at this Zalman Kahan's feet and tell him everything. That I wasn't a prostitute by nature, that my parents truly believed I was to be married but were tricked by those Goldenbergs. That I was smart once, and had excellent grades at a Warsaw gymnasium for girls. That I could name constellations in the northern sky, that I knew all the capitals all over the world.

But I heard Madam Perle's voice in my head, I felt her hands on my thighs. I looked at this man who was only a man, who was rich and who said to me, "Here's what I like."

He asked me to take his shoes off, to unbutton his jacket, to loosen his tie. Then he made a to-do about kissing me, he opened my robe, and I wanted to die. He pulled out his *shvontz* and said, "What do you think?"

"It's nice, I guess."

"I think so too. Lie down on the bed little virgin, and I'll show you the tricks it can do."

He lowered me down and lay over me, then he pushed into me. It hurt. He writhed and he thrashed and he whinnied, he sounded like a horse. He called me *b'suleh yefay*, pretty virgin, and this seemed to excite him unbelievably. He went wild. He started pumping and humping and I thought, what if I just left him here, climbed out from under him, what would happen, would he explode? And just then he did explode and he didn't praise God—he simply shouted, "Whore!"

He collapsed on top of me and was out like a light. I didn't know what I was supposed to do, squeeze out from under him or stay there. For all of Perle's lessons she never mentioned this. I lay under him, sticky, and I prayed to God he hadn't made me pregnant. If I had to have a baby here, I would kill myself for sure.

Finally I couldn't take his dead weight one more minute and I carefully pushed him aside. "Mister, wake up, it's over."

He grunted and sat up. He looked at his penis, shriveled up, and stuck it back in his pants, buttoning them quickly. "There, my dear, you are a woman now. You have been blessed by me in this, your first hour of pleasure."

I sat and stared at him. I was speechless and sad.

"Say thank you to me. For I have relieved you of the curse of virginity. For this you will be eternally grateful."

"Thank you, *Reb* Kahan," I said in my meekest Polish voice.

"Think nothing of it, *Señorita* Sofia. Now kindly help me get dressed."

Each trick drove me further from Warsaw, every Mack, every Johnnie, every Chaim and Sam drew a line through my memory. Each night before sleeping I recited my life out loud: Sofia Teitelbaum, sixteen years old, born in Warsaw, Grzybowski Street 42. Daughter of Bayla and Yakov, best friend of Tamar. Kidnapped by Tutsik Goldenberg in May 1913. But little by little the moorings came loose, I forgot the smell of our kitchen, the creak of the floor from there to the study.

The feel of the china plates under my hand, the smell of my father's pipe. The way the house felt when we all were asleep, my mother's tight lips as she kissed me good night. Worse than all that, I stopped dreaming.

For what strength did these sweet memories hold against the sorrow of my daily life? Although it became easy after a very short time to keep the *putz* customers pacified, especially if Marianna spiked the coffee, once in a while those Jewish johns came at us with straight razors, and one time, a kosher butcher from La Plata burst out of Rachel's bedroom wielding a pistol. That time Madam Perle herself came to the rescue and with her own hands grabbed the butcher around his thick neck and began to choke him until he dropped the gun and ran out the door. Even then he shouted, "Bitches, you pack of filthy sows!" The other men laughed their heads off in stupid relief, but we, the girls of the *shandhoiz,* huddled together and wondered what was to become of us next.

In those earliest days, when I still had it in me to cry when a mango was drunk or hit me, Madam Perle pampered me with a cup of tea. I wept bitterly while she fed me bits of chocolate, ran soothing fingers through my hair. And just when I was ready to jump out my window as I heard a girl from Red Ruthie's had done, Madam would come to me, she'd kiss me and say, "I'll show you now how real loving feels." She covered me everywhere with the same wild caresses she used to make crowned heads and geniuses blush. I thought at first this was an act of love but soon saw it was a trap. I was Perle's *neshomeleh* now, but before me it was Sara who was her beloved, and before her wasn't Rachel her fine little queen? And there would certainly be somebody else after me. Madam Perle was really a sultan, and we the whores of Talcahuano Street were not only her bread and butter, we were her many wives. These sorry facts I accepted about my new Argentine life.

— 5 —

OH, YES! IT WAS HORRIBLE, but working for Perle Goldenberg brought with it a most bizarre form of respect. For before her leap toward piety, Perle Goldenberg was not thought to be ridiculous at all. On the contrary. Among people who knew, both here and in Europe, Perle Goldenberg was considered to be the most learned of madams. Unlike her interpretations of the Bible, her reputation as a courtesan with remarkable intelligence and scholarly leanings was not a thing she invented. Her monumental library, which, Hankus, you saw with your own eyes, was a well-established fact and bragging point in Varsovia Society mythology, as were Madam Perle's mental and physical prowess. Visiting rabbis and the men of their flocks regularly found their way with pleasure and great determination to the doors of Talcahuano Street 154.

I suppose I might have felt honored to be counted as one of her many lovers, that my father's Shakespeare was shelved with her many volumes, if I did not feel such shame. Because it wasn't just holy men, or for that matter only men, who sought Perle Goldenberg out. It is rumored that back in the old country, *der Goldeneh Nafkeleh* (for that is what Madam Perle was sometimes called) rivaled Chopin as George Sand's favorite lover. As a young girl, Perle Goldenberg is said to have seduced an already aging Rasputin, who in turn went on to seduce the Romanovs, who, as we know, met grizzly ends at the hands of revolutionaries, though that is one set of troubles for which I cannot blame Madam Perle.

Sigmund Freud is believed to have traveled to Madam Perle all the way from Vienna to simply ask her, "What is it women want?" And it is common Varsovian knowledge that both Emma Goldman and Rosa Luxembourg sought Perle Goldenberg out for her ideas on free love, both theoretical and practical. This, of course, was long before Madam Perle had made her fractured peace with God.

There was talk that Perle Goldenberg had been mistress to one of the Rothschild grandsons. This Rothschild, no spring chicken, is rumored to have sent a private train for Perle in Warsaw, which brought her to Paris, where he rented the entire Hotel George V for a week. When he was done with her he sent her on to Monte Carlo alone. There she gambled her respectable whore's fee—the cash as well as the furs, the rubies and the diamond tiara—tripled her earnings, traveled back to Warsaw third class, sold her furs and liquidated her other hard assets. Then she booked passage for two and went straightaway with the profits and her younger brother Tutsik, who was then just seventeen, to Buenos Aires, to which place, it is said, she was advised to emigrate by another of her rumored clients, the philanthropist Baron de Hirsh. The good baron, as we know, Hankus, had taken to sending boatloads of Jews to Argentina in order to form a new Zion on the pampas, of which the little colony of Moisesville was a part. Madam Perle, through her own connections in the Warsaw underworld, had learned that whoring was perfectly legal in the City of Good Airs, and she liked the idea of being in a place where summer was winter and winter wasn't nearly as dreadful as it was at home. While she was far from eager to make her way as a pioneer on the Zion plains, she was very enthusiastic at the prospect of becoming part of the Buenos Aires *zoineh* frontier. For if ever there was a place where a woman could make a respectable living doing reprehensible things, this indeed was it.

And so the not-so-young Perle Goldenberg arrived in Argentina just as the 1890s were turning into the twentieth century. She and

Tutsik carried between them one trunk of clothing, a silver spice box, three brass candlesticks, and, as they say, not a pot to pee in after that. But each of them carried, sewn into their undergarments, their hems, and their overcoats, enough *zloty*, rubles, pounds, and dollars to convert their lives into very comfortable ones in no time at all.

Perle first of all purchased the flat on Talcahuano Street, in the Jewish barrio, just east of Once where the respectable Jewish people lived. For a few years, and with some discretion, she did all the whoring herself and provided her brother Tutsik with everything he wanted: beautifully tailored suits and silk shirts; shoes of fine, hand-tooled leather; steaks, even kosher ones, thick and tender. Yes, she provided him with all he wanted, except what he desired most—passage out of Argentina. He hated it here.

Unlike his sister, Tutsik Goldenberg detested that winter was summer and summer winter. He loathed that when it was winter it never snowed, only rained in a way so huge and horrifying it made even soggy Warsaw seem a desert. More than anything, the young Tutsik Goldenberg could not abide in the least that when a person went out the door in this upside-down city, left became right and right left. It was impossible for him to find his way even to the neighborhood candy store, or the *confiteria,* without becoming completely at sea, and this made him feel a fool, which, for Tutsik Goldenberg, was the most loathsome thing of all.

Tutsik didn't like the other young Jewish men he met in Buenos Aires. With their old world ways, they were silly little mama's boys at eighteen or nineteen, and look at him: he had no mama to speak of, just an older sister who was a whore. He wasn't tough enough for the *porteño* boys, either. No, those boys who had lived in Buenos Aires all their lives believed that, *takeh,* Tutsik Goldenberg was indeed a mama's boy, with his neat-as-a-pin clothes and his pink Polish face. Them he tried to impress with the fact that his sister was a harlot, but in Buenos Aires, Argentina, where almost anyone might be related to a prostitute, this held little currency and impressed no one.

In spite of this, the hard *porteño* boys let Tutsik hang around with them. They taught him how to drink coffee the *porteño* way, very strong with steaming hot milk and almost as much sugar. They taught him how to cheat at dice and how to look a woman up and down, which Tutsik became quite good at, although it gave him little pleasure.

Perhaps the best trick he learned, from a boy who sold papers up in Once on Rividavia Street, was how to hide and handle a blackjack. This activity Tutsik Goldenberg loved. He loved the weight of the blackjack in his hand and the coldness of it against his palm. He liked how a good blackjack gave just a bit, and he had to admit, although it shamed him at first, that he liked the feel of the blackjack against a person's head. This he discovered when some local boys took him down to La Boca and taught him how to roll sailors.

It was possible to roll a sailor without a blackjack. One could talk him into having sex, and then, just when his pants were down, bite on his dick or punch him in the eye. But this method reminded Tutsik Goldenberg too much of how his sister earned her money, and also he found himself just a little too excited at the thought of seeing a man's penis. He liked the idea better of coshing a person in the back of the head and reaching into his victim's pockets for cash.

From the thug boys he learned about blackjacks, but it was from the aristocratic Argentine boys, the sons of the mayors and governors who waited downstairs for their own turns while their fathers enjoyed Perle Goldenberg first, that Tutsik Goldenberg learned the value of a sharp knife and how to use it. With the blackjack, a man had to be sneaky; with the knife, well, half the fun of it was holding it under a person's chin and knicking him oh just the tiniest bit and then threatening to do much more. Tutsik liked to hide his knives in his shirtsleeves and make them appear as if from nowhere. He liked to snap his fingers and then find the knife open and gleaming right there in his hand. And Tutsik liked the look on the other man's face when he put out his free hand and asked for his wallet. "Turn it over," he'd tell them, and every one of them did.

Our Tutsik made his own pin money in this way, and while Perle wondered where he got it, she never bothered to ask. To live in a glass house and throw a stone was not something she liked to do. Instead she worked and saved. She befriended another *nafkeh,* a beauty called Ruchel in her hometown of Riga but Red Ruthie here in Argentina, not because she was an anarchist like Madam Perle's other girlfriend, the aforementioned Red Rosa, but because her hair was the color of copper, and her cheeks were ruddy, and all of her clothing, from stockings to corselet to kimono to dresses when she wore them, were the brightest scarlet. Red Ruthie was in Argentina now, not in dull

Lithuania. How she laughed at the thought of this all the time, how her *frum* Litvak family was sitting around their dull *Shabbes* table in black black black while she herself was dancing about her own parlor in magnificent fire-red underwear.

Red Ruthie and Perle Goldenberg were partners for a while. Ruthie paid Perle some rent to entertain her tricks in the Talcahuano Street *shandhoiz,* and the money they earned went fifty-fifty, each to each. Then one day, Marek Fishbein came knocking on their door and Perle Goldenberg began to lose her sense of independence in the City of Good Airs, although she also saw a way to rescue her little brother from the riffraff of the Buenos Aires streets and give him a job with a future.

Marek Fishbein was even then a *macher* in the Buenos Aires local of the Varsovia Society, the eastern European Jewish brotherhood of pimps and thieves. He wasn't the biggest boss of all, but he was close to it, and he had the big boss' ear. He was, even way back then, a repellent man.

Everything Perle Goldenberg was, this Fishbein was decidedly not. Where Madam Perle was a model businesswoman, frugal yet generous when generosity was needed, Fishbein was tight-fisted and a wastrel all at once. He thought nothing of buying huge and horrifying *objets d'art* from around the world—ancient Ming vases, paintings by masters such as Rembrandt and Goya, statuettes by Bernini—and then slashing and smashing them to bits in a fury. He was known to be this way with women as well, and both Ruthie and Perle had experienced this firsthand. More than once there had been a wild pounding on the door of Talcahuano Street 154 at five in the morning and some young girl in a ripped-to-shreds slip and an enormous black eye would be standing there in tears. "Please take me in," the girls begged, and Perle and Red Ruthie did for the night. But knowing Fishbein's reputation for efficient and violent retribution, they were quick to put the girl out before word got round the Jewish barrio that one of Fishbein's tarts was hiding there.

While Perle Goldenberg and her brother Tutsik—oh, he to the greatest extreme—looked tidy and immaculate, Fishbein was a huge mess of a man. No suit he wore ever fit him. The shoulders slid from side to side. The front flapped open to reveal a filthy white shirt whose cuffs and collar were frayed beyond repair, and a striped cravat that was a map of every soup he had eaten for the past week. His pants had crusty mud at the cuffs. His shoes were always in need of a new pair of heels and a shine. His wild beard and hair stuck out in every direction, no matter how often he combed them, and he wore an ancient black stovepipe hat, badly in need of blocking (if this would even help) which sat at all times loosely on his head and rested just atop his ears. In Fishbein's mouth was always in those days, lit or unlit, the stub of a bad-smelling cigar. This in spite of the fact that here in Buenos Aires it was possible to find slim, sweet-tasting coronas and cheroots for a fraction of what they cost back home.

Well, one afternoon while Madam Perle and her companion Red Ruthie were sitting at the same dining room table where you and I were to meet some years later, as they sipped their shared tea through a *bombilla*, gossiping and giggling about the business of the night before, there came an insistent rapping at the front door. Perle sent Marianna down to see about the racket. The cook returned followed by Marek Fishbein, sweating in his filthy shirt and ill-fitting collar and jacket, holding that stubby cigar in his teeth.

He arrived alone but made it clear that he had two lackeys waiting for him in a *droshky* downstairs. He bit down on the end of his cheap cigar and never removed it as he spoke, although he did tip his hat when Marianna brought him into the dining room. The two whores started laughing. They were expecting a john, but Fishbein wasn't even a trick; he was more like a practical joke. Ruthie recognized him immediately, but Perle had to put on her glasses because she had only seen him once before and that was in a crowded *cantina* on Tucumán Street.

Recognize him or not, Marek Fishbein was standing in their dining room and there was no reason either one of them could think not to invite him to sit down, which he did with a great scraping of his chair on the well-polished wooden floor. Marianna went back to the kitchen, and Red Ruthie asked if she might take Fishbein's hat. He made as if to hand it to her, then took it back. "It's a nice offer, but to tell you ladies the truth, no matter what the weather, no matter what the place, I'm never far separated from this old stovepipe of mine. My father wore it and his father before him. It was passed down through the generations and even in *shul*—and like you, Perle Goldenberg, I go to *shul* twice on a *Shabbes* weekend: once on Friday night to see our dear queenie in and once on Saturday to see her out—I don't ever wear a *yarmulkie*. No, just this old top hat. I get it blocked for the high holy days and in those few hours when it is off my head, I tell you, dear ladies, I go a little insane. There's no telling what I might do. Why just this past Rosh Hashanah I threw my best pal out my office window. True, it was only four flights up, it could have been worse, but to see him all bandaged up like that after the fact—ah, it broke my heart. I sent him honey and apples in the hospital for a week after that. And since it's business I come to talk to you of, it's best I think if I keep this hat on my head. Now, might I have a nice glass of tea—Odessa-style?"

The ladies looked at each other and shrugged. Perle went in to the kitchen to tell Marianna. Fishbein called after her, "And mix in it please a little schnapps."

Perle thought better to mix in a little arsenic. As she watched Marianna boil the water and fix the tea she heard Fishbein's low voice and Ruthie's girlie laughter. She put the glass on a silver tray and brought it out to Fishbein. "As it happens, *Reb* Fishbein, we're out of schnapps."

"Out of schnapps!" he said, hitting his head. "And you call this a whorehouse?"

"We call it nothing of the sort," Perle said.

"Well then, that's the problem. It's a very good thing I've come. Listen, you girls are running a business here. It's a documented fact, everybody up and down Córdoba Avenue knows it. You're doing reasonably well, and you've expanded, no?"

"What do you mean? It's just the two of us—"

"But it was only one of you apiece two years ago. You see my point. You girls think you're running an isolated little independent business here, but no one in Buenos Aires is independent, do you understand?" Suddenly he pounded his fist down on the table. His tea glass shook. "One hand washes the other. You scratch my back I scratch yours, *fashstais?* And here in Buenos Aires, in this foreign city far away from all we know and understand, we Jews must look out for one another. Because we don't know when these Argentines are going to turn their backs on us and send us on our way. We don't know when all those gauchos out there in the provinces are going to go a little crazy and decide that it's Easter and they miss their Jesus so they have to burn out all the Jews in Moisesville and our other colonies and when that's done come into the city and burn our houses down too." Perle and Red Ruthie looked at him blankly. "You ladies might think we're all better off and safe here, thousands of miles away from the Tsar and the Tsarina, far away from all those *goyisher* peasants, but mark my words: no matter where he lives, the Jew is never safe." Fishbein hit the table again. Perle and Red Ruthie jumped just a bit. He leaned toward them as if to let them in on a monumental secret. "And we, the Jews who provide life's secret pleasures, we are the least safe of all."

Fishbein took a grubby cube of sugar from his breast pocket, dusted it off, and placed it carefully behind his bottom teeth. He followed this with a long sip of hot tea and smacked his lips appreciatively. "Now *this* is tea. I can't drink it out of that gourd the way they do here. Tea is meant to be swallowed in hot little gulps, not sucked through a prissy straw." He noticed the *maté* between Perle and Ruthie and cleared his throat. "Look," he said, all business again, "you ladies may not be aware of it, but as part of our attempt to protect ourselves here, we Jews in Argentina have a society, a brotherhood as it were, to make sure we're all taken care of. You know what I'm talking about? You know what this is?"

"It's the Varsovia Society, so what?" Perle said. Red Ruthie shook her head at Perle and tried to signal her to shush.

Fishbein sucked some tea out of his mustache. "An attitude like yours will get us nowhere, Miss Goldenberg. An attitude like yours in a business like ours is no good, none at all. You listen to me. I have been back and forth from the old country to here fifteen, maybe twenty times in the past five years. It's my job, back and forth, back and forth, to bring home fresh blood. Young girls. You two are sweet now, but this is a business that ages a woman, and you, Perle, you're well past twenty and you begin to look it. If everyone else has a stable full of young girls here, fresh meat straight from the kosher butcher shop in Kiev, you get my meaning, who will come here to you girls for a piece of tough worn-out leather? Especially in Argentina, where beef is cheap."

Perle was going to put in her two cents about a lovely steak, aged and mellowed, but she didn't have a minute between Fishbein's lively sentences.

"Look," he said, as if he were doing them a great favor, "what's good for one is good for all and we Varsovians are a generous bunch. We'll cut you girls in so you can be just as equal with us men. All you have to do is join our society, pay dues once a year, protection money to the police and the mayor as needed, and you're in."

"And if we don't?"

"What is this, *if you don't?* You will. Because it's good business. *Señora* Goldenberg, you are known far and wide not just for your bedroom calisthenics but also for your fine business brain. You are well respected and well known, as is your partner here, Red Ruthie—incidentally, Ruthie, your father and my father were pinochle players together whenever he was in Riga. But if you two should decide to act stupid, you decide maybe you don't want to play by our rules, well, let me just remind you about that fire over on Pasteur Street a few weeks ago. A little flat run by Zev Brokhes and his lovely wife Ettie. Very nice business built up over time with real *haimishista* girls—two of them—their flat just so happened to be in that building on Pasteur Street. *Whoosh.* Nothing left. No one knows how the fire started, and you know, he wasn't a member of the Varsovia Society so there's no brotherhood money to help him out. Poor guy, he's ruined." Fishbein lit a match quite suddenly and waved it in front of Perle's face before he touched it to his dead cigar. "You're getting the picture, no?"

"You're painting it beautifully," Perle answered flatly.

"To join us is quite simple, ladies. Your fee is divided up into fifty-two payments which are collected weekly by a Varsovia Society official elected twice a year. We have meetings once a month at our headquarters on Córdoba Avenue. There we organize our buying expeditions to the homeland together so as to keep each other posted on any new obstacles we might encounter on the way. We like to hold the suspicions of the authorities at bay. The Buenos Aires cops could care less about how we make our money, but there is an unfortunate group of do-gooders from England and the United States who are on to us, and they watch for us here as we come off the ships. I, myself, had a young lady ripped away from me by one of those sour-faced old maids. I claimed I was her uncle, but the young lady caved in and started bawling her eyes out. Before I could get her to back me up she blurted out that I had stolen her from home. I hadn't stolen her. I'd paid her parents good money, but there was no time to explain that to the lemon face. I left them both there on the dock and pushed my way through the crowds. I got away, but not before that goody two-shoes got a good look at me." He held out a wrinkled copy of the Yiddish paper. There, gazing up at Perle, was a cartoon of Fishbein that looked remarkably like him. "It ain't a bad likeness," he said, "although frankly the beard's a little long. Anyway, in terms of trips from the homeland with girls as cargo, I'm afraid I'm all washed up. Which is another reason, dear ladies, we need you on the company payroll."

Perle glanced at Red Ruthie who had been sitting with her hand wrapped tightly around her mouth since Fishbein lit his match. "As a businessman, *Reb* Fishbein, you understand that my partner and I need to discuss your proposition."

"Yes, of course you do. It's to be expected."

"We'll get back to you at the start of next week."

"At the end of *this* one," he said as he rose and adjusted his hat. "Terrible thing about those Brokheses." He shook his head and clicked his tongue against his teeth. "And they were doing so well. I'll be at the *shul* Friday at seven o'clock."

"Indeed," said Perle, who saw him to the door.

"Afternoon, dear ladies."

"*Señor* Fishbein, good-bye."

Madam Perle and Red Ruthie didn't have to consult with each other very long before deciding that Fishbein was not a man to diddle with. If they wanted to prevent their flat from being destroyed, and themselves with it, they had no choice but to do as Fishbein asked and join the Varsovia Society. It was a fact that neither Red Ruthie nor Madam Perle was getting any younger. It occurred to them both that a little new material around the house might not be a bad thing. Also, neither one of them wanted to make the long trip back to Europe to look for girls.

So this is how Madam Perle's became a Varsovia Society house, and how that weasel Tutsik Goldenberg began his career as an international purveyor of diamonds and other fine jewels. At first Tutsik sailed as a lackey in order to learn the trade. Although he was just barely twenty by now, and to be a lackey was only fitting, it irked him. But the job paid well and it permitted him to visit his beloved

Poland twice a year. The boys who traveled back and forth for the Varsovia Society did it well. They dressed in fancy clothes and traveled first class. On the trip over to Europe they gambled with the cattle barons and made their expenses in the first two days. Thanks to his *porteño* pals, Tutsik found himself in the enviable position of being able to cheat not just at pinochle but at dominoes and craps as well. So excellent at cheating was he that he never bragged about it. And because he didn't brag about it, his Varsovia Society cronies thought he didn't do it, and so he cheated them as well.

Though the journey was long, and in spite of the gambling unbelievably tedious, when the ship pulled into the harbor at last, a little thrill ran through Tutsik, a thrill that lasted all the long train ride to Poland as he looked out his window and saw old ladies in aprons and huge brown shoes shepherding two or three cows along the river bank or through a meadow. It thrilled him to catch sight of a couple of Cossacks on horseback, though he knew that for some poor sucker Jew those quaint Cossacks would mean a saber in the belly before the night was through. And when he and the others got off the train in Cracow or Minsk, even in the early days when he was at the bottom of the pile and not the top of the heap, when he and the other Varsovia men wandered into a tavern, all of them together and you could smell the food—the *blintzes* and the *smetteneh,* the boiled cabbages and onions—oh, then was Tutsik Goldenberg the happiest of men. For nowhere in all of Buenos Aires could a person get a bowl of cabbage *borscht* the likes of which you could find everywhere in Jewish Europe.

His job that first year was as a details man, and as a details man he got to watch the bagmen very carefully. He saw how a bagman placed himself in a town and how he set his sights on a target. The men who taught Tutsik his trade used the Lothario approach. They seduced the women themselves, then got them to run away from home with them. They never involved the parents at all. While the Lotharios were busy luring and bribing the young women to leave all they knew for a life of adventure and lust, Tutsik Goldenberg and the other details men were busy securing false papers, finding more women, booking train and boat tickets, and carrying luggage. Some bagmen actually slept with the women or pretended to marry them. You know how it went: a fake rabbi in the back of some tavern over on Krachmala Street, a cheap rhinestone ring, and then a punch in the mouth on a boat going west. Others just got the woman to fall head over heels for them and swear that they'd follow them anywhere. Then the women got on the boat and the Lothario types romanced them all the way to Buenos Aires, saving the punch in the mouth until later. To be absolutely truthful, there were some women who knew what was up right from the start and went along with it anyway. For them, a whore's life seemed much more exciting than a thousand years stuck at their father's dull table, and a second thousand years stuck at a husband's dull table, and then an eternity as the dull husband's footstool in heaven.

But Tutsik Goldenberg didn't like the idea of having to romance a woman. He thought it was better and easier to court the girl's father, keeping the girl out of the picture right up until the last minute. So at the start of his career, Tutsik Goldenberg spent all those long boat rides figuring out exactly how to go about this. Because once a details man set up all the details, he had little to do except gamble the pants off rich Europeans en route to the new world, and dread his return to Buenos Aires. Thinking and thinking as he watched the grey water slip under the ship all the way home, Tutsik Goldenberg struck upon the plan that brought me and many women before me, and not a few after me, to sadder times in the City of Good Airs.

Tutsik Goldenberg soon convinced the Varsovia Society to let him lead expeditions to Poland and do the bagging himself. In the months that followed he procured enough women for Red Ruthie and Perle to be able to split off and run two houses in a kind of independent partnership: four women for Red Ruthie, and for Perle he snagged Rachel and Sara. In between he provided women for Jewish bordellos in the provinces. He was paid handsomely for them, but he soon gambled away the money. At last Tutsik Goldenberg dragged me to Madam Perle's house and, with Sara and Rachel, we were a stable of three.

By the time I was situated and broken in at Talcahuano Street, Madam Perle herself took only customers for whom she had some sentimental attachment. That is to say, only if she liked their faces and they could quote from the Gemara as well. Her oldest associate was her cook and confidante, Marianna, a Jew from Toledo, Spain, who had been with the Goldenbergs practically since the day they arrived in Argentina. Madam Perle stole Marianna away from a kosher restaurant in Once, then trained her in Polish cooking. The creams and cheeses were hard to come by in Buenos Aires, but onions and garlic were plentiful, and it suited Perle that Marianna would from time to time throw a hot chili pepper into the *tsimmes,* or sprinkle the brisket with cumin and ginger. It made her feel as if she were having the best of all worlds, and she passed this small pleasure on to us *nafkehs.*

In her spare time, long before I arrived, Madam Perle Goldenberg began to take great care over the holy books in her library. She was after some meaning, some unbreakable deal with God.

To the careless eye, I seemed to thrive at Talcahuano Street, for Madam Perle and Marianna fattened me up like some cow. Though I was pale from lack of sun and air, I became *zaftig* and lovely, or so the johns said. Rachel, who hailed from Grodno, was *zaftig,* too, and she seemed almost happy. Not so my Sara, who ate, but rarely with joy. Once she had delivered me to Talcahuano Street and was back in Buenos Aires for good, she began to waste away before our eyes, in spirit as much as in body. Those crook Goldenbergs decided that she was of more use to them flat on her back in the whorehouse than as a traveling companion in Europe. There would be no more trips for her then, and Sara, who was naturally thin and tall to begin with, started to shrink away. The dead look in her eyes became deader still and her mouth set deeper and deeper into a horrible smile.

Did anyone else see it? I couldn't say. I only know that even I, who was being worked to the bone in Perle's big bed and at the hands of the men, even I noticed Sarah wane and harden, and this left me more desolate and lost than ever before.

I wanted to show her love, but since my first week in Madam Perle's bed, Sara only averted her eyes and drifted away when I reached for her. I craved her nearness, for in an awful way, she was the link between my two lives. I remembered those long Sara nights aboard the *Viktorius* as we steamed our way to Argentina. Once or twice in that cursed bed she actually looked into my eyes while she lay on top of me. She spoke my name then, while she pushed into me. She laughed when I wriggled and moaned. These small gestures impressed her forever onto my heart, as Tamar was impressed in another, more dangerous spot.

But there on Talcahuano Street, when we shared a bed together as we sometimes did to escape a damp night, the novelty of my noises and surprise was gone for her. She touched me in the same places she always did, but it was a ghost touch. She kissed me but her kisses were blank. I could understand her coldness when she took me to bed at the demand of some *yentzer* who paid to watch. But at every turn in our day, at breakfast with the others, or alone in the parlor when no johns were there, I tried to curl up, lay my head upon her naked lap, hoping only that she would caress my hair. Once or twice she brushed it for me, but her strange, lonesome hands never lingered.

I tried to tell her that my time with Madam Perle was at Perle's request, not my own; that left to my own devices, it was Sara I'd pick each time. When I whispered these facts into her ear and ended them with kisses, she brushed me off with the slightest flick of her hand and a sad smile, then disappeared into her room.

At first I took her condition as entirely my responsibility. If only I could say no to Perle, if only Perle would stop paying so much attention to me and offer some to Sara. But then Rachel, of all people, pulled me aside and put me wise. "Look," she said, "Sara is always a little *tsedrait* when she gets a taste of the big world and then has to come back to Talcahuano Street. Once she starts *shtupping* again for money, she's gone. And now that Tutsik don't want to take her no more to Poland, well, we'll see how long she stays alive."

"What do you mean?" I was horror-struck.

"I mean we'll see if she don't kill herself. You haven't been here long enough to entertain the thought, but me, I think about it all the time. And for Sara, it's a secret key she keeps tucked behind her tongue. The thought of ending it all, that's Sara's only hope."

I looked at Rachel with great alarm. When first I came, I thought that she was simpleminded. What else was I to think? She laughed at every joke, even the ones the most despicable mangoes made at our expense. She giggled at the sight of straight razors, took blades and brass knuckles in stride. She never lost her temper and smiled all the time. She was rosy cheeked and cheerful and, until just that moment, I believed empty-headed. Rachel was twenty-two by the time I arrived in Buenos Aires and had been with Madam Perle already seven years. She was the first of Tutsik's solo conquests. Looking at her closely, I just then saw there was a hollowness to her cheer.

"Don't look so scared, you little *yold*." She slapped me on the behind. "As long as Tutsik Goldenberg keeps Sara on dope she'll be too gone to take a powder."

I looked at Rachel carefully. Her eyes never left mine. "What's *dope?*"

"What a baby. Did they snatch you right out of the kindergarten schoolyard or what? Dope is opium—that sticky stuff she and Tutsik smoke in pipes all the time. What did you think it was, just another way to drink tea?"

I didn't say anything.

"I'm surprised they haven't introduced you to it. Didn't Perle mention it was one of the secret tools of Jewish womanhood? Anyway, they try to offer it to me, but I say no. You'll refuse it too if you know what's good for you. It makes you so stupid you think you're happy, but really all you are is gone. Like our Sara. Find yourself another girlfriend, dollface." Rachel winked at me the way I'd seen her wink at johns. I hate to say so, but I felt a tiny thrill in my *peeric* when she did it, but I knew she was doing it to torment me. Then suddenly she softened. "Sara covers her sorrow with a chilly mask, *neshomeleh*. Be careful or you'll end up doing that too."

There were some men who came to the Talcahuano Street *shandhoiz* who were not johns. They were pals of Tutsik Goldenberg, there to play cards in the parlor and smoke. One, Mordechai Dorfman, who frequently accompanied Dov Hirsh, was a doctor who inspected us against the clap and showed me how to clean myself with vinegar so I wouldn't get pregnant. All of them drank tea in tumblers and schnapps in shot glasses that Perle brought from Poland a long time ago. Those men rarely took us to bed, but we were theirs to touch as much as anyone else's. This drove me insane. At least when the *mohel* from La Plata came up for a good time you were likely to get a tip for your trouble. When that vampire Dov Hirsh came to call, with or without his friend Dr. Dorfman, all you got was pinched—maybe even slapped in the face—and not a *peso* to be made for all of that. Dorfman seemed not such a fiend as Hirsh, although we learned different later on. He wasn't as bright, and on the surface he wasn't as mean. I never saw him wield a knife except one time when Rachel had an abortion, and this he did with the greatest care.

But Hirsh, he was another story. He'd arrive with Dorfman, maybe alone, at seven exactly. He'd sit down beside me, or Sara, or Rachel, and proceed every evening to pare his nails with an evil-looking knifeblade that was twice the length of his hand. He liked to point it at our lips and heart. Once he slipped it under the strap of my slip and made as if to cut it open. But at the last minute he pulled it away and he and the other fellows around him all laughed.

I continued to be terrified of him, as I had been on the ship, and sat the whole time with my dressing gown pulled tight around me. He'd sit and read the Yiddish paper, slowly it seemed, one word at a time. I'd stare at him and wonder how could I get that long knife and run it through his breast and run it through mine and be over and done and die.

If Perle caught one of those *shnorrers* playing with knives or grabbing a feel, she told them hands off fast enough and made them stick a few *pesetas* in a metal bank she kept for charity. But suppose she was busy with her own customers, or out praying at the synagogue, which she began to do more and more. Then Dorfman and Hirsh took free handfuls whenever they liked and slapped us on the rump besides, which gave the paying customers the idea that they, too, could take liberties with us. They were bad for business, that Dov Hirsh and Mordechai Dorfman, but more than that, they were bad for my heart. And without Sara to laugh or complain with, I felt desolate.

There were wonderful sights in Buenos Aires. I knew because I read it in Madam Perle's books. There was a cemetery where everyone was vaulted in tombs above ground. There were statues of those people in front of their tombs looking regal and profound. There were huge theatres and concert halls, some built by the Varsovians themselves to get in good with the common Jews. There were dance halls in those days and fabulous plazas that stand even now. There was the flea market in San Telmo, and there were marvelous squares. I was not permitted to see any of this in my early Buenos Aires years. Although we were fed and allowed to keep clean, although we were kept disease-free, we were never allowed outside the flat without a companion screw. Since the screw was usually Perle herself, we saw little besides the inside of the Thieves' Shul, where we were shunned and derided all the way up into the women's balcony and then silently spat upon once we were finally there.

This broke Perle's heart but she brought us anyway, every Friday night. Can you imagine, four Jewish whores walking to Once in their

Sabbath best, four Jewish whores in white cotton dresses? A remarkable, laughable sight. For a while, Sara came back to life in the women's balcony. When the reputable Jewish women scoffed at our piety, poked each other and rolled their eyes, it was Sara who sneered back and barked like a dog while our good Madam Perle put her head down and cried.

I had hope then that Sara would stay alive, would be my companion on those long walks home. But as soon as the service was ended, as soon as we pressed through the venerable crowd, icy Sara sunk back to the heart of herself and said nothing, just muttered and frowned.

We came back on Friday nights to *Shabbes* dinners I could almost enjoy. It was the only time on Talcahuano Street I was close to happiness, until I remembered that Tutsik Goldenberg stole me away at a meal such as this, and that my own candlesticks were long gone. On Friday nights and Jewish holidays, the *shandhoizen* were all closed. Red Ruthie and her *kurvehs* joined us for dinner and tea. It was then that we drank up our brandy and ate our honey cake with no fear. For the evening was ours, just us whores. Madam Perle allowed no smoking on these nights, so Hirsh and Dorfman left with Tutsik Goldenberg right after dinner, went out to the *cantina* to smoke and drink there. They harassed and belittled the *goyisher* girls for a change of pace and left our asses alone.

Cursed Goldenbergs, thieves of my childhood! Thanks to you I was old by seventeen. I had no wild youth. I watched Rachel's empty smiles, tried to coax love from dead Sara, saw that I was destined to die here, too. I swore that one way or another I'd be delivered from this place. On the back of a man or underneath him, I would walk out that door and be free.

PART TWO

South American Handcuff Release
(1910–1915)

I

MEANWHILE, HANKUS, IN ANOTHER COUNTRY, some years earlier, something so terrible has happened that you find yourself walking in the pouring rain on a dirt road to Cracow and you've no idea why. You are wearing filthy trousers too big for you tied around your waist with a rope, a ripped linen shirt with a round collar, and over this a mud-caked, blood-smeared black frock coat. Your slender feet are bare. On your head you wear a wool cap covering your hair. It used to hang down to your hips; now it stops unevenly above your ears.

You walk through puddles along the road, your feet wet and freezing. You carry something in your hands, and though you know you must never lose it, you cannot bear to look down and see what it is you hold.

Men on horseback pass you by, and twice, three times, a coach full of men and women in fancy clothes splash past, and what do they see when they pass you? Anyone? Anything? Once an ox-cart driver leans over to ask you, "Little boy, do you want a ride?"

You take to the woods, run into the forest, sit down on a tree stump and cry. You have no idea what your name is or what you are trying so hard to forget. Yet once in a while you hear voices, men shouting, and women and men shouting back. You see flashes of metal and flashes of blood. The more you remember the faster you run.

At last you arrive in Cracow, you sleep on the banks of the Vistula. You wander to Kazimierz. Slowly your panic begins to subside.

You find food in the alleys behind Jewish cafés—beef bones and bread with some bites taken out, an all-but-devoured stewed leg of lamb. You beat the feral cats at their game, grab what you can and run. You sleep in doorways by night or you walk. In the day you live in the public park. You study the Vistula, flat and narrow, as it runs its lazy way north to south. When soldiers stroll by you hold your breath. You become invisible, that's how you live.

The days go by and the days go by, for how long you don't really know. You're a ghost in Cracow, you hold a small bundle, and where your feet take you that's where you go.

Then one evening, outside a café that has better garbage the more you come 'round, there's more than a bone: there's a bowl full of soup and a spoon, and a hunk of black bread. At first you think—best to leave it alone, it's not meant for you, just ignore it. But a big red dog with a sneer on its sorry face ambles directly for it. Even though the dog is huge, the thought of that mutt slurping such beautiful soup with his ugly tongue makes you wild.

"*Paskudnyak!*" you shout, "stupid dog. Get out of my way, it's *mine!*"

The dog snaps its chops, you snap yours; the dog growls, you growl, too. Then before you can lunge at each other's throats you hear a man's voice say, "Hey, Motke, it worked, we caught him." He grabs at your frock coat. You try your best to wriggle away. You kick and scream, you scratch him, but the man has both your arms. "Shush, little *vildeh*, shh, shh, shh. I'm Max, hush, *shh*, quiet down. We seen you around for a couple of weeks. Neither Motke or me's going to do you no harm."

He holds you tight while you fight him, he holds until you can't push anymore, then he wraps his arms around you, and you sob while he brings you indoors.

It is not until they bathe you, the water hot and soapy in a steel tub in the kitchen of their little apartment behind the restaurant, that the two men, Max and Motke, see you for who you really are. They are big men, both of them, tall and heavy with trim beards. Max has a pot belly and giant hands, Motke's are dainty and quick.

Before your bath they bring you back through the café. Max sits with his arms around you in a wood rocker and holds you until you stop crying. Then he asks kindly, *"Tsir reit ir* Yiddish?" When you nod your head a tear forms in his eye. Motke fills up the tub with water. Max gingerly pulls off your shirt. They don't notice then, but when your pants come down Max covers his mouth. "*Gottenieu*, Motke! A girl!"

Motke washes you sweetly, scrubs your back without hurting, offers the wash rag so you can wash your most private places yourself, then he carefully pats you dry. He dresses you in one of his own shirts, which is enormous on you, pulls a huge wool sock onto each of your feet. Then he sits you down at the table. "*Tochter vildeh,* wild daughter, let's see what our Maxie has made you to eat."

There before you sits a feast: red soup full of cabbage and chunks of meat; potatoes roasted with onions; pickled tomatoes and steaming beets; and a tall glass of black tea with sugar. All you can do when you look at this banquet is cover your face and sob.

The two men get you to eat that night just a little bit at a time. They hold the spoon while you sip your soup. They never ask your name. They make you a bed of blankets at a warm place by the stove, and just before you drift to sleep they give you your bundle to hold. It's when you unwrap the cloth, an old dish towel, that you start to unravel yourself. For here are your mother's candlesticks. You saved them with your own life.

Max and Motke took you in. They never asked for your story. There was a pogrom in a village up the river and everyone was presumed dead. But when they saw the look in your eye, they guessed that maybe just one had survived. For they'd seen the look before, the wide-eyed look of a person who climbed out of an oven or out of a closet or out from behind a locked cellar door. Or someone like you who saw everyone murdered while she herself was ignored. They did not press you for details. They assumed you couldn't remember anyway.

You thought your name might be Hannah, they believed this was so. They figured you for thirteen and you said that sounded right.

You were flat-chested and lanky, and *dafkeh*, you looked like a boy. "We'll say you're our nephew from Lublin, our sister Bronia's son." Motke surveyed their apartment. "For now you can sleep over here by the stove, but we'll make you a place in the study. For a girl must have her privacy, even if she's a young man."

Now anyone with a brain in their head knew that Max and Motke weren't brothers. They shared a bed and they kissed good night. They were sweethearts, married lovers. But the whole town agreed to the story: two brothers, Max and Motke from Plock, who owned the Alef Bais Café. And now their nephew Hankus was here, who arrived just yesterday by train. Had the rest of the town seen you groveling from trash can to trash can on chilly spring nights? Or did they just believe you sprung off the train, a visitor in their midst? It didn't matter. From the minute you started washing dishes in the Alef Bais Café they believed you were who you said you were, the nephew who carried the tray of gravy-stained plates and bowls from the front of the joint to the back, who bowed when he wiped down their table. When they asked you, "*Bar Mitzvahed?*," you nodded. That was the end of that.

Max and Motke kept you a boy because for all the pretense it took it was still a good deal easier than living with them as a girl. For one, there was the way it looked to the outside eye. A nephew living with two bachelor brothers was one thing, a niece quite another.

You didn't mind the clothing part. You welcomed it, in fact. The dresses and pinafores you wore back at home always left you feeling confined. And Max and Motke were quick to point out the other benefits that would befall you in your new gender. "Religiously, you're much better off, of course," said Max, as he scrambled some eggs with onions in a big cast-iron skillet. "They'll let you sit right on the main floor if you ever go to *shul*."

This didn't seem like much of a bargain, for you were never a great believer in God. Especially after what happened to your people back home. Still, there were other advantages that you'd not have thought of on your own. "Those matchmakers," Motke nodded, "they still might chase after you—a nice boy, handsome, a good catch. As a girl you'd have to entertain future husbands every night, which, believe me, gets tedious after a while. But as a man, whether actual or in- vented, if you tell them you have better things to do, they pretty much leave you alone."

"Plus," chimed in Max, "there is also the problem of your safety in the bigger world."

"Absolutely," said Motke. "It's bad enough to be a Jew in Cracow—"

"In *Poland*." Max shook his head mournfully.

"In Poland!" continued Motke, "but as a woman there's no telling..." His voice trailed off softly, and sadly you understood why.

For you saw what those soldiers did to your sister and mother. You tried not to remember, but once in a while as you carried a tray of greasy crockery into the kitchen, or nodded your head when a customer asked for a nice glass water, something in a man's laugh at the other end of the room brought forward your sister's face, your mother's, and you became silent then, traveled back almost as far as you had walked in that muddy rain, lost the thread of where you were in time and space, even in the middle of one of Motke's uproarious jokes or Max's magic tricks. Even as you were setting down a plate of roast duck with what seconds ago had been the greatest care in front of a customer who had been coming to the Alef Bais for years. You didn't drop the plate. You let it slip down in front of the customer quietly, then just as quietly you disappeared. A little while later Max or Motke found you in a corner of the cellar, sometimes shaking, sometimes in tears.

They kept you close by them and loved you. They found you clothes from the Ladies Benevolent Society, and Motke made you a wonderful shirt. In turn you washed all the dishes, bussed tables, and kept them clean. Motke cooked, Max took orders and *shmoozed*. You brought out the food when the café was busy. In the off times Motke taught you his secret recipes and Max taught you magic tricks his father and uncles had taught him. He showed you how to make coins vanish right from the palm of your hand. He taught you how to free yourself from all kinds of knots, secretly pick a lock so it looked like you did it by magic. From him you learned how to conjure a pigeon from out of a person's ear, then once it was resting on your finger, make the pigeon disappear.

Then one day, completely by accident, you emerged into your truest magical vocation, your life dream come true. It was a crowded lunchtime in the Alef Bais. Gentile salesmen from Cracow proper were crowding the little tables, making deals with Jewish businessmen, ladies who were out to market with their daughters decided to stop for a cup of Motke's, God bless him, beautiful chicken soup. As quickly as you and Max brought the food out, Motke was handing you more. There were men and women waiting for tables all the way out the door.

You lifted a tray full of dishes on to your shoulder and were headed toward the back. Yossel Shimkes, the traveling shoemaker, was, at the very minute you passed, impressing his pal Shmuel Sadowsky with facts about the magnitude of the L'vov rabbi's feet. "Big. I ain't seen such a big foot on a man in thirty years. Not like us, little-bitty size eight, nine. I'm talking a giant foot to reflect the man's great brain, giant, I tell you, like so—" and he flung his arms wide to demonstrate at the very moment you walked by with your tray of dirty crockery. The tip of the rabbi's enormous learned toe knocked you off your balance, the tray slipped, and everything on it went flying. The entire clientele of the Alef Bais Café braced themselves for a crash.

Instead, what they saw was a miracle. For there before them, calm as could be, stood you, young Hankus Lubarsky, spinning and juggling dirty cups and saucers, platters and soup bowls, silver knives and forks effortlessly through the air. It was a sight so breathtaking that gesticulating *kibbitzers* stopped midsentence and voracious eaters put their well-stuffed sandwiches down.

Max and Motke emerged from the kitchen with towels on their arms to see what had caused all their chatty customers to suddenly go mute. And there you were, their pride and joy, keeping everything but the kitchen sink swirling and twirling high above your head. Then as quickly as you began, one-two-three, you piled the dishes as if by magic into neat, manageable stacks. The lunch crowd at the Alef Bais Café exploded into cheers and stomping feet.

Yossel Shimkes grabbed Max by the shoulder. "I know what I'm talking about, Maxie. That boy is going to be big."

You bowed, then brought the dishes back to the kitchen and started washing them. But Hankus, you were hooked.

From that day forward you worked at the Alef Bais only Friday and Sunday lunch and alternate Thursdays. The rest of the time Max and Motke wanted you to practice magic and acrobatics, your new craft. Max spotted you for handstands and backflips. Motke found you some Indian clubs. You practiced in the park by the Vistula, and once in a while you took the trolley to the old city up the hill. You juggled then for the *goyim* who threw *groschen* your way and applauded every trick. You perfected your rope and handcuff escapes just outside the marketplace. Max swore he wanted to get you a theatre, but instead they relinquished Thursday nights to you in the café. They built you a tiny stage. Motke painted a sandwich board that read:

REAL JEWISH MAGIC AT THE ALEF BAIS CAFÉ
HANKUS LUBARKSY, ESCAPE ARTIST
JUGGLER AND MASTER OF SLEIGHT OF HAND
THURSDAYS 8:30
INQUIRE WITHIN

Two local musicians accompanied you, one on cornet, one on drum. You started your evening with handstands and flips and then you went on to perform Motke's vanishing *groszy* trick. You did it with a gold coin. You juggled some dishes for old time's sake, followed by your Indian clubs. You finished that segment by juggling a platter of Max's famous *knishes*, then passed them out for the audience to eat. Once a night you were challenged by anyone who chose to cuff your wrists with a lock or tie your hands with a length of rope. And no matter what they brought you, from what far corner of the earth, in a matter of minutes you freed yourself. The crowd burst into cheers.

For your grand finale each Thursday night, Max and Motke appeared on each side of you, *sans* aprons, wearing beautiful embroidered vests from the Holy Land. The music became mysterious as the brother lovers brought forth a fabulous wine-red cloth. They covered you with this, spun you around three times, clapped their hands together, and the cloth fell to the ground. They lifted the cloth to reveal that you were gone. The crowd caught its breath, the drummer rolled. The door of the café flew open and in you sailed, head over heels.

Then the little crowd on Jozefa Street went insane with delight. They came again the next Thursday, and this time they brought all their friends. Thursday nights at the Alef Bais in Kazimierz Cracow became known to Jewish travelers far and wide. If Tutsik Goldenberg saw you there first, I wouldn't be surprised.

You more than earned your keep with the lovers Max and Motke. By the time you were sixteen you were doing two shows nightly three nights a week. They hired another waiter. Other acts performed. You were the center of Jewish cabaret life in all of Cracow, and Hankus, there was nothing you loved more.

The more you performed at Max and Motke's Alef Bais Café, the more Polish gentiles found their way to Kazimierz to watch you. There was talk of an impresario, there was talk of a tour to Warsaw, but one night two strapping Russian officers came in. They sat down at a table, ordered two beers, tapped their feet to the *klezmer* music, and clapped and cheered right along with everybody else. They were especially impressed when you vanished into thin air.

They tipped the brothers lavishly, the musicians as well. When the hat went around to pay you they didn't put a penny in. The next day they came back looking for you. Motke greeted them at the door. "Gentlemen, what can I do for you?"

"We're looking for the boy."

"My nephew the magician?"

"He's the very one. The Tsar would like his services in the army."

Motke scratched his beard. "You know, I'm sorry to say that Hankus has gone off to Kielce. He's performing there for a fortnight beginning Monday."

"He'll be back?"

"Indeed," Motke said, "although exactly when we're not sure. This show in Kielce is the beginning of what might be an all-Poland tour. He'll be traveling to the big cities and we're not sure when he'll return."

"We'll keep an eye out for him." The soldiers winked and walked out the door.

The lover brothers panicked. This was just like the Tsar's army. Once every month or so they came into a town and looked for Jewish boys to make into cannon fodder. The more talented the boy, the more clever, the better for them. They liked to watch smart Jewish boys walk the front lines. They chuckled over their bloody bodies when they fell.

As soon as the soldiers left, Motke went back into the kitchen to find Max. The two of them slapped themselves on the face over and over. "Terrible, it's a terrible thing. They can't put our Hankeh into the army...for one thing, she's a girl!" They slapped their faces some more. "And we can't tell everyone she's a girl because as wonderful, as remarkable as we think this is, to the rest of the world we've tricked them and this is a *shandeh,* a shame and a sin."

The two men paced back and forth in their little kitchen, then Motke ran down the street to see his old friend Pipke Grosze, the Zionist. When he came back, it seemed your problem might be solved.

Motke got Max at the café, then they went together to find you. You were just waking up from your hard night's work. The two men looked as if they would cry. Without saying a whole sentence, Motke threw his arms around you and started weeping. Max stood and watched until he began to sniffle. You blinked your eyes once, twice. "Soldiers," was all the lovely men said, and you, Hankus, you sobbed too.

It was decided then and there that you should book passage on the next boat in Baron de Hirsh's fleet and sail away to Argentina. "It's a wonderful place," Motke said, as he unfolded the leaflet Pipke had given him. "Jews!" it read, "BECOME A PART OF HISTORY! SETTLE THE NEW ZION ON THE PAMPAS. SAIL WITH THE BARON DE HIRSH AND BE-COME A CITIZEN OF THE JEWISH COLONY OF MOISESVILLE!" There was a drawing of a man on a horse who seemed to be riding very fast. In his hand, up above his head, was a long rope with two balls at the end. "That," Max told you, "is a gaucho—an Argentine cowboy. Only be-cause this is a poster for the Zion on the pampas, he's a Jewish gaucho."

"Imagine it," Motke continued, "riding along on the open plains all day long, swinging one of them ball ropes in the air."

You looked at them with some considerable question in your eyes.

"It's not all horseback riding and fancy clothes there, Hankus," piped in Max, "it's a little village, self-sufficient. Some people are farm-ers, some raise cattle, everybody shares everything, when things go bad they help each other out. Oh, how I envy you..."

"Yes, to be part of a new way of life right from the beginning."

You thought about the mud and the wind, the sad distance in country life between one house and another. Your home before Cracow was a little village—now all who lived there were gone. "If you like it so well, why don't you go?"

Max and Motke looked at each other. "Why don't we go, indeed," Max said, "this is an excellent question—"

"But the answer's not so hard. We are old," Motke answered flatly. "The cowboy life appeals to us, but do we have it in us to ride horses at this late date? Decidedly not."

You thought about this. Then you asked, "Why can't I just go to London and make my fortune there? I could be a magician as well there as I could be a cowboy in Argentina, and a magician is what I truly want to be."

The lovers scratched their beards. "This is true, Hankus," Motke conceded. "England is not so far away and there are Jews, we are told, in England. But Moisesville is a whole colony of Jews. It's like Palestine only without the religious claptrap—"

"And Baron de Hirsh provides the journey cheap. You need only sign a contract that says you will work for a year and then there you go, off to Argentina."

"One other thing," Motke pursed his thin lips. "There is the fact of your sex. I don't know why, but intuition tells me that your guise will last longer in a faraway country than it will in England—which is England after all, and not Europe, but still not so far from home. If, for example, you are performing in Covent Gardens, and your mother's brother Berle, for example, if such a man exists, happens to be in England on business, and there you are, juggling up a storm, what's to stop him from recognizing you—"

"But the likelihood is so small," you said.

"Sure, sure. But humor us, Hankeh. Humor us, dear. We like the idea of you being a Jewish gaucho in Argentina much better than the idea of you being a world-renowned magician in London."

"Besides," Motke said, "there is competition in England and America—there you have Houdini. In Argentina, if the cowboy business doesn't work out, how many escape artists could there be? And there is talk of a war—"

"There's always talk of a war," you said.

"Look, Hankeh," Max said, "War, *shmar*. England looks good because they don't speak Yiddish there. But is the Jew really welcome? According to Pipke Grosze, the Jew is not only welcome in Argentina, there's also plenty of room. The Jew is welcome in Argentina and encouraged to build a Palestine on the pampas. We'll miss you, darling Hankeh, but those officers will be back, and we have to send you off soon."

2

AND THAT IS HOW IT CAME TO PASS that on another boat, two years later than I, just as Europe was bursting into war with itself, you landed, Hankus, with your own set of secrets, on Buenos Aires' shores. Because you were young, your sea legs lasted only as long as the walk down the gangplank to the dock. You were steady on your feet by the time you tipped your hat boldly at the customs men, who waved you through without so much as a glance at your carefully signed papers. Like a colt who's been held too long in a tiny pen, and like a young man who is happy at last to see dry land (no matter that you deemed your ship ride marvelous, no matter that the Buenos Aires streets were damp and cold as the deck you slept on all those long days), you, young Hannah Lubarsky, now to be named forever Hankus, went wandering the cobbled streets beyond the Buenos Aires harbor and, for all intents and purposes, got lost.

Truth be told, as much as you resisted the idea, you had every intention of keeping your promise to Max and Motke. Absolutely.

You intended to travel with your fellow settlers by train all the way to the pampas, to the colony of Moisesville, where you were to live as a farmer and a gaucho, a Jewish cowboy, for the good of your people. That was what your papers stated, that was why your passage was free. Max and Motke had arranged it all, had made, through Pipke Grosze, an appointment with the representatives for the new Zion on the pampas, Cracow Division, had sat with you while you filled out your application, Hankus Lubarsky, male, age eighteen. They bought you lovely and appropriate clothing: tall boots and a short jacket, heavy trousers for riding. And wasn't it just like Motke to make you two new shirts, one for best of fine white linen, the other for the everyday work of the gaucho, a cotton shirt with long sleeves and a sash such as the dreaded Russian cavalry men wore around their waists. Quite dashing, and on you, Hankus, well, it must have been breathtaking! These were in addition to your magician clothes, also constructed by Motke, with hidden pockets and magical pouches. He gave you a specially made bag in which to store all your magic: your picklocks, your handcuffs, your magician clothes. Because who knew—you could yet become a magician on the pampas. The greater accomplishment though, Max and Motke were convinced, was for you to learn to ride a horse.

Ah, Hankus, this was truly what you meant to do as you walked down that plank and past those customs men. You had the letter with exact directions to the Buenos Aires train station, complete with the name of a *haimish* hotel very close by, absolutely kosher, positively safe, where a weary sojourner in the new world might rest her seaworn bones before setting off to the grasslands by rail. Oh, and weren't you walking in just that direction with your valise full of new clothes under one arm, your bag full of old magic under the other, new boots on your feet, a wonderful broad-brimmed hat on your head, a free train ticket to Moisesville tucked away in your pocket, and, luckier than me, your mother's candlesticks, too? Oh, you promise, you had every intention of doing exactly what Max and Motke had made possible for you to do, when on your way from harbor to railroad you came to a plaza, a magnificent plaza long and white, bordered by palaces on two sides. Yes—palaces, and one of them pink! Unlike the squares in Cracow this plaza was full of palm trees and flowers, with not one fountain but two, and who should be right smack in the middle of the plaza, surrounded by a crowd of entranced onlookers, but a motley troupe of acrobats and jugglers?

And Hannah Lubarsky, now forever to be called Hankus, you watched those acrobats and jugglers in their magnificent satin vests and pantaloons, as they spun fire and jumped through hoops, stood atop one another's shoulders and leapt into one another's arms. You could barely stop yourself from jumping in as the tumblers rolled forward and backward in somersaults and flips. Even after the last spectators had thrown their *pesos* into the passing hat and departed, Hankus, you were sitting on the side of the fountain, completely and totally enthralled.

The acrobats began to pack their tools away and still you sat staring, a huge grin on your handsome face. You didn't know what possessed you, tired and shipworn as you were, but as the men were packing away their barrel hoops and Indian clubs, you reached over and started juggling the clubs yourself.

At first the men stood staring at you. Then one of them tossed you a hoop, which you juggled in without missing a beat. Next you passed the Indian clubs one by one to the hoop thrower, who juggled them back. Suddenly, there you were with a complete stranger making music out of flying hoops and clubs, and a new crowd began to form and throw *pesos* into a hat until the stranger, whose clubs and hoops these really were, backed away exhausted, and you tossed the clubs to him one, two, three. For a finish, you grabbed the barrel hoop and somersaulted through it midair. The crowd went wild. The acrobats were speechless until they, too, clapped and jumped and rushed to pat you, grinning Hankus, on the back.

When at last all the juggling tools were packed away and you had retrieved your belongings, the little troupe tried to talk to you. One fellow said something in Spanish, but you could only shake your head and open your arms. He tried Italian, then English, then French. Still, Hankus, you shook your head. When one of the jugglers at last asked in a not-so-convincing accent, "*Fu vanen kumt ir?*" you grinned an even wider grin, reached out and hugged the man, and said, "*Ich kum fun* Cracow."

"He's from Poland," the juggler told his fellows in Spanish.

"*Ich kum fun* Cracow," the little magician repeated in Yiddish, "but now I am home."

You spent your first endless Argentine night with those jugglers and tumblers, beginning at a *parrillado* on Corrientes Avenue, where you witnessed for the first time the Argentine habit of cooking whole cows, split and splayed, over an open fire right in the window of a restaurant. Not for a minute did you have a crisis of conscience over whether or not to eat that cow, kosher or not, for on your way across the ocean you had made up your mind that here in this new land, as a cowboy or a magician, or simply as a citizen of the world, you would eat what you were given, kosher or *traif*. You had also made up your mind that you would observe the holidays, but only in your heart. Were you an apostate? No. You were a New World Jew, and a Jewish *man* at that, and, as you observed, Jewish men made up their own minds about when to go to *shul* and when to sit and play cards.

There you were, like a regular Jewish guy, about to experience your first encounter with a genuine Argentine steak, which you began to dig into in the company of three professional tumblers (one of whom was Maishe, the Yiddish speaker), two jugglers, and a tiny trained dog. All six of the humans and the dog were seated round a table covered with a white cloth. The waiter appeared with a platter full of sausages, ribs, steaks, and chops, and the hungry performers dove into it, but not before ascertaining that this was your first day in Argentina. To honor you, the jugglers put on your plate the choicest piece of steak, three inches long and at least an inch thick, charred black on the outside but when a knife was sunk into it, juicy and red inside. All of the performers, hungry as they were, stopped and watched, breath held, as you chewed your first mouthful of their nation's most prized culinary treat.

You chewed and chewed and chewed. True, Hankus, you had just come from a fourteen-day journey during which you had eaten nothing but dried salami, dry bread, and sour pickles, alternated (thanks to Max and Motke) with cabbage soup (cold from the jar), pot cheese, and a dozen apples ("One," said Max, "for each traveling day!"). True, those provisions were stretched and saved, and sailing across the ocean to a new life is hungry work, and it's safe to say that you landed in the new world famished. But it is also true that that *traif* steak, juicy and red, cooked right there in the window where anyone walking down Corrientes Avenue could see it, was like nothing you had tasted in your life.

The others drank wine, which you did not, and yet, sweet Hankus, you felt drunk. When that platter of meats was empty, the jugglers called for another, and this time they watched with profound pleasure as you ate grilled sausage and lamb chops, more steak, and baked potatoes. When you were done, they applauded.

It wasn't until the third platter was empty and the coffee drunk, the bill paid by the performers from the day's proceeds, that the matter of where you were to stay your first night in Buenos Aires came up. Through signs and facial expressions, voices raised loud, and Maishe's terrible Yiddish, it became clear that the performers wanted you to stay with them. "But why?" you asked in Yiddish. "You hardly know me."

"We know you, we know you," Maishe said. "Come, little brother, to our sumptuous flat."

You spent that night in the jugglers' flat in San Telmo, dressed in all of your clothes, your arms wrapped tightly around your bags, just as you had all those nights on the ship. The men tried to persuade you to take a bath. They went so far as to fill the tub with hot water and bring you huge towels. But the tub was in the middle of the flat and there was no privacy. In fact, the men washed one another, poured warm soapy water over each other with a big stone pitcher. They used the same water again and again, then offered it up to you.

Although you were covered with two weeks of salty grime, and these men had fed you and given you a corner of their floor to call home, you still could not risk being naked before them. For among those many resolutions you made as you stood on the deck of Baron de Hirsh's ship, the grey on all sides of you whipping by, whipping by, was one where you promised never to reveal to anyone, stranger or longtime acquaintance, the truth about your gender. Here in the City of Good Airs, you would always be a man.

In the morning (which for the *porteño* acrobats did not begin until noon) you demonstrated some tricks of your own. As Max had taught you, you freed yourself from handcuffs and all kinds of knots, and it must be said that these men, who knew so much about leaping through the air and landing on their hands, became mystified at your sleight of hand. With each disappearing coin, each multicolored scarf that vanished and reappeared, the five men gasped and cheered. When the juggling began again, the men were completely won over, for you could keep up with the troupe so well that in a matter of minutes everything in the flat, with the exception of the bathtub and the heavy furniture, was up in the air. When you were finished, all five of them took you up on their shoulders and carried you through the streets of San Telmo as if you were a war hero.

That evening, after you made it very clear that you could not live on the floor of their flat for the rest of your days, the acrobats found you a furnished room a few doors down from their place on Chacabuco Street. The rent wasn't cheap and the room was small, but there was a huge bathtub in a room with a door that locked just down the hall. All of them agreed that this alone was worth the cost. They made the transaction for you in Spanish and insisted on paying the first week's rent.

As soon as the acrobats left, which you told me was three in the morning, you filled the bathtub with the hottest water you could summon from the tap, locked yourself in the tiny room, and soaked and scrubbed and soaked more. Layers of salt and filth washed off you, and when you scrubbed a second time, off came more and more. You emptied the tub and filled it again, then slid down and submerged yourself. You held your breath and counted as you lay there, looking up at the ceiling. When you reached three hundred you could stand it no longer and surfaced with a splash like a dolphin.

You were new now, and clean, and in Argentina. You would not be a gaucho but a showman at last.

— 3 —

THERE WAS A RUMOR FLOATING ABOUT the Jewish *barrio*, Hankus, that Tutsik Goldenberg and his cronies discovered you on the streets of Buenos Aires while you were juggling up a storm with Maishe and his buddies in the Plaza de Mayo. You started that rumor, and it was false.

True, in your earliest days in Buenos Aires you performed with Maishe's troupe, everyone was generous with the collected earnings, and Hankus, you always got your fair share. But the economic facts of an escape artist's life soon caught up with you. Rent in your tiny Chacabuco Street room cost money. With a little guilt you sold that free train ticket to Moisesville to buy you a month of the acrobat's life. You thought to sell your leather boots, but when it came right down to it, you could not bear the thought of that. Then there was that jacket in the haberdashery on Maipú Street that you really had to have—a snappy, fine linen jacket, perfect for the Buenos Aires spring, which, coming as it does in September, was upon us now. The jacket was splendid, hung perfectly about you so that you never had to worry how much of your slim physique was revealed. You simply couldn't pass it up, and since that jacket cost just as much as your train ticket to Moisesville, before the next month's rent was due you were forced to find a job.

So the actual scene of the event that was ultimately to save my life and change both our fates was a posh kosher *parrillado* on LaValle Street. You worked your way up there, first juggling dishes from blood-stained to sparkling clean in a few seconds flat in the kitchen sink. Then tossing glasses and full bottles of champagne into the air in such a way that the glasses seemed to fill themselves midflight and land gently before delighted customers. Finally serving full dinners with flamboyant abandon (flying dishes, flashing silverware, flaming plates of steak that were extinguished with the snap of a finger to reveal an exquisitely rare filet that could be cut with a butter knife, and for dessert, with the snap of another finger, out of nowhere appeared a steaming *demitasse* of coffee and a perfectly browned dish of the most extraordinary *flan* one might taste on three continents).

So remarkable were you, Hankus Lubarsky (or "that daredevil waiter" as you were commonly known), that you soon drew as many patrons to Casa de Yale Levine as the enormous carcasses of fine beef standing splayed in his windows over burning coals. It was not unusual for a regular at Casa de Yale to wait a full hour for the privilege of having you serve dinner to him and his guests. But for the hungrier, less well-fixed souls, the mere spectacle of watching you serve others in a whirlwind of clattering china and sparkling cutlery was pleasure enough.

It was the kind of restaurant that Tutsik Goldenberg, even with his share of the Talcahuano Street profits, could barely afford, and that his sister Perle, who could afford it, would never agree to walk into. It is doubtful that if this had not been the evening before Rosh Hashanah, and Yale Levine himself were not completely occupied with the business of closing up shop for eleven days, that Tutsik Goldenberg, dressed as he was, would have even been allowed past the front door, let alone shown to a table. For what was sharp dressing for a Jewish mackerel was *déclassé* for Buenos Aires' more upstanding wealthy Jews. Yale Levine himself would have brushed Tutsik Goldenberg and his green-checked jacket and yellow trousers out into the street in a second, no matter how well-pressed they were.

But Yale Levine was in the back room of his fancy restaurant counting his cash and writing up orders for the day after Yom Kippur, and the young *maître d'*, who had his nose in the air but didn't have the experience to keep it there, was convinced, if not by the gold *peso* Goldenberg slipped him as soon as he walked in the door, then by the sharp blade his dining companion, Dov Hirsh, suddenly used to clean his nails, to seat the duo at a table in a corner dark enough so that none of the important customers could actually see them.

When a waiter finally noticed them, the two roughs asked him only for a match, a cup of coffee, and an *agua minerale, sin gaz*. "But *Señors*, this ain't no *confiteria*, it's a *parrillado*—"

"I'm aware of that," Goldenberg answered. The glint of Dov Hirsh's stiletto persuaded the waiter that this was all the gentlemen wished to order.

When the waiter came back with their drinks, Tutsik Goldenberg leaned toward him. "When does the floor show start?"

"*Señor?*"

"The juggling waiter."

"He's no floor show, *Señor*, he's a regular employee. His station is those tables in the center of the room."

"Those well-lit round ones with the swells in monkey suits?"

The waiter cleared his throat and adjusted his head at the top of his neck. "The very ones, *Señor.*"

"So I can sit here and sip my coffee and watch him in action?"

"I suppose, *Señor*, although there is a ten *peso* minimum."

Goldenberg flipped a ten *peso* note from his breast pocket and handed it to the waiter.

"*Gracias, Señor.* If there is nothing else—"

"Yes, there is something else. Bring my friend here a lamb chop. A small one. And me another cup of coffee. And when the juggling waiter comes out and serves those swells, you come back over here."

Tutsik Goldenberg had been tipped off about this juggling waiter, and *peso* signs flashed in his head. He was looking, at last, for a way out of the whorehouse. Not that he didn't like to be surrounded day in and day out by pretty girls in their underwear, or act like a big cheese and pass out his sister's schnapps and brandy to all of his friends. But that was the point. It was his sister's place, his sister paid the bills, his sister got the money. He was just the brother of the madam, the buyer, and during busiest times, the bouncer. This entertained him, because quite frankly he liked nothing better than the feel of his fist up against someone's flabby cheek. He liked to push a fellow to the wall by the shoulders and knee him in the groin, or for that matter, to pick a woman up and throw her against a wall. But what he really wanted out of life was to be the boss.

That was why he kept the likes of Hirsh around; he liked it that he could snap his fingers and Dov Hirsh would scare people for him. He never carried a weapon himself. Well, yes, he did keep that thin blade that opened with the touch of a thumb tucked away in his back pocket, but that was mostly to make an impression. As time passed and he got older, Tutsik Goldenberg had come to prefer the impact of skin to skin. The thud, the slap, the crunch and pop of real muscle and bone. One might never know this to look at him, for compared to Dov Hirsh and Dr. Mordechai Dorfman, his *aides de camp,* or even compared to Marek Fishbein, that lummox who had worked his way up to being one of the biggest hoo-hahs of all the Jewish pimps in Buenos Aires, and to whom Goldenberg was in for too many gambled *pesos* besides, Tutsik Goldenberg looked like a real gentleman.

But I knew him for the violent man he was. Sure, Tutsik Goldenberg would never ruin the line of his suit with a big fat gun or a pair of brass knuckles, but he was a lady killer in the truest sense of the word. I knew it from my beating on the boat coming over, and daily it seemed I knew it again. Why, just a few months before you started to come around, Hankus, Tutsik Goldenberg cut into the sad face of my icy cold Sara.

It was a Saturday night, the parlor was full of johns and gambling men, when all of a sudden from the dining room there was horrible yelling. "Give it to me, you sow!" shouted Goldenberg. We all became quiet and looked into the dining room.

"It's mine, I earned it!" Sara held something small in a tight fist close to her breast.

"You maybe earned it, but I get 50 percent!" shouted Tutsik Goldenberg.

"It's the last speck of opium in the house," Sara's voice was shrill now, "and you know it's mine!"

Before any of us could burst in and stop it, Tutsik Goldenberg took out that mean-looking knife, and in front of all of us witnesses he charged right for Sara's face. Poor Sara looked like a mad tiger had fallen upon her by the time Madam Perle could pull her brother off. Mordechai Dorfman fixed her up as best he could, but he was drunk, and she was screaming, and my Sara's face was never the same after that. Neither, as I shall tell, was her heart.

As for Tutsik, the very fact that he could take a knife to the face of one of his meal tickets let him know that after ten years of faithful service he must find another line of work, once and for all. That and the fact that he had begun, as of late, to hate Poland with its meat-locker winters, its flat spaces. All those picturesque cows he used to love watching as they waded up and down the Vistula appeared to be so many hippopotami. It was becoming unbearable courting those girls' fathers, eating all that Polish peasant food at poverty-struck Jewish tables. The private drinks with the same fathers in the backrooms of taverns, then the sweet-talking of the mothers over watery black tea and cookies so hard you could break all your teeth.

Most of all, Tutsik Goldenberg hated the magic act—the long *droshky* ride from East Nowhere to the train; the train ride from Poland to Hamburg or Nice; the interminable boat ride home, if a person could call this upside-down city home. All those boat rides back and forth might seem like fun and games to rich Jews, but for Jews like him they were just so much sea sickness. And even though he only did it once a year now, instead of two times or three, he was really beginning to detest it. Weeks it took, even on the most well-appointed steamers. What he needed was a cushy job and a ticket to New York City. There was the real land of opportunity: *Nueva York*, with its Statue of Liberty. That's what Goldenberg wanted, an easy job where yes, he might be required to beat a woman up once in a while, or throw a man half his size out a window, but certainly not all the time, and in a country where people spoke that civilized tongue, English, and drank tea in a cup.

Goldenberg knew just the line of work, too. One of our regular customers at the *shandhoiz*, a tiny little man with fancy three-piece suits and a pencil-thin moustache that stuck straight up on either end, a man who spoke Yiddish with a French accent, named Epstien, was an impresario. He managed actors and singers and, according to him, what Buenos Aires really needed was some novelty acts. Novelty acts were the coming thing, and if he planned it right, if he found just the right people to manage, Tutsik Goldenberg could find himself an easy door to open in the United States. Because face it, the Jewish theatre circuit had almost a direct line from New York City to Buenos Aires. It was an established fact.

Epstien himself couldn't actually take any new people on now, and if Goldenberg wanted to do a big service to the Jews of Buenos Aires, bigger even than building a new opulent *shul* (as his sister and her Varsovia Society cronies had done—and look at the thanks it got them), or a new theatre like the Broken Heart, also courtesy of the Varsovia Society, what Tutsik could do was organize a few topnotch jugglers or magicians, a couple of belly dancers and sword swallowers. Not circus acts exactly, but close—full of splash and dazzle. "In fact, if I might be so bold," Epstien said (and I remember overhearing this conversation myself while I was languishing on the fainting couch, praying that there was a plague upon the city and no johns would come), "let me suggest a boy, a young man who is currently tossing all kinds of fancy dinners into the air at Casa de Yale Levine over on LaValle Street. Perhaps the boy could be persuaded," the Frenchman rubbed his thumb and forefinger together slowly, "to give it all up and juggle dishes on the stage."

And so Tutsik Goldenberg found himself at Casa de Yale Levine on the last night of the Jewish year, sipping *un corto* while his crony Dov Hirsh sucked the lamb juices off his slender fingers, when a whirlwind spun from the swinging kitchen door. A red-and-black blur was all Goldenberg could make out as you, Hankus Lubarsky, rotated to the round table in the center of the room holding a huge tray of covered dishes over your head. In a moment, plates and silver whirred in the air, while sizzling platters of delicately grilled steaks, chops, and ribs, a half a chicken and three *ensaladas mistas,* which you tossed and dressed right there at the table, arranged themselves in front of the diners. Soon each of the beautifully dressed guests had before them a miraculously gorgeous dinner. You, the *mozo,* stood still, but just long enough for all to admire your sharply creased black pants, your sparkling white shirt, black bow tie, your red *mozo* jacket, a tidy white towel draped casually over your left arm. Then, as quickly as you had arrived, you shouted a loud "Hey!" and somersaulted backward to the kitchen, disappearing through the padded kitchen doors.

The entire restaurant went mad with pleasure, and when you somersaulted out again, this time holding a carafe of wine and six glasses, all the patrons were up on their feet stomping and clapping. You stopped only long enough to bow, poured each glass of wine calmly, clicked your heels together, then sprung backward into the kitchen once again.

"Absolutely amazing," Dov Hirsh said, on his feet, making a racket. "More!" he shouted, "More! More!"

"Don't be ridiculous. This is a restaurant, not a cabaret," Tutsik muttered. "He comes back only when it's time to pay the check. Sit down, you look like a fool." He snapped his fingers at his own waiter who seemed meager, indeed, compared to the *mozo* who waited the center tables. "Deliver this note to that boy we just saw, please."

"If you're asking him out on a date, he don't get off 'til 3:00 A.M."

"Very funny, young man. Just deliver the note. And bring me another *corto,* and my friend another chop."

The waiter snapped his heels together and bowed the way all the ordinary waiters in Buenos Aires did, then took Goldenberg's note to the kitchen. In a minute, you, the acrobat waiter, strolled out with Goldenberg's *corto* and set it down before him. "Hankus Lubarsky at your service, *Señor.*"

"I am Tutsik Goldenberg, and this is my associate, Dov Hirsh. Please, sit down."

You glanced over your shoulder at the table center stage. The men were still gnawing on their steaks, the ladies were giddy over salads. You slid into the empty chair at Tutsik Goldenberg's table and sat down just as the other waiter appeared with the lamb chop. "You want him to toss it in the air before you eat it?" Goldenberg asked Hirsh. Before he could answer, the waiter plunked the dish down unceremoniously in front of the thugs and left.

"You Jewish?" Goldenberg asked, while he looked you up and down. Lubarsky, you nodded.

"How long you been over here?"

"A few months. I was supposed to go to the Jewish colonies in the provinces when I first came but I somehow never made it."

"That whole pampas scene never thrilled me, either. Too many cows."

"You like them better on a platter, eh Tutsik?" Dov Hirsh clapped Goldenberg on the back, laughing.

Goldenberg pointedly ignored Hirsh. "You got plans for the holidays?" Tutsik looked past you to the swells in their tuxedos.

"To put my feet up for a day or two, then practice my other tricks."

"What kind of tricks?" Hirsh asked.

You picked up a spoon and snapped your fingers. It disappeared.

"Look how clever he is, Hirsh." Tutsik lit a cigar and offered it to you. You shook your head. "Quite clever. A clever Jewish boy alone in a foreign country on the holiest day of the year is a real *shandeh*. One needs a good meal on Rosh Hashanah. A little *cholent*, a little *matzoh* ball soup, a little honey cake and schnapps."

You checked your tables. The men in tuxedos were beginning to fidget and look around for you. "You'll have to excuse me." You began to get up.

"Of course," said Goldenberg, "of course, of course. But young man—"

You turned and looked him dead in the eye. *"Señor?"*

"If you would be so kind as to meet *Pan* Hirsh and myself outside the Thieves' Synagogue just before evening service tomorrow night, I can guarantee you a meal you could die for."

You nodded. "I don't go in much for the religious life."

"Neither do we. We meet a physician friend in front of the *shul* and play pinochle in the *confiteria* down the street until the *shofar* sounds, then we go to my sister's and get a little something to eat."

The men in tuxedos at the center table were waving discreetly at you now. "I'll think it over."

"There's more than a tasty dinner in it for you if you come." Goldenberg rubbed his thumb and forefinger together. "I'm talking opportunity. I have connections. At the Broken Heart Theatre."

You raised one eyebrow. "I'll take that into consideration."

"The Thieves' Synagogue at 6:15," Goldenberg repeated. "You know where it is?"

"Up in Once," you answered.

"Precisely." Tutsik snapped his fingers at his own waiter. *"Mozo, la cuenta, por favor."*

"Certainly, *Señor*. You are satisfied?"

"Absolutely," said Goldenberg, who handed the waiter a bill that just barely covered the check. The waiter looked at Goldenberg expectantly as he tapped the well-blocked bowler on his head. "Of course, *mozo.* You may keep the change."

At closing, while the waiters added up their bills and counted their tips, the one who tended to Tutsik Goldenberg and Dov Hirsh put his finger on your shoulder. "Hankus, you were getting kind of chummy with that lot at table six. I'd watch my back around those, Pimps, I think. The unctuous one in the yellow pants runs a house on Talcahuano Street, and the other one is either his boyfriend or his goon—showed me a knife for no reason at all. I'd be careful of those, I would."

"Thanks for the tip, Hamer, but I'm not too worried. They want me to join 'em at *shul.*"

"That's how they start it. All religiouslike. Before you know it, you're into them for your soul."

You nodded your head toward Hamer. "Happy New Year," you told him, then were on your way home.

The notion that Tutsik Goldenberg and his friend were pimps wasn't as interesting to you as the fancy dresser's parting comment. *Connections at the Broken Heart Theatre.* That was all you needed to know.

You slept late into the next morning, then spent the afternoon planning your evening costume. You took coffee in the *confiteria* downstairs from your Chacabuco Street room, came back and practiced sleight of hand for an hour, then bathed and proceeded to dress, slowly, carefully, as if for a first tryst with a most intriguing lover: black silk trousers, immaculate white shirt, gold cufflinks, velvet vest. You wore those leather boots you couldn't bear to give up, and your wide-brimmed black felt hat. You carried a black walking stick with a brass tip. Although it was still a bit chilly, you wore your new linen jacket.

You put a pack of marked cards into your vest pocket, adjusted your hat just so, and went out to meet your fate, which, as it turns out, would save me from mine.

To those who saw, Hankus Lubarsky arrived as requested in front of the Thieves' Synagogue at exactly 6:15 on *erev* Rosh Hashanah. Most congregants were just beginning to make their way into services. Men smoked their last cigarette for forty-eight hours in order to welcome the Jewish year with pure bodies and open hearts. Women in their holiday finery prepared to walk the stairs and sit in the balcony, hidden behind a thick velvet curtain so that their prayers might not distract the more serious work of the men below. You recognized the men from the restaurant. The one who did most of the talking and called himself Tutsik Goldenberg was dressed superbly in a well-pressed navy blue suit, spats on his shoes, and a bowler hat. He had two henchmen with him this time: the one who was with him the night before, tall and thin, had a freckled face and was called Dov Hirsh. The other man you noticed was bigger and dopier looking than the other two, and while I knew this man as Dr. Mordechai Dorfman, you had never seen him before.

You must have cut quite a figure as you rounded the corner from Rivadavia Avenue to meet the three men. At the sight of you, how light Tutsik Goldenberg's heart became. "Look, there he is, I told you he'd join us!"

Hirsh flicked his cigarette into the cobbled street, the other man adjusted his tie. "Mordechai Dorfman," he said, extending his puffy hand.

"Hankus Lubarsky," you said. "So, gentlemen. Is it cards or a little date with the Lord our God?"

"Cards, I think," Goldenberg said, patting you robustly on the back, "and a bit of schnapps. Then, my boy, a dinner that will make you long for home."

The men guided each other to a tiny bar just around the corner, dark and smoke-filled and not at all Jewish. The bartender greeted Tutsik Goldenberg by name, waving the men to a table in the very back. Goldenberg broke open a deck of cards and offered them to you.

You cut them once, twice, then handed the pack back to Tutsik, who dealt the cards, and the play began. At first you lost hand after hand, then slowly began to take the men on. You didn't even need your marked deck. Your shuffling and dealing became what was interesting to the men at the table and those around the bar, for as flamboyant as your table-waiting was, so was your finesse with cards. The men stopped playing altogether and watched you do your handiwork with open mouths and approving grins. At 8:55, as you were raking in your New Year's earnings, the man who called himself Dr. Dorfman bade the whole bar shush, then the four of you listened as the *shofar* sounded from the synagogue. Everyone gathered their cards, their hats and cigars. Goldenberg put a gold *peso* on the table, and you four *compadres* made your way into the crowd of pious Jews who were going home, some to ones like mine, some to ordinary houses, for *kreplach* and boiled chicken, brisket and fish.

"You have been in Buenos Aires for some months and you've never been to my sister's house?" Tutsik Goldenberg asked, close to incredulous.

"Why should I be there?"

"All young men find their way to Talcahuano Street 154 sooner or later, Lubarsky. Because the meat there is strictly kosher."

"And not bad to look at either!" Dov Hirsh burst out laughing.

Dr. Dorfman continued to walk in silence.

"We'll eat a good meal, you'll enjoy yourself, but be forewarned: my sister has recently become something of a religious fanatic and none of the young ladies will be permitted to work tonight. So you— who by the way must tell them all we met by chance at *shul*—can look, and meet the girls, and possibly even get to lay eyes upon that great baboon, Marek Fishbein (may he and all those *pesos* I owe him fall into a vat of boiling oil), to whom we are all, unfortunately, indebted one way or another. For I believe my sister has invited him and his cronies to join us for coffee and *taiglech* later tonight. In the meantime, might I remind you, young man, of my suggestion to you?"

You jingled your pinochle winnings in your pants pocket. "Refresh me, *Señor* Goldenberg—you'd like me to become a whore?"

Everyone but Goldenberg burst out laughing. "Not at all, my boy, no, not at all. Why, your considerable talents would go to waste in the Talcahuano Street bordello. No, my *yingeleh,* you will recall I mentioned I have connections at the Broken Heart Theatre. Perhaps you will allow me to mount a show for you there. Provide you with an opportunity to juggle dishes on a stage instead of simply for the hoity-toity Jews at Casa de Yale Levine."

You looked at Tutsik Goldenberg and hid the hope you felt, for not a day went by when you did not wish for such an opportunity. "Of course I'm interested, *Señor* Goldenberg, and not just to juggle, either. As you saw with your own eyes this evening, I can make an eight of spades turn into a ten of hearts in five seconds flat. Better than that, I can clap my hands and make whole wedding cakes disappear. In the blink of an eye I can free myself from any set of handcuffs."

"It's in your future, dear boy. You have need of a decent impresario, this is all."

"And where do I get one?"

At this, both Hirsh and Dorfman guffawed. Goldenberg still didn't join them. "Why, Lubarsky, I'll be your impresario. You'll open a show at the Broken Heart Theatre or my name isn't Tutsik Goldenberg!"

"You?" Dr. Dorfman said out loud. "Pimping women is one thing, Goldenberg, but pimping a magician something else entirely."

"Yes, how do you get this one to marry you on the ship?" sneered Dov Hirsh.

Tutsik Goldenberg took you by the arm and steered you away from his henchmen. "You'll have to forgive my friends. The Jewish New Year makes them giddy. All that possibility of redemption. Think this over, will you? I'm willing to provide you with all of it—funds, publicity, even a lovely assistant. In return for your trust and a very small percentage of the profits. It's all for you, my boy, all for you."

"But you don't even know me. You've no idea if I can do what I say. And even if I can, what makes you think Jews will come see me in a Varsovian theatre?"

Tutsik took your face in his hand. For a minute you thought he would kiss you. "Listen, Hankus—may I call you Hankus?—you can do what you say, and you must. I will get people to come see you, and they must. Because I can't stand to be a lackey to my sister and her filthy women one more minute. Not one second more. You will release me. You will be my key to freedom. Do you understand me?"

You looked directly into Tutsik Goldenberg's pink and desperate face. "Well," you said, "I'll certainly consider it."

Goldenberg grabbed you by the shoulder of your new linen jacket. "I beg of you, young man. Do not consider it, accept it!" You thought you detected just a hint of a tear in his beady eyes. "Dear boy, you must accept!"

Mordechai Dorfman and Dov Hirsh turned up a narrow street and were waiting now in front of a tidy brick building whose second-floor lights burned brightly behind slotted blinds. Tutsik Goldenberg pushed past them, pulled a key from his pocket, and worked the lock on the door. He turned to you just as the door swung open. "I beg of you, Hankus Lubarsky. It's an opportunity to save a life in the coming year."

— 4 —

FROM MY EARLIEST DAYS at Talcahuano Street, to the first time you walked in the door—yes, even in those three short years—everything had changed. Tutsik Goldenberg was not the only member of our *shandhoiz mishpocheh* who wanted relief from his life of sin. As I craved freedom, as scratched and sorry Sara wasted away to nothing, as Rachel moved from cheery to cynical smiles, so Madam Perle moved quickly and quickly toward even more heightened religious zeal.

In the beginning it wasn't righteous zealousness so much as a lust for the approval of the ordinary Jews of Buenos Aires. What did it matter, for example, if the greatest artists and intellectuals of her time sought her out for concubinage and conversation when her neighbors down the street spat on her?

Even in Perle's old days in Poland, she wanted nothing more than the love of her neighbors. Failing there, her journey this long way to Argentina was meant to start her life in every way anew. Madam Perle hoped against hope that by living an observant life in a new and distant country, where the very seasons were opposite the Polish ones, she would gain at least a nod and a "Good *Shabbes*" on Friday evenings as she made her way to *shul*. With each day, she made her observances stronger. And ours as well.

Perle kept the larder in the Talcahuano Street kitchen strictly kosher; neither we *nafkehs* nor our customers were allowed to mix the meat dishes with the milk. Madam Perle forbade us to work on Friday nights and forced us all to join her at services in the new *shul* the Varsovia Society had built, which was located on Paso Street, but which was known as the Thieves' Shul and was disrespected accordingly.

In fact, long before I came to Buenos Aires' sad shore, it was Madam Perle herself who had persuaded the Varsovian brotherhood of pimps and thieves to build the spectacular synagogue in the first place. She had used her influence as a superior businesswoman to convince Fishbein and the other pimps and fancy men who filled the Varsovia Society's monthly meetings that a beautifully built house of God was a marvelous gesture of good will. "What better way to prove to those more conventional Jews, even to the *frum* Jewish settlers, that we, the pimps and madams of the Buenos Aires Jewish community, are a bunch of hard-working *mentshen* just like the rest of them?"

"Please, please," Fishbein waved the suggestion away with his fat cigar and scratched the unruly hair on his chin. "We've built those Jews two new theatres and a cemetery and they still hate us. If they can't tell by now how hard we work, to hell with 'em." He poured himself a glass of vodka and belted it down noisily.

Other Varsovians nodded and mumbled in agreement with Fishbein, but Perle Goldenberg persisted. "Not just hard-working *mentshen* then, but good religious citizens with aspirations just like they have to get one foot at least through the door of heaven, to lead decent, *haimishista* lives. Let me be the first to pledge one hundred gold *pesos* toward the building of this fabulous new *shul*."

All the other madams thought this an excellent idea. "What harm could it do?" Red Ruthie asked matter-of-factly. "I wouldn't mind a new *shul*, maybe with room at least to breathe in the women's gallery. On the high holidays especially, with all our girls in there, you could die from no air. Count me in for a hundred gold *pesos* as well."

Once the women agreed with Red Ruthie about the women's gallery, a long discussion ensued about the fact that a roomy women's gallery was very nice, but who would see it but a bunch of women? The men, not to be outdone by their sisters and wives, went on to pledge their own *pesos,* in order that they might have pews built of the finest ebony and oak, that the Holy Ark be draped with fine silk imported directly from the Holy Land, that the *bima* chairs be covered in plush blue velvet, and above all, that every seat have a breathtaking view of the western wall. By the end of the evening it was agreed that the Varsovian synagogue would be the grandest, most magnificent *shul* that anybody's money, sacred or profane, could buy.

This pleased Perle greatly. Now, hundreds of miles from the foul streets and back alleys of Warsaw, because of her visionary goodwill, an extraordinary tribute to the God of our fathers would fill an entire block of Jewish Buenos Aires. Through this excellent deed, Perle Goldenberg would at last be liberated from the old ghosts of Poland. She might not only understand the laws and precepts of the Talmud Torah, but live by them and revel in them as well. Madam Perle Goldenberg hoped against hope that by performing this ultimate *mitzvah* here in her adopted homeland, she would shed her old sin-filled skin like the moth-eaten fur coat it had become, and stand before God naked and renewed in the healing breezes of the City of Good Airs.

But for Madam Perle Goldenberg there was no such luck. The Jews who journeyed to Buenos Aires all the way from Europe to make new lives within the respectable bounds of convention turned a cold shoulder to Madam Perle and her *nafkehs,* just as they shrugged in disgust at the beautiful Thieves' Synagogue, which was not only the loveliest and most up-to-date synagogue in all of Argentina, but was also built in record time.

True, the common men of Once saw fit to sway from side to side in its shiny oak pews, to pray solemnly before its magnificent ark and glittering Torahs. And yes, the Jewish women who lived ordinary lives were content to sit behind the elegantly embroidered curtain in the women's gallery, to gossip or pray as they saw fit, because never in their lives, in European synagogues or in Argentinean ones, had they had so much space to stretch their legs and inhale. And it couldn't be denied that the Varsovia Society had gone out of its way to provide a cantor with the most extraordinary voice, a voice that spoke to the prayers of heaven and Poland all at once, a voice that let the Jews of Argentina forget, if only for a few hours on a Friday night, that they were living in exile in a huge country at the bottom of the world.

But the fact that so many good Jewish citizens of Buenos Aires, the Jerusalem near the pampas, partook of the Varsovia Society's generosity of a *Shabbes* eve or Rosh Hashanah holiday in no way meant they harbored any warm feelings for its members, whom they commonly referred to as that pack of two-bit *yentzers,* those *chazzers,* those crooks.

Madam Perle Goldenberg, for all her good intentions, got no more respect for her *tsedokeh* than Fishbein, Red Ruthie, or any other Varsovian pimp got for theirs. The immigrant shopkeepers viewed her on Calle Talcahuano the same way they viewed her on Ulica Grzybowski: as a whore with a whore's irreparable soul, generous or not.

Very well then, she thought. Let them see her that way. But she would not let their bad opinion of her stand between this life and heaven's gate.

As time passed, she became more and more obsessed with the scholarly teachings of the Talmud Torah, the Gemara, and all the rabbis of Europe and beyond. She made it a point for all us whores to be seen in the holiest places, for had we not the right? Were not concubines and prostitutes at one time revered as the most devout women, protectors of the Holy Temple? Did not the common people hate us only because we pointed up their shame?

So on the night you first arrived at Talcahuano Street on the arm of Tutsik Goldenberg, Hankus, we, the property of Perle Goldenberg, had just returned from our duty as Jews on a Rosh Hashanah afternoon. We had come from casting our sins away into the Plata River, from praying and making *tashlich.*

What a sight we were, four whores dressed in white from top to toe: underwear, slips, stockings, slippers, then finally (and completely contrary to what the *frum Yiddishe porteños* wore for Holy Day best), loose-fitting white dresses. We walked in a line down Paraguay Avenue, over the railroad tracks to the Rio de la Plata, along with Red Ruthie and her girls. Once arrived, together we fed our sins into those muddy waters that flowed between our Buenos Aires shore and Montevideo, where still other Jews tossed other sins, most not as provocative as ours.

We tossed our tiny pebbles into the quiet water: Sara, flat-faced and now, thanks to Tutsik Goldenberg, knife-scratched, deader and deader in the eye, spitting whispers of hatred from the corners of her mouth; Rachel, face to the sun, smiling, tossing her stone sins into the river like wildflower petals with firm conviction that it might do some good; Perle, so serious and dignified, as if she were the head rabbi of Argentina herself. The more adventurous Red Ruthie and her girls stood, skirts hiked up, knee deep in the harbor, tossing and laughing all their whores' sins into the waters of time. To what end, I asked myself, for what? I stood as if outside them all, dropping stones and watching the ripples they made, wondering what good these little rocks could do me, what salvation I might acquire after all this time. With each pebble I dropped I whispered to God only, *Free me, free me, free me.*

The other Jews made a point of standing many paces away from us, but not so far that they couldn't get a good look. Our kerchiefs blew up in the wind and our skirts also, but Madam Perle was determined to release us from worldly sin. Yes, she wanted to make certain we were sealed into the Book of Life so she could get another year of profits off our otherwise-damned-to-hell souls.

There was a joke Red Ruthie told us, made by the pious women of Once, that we Talcahuano Street whores might as well throw our whole selves into the water for *tashlich,* and save the bits of bread and pebbles. Red Ruthie was outraged. "It's them that make us who we are. If those *frum* women treated their husbands right, they'd not come down here to the *barrio* to *shtup* the likes of us!"

I disagreed with Red Ruthie, but to myself. In my short experience, men came and complained to us about their wives—but also their mistresses. They complained to me about Sara and to Sara about Rachel and to Rachel about Madam Perle. To Perle they complained about Red Ruthie and all of Red Ruthie's whores.

The men who came to visit us were no lovers of women, any women at all. But their wives were right: perhaps we should have thrown ourselves into the river and cleaned our entire bodies, for we were indeed the repository of much sinful scum. Those men performed *tashlich* on our backsides every day of the year.

After this, my third Buenos Aires *tashlich,* we went back to Talcahuano Street—Red Ruthie and her whores too—to our flat. Not to work but to rest, or, as Perle would have it, to meditate until dinner.

Madam Perle herself changed into a most beautifully made black linen dress, put on a black bonnet and veil, and went directly to *shul* for the *maariv* service. Everyone was welcome to go, although to her credit, Perle didn't require it. We all declined, for we had had our bit of religion by the water's edge, and for myself, I saw no point in making peace with God while hidden behind a curtain, no matter how rich and velvet it was.

Marianna prepared the dinner: *cholent* Spanish-style, with fava beans and barley, succulent raisins, and from our own kosher butcher, the most delectable Argentine *flanken*. This cooked and bubbled as it had been since dawn in the clay oven Rachel brought with her from Odessa as part of her imaginary trousseau.

We who lived here lounged in our tiny rooms and waited for dinner. I went into Perle's boudoir library and picked out the English novel *Jane Eyre*, translated to Yiddish, then came back to my bed and read in my underwear until the sun began to set. Although it was forbidden because of the holiness of the day, Rachel wrote letters. Sara, in a rare act of community, sat staring sadly out my bedroom window, while Red Ruthie and her three whores drank tea and played cards downstairs.

The house, thanks to Marianna's talents in the kitchen, smelled like heaven.

Madam Perle arrived home from synagogue before the men, with the look of a woman transformed by God. She went straight to her rooms and locked the door. Sara, in an unusual moment of playfulness, put her ear to the wall and a finger to her lips. "What's she doing?" I whispered. "Let me listen!" I put my own ear to the wall.

"She's weeping," whispered Sara.

Indeed she was. Between sobs I heard her praying. "Oh woe is me, dear God," she crooned, "release me from lo these many sins!"

Half an hour later we had, all but Madam Perle, dressed and descended to the parlor. Then the men arrived. Dov Hirsh and Mordechai Dorfman, laughing and hitting themselves. Even Tutsik Goldenberg seemed to be in a festive mood. He was chatting up a young man we none of us recognized, remarkably well-dressed compared to them, breathtaking to look at. This *bacán* had Poland and the pampas written all over him: his wide felt hat, his beautiful jacket and walking stick, his boots of fine black leather. Marianna took the hats, she took the new gentleman's stick, and there you stood before us, black curls falling into your eyes, silken white shirt, wine-red velvet vest. Yes, Hankus, there you stood before me, remarkable in your beauty. But I did not recognize you yet.

"Ah, the ladies, you must meet our ladies!" Tutsik Goldenberg told you with too much warmth in his voice. He gestured to us, languid in our parlor chairs. "The lovely Sara (she looked at you carefully, then looked away), our Miss Rachel (she smiled, but curtly), and our most delicious *chuleta cordo, Señorita* Sofia." Did Tutsik expect me to curtsy? I did not. I barely gave you, that marvelous stranger, the courtesy of an upturned face. Another kosher john, I thought, one more man who will treat me like a cow.

"And us?" Red Ruthie slapped her cards down onto the table. "We don't live here, young man. I own another house, on Tucumán. You are just as welcome there as here most any day, *Señor...*? Tell us his name, Tutsik, he's such a pretty thing!"

"So rude of me, I'm sure..." Tutsik Goldenberg pulled his own vest down and cleared his throat. "Red Ruthie, loveliest ladies, I present *Señor* Hankus Lubarsky. A Jew from our own Poland who we met completely by chance in the lobby of the Thieves' Shul."

Red Ruthie extended a bejeweled hand. The new gentleman held Red Ruthie's eyes dramatically with his own and kissed it magnificently.

"Oh, my," Red Ruthie sighed, and blinked at your brightness. I had never seen her so disarmed by any man's charm.

It was obvious that Goldenberg was entirely pleased with himself, to bring into our midst such a dapper and spectacular lad as you, Hankus Lubarsky. So pleasing to the eye, such well-bred manners. You bowed to us whores with great flourish, went from Ruthie's women to Rachel then Sara then me, took each of our hands into your own and brought it sweetly to tender lips. Then in a minute pulled a blue silk handkerchief from your vest pocket, rolled it into a tiny ball, rubbed it between two palms, blew on it, snapped two lovely fingers, and with a lively flourish brought forth three handkerchiefs—red, blue, black. If I were a proper young lady as I should have been and not a jaded doxy, I would have giggled, which all of Red Ruthie's crew did, joined, of course, by our Rachel. The men, except Tutsik (who watched the trick proudly as if he had done it himself), stood with open mouths, amazed. But Sara ran a finger of her own across the knife marks on her face, stared blankly at our magician, then walked toward the stairs. Myself, I nodded polite as I could and tried to figure what it was about this stranger that pulled me more and more into your eyes, toward your mouth. Just another john I said again, to still a furtive hope I felt rising madly in my heart.

Rachel and Red Ruthie were truly fascinated and so begged you, little magician, for another trick. You proceeded to pull a *peseta* out of Rachel's ear (my uncle used to do this to each of us nieces every Saturday night) and then make it disappear again. I stifled a yawn.

Then, Lubarsky, you snapped those miraculous fingers and there in the palm of your hand was a gold *peso*. Snap again, the *peso* became a golden egg. One last snap and out of nowhere appeared a white dove holding a tiny pink rose in its beak. I was in it now, in this fabulous world created by you, radiant stranger. It was a kind of romance, for I had seen a little of these tricks before but none so spectacular in my own parlor, and certainly none performed by such a handsome beauty as you.

Before we *nafkehs* could gain back the breath we lost around your golden egg, your dove, your roses, before we could bring our hands together and clap our appreciation for you, Hankus Lubarsky, a door slammed shut at the top of the bordello stairs, and there stood Madam Perle, in her serious black dress, tapping her *pince-nez* against the banister like a schoolmarm. Her voice was cold and joyless. It was hard to believe that this was the same queenly seductress who brought me full force into my *shandhoiz* life. "Even for whores you sound like a bunch of animals. This is Rosh Hashanah, one of the holiest nights of the year. You act as if it's a circus."

"And well it is," Red Ruthie said, her arm around our guest. "This here is a friend of your brother, a very talented lad." Ruthie kissed him on the cheek. "Clean-shaven, too. He's only entertaining us until dinner, which we might have eaten an hour ago if you weren't so fascinated with your own private prayer."

Perle walked slowly down the stairs. "It's the birthday of the world, and I'm forced to celebrate with sinners," she muttered.

"You might as well enjoy it, too!" Red Ruthie guffawed. All the women giggled. The men, but for our honored guest Lubarsky, mumbled each to the other under their breath.

Perle rang a tiny bell. When Marianna pulled the dining room doors open, it was clear she'd worked a magic of her own. Before us was a table fit for royalty: Perle's most special china, dazzling white with gold edges ordered from Warsaw and shipped at great expense to Buenos Aires. Tall glass goblets, hand-blown in Mexico, a fine lace tablecloth tatted in Mendoza. In the center of the table were the lit holy day candles, set in ancient brass sticks that came from Palestine itself, sent long ago to Madam by an apostate Jew so struck by her great sensuality that he went posthaste to Jerusalem to repent. Between those sticks, in a cut-glass vase, sat the most delicious bouquet of gardenias and irises, and around all this were laid sweet wines, golden sauces, steamed green vegetables, fresh-made *challah*, and, at either end of the table, huge platters of the delectable *cholent* which Marianna had cooked in Rachel's pot with such care.

And so we all sat, Perle at the head of the table like the Queen of Israel, the rest of us her odalisques and bond slaves, but for you, the intriguing Hankus Lubarsky, who sat directly across from her, with Red Ruthie to the left and Tutsik Goldenberg to the right. Oh, handsome magician with your most remarkable mouth and brilliant eyes, you were mine to gaze upon from my place at Perle's right hand, mine to study across a sea of most delectable foods. Pleasure all around me, even here at Talcahuano Street.

Perle tapped her wine glass until we were silent, then bowed her head, though none of us followed suit. "*Baruch attah adonay, elohaynu melach ha olam, boray pree ha goffin.*" She waited but a second, then looked up at all of us. "Well?"

"*Oymain,*" we grumbled.

"Drink," she ordered. Dov Hirsh gave a terse laugh—the men had clearly dipped into their schnapps already this evening—but we all sipped our wine, that is except for Tutsik Goldenberg, who gulped his down all at once and waved Marianna over to the table in order to pour him more.

"Not yet!" Perle shouted. She glared at Marianna, who backed away from the table, shaking her head all the while. Then Madam dropped her head again and covered her eyes. "*Baruch attah adonay, elohaynu melach ha olam, ha motzee lechem min ha aretz.*" She looked up at us again.

"*Oymain*," we offered.

"Very well," Perle said. She tore a hunk off the *challah* and passed it to Rachel, who took a chunk and passed it to Mordechai, who took a handful and so on until it was my turn and I handed what was left of the sweet white bread back to Perle.

Lubarsky, you leaned across to Ruthie and whispered loudly, "Why does she not bless the candles?"

"Women's work," Red Ruthie whispered back. "It's our little Perleh's greatest sorrow that she wasn't born a man. Isn't that so, Perle?" Red Ruthie asked in her true voice.

"True enough," Perle said, helping herself to a large serving of the meat which she began to devour before anyone else had taken theirs.

"We stand on no ceremony here," Tutsik Goldenberg said without apology as he put double the amount of Perle's serving onto his own plate. "Eat, eat," he pointed to the platter of meat that sat before you. "Good *Yontiff*, everyone!"

"Yes, good *Yontiff*," echoed Red Ruthie, who pinched your magician cheek as she piled slice after slice of the beautiful *flanken* onto your, our new guest's, plate. "Good *Yontiff* and a merry, merry new year."

— 5 —

AND SO, HANKUS, you found yourself on Rosh Hashanah eve at the Talcahuano Street bordello enjoying the most spectacular dinner you had eaten since you left your beloved Max and Motkeleh behind. The fact of your fabulous appetite was not missed by Red Ruthie, who clapped her hands together with delighted pleasure at every bite you took, nor by Tutsik Goldenberg himself, who summoned Marianna again and again to bring his flushed guest more *kreplach*, more beans, another glass of wine, long after the ladies of the house had pushed their well-cleaned plates away. Even Madam Perle leaned her strictly painted face into a balled fist and watched with fascination as you swallowed slice upon slice of meat, mouthful upon mouthful of potatoes, even green vegetables. "He has an appetite of biblical proportions, Tutsik. Where did you say you found him?"

"The truth is," you said, holding up a hand to prevent Marianna from providing you with one more drop of anything, "it was I who found your generous brother and his friends. It was an act of fate, pure and simple. For there was I, stumbling down those few steps from the synagogue into Paso Street, not a friend in the world here in the City of Good Airs, when who should put his palm out to me and say, 'Lad, stop! *Detengas!* Please join my fellows at my sister's house.'"

"Yes, and did he tell you just what kind of house this was?"

"It was easy to know, *Señora* Red Ruthie, from the address and the decor."

"But not," jumped back Red Ruthie, a laugh in her voice, "from the ladies themselves?"

You opened your magician hands and shrugged. "What can I tell you, *Señora?* Although I might add I've never seen such a pious-looking bunch of *nafkehs* in my whole life."

The truth was that you had never seen any *nafkehs* of any religious stripe before tonight, but your bravado covered this fact nicely.

"Yes, well, we'll be having after-dinner services upstairs soon as we all digest," said Sara with a sullen smirk. The rest of us women, including Ruthie's bunch—but not Madam Perle—laughed.

In time, Marianna cleared the table. Just as the tea was set to boil upon the stove, the doorbell rang and into our midst stumbled none other than Marek Fishbein and two of his lackeys, Sholem Big Sam Horowitz and Fishbein's brother-in-law lawyer, Moritz Shatz. To look at them one would never have guessed that they represented the top of the heap in the business of Jewish pimping in Buenos Aires, nor that it was one of the holiest days of the Jewish year. Fishbein, in particular, looked as he always looked, his thick brown hair sticking every which way out of his battered (although somewhat cleaner) top hat, his big face ill-shaven, his filthy shirt open under his cravat at the collar and at the wrists as they poked out of his tattered suit jacket. His shoes were scuffed and down at the heel. But for the stained velvet cape on his shoulders and the dead end of the hand-rolled Cuban cigar perched, as ever, between his lips (yes, Fishbein's taste in tobacco had improved over time), a person might never guess that this was one of three men in five Argentine provinces who wielded more money, power, and fear than the North American bankers J. P. Morgan and J. D. Rockefeller combined.

Tutsik Goldenberg stood immediately and practically bowed. *"Reb* Fishbein, friends of *Reb* Fishbein, welcome, welcome to our humble house. Marianna—" Goldenberg gestured in the direction of the newly arrived guests, and the housekeeper took Fishbein's cape and gloves.

After all these years she knew not to ask for his hat. "We were just about to retire to the parlor for a bit of tea and holiday brandy, *Reb* Fishbein. Please join us and perhaps have a little smoke—"

"To smoke on this holy day, here, in the frum *heizel* of the exalted Madam Perle, *Reb* Goldenberg? I wouldn't think of it." Fishbein handed the butt end of his fancy cigar to Shatz, who produced a silver tube, just its size, and slid the remains in. "For another day," Fishbein said, smiling almost brightly to all assembled. "It is a very good cigar and so I must be careful to cherish it as I do all my other pleasures." With this he tipped his hat to Madam Perle. "And speaking of such, a very warm *shana tova* to you, Madam Perle. May you be inscribed in the Book of Life for at least one more year."

Perle looked at Fishbein coolly and made just a hint of a curtsy. "And also you, *Reb* Fishbein, and your brother-in-law Moritz..."

Moritz shuffled his feet and whispered hoarsely, "*Shana tova...*"

"...and to you as well, *Reb* Horowitz."

Sholem Big Sam Horowitz nodded his head but barely met Madam Perle's eyes. "*Shana.*"

Perle Goldenberg drew herself up and put a hand to her bosom. "And now, dear friends, I must myself retire. Marianna, please see that our holiday guests get whatever they desire. I will take my tea, and one *taiglech* only, in my room. Tomorrow I must rise at dawn to take in the early morning service at the *shul,* and so I ask that you all keep the festivities down to a reasonable roar. Red Ruthie, Dov Hirsh, Doctor Dorfman—good night."

We all watched Madam Perle ascend from our place in the dining room archway. As soon as she was up the stairs and her door clicked shut, Fishbein pointed a thumb at Moritz who produced not only the silver tube with the cigar end in it but six brand new cigars as well. Fishbein handed them around to all the men like a new father. When he came to you, Lubarsky, he gave you a *shockle* under the chin. "And who is this little dandy? Could it be you are the waiter who served me up such a magnificent storm at that *parrillado* on LaValle just last week?"

"The very one," said Tutsik Goldenberg before you could get in even one word. He held a lit match to Fishbein's cigar, then turned it back to his own.

Fishbein squinted at you through a cloud of grey smoke. "You know, I've been thinking of opening a *parrillado* of my own to rival that Yale Levine. What would it take to steal you away?"

Again it was Goldenberg who chimed in. "Talking business, *Reb* Fishbein, on such an awestruck night? He may be a waiter on common nights, but this evening he is a partner in prayer. We met for the first time just hours ago at the Thieves' Shul."

"The Thieves' Shul? Is that true?" Fishbein held your fiery eyes with his own glassy ones.

"*Sí, Señor,*" you replied.

"So interesting," Fishbein returned his attention to Goldenberg, "because my brother-in-law Moritz and my friend Horowitz and me, we also prayed at the Thieves' Shul tonight. I had my eye out for you, Tutskeleh, but I didn't spot you."

"We were there, *Reb* Fishbein, just not in our usual spots. We stood near the back so as not to interfere if we felt moved by God to walk out and smoke."

"Interesting," said Fishbein, puffing gently on his cigar, which Goldenberg could tell from his own draws of smoke was a very fancy cigar indeed. "Interesting, because we too stood at the back of the *shul,* thinking you might be just there."

At that moment the beleaguered Marianna appeared with a kettle filled with strong tea which she carried to the buffet and poured with great care into Madam Perle's cherished samovar. Sugar and lemon were arranged beside the samovar in silver servers, along with cups and saucers that matched the dinner dishes. Beside these was a great bowl filled to the brim with hard, sticky *taiglech* and a square plate containing slices of Marianna's famous honey cake.

We ladies, along with Dorfman and Hirsh, took our tea and sweets into the parlor and arranged ourselves on various couches and easy chairs. Without our customers littering the place it wasn't nearly as unpleasant as usual.

"Perhaps our young guest would favor us with a little more magic?" Goldenberg's eyes met yours hopefully.

"I'm afraid I used up my most dazzling tricks before dinner. But if you're a fan of card magic, I've a few things...up my sleeve."

Red Ruthie laughed heartily. "A boy with a sense of humor—when was the last time we saw such a one as this?"

"Yes, card tricks are an excellent idea!" Tutsik Goldenberg made for the decanter of brandy that stood at the far end of the buffet and poured himself a teacupful. He began to follow the small crowd into the parlor when he was stopped by Sholem Big Sam's hand on his shoulder.

"I believe we were in the midst of a discussion," Fishbein said with no smile in his voice.

Goldenberg looked at the three men and took a tiny sip of brandy. "Yes, a pity we missed each other this evening, but now you are here."

"Yes," Fishbein told him, "after all, here we are now visiting on New Year's eve. Moritz, what year would this be?"

"Fifty-six seventy-six, Marek."

"Fifty-six seventy-six. It's lovely, ain't it, how we Jews are so much advanced in time than your average Catholic Joe. They're still stuck at the start of the twentieth century, but us, we're already close to the end of the fifty-seventh." Fishbein put his face very close to Goldenberg's. "It boggles the mind, don't it?"

"Boggles it," said Goldenberg, clearing his throat. "Now, if you please, *Reb* Fishbein, this boy is such a talent, we won't want to miss even one trick."

Moritz and Sholem Big Sam suddenly had their arms around Goldenberg and blocked him from the rest of the company's view. They herded him back to the buffet, where Fishbein put his face very close to Goldenberg's.

"Have you any idea, Tutsik, why I might have had an eye out for you? Why I took it upon myself to leave my wife, my poor homesick mother"—this was a lie, for Fishbein's mother was so well set in her little villa on the Tigre River just outside the city limits that she made a point at every turn in a conversation to curse not just the old country, Russia, but all of Europe besides—"in order to travel to Talcahuano Street to eat *taiglech* with the likes of you?"

Goldenberg took a good-sized gulp of brandy and a puff of his cigar. "No, Marek, I can't say as I do."

In a second Fishbein put his whole hand around Goldenberg's skinny neck and pinned him against the wall. "There is the little matter of a certain gambling debt."

Goldenberg sputtered. His face turned red. Hadn't he just thought about that gambling debt on his way home from *shul?* It was one he'd acquired when Big Sam caught him cheating. The worst kind. He looked over Fishbein's shoulder into the parlor for help but saw only his gathered guests and employees watching intently as the little magician made what appeared from Tutsik's less-than-perfect vantage point all of the red cards in his deck disappear. "A gambling debt, yes," Goldenberg finally squeaked out, "in the sum of five hundred gold *pesos.*"

Fishbein opened his hand and Tutsik stumbled forward. "I see you've not forgotten entirely."

"Not entirely? Why, not at all! I owe you five hundred gold *pesos, Reb* Fishbein, which I have every intention of paying back. On the due date."

"The due date being?" Fishbein asked.

"Why, the end of the year."

Fishbein held his hands up over his head, then put them down by his sides. He grabbed Tutsik Goldenberg by his well-made lapels. "And what day is it now?"

"Why, September twenty-third."

"And what is significant about September the twenty-third, nineteen hundred and fourteen?"

Goldenberg looked back at Fishbein, a complete blank. He thought and thought, but nothing came into his head. "As far as I can tell, *Reb* Fishbein, I still have ninety-nine days to make good on my debt."

Moritz and Sholem Big Sam each folded their hands. Fishbein himself turned purple and, without raising his voice, screamed into Tutsik's ear, "*Shlemiel!* Idiot! *Paskudnyak!* What is the entire point of tonight's meal?"

"It's Rosh Hashanah, New Year's—"

"Exactly right!" Fishbein hollered in his full voice. "It's the New Year! The end of the Jewish year! WHERE ARE MY FIVE HUNDRED GOLD *PESOS?*"

There was a slight pause in the parlor chat, a rumble and some tittering, then we all were back to your cards.

"Ah," said Tutsik Goldenberg, shaking his head to make the ringing in his ears stop, "ah, now I understand. We have a misunderstanding based on time. Yes, it's quite clear. I think I have until January first to pay you your money; you feel the money is due you tonight. No wonder you're upset, *Reb* Fishbein. I honestly can't say I blame you. But there's a little problem here, a tiny," Goldenberg held a thumb and forefinger together and shook them before Fishbein, "teeny," he did the same with his other hand, "little problem. Where as I know for a fact I can have the money delivered to you without a doubt on the eve of December thirty-first—I know this absolutely, based on a business endeavor that just this evening has been settled—I also know absolutely that I have nowhere near five hundred gold *pesos* to give to you tonight."

"No gold *pesos* tonight. What about Perle?"

At the mention of his sister, Tutsik Goldenberg's demeanor changed completely. He pulled his crumpled suit jacket straight and dusted himself off with his hands as if to do so would automatically restore his dignity. "*Reb* Fishbein," he said, an angry quaver in his voice, "I am sure that somewhere, hidden in this house, there are at least one thousand gold *pesos*. But those gold *pesos* are Perle's, *Reb* Fishbein, not mine, and if you wish to have them, I'm afraid you must ask for them yourself."

Fishbein seemed not to notice the change in Tutsik Goldenberg's manner. He pushed up close to him and put a dirty finger exactly on Goldenberg's heart. "I'm telling you to get the money from her."

Goldenberg, with the back of his own impeccably manicured hand, brushed Fishbein's finger away. He straightened his tie and patted his hair into place. With his head high, his feet together, and not a trace of fear in his voice, he said, "*Reb* Fishbein, with all due respect, I am a man of my word. I have never welched on a gambling debt in my entire life, although, permit me, I have had many opportunities to do so. To assume that I would take a chance on getting on your bad side over a few hundred measly *pesos* given the power you wield in this city is patently absurd. And then, to assume that I would look to my sister—of all people—to get me out of it is even more absurd. You shall have your five hundred gold *pesos,* you can depend on it. Ten days from now, on Yom Kippur night, as soon as it becomes kosher for money to pass hands, you shall have your winnings."

Fishbein took a step forward with a balled-up fist. Goldenberg stood firm. Moritz put a hand on Fishbein's shoulder and Sholem Big Sam gestured with his head toward the parlor, where we women all raptly watched our magician remove wrists from an array of knotted kerchiefs and belts. Goldenberg's two men, Hirsh and Dorfman, however, were beginning to crane their necks in the direction of the dining room. Fishbein rubbed his hands together, pulled down his filthy cuffs, and straightened his hat. "Very well then. Five hundred gold *pesos* by Yom Kippur night. Plus ten percent interest per day late fee which figures to," he snapped his fingers and Big Sam whispered into his ear, "five hundred more gold *pesos*, bringing our total to one thousand gold *pesos*. Which you will deliver to my offices on Maipú Street as soon as the last *shofar* sounds. Are we agreed?"

It took every ounce of Goldenberg's composure not to burst into tears with the addition of the penalty fee, but in spite of himself, he rather smartly ran a finger across his eyebrow and said, "Agreed."

"You know, it's a shame that you and your sister don't share assets. I would have settled for a few weeks with that Sofia." Fishbein winked at Goldenberg, who nodded his head noncommittally.

"I should be happy to accommodate you, *Reb* Fishbein, but the merchandise of this house is, alas, not mine to give away."

"Pity," said Fishbein, "pity indeed." He pinched Goldenberg's cheek and popped two pieces of honey cake into his mouth at once.

Goldenberg pulled down his suit jacket one more time. "You will join us now for what remains of *Reb* Lubarsky's little magic act?"

"I'd love to," said Fishbein, "but look at the time. My mother, poor thing, must be worried sick."

"I'll ring Marianna to get your things."

"Yes, do that," Fishbein smiled. It was a warm smile, but his teeth glinted through it. "Join your friends. My colleagues and I will see ourselves out."

I have said to you how on that first night in our brothel home there was something in your magician eyes that held me all through dinner, something in your generous mouth. But I must tell you, as much as those eyes smoldered and those lips beckoned, it was your hands that kept my curiosity kindled. Long after you, our honored and talented guest, successfully identified every card we pulled from the deck; rendered invisible and re-produced household objects of all sizes with the help of only a large silk scarf (the most impressive being Madam Perle's prize gramophone); managed to make short work of every knot tied around those skillful wrists by any of us, including Red Ruthie, renowned up and down our red light district for her knot-tying expertise; and even got out of a pair of regulation Russian army handcuffs provided by Mordechai Dorfman who had been carrying them around with him since his dishonorable discharge seventeen years before, I was thinking only of those hands.

I myself did no tying or card pulling. Wait, I pulled out one, an ace wasn't it? Of hearts, too, which I remember gave everyone a little something to giggle at. But by and large I sat back at a comfortable distance on the velvet fainting couch and watched as you captivated everyone for more than an hour, and not only never grew tired or bored, but also carefully deflected the curious questions about how such and such a trick was worked by working yet another trick more intriguing than the one before.

Tutsik Goldenberg never joined us. When you had emptied your entire bag of magic tricks and were ready to have a cup of tea like the rest of us, I went to find him.

"Hey, Tutsik," I called from the dining room door, "your dinner guest will be looking for his hat and stick soon."

"What's that?"

"Lubarsky. He's getting ready to go off in a bit. Since you missed all his magic, it's only polite that you come out and join him in a cup of tea."

"I've had my tea," Goldenberg rumbled. "I've had my tea and cake besides."

"You invited the boy here for dinner. The least you can do is spend two minutes with him before he goes home."

"Well, aren't you the picture of polite society. Can't you see I'm busy?"

"All I can see is that you're drunk on your ass and sitting in your sister's chair besides."

"Yes, drunk on my ass and in my sister's chair besides. Her throne, don't you mean? Queen Perle Goldenberg the First, and me the court fool." He pulled himself out of the chair and staggered toward me. "Have you got a thousand *pesos* you can lend me, *neshomeleh?* Just for a month or two until I can get on my feet?"

I backed away from him and he nearly fell over. "I? I have no money of my own. You and your generous sister have seen to that. If I had ended up in the Warsaw prison I'd have more money for my trouble by now."

"Just a thousand gold *pesos*. Is that so much to ask from a man who changed your life?" He collapsed back into Perle's chair and tried to suck the last drops of brandy from the decanter. When this proved fruitless, he tossed it over his shoulder. It shattered against the wall. I didn't move, but at just that moment Dorfman and Hirsh stood stupidly in the doorway.

"Ho-ho, old man," Mordechai laughed. "What did you do, empty the bottle?"

"Emptied it, yes," Goldenberg spat. "Emptied and smashed it, just like my life in this stupid country!"

"Well, your new boyfriend is getting ready to leave and he'd like to say good-bye," Dov Hirsh offered.

"Tell him to go to hell."

Dorfman went over to the buffet and picked out a perfectly round *taiglech*. "That won't do much for your business prospects. Remember you invited him over here with a tease about work?"

"Well, that was before that *ganef* Fishbein came in here and ruined me."

"Did you get ruined again, Tutsik?" I asked, although I knew it was probably better if I did not. "I was under the impression it was your sister Perle who ruined you."

"Oh, don't you wish it," Goldenberg sneered, "don't you wish my life had been ruined by Perle. You useless slut, get out of here! How can a man think when he's surrounded by women like these?"

"You brought me here in order to surround you, you stupid pig!"

"I should have thrown you in the ocean when I had the chance." He lifted his fist to me. Mordechai Dorfman caught it with his hand.

"Go out and tell Lubarsky that Tutsik's indisposed. He should call on us later this week," hissed Hirsh.

"Where? At his private offices?"

"Don't be smart. Tell him to come by this week sometime for a pinochle game and Tutsik will talk to him about his proposition—he'll know what you mean."

"What, you're making him a pimp, too?" I muttered.

"Slut!" cried Goldenberg. "Whore! I'll break that bitch's neck."

And so it was my job to see you, our guest Lubarsky, to the door on the first night of the Jewish year in Buenos Aires, Argentina. I found your hat and stick among the others on the coat tree and stood with them while you made your rounds, kissing the hands of Red Ruthie and the others, all the while acting like it was us who did the favor of watching instead of you who did the favor of keeping our minds off our lives for an hour. "And where is *Sénor* Goldenberg?"

"Indisposed," I said flatly from my station at the coat tree.

"I see," you said. I couldn't tell if you were disappointed or not. You reached for your hat and with great flourish placed it at a jaunty angle on your head.

"He says to stop by for a game of pinochle sometime next week. Perle will still be up in her room praying for all our salvations, but Tutsik will do his business."

"Yes, we were to talk business tonight, but *Pan* Fishbein's visit seemed to cut that short."

"Frankly, you wouldn't want to try to talk to him now. He's likely to knock you over. That crash you heard a few minutes ago was him bemoaning the current facts of his life."

"I see." You smiled up at me warmly, took my hand in your own, and once again tried to hold my eyes while kissing my fingers.

Of course, it was then I knew. Not the eyes nor the lips at all, but the hands were what told me why such a man as you was no man at all, had no interest in us whores as whores but only as sisters. And lovers, perhaps, maybe that, too. I knew instantly why it was your eyes and mouth attracted me so: they were not meant to dazzle me into submission—they were meant to keep me from seeing you and your hands too closely.

It was impossible to look at your hands without learning their secret: Hankus Lubarsky, you were no boy wonder from Cracow, although you were truly a remarkable magician. No, your hands, Hankus Lubarsky, were a woman's hands. Indeed, how could they not be? Not only were they small, they were nimble and deft. And you were so good at keeping everyone's eyes away from them because, as beautiful as were those hands, so much more riveting were your odd eyes, eyes which held and released a person, dared a person to look and look away. You wanted it that way. If a person looked too closely, of course she would know the truth.

One would think. I had no doubt that the men of the house didn't have a clue. Tutsik Goldenberg looked only at a woman's shape and the length of her hair, and Dov Hirsh looked at what Tutsik looked at. Mordechai Dorfman might have noticed, for he was, after all, a doctor. But he was also a drunk and tonight he sat like a little boy and *kvelled* while you worked your magic, or else he tied sloppy knots around your wrists and then his interest was mostly in the knots themselves and not the wrists beneath them. As to Red Ruthie and her girls, who knew what they noticed? All of their senses were dulled by liquor, the holiday, and tonight, also, opium smoke. I was certain Madam Perle didn't notice, for her mind was on her visit to heaven and she saw only what God whispered in her ear. But Rachel and Sara, dear Hankus, I was certain that they knew it too.

I decided it was best to play along with your ruse of manhood. I would watch and welcome you into this house as if you were a man, and not any old Johnny, either. I would treat you with more respect than I gave any of them, lure you close to me and earn your trust. I would act as if I never knew the true secret of those magnificent hands until it was the perfect time.

You would be my salvation. I wanted it so.

6

DESPERATION MADE TUTSIK GOLDENBERG a more enter-
prising thinker than usual. It was clear to him five minutes after Marek
Fishbein left our house on Rosh Hashanah eve that there was no human possibility he could come up with a thousand *pesos,* gold or paper. He would not, under any circumstances, not even threat of death
by one of the many colorful accidents Fishbein and his boys liked to
engineer—death by *droshky,* death by house fire, death by falling drunk
off a pier in La Boca (Tutsik knew them all)—not even under threat
of these would he stoop so low as to ask his sister Perle for the money
he owed.

   He drank himself into the stupor I found him in. After you left,
Hankus, Dorfman, and Hirsh carried him up to his rooms, where he
collapsed into a slobbering heap on his bed. When morning came,
however, he woke up brilliant. Just as God provided ten days between
the New Year and the Day of Atonement in which to repent unconditionally for one's sins, so had He allowed ten days in which a man
could convert himself from a *shlimazel* to a big winner. And today

was Tutsik Goldenberg's day.

He bounced out of bed, went straight to the bathroom, and soaked in the tub for half an hour. He shaved, he perfumed himself, and dressed in his yellow pants and checkered jacket. He chose a small green bow tie and, to add a jaunty air, his straw boater. This outfit, but for the hat, the very one he wore the night he discovered you, he called his impresario costume. He put it on carefully, picking off all lint and smoothing all wrinkles. He brushed back his hair and patted it down with tonic. He inspected his jacket shoulders for any trace of dandruff. Then he picked up his boater and trotted downstairs. Even he was surprised by the lightness in his step.

More surprising than his jauntiness was the way he spoke to all of us women that morning. There we sat, sipping our strong South American coffees, eating our sticky sweet rolls, waiting for that storm cloud of a Goldenberg to weigh us down with his *shmulkiness*. Here comes he, with a big smile on that maddeningly handsome face of his. "Ladies," he greeted us, and for the first time in three years I heard no disgust in his voice.

"Where's your hangover, Tutsik?" I couldn't resist.

"What's that?" Perle asked. She was until that moment absorbed in a thick and ancient-looking book written completely in Aramaic. I wondered that she didn't worry about spilling coffee all over it.

Tutsik glared at me. The old venom came back into his face, but just as quickly faded away. "Sofia, I've no idea what you're talking about." He smiled pointedly and signaled Marianna to pour him his coffee. "Thank you," he told her. She looked at him as if she would faint. Tutsik took a long sip and smacked his lips. "Perfectly done, Marianna. The perfect cup of coffee, and to think I had to come all the way here to this godforsaken country to find it." He took out his pocket watch. "Ah, look at the time. I must dash." And before his sister could ask even one question, Tutsik Goldenberg had his boater on his head and was out the door and down the stairs.

He made his way from Talcahuano to Maipú Street almost whistling. "Saved, I've been saved!" he sang out. "At last, at last! I'm saved!"

Now I myself have never been there, but you told me, Hankus, that Marek Fishbein's private offices were two flights up a dark set of stairs. At the top of those stairs, in a chair in front of the office door, a goon in a nicely pressed suit and a Panama hat always sat. On this day, the goon played mumbletypeg with a nasty-looking blade on the landing. "Help you?" he asked, without looking up, as Tutsik Goldenberg stood before him and straightened his tie. The goon tossed the knife. It landed straight up between Tutsik Goldenberg's feet.

"I'm here to see Fishbein," Goldenberg said, trying to hide the sudden shallowness of his breathing. His fingers crept to his back pocket to make sure he felt his own little knife there.

The man reached over and pulled his blade out from the floor. He held it just a fraction of an inch away from Goldenberg and ran it up the length of his body.

Goldenberg resisted the impulse to tumble backward down the stairs. "It's a financial matter," he managed.

"Ah," the goon said. He flipped his knife into the air, caught it by the handle, then pointed the tip at Goldenberg. "Lending or borrowing?"

Tutsik pulled himself up and adjusted his boater. "Settling a debt."

"Good boy." The thug leaned back in his chair and without turning round rapped on the door with the handle of his knife. "Name?"

"T. Goldenberg."

The man licked his teeth under his tightly closed lips and nodded. The door opened just a crack. Fishbein's brother-in-law Moritz stuck his head out. "Yeah?"

"T. Goldenberg to see Fishbein. Debt-settling."

"Oh, really? And to think, just last night he was crying in his brandy about a few trifling *pesos*. Well, let me see if Mr. Fishbein is available." The door slammed shut. Tutsik stood bouncing on his toes on the landing, trying to diffuse his contempt. Moritz Shatz was the perfect example of why a person ought never work for one's relatives. Here was a man, a solicitor by trade, a lawyer, reduced to being a receptionist. Goldenberg was thrilled to have a real plan to present to Fishbein. A real investment possibility. A partnership. His days of kicking deadbeats out the Talcahuano Street door for Perle were soon to be over.

Goldenberg bounced for another minute, and another minute after that, and then stopped bouncing and stood still. After a few minutes he began to pace. The goon in front of the door had by this time put his knife away and was reading a girlie magazine. "Take a look." He offered it to Tutsik, who shrugged it away.

"No thanks, I have to look at the real thing all day."

"Too bad," said the man.

"What's taking him so long?"

"Marek Fishbein is a busy guy," the goon said. He turned the page and gave a low whistle. "It's unusual to just walk in without an appointment."

"I'm a busy man, too."

The thug looked up from his magazine and winked. "Ain't we all. Have a seat."

When Tutsik looked around him for a chair the man pointed with his chin to the top stair. Tutsik paced some more, then looked at his watch, and finally sat on the step. Within seconds of his doing that, the door opened another crack and Moritz stuck his head out. *"Pan* Fishbein will see you now."

Goldenberg stood up abruptly and dusted himself off. He pushed his boater back on his head as he followed Moritz. The goon at the door whistled at the magazine again and shook his head.

The office was as one might expect: a cavernous set of rooms with high ceilings and no natural light, although there were window blinds which Fishbein never saw fit to open. On every imaginable surface was an ashtray, and each ashtray was full to brimming with ends of cigars. There were piles of papers everywhere, and bottles, empty and full, that contained or once contained every kind of alcoholic beverage known to man. There were ledgers and half-eaten sandwiches and dirty coffee cups spread all over. Yet as filthy as the whole place was, there was a strange orderliness to it. One got the eerie sense that at any time, at any moment, Marek Fishbein could put his hands on just the piece of paper he needed and shove it down your throat.

Tutsik Goldenberg stood for a second in the entryway as his eyes adjusted to the dark. In a corner by a closed-up-tight window was a desk; at that desk sat Fishbein himself. Tutsik could just make out his silhouette against the burning ember of his cigar. At another desk, Sholem Big Sam Horowitz sat under a bright desk lamp figuring some numbers. He looked up when Tutsik cleared his throat, then went right back to work. Moritz was whispering something into Fishbein's ear.

"Ah, Tutsik! Tutsik Goldenberg, *shalom alaichem,* as our brethren in the Promised Land like to say."

"*Alaichem v'shalom,*" answered Goldenberg tersely.

"Moritz tells me you've come to settle up. That's good, because I was worried about you. Finding five hundred *pesos* in ten days is one thing. A thousand *pesos* quite another. I would have hated to have to rub you out so close to Yom Kippur. Sit down."

Goldenberg made himself as comfortable as he could in the straight-back chair across the desk from Fishbein. They sat for a minute in silence.

"I hate to be pushy," Fishbein said at length, "but as you can see, I'm a busy man."

Goldenberg nodded.

"So where's my money?"

"I said I came to settle my debt, *Pan* Fishbein. I didn't say with cash."

Fishbein stared at Tutsik through the murky air. He turned his glance to Moritz who stood obsequiously by his side. "Am I hearing things? Did he say he was here to pay a debt but he's going to do it without money?"

"That's what he said, Marek."

Fishbein puffed out his cheeks and nodded his head. His top hat wiggled just a bit. "You have what, Palestine bonds?"

"No bonds," said Goldenberg calmly.

"The man is obviously insane," said Moritz.

"Shut up." Fishbein's voice was soft and very controlled. "If you have no cash, and you have no bonds, just how do you intend to pay me back?"

Even Sholem Big Sam stopped his paper work and looked up at Goldenberg.

Tutsik took a cigar from the box on Marek Fishbein's desk. He reached over an unruly pile of papers and snatched up a match, which he lit with his thumbnail. Moritz watched Fishbein from the corner of his eye. Fishbein chewed his own cigar.

"I have a plan, *Reb* Fishbein. I have a property, and a plan. And the property in the form of an investment is, you will see, a very good one, a very smart one." He took a draw on his purloined cigar, then leaned back in his seat and exhaled smoke rings. "And I would say that your half of this investment could be worth exactly five hundred and fifty *pesos*. Shall I tell you more?"

No paper was signed, it was all done with handshakes, gentleman-style. Tutsik Goldenberg offered up half of your ass to settle his debt with Marek Fishbein (an ass he didn't own at all), and Marek Fishbein accepted it. In that moment, in their own pimp minds, you came to belong, however briefly, to them both.

You yourself had no idea that such a deal was being struck. No, at that very moment, you yourself were busy wondering if this Goldenberg chap was serious about helping you or not. Oh, what luck what luck if he would, for you had not the resources to make yourself as famous as Harry Houdini.

You sat in your Chacabuco Street room with your own strong coffee, looked out your window onto the street below, and your mind drifted to the night before. Your first night in any whorehouse. It was pleasant enough, but you didn't like to think about the fact that it was a *shandhoiz* much, because if you did, you had to remember that you were a woman like the rest of us, that it could as easily have been you in a silk kimono with no underwear on as any of us. You preferred to be sentimental about the company: the dour but impossibly sexy Madam Perle and ribald Red Ruthie could both pass for aunties. The goofy gangsters, you could imagine them the uncles you never had. But then—if Red Ruthie's girls, if Sara and Rachel and me, if we were not whores, what were we? Surely not your cousins from Zamosc!

No, no, Hankeleh. Sara, Rachel, and me were the undeniable *bisteca* and *chuleta cordero* on Perle Goldenberg's kosher table—the *zoinehs,* the *putas,* the doxies, the *tsatskelehs.*

You thought for a minute about the look in my eye when I bade you good night. You wondered if I hadn't guessed you were a woman like me, if I hadn't recognized you by your nimble fingers and smooth chin. But these thoughts you quickly put out of your mind, for as you knew better than anyone, you were no woman like me at all.

Where I was round about the breasts and ass, you, Hankus, you were slim-hipped and flat-chested. You wore your coats long in the sleeve (the better to hide your pick locks, your matches, your white doves and roses, your give-it-away fingers). I was allowed to wear no shirt at all. Around your neck you wore a string tie like the gauchos, or else a silk cravat like the *bacáns* who trafficked with us. My neck, by professional obligation, was completely exposed.

Not only that, but no one had ever smacked you in the face. The men you met in your daily Buenos Aires life treated you respectfully:

they looked you in the eye; they talked to you as if you had more than half a brain in your head; and not one man sitting across a card table from you, no matter how badly you had beat him at pinochle or poker, ever raised a fist to you let alone knocked you halfway across the room.

It crossed your mind, as you sat looking out the window onto Chacabuco Street, sipping your coffee, contemplating your future, that those thugs, Dov Hirsh and Dr. Mordechai Dorfman, would surely lift your slender magician self by those well-made lapels and mash your generous mouth into a pulp were they to discover your secret. If Tutsik Goldenberg, who took the most pleasure in offering to knock his sister's women through a wall, realized that his *goldeneh yingeleh,* the magician Lubarsky, was a woman in men's clothing, there was no telling what parts of your body he would figure to brutalize with his bare and calculating hands.

I didn't wish it on you, although I, who spent my days and nights on my back and all fours to fill the pockets of Madam Perle Goldenberg, certainly envied you. For you were a woman unfettered by silk stockings and garters, free, it seemed, to walk the cobbled streets alone, day or night.

But now, without you even knowing it, Fishbein and Goldenberg had put a money value on your behind. I felt bad for you when I heard this, but I wouldn't betray you. It is true, though, that in order to get out of Talcahuano Street, I was not above threatening to do just that.

PART THREE

*Sawed in Half
(1915–1916)*

I

NOW, AFTER NEARLY THREE YEARS in which the most that had happened was that my virtue was compromised in every imaginable way, there began to be motion in the Talcahuano Street bordello, motion that hurtled me toward freedom. And even though there was a world full of history outside the *shandhoiz* walls—revolution brewing in Russia, women in England and America agitating to vote, a war beginning that would consume entire nations—it was not history that dictated my fate, but the whim and cross purposes of those cursed Goldenbergs. This time, sweet Hankus, because your life was knotted into theirs, your fate was in their hands as well.

Things began to change, as I remember, after the Jewish holiday of Simchat Torah. We whores had languished through our Yom Kippur fast, we complied with Madame Perle's wishes and spent a week eating Succoth meals in a little booth in our courtyard (this not without derision from our not-so-pious neighbors). You were the honored guest at all of the holiday feasting, Hankus.

It was unclear as to whether you retained your job at Casa de Yale Levine, for you were at the *shandhoiz* more and more, and when you were not there of an evening, Tutsik Goldenberg always made noises about going to collect you at your flat on Chacabuco Street, to tear you from your practice. There was a conspiratorial mood between you two, a back and forth winking at these dinners, and not a little giggling besides. Rachel wondered to me out loud if the two of you had not become lovers. I felt a horrible sinking in my heart.

Then *voilà*. Succoth moved to Simchat Torah, the Torah was finished and begun again. Madam Perle herded us all to the balcony of the Thieves' Shul so we might poke our heads through the curtain and watch as the men below threw Torahs into the air, danced with them like sweethearts, carried them on their shoulders like babes.

You, Hankus, you were down there with the men. And how the crowd thrilled as you juggled those Torahs, oh, it was better than watching any steak dinner be whipped through the air. No Jew in Buenos Aires will ever forget that electric moment when you stood on your hands and balanced the most beautiful scroll by its ebony handles on the balls of your upside-down feet.

I admired you, I was furious, I was heartbroken. True, there was no love lost between me and that Torah, and yet, I longed to touch it. And it wasn't just my harlot's hands that restrained me. In the eyes of God, just the fact of my womanhood made me unfit to enjoy even the pleasure of a kissed finger on its satin coat. There was I, up in the balcony, that damnable velvet curtain holding me back, and there were you, to the untrained eye a young man, on the floor of the temple, not just touching the holy Torah, but tumbling with it as well.

When we returned to the brothel for dinner, I could not look at you across the *blintzes* and cream, so angry was I. For you were among us, but you were not of us. Well, you were, but your secret had not yet been loosed upon the world.

There was a new girl at our table by this time, a young thing named Magda whom Dr. Mordechai Dorfman had lured to us through letters to her poverty-struck mother, his third cousin Hindeleh from Lodz. You tried to charm her along with the rest of us throughout dinner. Little Magda, who prior to this moment spent all her time weeping, succumbed to your charms and giggled at your silly wiggling ears and dancing biceps. I would have none of it. I ate my sweet creamy food and went back up to bed.

I kept you in my sight as the months passed. Sorry to say, I felt nothing but disdain as your confidence among us grew. Nightly you would join the other men of the house at their card games and at dice. Once a week at least you would juggle Madam Perle's fine china or her gramophone records, thrilling all with your daring, never once dropping a plate or exposing who you really were. When asked a question about your past, you politely deflected it. When asked a question about your future, you simply shrugged.

Oh, yes, you were Tutsik Goldenberg's *goldeneh yingeleh*. You enjoyed your manhood, and oh, how it protected you. By the time *Pesach* came upon us, I spent day and night dreaming, under the customers and over them, how to best use what I knew about you in order to free myself. For the more confident you became around the johns, the more useful you would be to me in the long run. Yes, I knew how things were shaping up. When we had our whorehouse *seder*, it would be you who sat reclining and we who would be straight and tall in our wooden chairs. Ah, Hankus, it breaks my heart to think of it now, how much contempt I held in my heart for you then.

But I was a concubine, not a prophet. I did not see the way things would later turn.

I have said how Madam Perle, since my arrival at her bordello, had moved more and more toward a life with God. I've no doubt that if we Jews had nuns, our Perle by this time would have found her way to the nearest convent. Perhaps Talcahuano Street was that very place.

I have talked about her reading tomes at breakfast, how she had taken to praying in her room while the rest of us were busy playing cards or working. She kept herself locked up for weeks before any holy day. Most surprising of all, when little Magda arrived on our doorstep, Perle had nothing to do with her. Her initiation was assigned immediately to Rachel, and that was the end of that.

During the months between Simchat Torah and *Pesach*, small, heavy parcels started arriving at our flat with return addresses from Jewish bookstores in London, New York, Paris, and Berlin. Letters came to Madam Perle all the way from Bucharest, Budapest, and Minsk.

Then, just two weeks before Passover, strange men whom none of us had ever seen before began to visit Madam Perle. They were religious Jews, to be sure, but other than their broad-brimmed hats and *paisim,* they dressed in modern clothes like Tutsik Goldenberg and

Dov Hirsh. Sometimes these men came empty-handed, but more often than not they bore large packages wrapped with brown paper and twine. These men never purchased tokens. They were shown by Marianna directly up to Madam Perle's boudoir, where they were admitted and stayed sometimes for hours on end. When Sara or I put an ear to Madam's bedroom door, instead of moaning and panting we heard whispered talk and chanting. "She's gone off the deep end," Sara said, which coming from her was quite a statement.

One might with good reason believe Perle Goldenberg had lost her senses. She took breakfast with us, but had Marianna serve her only a bowl of cooked groats with no milk or cream. She eschewed her breakfast coffee for strong black tea. Lunch and dinner she ate when we did, but took no meat, fish, or fowl, no eggs or butter, cheese or cream. Most peculiarly, she left all collection of money and distribution of tokens to Marianna.

So by the time of this breakfast, this day before *Pesach desayuno*, Madam Perle sat amongst us in a long-sleeved black dress with a tall black collar that completely covered her neck. The hem of her dress dragged along the ground and she wore heavy wool stockings on her shapely legs. I wondered what had happened to that shiny green dressing gown, or if underneath that strict covering she still wore her black corselet.

We were enjoying our usual coffee and sweet rolls, our last before we would be dining on dry *matzoh*. Tutsik sat with a newspaper in front of his face. Perle took her seat and signaled Marianna, who brought a bowl of plain groats to her immediately. Perle made quite the point of looking slowly around the table, then saying to Tutsik, "What, that *shnorrer* Lubarsky's not here? Ah, that's right, he comes for the expensive meals, never the cheap smaller ones."

"I see the lady of the house is in an exceeding good humor today." Tutsik Goldenberg barely looked up from his paper as he dipped a corner of his roll into his tiny cup of coffee. We all, even the new Magda, held our breath carefully. "Tell me, Perle, has the young man done anything but join us as *mishpocheh?*"

"He eats but he never purchases anybody's services." Perle took a spoonful of *kasha* into her mouth and chewed purposefully. Marianna poured Madam a second cup of tea from her special silver pot.

"Has he ever laid so much as a finger on the goods? Not once,"

Tutsik asked and answered, his head still hidden in the paper. "Has he ever smashed a glass or broken a chair or table to bits?"

"He eats us out of house and home and gives nothing back." Madam Perle took another mouthful of groats and chewed.

"He's a member of the family. I bring him here to join us for dinner. Tomorrow night he'll honor us by saying the *Fir Kashas*. Is something wrong with that?"

"For a special holiday, nothing, but this goes on since Rosh Hashanah. He's here every single night. It is now nearly *Pesach*. What does he want?"

Tutsik Goldenberg dropped his paper and snapped for Marianna, who brought him more coffee. She poured for him and silently offered to pour for the rest of us. I nodded and thanked her, as did Magda. Rachel and Sara said no.

"You have a big business, Perle, but you have a small mind." Tutsik Goldenberg sipped his coffee noisily. "You see a young man come nightly to our table for months and all you can think is, *He's not paying for the food.*" He sipped his coffee and smacked his lips. "In the long run this boy is going to make *pesos* for us, not the other way round."

Perle brushed a grain of kasha from her lip with the corner of her napkin.

"For another thing," Tutsik Goldenberg went right on, "just like a woman you ask the wrong question. Instead of asking, what does Hankus Lubarsky want from me, you might ask, what do I—Tutsik Goldenberg—want from Hankus Lubarsky?"

Rachel, who sat beside me, tapped her knife nervously on her plate. I wondered myself what Tutsik was talking about. Had he discovered your secret? Was there a new demand for women who passed themselves off as men?

"What could you possibly want from him, Tutsik, unless you are changing your sexual appetites—which wouldn't surprise me." Perle placed her dry spoon down by her plate.

"Sure I am." Goldenberg started laughing, then he pounded the table with his fist. "That's how come I can't keep my hands off these ugly, idiot women."

Magda immediately began to cry, but Rachel interrupted. "*Tsk-tsk*," she said flatly, "Sofia is one year short of a degree from the girls' gymnasium in Warsaw." For some reason we all started laughing, even Magda.

Goldenberg slapped his palm onto the table. The coffee splashed out of his cup. "You shut up. All of you. I outsmarted every one of you. Never forget that—"

"Not Magda, that was Dorfman's doing," said Sara.

"You outsmarted my father, not me," I added coolly.

"Keep your mouth shut, Sofia, or I'll mess it up for you good."

I did shut up then because messing us up was one thing Tutsik Goldenberg did well. The little slices around Sara's eyes were evidence of what he could do when tempted and there was no one to stop him. I pulled a long sweet roll in half and stared at Goldenberg while I took a bite.

Tutsik Goldenberg took out a cigar and lit it right at the breakfast table. A cloud of sticky grey smoke unfolded just above our heads. To his sister he said, "It just so happens that Hankus Lubarsky has his own talents, which have nothing to do with *shtupping* or being *shtupped.*"

"And you are interested in them?" I couldn't resist.

Madam Perle looked at me sharply but went right on castigating her brother. "So he's a sleight-of-hand artist, so what? Of what value, Tutsik, are Hankus Lubarsky's talents to you?"

Tutsik Goldenberg looked his sister dead in the eye. "Wouldn't you like to know."

"Actually, I would." Perle smiled at her brother demurely.

Only I kept a straight face while Tutsik glared at his sister. "You can make your little insinuations, *Madam* Perle." Tutsik's face was red, his eyes bulged. "You can laugh at my attempts at enterprise and self-sufficiency. But when Hankus Lubarsky opens on the stage of the Broken Heart Theatre, when the place is packed and there are Jews overflowing from the balconies and standing in the aisles cheering and stomping their feet, when the receipts are counted and I've brought in more in two hours than all of you *zoinehs* could bring in together on your backs or in any other position in a week, you can laugh all you like. Yes, choke on your laughter for all I care. I'm an impresario now. I'm the manager of a property so hot he'll burn that asinine laughter out of all of your throats. And if I want to treat him as a guest in a house that's rightfully part mine, and if he decides to keep his hands to himself, that's none of your concern. Any of you, you empty-headed whores."

Perle herself was not laughing. "You mean you intend to make a fortune out of a few simple-minded parlor tricks?"

"Parlor tricks? Simple-minded?" Tutsik was absolutely indignant, his face beet-colored. "That boy doesn't do parlor tricks. You, you women do parlor tricks! What my boy Lubarsky does is art, capital *A* art. The man is a *magician*. A *juggler*. An *Escape Artist*. You've seen it with your own eyes here and in the synagogue. The boy is a *genius!*"

"Indeed," Perle said flatly. "Here is a young man who can wiggle out of a pair of Red Ruthie's silk stockings tied delicately around his wrists, who can pull his skinny little fingers out of Mordechai Dorfman's antique army handcuffs." Perle stood at the table with both fists pressed down tight. "I could do those tricks with my eyes closed."

"You have," giggled Rachel.

"She has," Sara added.

Tutsik threw his napkin down. "Why do I waste my time explaining great genius to stupid women? What you have witnessed here in this house was the tip, the very tip of an enormous iceberg, the merest whisper of what that boy can do! I do not lie around in a dark flat all day in my underwear filing my nails. I go out in the world. I see things. I do things. And one thing I have done every single day for months is visit my friend Hankus Lubarsky at his little room all the way over on Chacabuco Street. It's like a museum that room, a magic shop, one you'd find on the main thoroughfares of Warsaw. Hanging from the walls are hats, scarves, locks, and handcuffs no customer would ever bring into this house because no Jewish mango knows how to get out of a pair of cuffs like these. Some of them were made for the lad by complete strangers with the express purpose of tripping him up. But no one could trip him up, no one can ever trap him. And why? Because there is not one pair of handcuffs on the entire planet that Hankus Lubarsky cannot escape from! There is no straight-jacket, no locked room, no ball and chain! What you have seen here in this house are party tricks!" Tutsik leaned across the table, his eyes became wide, his voice full of awe. "But I have seen the real goods with my own eyes. The boy is a genius. An absolute genius. And he will do for me what none of you women could ever do—he will make me rich. You have heard of the American magician Harry Houdini? My boy

Hankus Lubarsky is better than Houdini!" Tutsik Goldenberg rose, so full of himself he didn't even notice he was bragging to women. "Hankus Lubarsky is better than Houdini, because unlike Houdini, Hankus Lubarsky belongs to *me!*"

"It takes money to own a man like Lubarsky, Tutsik. And as far as I know, you have none."

"Then you know nothing, Perle. Perhaps all these months I have had a backer. A very big backer."

"It wouldn't happen to be a backer to whom you owed a good deal of money to begin with, would it?" Perle sipped her tea and stared her brother in the eye.

Tutsik stood very straight and very still when he met his sister's gaze. "Perle, you have your affairs and I, for once, have my own. I, for once, have found a way to get respect from the men of the Varsovia Society without your influence, without your meddling."

"Have you gone into this thing with Marek Fishbein? If you have, you'll never see one *peseta.*"

"I will see thousands of *pesetas.* Millions. Because we are not talking about pandering here, we are not talking about taking some little money from a few *shlub* greenhorns from the pampas who ain't seen a woman in a hundred years. Fishbein is putting up half the money to give Hankus Lubarsky the stage because he knows he'll make it back three times over. He can scrape that five hundred and fifty gold *pesos* I owed him right off the top, because after that, and after the original expenses, it's all gravy, Perle, and for once the gravy goes to me!"

"Yes," said Perle, now completely occupied with some invisible particle under her fingernail, "and if you deal with the likes of Fishbein, the gravy is likely to be splattered all over your tie."

Tutsik straightened that immaculate, expensive tie, and sat, his hands folded, without moving a muscle. "Have you, my dear sister, a better idea as to how to get the millstone of dependency, which you yourself have tied there, from off my neck?"

"There might be a way." Perle Goldenberg's eyes took on a wicked glint.

"Short of murder?"

"Oh, quite short of murder, and sooner than you think."

"Well if it is short of murder, it better happen soon because I cannot stand to be beholden to you one more minute!"

We all shifted slightly in our seats. It was clear that the conversation would soon take us once again to the back alleys of Jewish Warsaw where the young Perle had made her first sacrifice of the flesh for the good of her poor orphaned brother Tutsik, and that this was all the thanks she got for it—abuse, threats of murder, not even a monthly rent check.

Rachel looked about her for a polite way to exit. Sara didn't stand on ceremony. She finished her coffee and shoved away from the table. I wrapped my shawl tight around me and got up as well. Only Magda sat timidly, without moving.

"Sofia, where are you going?" Perle Goldenberg demanded as she poked at a tooth with an ivory pick.

"Up to my room, Madam, to catch up on my beauty sleep. That is, if the racket permits."

"Ha," muttered Tutsik, who stuck his nose fiercely into the paper again, "that will require more than forty winks."

"Forty or fifty," I called over my shoulder. "As many as it takes."

"Mind," said Madam Perle, her voice still full of the chilly exasperation she had previously directed at Tutsik, "I'd like to see you in my rooms in half an hour."

"I, Madam?"

"Yes, you Sofia. In half an hour."

"But you've not requested my company in months."

"In my rooms in thirty minutes." And to Tutsik she said, mysteriously, for all to hear, "You'll not need Marek Fishbein very much longer to free yourself from the likes of me."

Thinking about it now, the deed was done months before that breakfast. Perle and Fishbein most likely put their evil heads together within hours after that big lummox pretended to accept Tutsik Goldenberg's partnership plans. For one thing, Fishbein, greedy as he was, wanted not only to have his little magician cake, Hankus Lubarsky, but to eat you, too. And Madam Perle, never one to pass up an opportunity to have things just the way she wanted them, saw a way to perform her own now-you-see-it-now-you-don't on her brother Tutsik.

I can imagine how they worked it:

First, a note was delivered to Madam Perle Goldenberg by one of Fishbein's henchmen: *Meet me at Café Victoria for coffee and cake at*

2:15 P.M., written in Fishbein's impossible hand. Fishbein went to the *goyisher* café by *droshky;* Perle, in her long black dress, walked from Talcahuano Street. They met in a booth toward the back of the establishment, away from the light of day. This was Fishbein's regular place of most secret business: gentile, mahogany, deep and dark. There was little possibility that his intrigues would be discovered when transacted here, although there were sometimes spies.

On this day there were no spies. On this day, at 2:15 in the afternoon—well, in Jewish Argentine time, 3:00—Perle Goldenberg, severe but still attractive in that long black dress, slipped into Marek Fishbein's other office. He was settled in the booth waiting for her. "Ah, Perlie," he sipped his *café con leche,* "so glad you could meet me. We've much to discuss."

"Have we, Marek?" Perle asked with no warmth.

Fishbein chewed his thick cigar. A waiter came by and nodded at Madam Perle. "*Señora?*"

"*Solamente té.*"

The waiter clicked his heels and looked to Fishbein. "*Señor?*"

"Cheesecake," answered Fishbein loudly in Yiddish. The waiter nodded and disappeared. "I hope he knew what I meant," said Fishbein.

Perle said nothing.

They sat together in silence for a minute until the waiter came back with the cake and Perle's tea. Fishbein took a huge mouthful. "Oh, this is lovely cake. You're sure you won't have some? No? Because I'll order you one—" Before Perle could object, Fishbein shouted "*Mozo!,*" and in terrible Spanish ordered Perle a piece of cake. The waiter once again clicked his heels and in that second was gone. Fishbein winked at Perle. "If you don't eat it, I'll have it. I love to come here. It's so British. So refined. I'm thinking of opening up a place like this over in our neighborhood. Give those Jews a little class." The waiter came back with the second cake and placed it before Perle.

"*Más café, Señor?*"

"Waddee say?" Fishbein asked.

"He wants to know if you want more coffee."

"You see, you get one thing from them, right away they try to sell you something else. *No, Señor, no más café!*"

Very politely the waiter bowed and went away. Fishbein sat for a moment—sipping his coffee, eating his cake, chewing on his cigar. Perle poked at the cake with her fork, then pushed it away. "You've asked me here for advice on an English café?"

Fishbein swallowed the dregs of his coffee and slammed the tiny cup down. "No, I have a better offer. You know that no-good brother of yours is into me for over five hundred gold *pesos?* He's a horrible card player. Do him a favor. Burn all his decks, it's ruining his life."

Perle reached immediately for her purse. "That surprises me, Marek. Tutsik used to be a sharp—"

"Yeah, used to is right. My brother-in-law Moritz caught him in the act and did all the dealing himself. It was downhill after that."

Perle looked up at Fishbein. "How much does he owe you? I'll give you the money now."

Fishbein waved her purse away with his cigar. "It's not you who's to give money to me, Perlie. It's me who wants to give a bundle to you."

Perle, taken completely aback, swallowed a forkful of cake although she had, for religious purposes, sworn off sweets. "I don't understand your meaning."

"Your brother and I have an arrangement with that magician Lubarsky. I'm the silent partner and Tutsik claims he's managing the act. But let's face facts. Tutsik knows maybe how to get a girl from Minsk to Buenos Aires, but in terms of making big dollars out of a *kuntsen macher fum* Cracow, I don't think he has it in him, if you get my drift."

Perle wiped her lips daintily with her linen napkin. "*Pan* Fishbein, I'm not certain I *do* get your drift."

Fishbein looked around him. "Where is that waiter? I'm *chaleshing* for coffee. *Mozo!*" The waiter ran over to the table and bowed. "*Shvartzeh kaveh,*" Fishbein demanded. The waiter nodded his head and disappeared. "They're so dignified here," Fishbein sighed. "Listen," he smacked his hand down on the table. "I want to own all of Lubarsky. Your brother, he don't think that's such a good idea. He wants to be a big *macher,* he wants to strike out on his own. My thought is this is not so hot. Facing facts, your brother Tutsik is a *fantazyor*—he makes his circumstances up in his head. Speaking strictly from my heart, he'll never amount to anything." Fishbein pounded his chest with his fist. The waiter arrived with his coffee. "Perle, we go back a long way. I've opened doors for you, and have I ever asked for anything in return?"

Perle wanted to laugh but she did not.

"Just grant me this one favor."

Perle studied Marek Fishbein, her bully, her boss. There he sat across from her in his filthy shirt and tie, his too-small jacket, and his moldy top hat. This slob of a man was one of the most powerful men in the Argentine underworld. He had grown men killed regularly for looking at him cross-eyed or playing the wrong card in a pinochle game. He beat women up without giving it a second thought. Now he stared Madam Perle Goldenberg, easily one of the most powerful women in Buenos Aires, dead in the eye.

"Listen to me," Fishbein said, "I want to buy your brother's share of the escape artist, but I feel it best if we leave him out of the trans-action altogether. Let him continue to think he's managing the show. It will give him something to do, get him out of your house for hours at a time. Let him be the one to encourage and coax the little *yingeleh* into doing fabulous magic, make all the arrangements for the Broken Heart. But after I give you these five hundred fifty gold *pesos,* all of Hankus Lubarsky's magical *toches* belongs to me."

It was clear from the way Fishbein held his cigar in his mouth that he was expecting some kind of argument. That Perle was going to tell him to take it up with Tutsik if he wanted you so badly. Quickly Fishbein reviewed his catalogue of possible threats in hopes of select-ing just the right one to make Perle comply. But no threats were needed, for as I have said, Perle Goldenberg had a plan of her own. This offer of Fishbein's suited her perfectly. She pushed her cake plate away and stared right back at him. "Make it six hundred gold *pesos* and you have a deal."

Fishbein chewed his cigar for a second more, then started to laugh. "Shrewd, very shrewd, Perlie. Six hundred it is."

"Well, then," Madam Perle said, "the little magician is yours."

So all fates were settled months before that rainy morning Perle Goldenberg asked me to her rooms: Tutsik's fate; your fate, Hankus; and as I was about to discover, Sara's, Rachel's, Magda's, and my own.

It was odd to go to Perle now, it had been so long since I was last invited. And I'm ashamed to tell you that I missed my time with her. For in those days that seem oh so long ago, under Perle Goldenberg's gifted hands and tongue, I gave myself, as I have said, willingly, although not without regret. As Perle leapt more and more toward her spirit life, she leapt also further and further away from us—from me. It was not just her sex she took. It was all that warmth, true or false, that bathed over me in my early Talcahuano Street days. That was gone now, to God I supposed. But just how far, and in what shape, I never knew until I entered her rooms that last morning before *Pesach* began.

I must say I was a little shocked by what I saw. For there sat Madam Perle in a wooden chair, in that same austere black dress, with what looked for all the world to be a *tallis* on her shoulders, and a *yarmulke* on her head. Before her on a writing table lay an unruly pile of notebooks and Hebrew volumes, some stacked open on top of others, some upside down or falling off the side. A pair of spectacles was perched upon her nose. There she sat, bent over a notebook, copying a page from the fattest of those books with a steel pen. She looked more scribe than madam.

She glanced up at me and became for a second the old Perle, her voice full of that alluring purr. Any traces of her argument with Tutsik just half an hour earlier were gone. "Sofia, my love, come in, come in." Perle slowly copied one last word, then set her pen down. She took her spectacles from her nose, gestured to the bed. "Sit down, darling, here by me."

Thinking she meant to have me, I opened my robe.

"Sofia, please. I don't indulge those whims any longer. I've called you in today to talk about the future. Yours and mine."

I almost laughed. What future could she possibly mean? For the likes of me there was no future in this house, and unless I could persuade someone like you to free me, Hankus, there was no future outside of it either.

Perle passed me her *maté*. Although I wasn't such a big fan of Argentine tea, I sipped through her *bombilla* to be polite. I made as if to pass it back. "No, no my pet. Keep it for a while. The sharing of tea here is such a quaint custom. One of the few I shall truly miss when I leave this godforsaken place, although to tell you the truth, where I am going I expect to drink my tea in fine china cups."

"Madam is going away?" All breath left me.

She appeared not to notice. "Yes, Sofia. Yes indeed." Madam Perle took her spectacles from her nose and tapped her notebook. "Women of a certain age, as you know, undergo a change of the inner chemistries. Some grow tense and angry, others take the opportunity to follow new paths. I, for example, have determined to give up this life of sucking the juices out of men for a living. I would like instead to marry a fine gentleman and become, in the afterlife, his footstool in heaven."

"You, Madam Perle? You would become a man's footstool in heaven?" It was all I could do to keep myself from laughing, though I could see by the look on her face just how serious she was.

"Unlikely as it seems, child, I am working toward that now." She tapped her notebooks again. "For you see, I am engaged to be married."

"No!" It was out of my mouth before I could swallow it. My doubtfulness didn't bother Madam Perle.

"Yes, Sofia. My betrothed is none other than the famous scholar and wonder rabbi, Eleazar ben Yahud ben Yaakov of Chelmno. His are the followers who wear fifteen fox tails on their *shtrimmels* and keep always one tiny emerald at the tip of their beards."

I thought about the arrangement of Madam Perle's private beard and wondered if all of *Rebbe* Eleazar's women followers wore their secret hair thus.

"In just a fortnight," Perle continued, "the *rebbe* will come to collect me in a fine coach. We will travel first to meet his brother in Rosario, then to his enclave in La Plata. From there we will sail back to Europe and take his own train to Chelmno, where we will marry." Perle sighed deeply; it was nearly a swoon. She took the *maté* from me and had a deep swallow. "And what a wedding it will be, darling Sofia. I wish that you, of all the *nafkehs,* could see it, for it will be a thing of supreme beauty and dignity.

"*Rebbe* Eleazar will be carried into the synagogue on a golden chair, I on a silver one. A clean white sheet will separate us. Through it, we will exchange our vows. Then *Rebbe* Eleazar's followers will lift both chairs high above their heads and we will be carried out of the synagogue like the royalty of Egypt. The Jews of Chelmno will eat and dance and sing for days. No one will sleep until finally, the women of the congregation carry me away, bathe me in purified waters, anoint me in sacred oils, wrap me in sanctified white linen, and bring me to our wedding bed.

"Once there, what my beloved Eleazar knows of spiritual ecstasy and I of ecstasy on the material plane will join in what the yogis call tantric love. Mark my word, dear Sofia. On that night, you will feel the magic of our union all the way here in Buenos Aires. Yes, on that day a kind of history will be made."

I looked at Madam Perle, whose countenance was completely transformed by thoughts of the carnal sorcery to come. I wondered how it could be that a woman with her appetites might travel from Rosario to La Plata and then across the ocean with a man, saving herself the whole time until after the wedding.

I also thought back to the hell that Madam Perle and her brother had caused me, the money they had raised on my back, on the backs of Sara and Rachel, and now Magda, and tried to put that together with a picture of Madam Perle's ultimate rest as some holy man's footstool in heaven. In a way it seemed a fitting end.

"Imagine, Sofia, after years of calling for him, begging him to save and accept me, God at last has opened his arms. I am leaving this desolate Talcahuano Street forever." Suddenly she adjusted her spectacles and tapped her steel pen against the desk. All sense of her future ecstasy left her; her voice was full of business. "My brother Tutsik will be taking over the *shandhoiz* and have responsibility for your wretched little lives."

I pulled my robe close around me. I reached for a cigar and lit it. I willed my face to go blank but I couldn't stop my voice from quavering. "What about Tutsik's big plans for Hankus Lubarsky?"

"That was taken care of months ago. His silent partner has been 100 percent owner of that *pisherkeh* magician since the High Holy days."

My mouth fell open.

"Of course I haven't yet had the heart to tell Tutsik. He takes all of my gifts as slaps in the face, and as you could see from his performance this morning he's in a very foul mood. Besides, Fishbein has been perfectly willing to let my brother do the hardest work. Watch, when the time comes, he'll give Tutsik none of the credit."

My throat was tight with things I could not say. I saw our whore lives flash before me.

"Since none of you girls has any respect for my brother—I dare say I don't blame you—I want you to explain the situation to the others. You are my favorite, and while Rachel is a bit more level-headed, I think the others respect you more. You have an education and they do not. In truth, I wanted to pass the business to you, but I was certain Tutsik would kill you for it. The library, of course, except for my holy books, I give to you. You may do with it what you wish. Sell it if you like. But I think if you keep the books you will be provided with a much richer reward."

I studied Madam Perle, whose eyes had begun to stray to her open notebooks. "Let me understand this, Madam. You are getting married to a wonder rabbi from Chelmno. Your brother Tutsik, who wants nothing further to do with this bordello, will inherit it by default. He has no choice but to take it now because you have sold his only chance to get out of this business to an impossible villain. It is my job to tell the others that a mad dog is about to take complete control over all of our lives—"

"Precisely."

"Why don't you just end the business altogether and let us go when you do?"

"And leave my brother at the mercy of vampires like Marek Fishbein? Unthinkable. Ours has always been a close-knit family, and I could never leave him scrabbling for money. At least with this *shandhoiz,* he'll always have something to fall back on."

"Madam Perle," I said, standing, "you might as well give him a gun and tell him to shoot us."

Madam Perle now had her spectacles in place and was turned completely toward her notebook. "Yes, well, my dear, you know enough by now to quite capably talk him out of anything like that. Now, if you will excuse me, I must get back to my studies."

I took Perle's face into my own hands for once, drew it away from her books. "He won't think twice about beating us all to a bloody pulp once you've left us, Perle."

She lifted my hand from her cheek and held it in her own. "Nonsense, *neshomeleh.* Except for that unfortunate incident with Sara, he's been smart enough not to damage the merchandise." She turned again from me, picked up her pen, and began to copy. "Mind the door," she said.

She didn't look up as I saw myself out.

2

AND SO I WAS THE MESSENGER NOW, and what I had to tell
was sorry news for all—not just us whores, but for you too, Hankus,
and maybe Tutsik Goldenberg most of all. Just when Madam Perle
planned to tell her brother that you were no longer his to brag about
I had no idea. Or when she would tell about her wedding plans. Perhaps she was waiting until I told Rachel, who would tell Magda, and
then Sara, who was so far gone she could be trusted to say nothing to
anyone. Perhaps Perle was counting on gossip to get the facts to her
brother and she wasn't going to tell him the truth at all.

You have heard about the practice in certain ancient cultures of
murdering the bearers of bad news. Make no mistake: if Rachel or
Sara had been alive enough to hear my news, I would be dead right
now for many years. But when I told each in the privacy of their
bedrooms, it was as if I had no news to bear at all. As it turns out, my
news *was* no news to Rachel. But to this day, I am not certain if Sara
even heard me.

I knocked softly on her door and it swung open slightly. She sat on her bed, stuffing opium into the pipe laid out before her on a silver tray. The air around her was already thick and sticky. This is useless, I thought to myself, and I turned as if to go.

"Wait a minute, little niece..." I was taken completely aback. Sara had not called me this in months, and to be sure, I wasn't even certain she still knew who I was. But she patted the bed beside her and said my name. "Come sit, Sofia. It's been the longest time."

There was a snap in what was left of my heart. I did as I was asked, and when I was beside her, the bed sagged only a bit under the weight of us both. Sara's eyes were hooded; the drug had made her face seem soft and dreamy. She put her arms around me then and gave me a most remarkable kiss on the mouth. It tasted smoky and sweet. All parts of me surrendered to it immediately. Then, to my dismay, she pulled back and relit her pipe. She filled her mouth with smoke and leaned in to kiss me again. I pushed her away. Sara burst out laughing, a cloud of opium fumes flying out of her mouth. She looked like a dragon. "What's the harm of a little pleasure once in a while, eh Sofia? Listen to your auntie. Didn't I teach you the best ways to love?"

It was tempting, I had to admit, particularly now that I knew we would likely all be killed by Tutsik Goldenberg in a matter of weeks—if not by the brutality of his rageful hands, then by his malevolent neglect. But I remembered Rachel's warning against the stuff, which had served me well these many years. I put up my hand and refused.

"Well, then," Sara sipped again at her pipe, "if you don't want to kiss me, and you don't want to smoke, what do you want?" A dry smile settled across her lips.

I was tempted to forget the whole thing until she became less cloudy, but Sara was never much sensible anymore. I took her hand just as she slid backward across the bed, just as her heavy eyes closed. "Listen to me," I whispered. "Madam Perle is leaving here for good. We're stuck with Tutsik unless we come up with a plan."

"Perle leaving? Lucky her...," she murmured sleepily. Her smile, under these circumstances, was ludicrous.

"Yes, she's marrying some rabbi from Chelmno."

"Well fine, then," Sara said, smiling still. She was further and further away from me. I couldn't drag her back. I wanted to slap her, to wake her, but I knew it was hopeless. I left her and went across the hall.

I found Rachel sitting in her underwear darning up a hole in one of her silk stockings.

"Listen," I told her, tears in my eyes, "we're in terrible trouble. Perle is leaving us in the hands of her maniac brother."

"Yes, I know," she said without looking up. "She's marrying that mail-order rabbi from Chelmno."

"But how did you know? I thought I was the only one burdened with the facts of Perle's private life."

"I know everything, haven't you heard? I'm a fortune-teller."

I looked at her blankly. "You've a crystal ball in here, Rachel?" I was relieved I didn't have to break the news to her, but I was furious now with Perle for making it seem as if I did.

Rachel looked over her darning and winked at me. "In a way, young Sofia, in a way. Perle and Red Ruthie had a little talk the other day, right under my window. I know everything. Except how to stay alive in here."

"We'll get out," I said. "We'll jump out the window and escape."

Rachel put down her stocking and took a sip from her *maté*. "You don't seem to understand certain facts of our life, Sofia, which surprises me since we've been in this together now for a number of years. You can jump out the window and you can maybe make it without breaking both your legs. But whether he wants this whorehouse or not, Tutsik Goldenberg will find you, and when he finds you my guess is he won't even bother to kill you, he'll carry you right down to La Boca and put you in a crib."

That stopped me all right, the idea of a crib in La Boca, which was the worst of all possible fates for a woman like me. For what were those cribs but stables full of straw with maybe a table and chair, maybe a chamber pot. They were cells, really. Tiny, and you were locked in from the outside. The men who used cribbed women were the lowest of the low, the cheapest sons-of-bitches or the most poverty-struck. They came in, they fucked you, and then they went away. A person ate whatever her pimp brought her. In the winter she was cold and damp. Ultimately, if she was lucky, she died there. Whether they buried her or dumped her in the La Plata river depended on how many friends she had on the outside, or on how sentimental her pimp before this one was. Some girls, poor unfortunate souls, got put there when they were first brought to Buenos Aires, but most Jewish girls didn't see the inside of a crib until it was the end of the line.

I didn't want it to be the end of my line—I wanted out of that cursed dive while I still had the will to live. I wanted my freedom as soon as I could take it. The pieces were all there, I needed only the proper conditions to put them in place. You were the center of my plan, Hankus. Now that I knew the others were just as happy sitting on their sad behinds exactly where they were, that I was clearly on my own and beholden to no one, I waited impatiently to find my time to act.

Then, as if by magic, I was passed the key.

It was as quiet as can be in Madam Perle's kosher whorehouse, the shutters still closed, only the faintest sunlight squeezing through the blinds. The cats on the street had stopped howling, the parrots in the courtyard clicked their beaks and claws, and all the women were fast asleep. All but we two, locked in one another's arms. Me, Sofia Teitelbaum, most tasty morsel on the menu at Talcahuano Street 154, this month's most valuable *nafkeh,* earner of the most *pesos* per minute, spitfire, whore most likely to bite back when slugged in the stomach or punched in the mouth. There I was with you, the escape artist Hankus Lubarsky, a man no longer in these desperate arms.

I have said many times that I planned to extort you. I was, after all, a whore with some years practice, a quick study who knows a golden opportunity when one falls down drunk on the floor in front of me. Get me out of here is what I imagined I'd tell you, take me with you the next time you go. And when you asked me how did I think you, a woman dressed like a man, could do more than I, a woman dressed like a slut, could do for myself, I was going to beg you to buy me, trade me for a week of magic show profits, rescue me with your quickest wits. Because what I had on you was huge. Huge. Once Tutsik Goldenberg and his thug cronies got wind of the fact that their *wunderkind* Hankus Lubarsky was a woman in disguise, you were no better off than I—and even more despised. You, too, would know the feel of a fist against the eye, a hard *shlang* shoved up the *toches.* One-two-three boom, and all one had to show for it was an asshole full of kosher cum, and then they spit on you besides.

Before Madam Perle passed on her awful news, I spent my afternoons idly scheming. Now that I knew for a fact that my days were numbered, I became obsessed with how I would trap you, trick you into showing me your secret self, seduce you into opening your shirt for me, and then at my mercy you would be.

One night, two weeks after *Pesach,* yes almost exactly three years since I first set foot on the slippery ground of Buenos Aires, such an opportunity fell into my lap.

Perle Goldenberg had left Buenos Aires on a mysterious business trip. I knew just where she was because now that she had trusted me with some of her affairs she trusted me with all of them. I found myself in the horrible position of being Madam Perle's best girlfriend, her new secret confidante. She still spoke to Ruthie and Marianna as if they were her closest friends, but I, I was the one who knew everything. I felt greatly burdened by this, but also thrilled, as if the old Perle had welcomed me home, as if even though she was leaving us, I had her back again that I might once more become the center of her heart. She requested my presence now once a day in her library boudoir. In this way I learned all details, sordid and otherwise, about her impending departure. "Sofia, my dear," she teased me this one time, never looking up from her books, no, never looking up, "I'm off to Mendoza. Why do you think this is?"

I stared at her, waiting for her eyes to meet my own. When it was clear they would not I answered, "I've no idea."

"Well, in Mendoza is made the finest lace in all Argentina. The purest lace, and the most spectacular. And in Mendoza also are the most miraculous dressmakers. Generals and governors travel from all corners of this enormous country to have made for their wives and their daughters the most fabulous dresses and wedding gowns. To-morrow, I board the train with Red Ruthie and off we go to Mendoza. When I return in one week, for that is at the very least how long it will take, I will have with me a remarkable wedding dress, white and full and delicious, fit for the wife-to-be of a rabbi. With pleasure, Sofia, I will pass it on to you when I am done."

"But, Madam, you forget. I've already got a wedding dress of my own."

"Ah, yes," said Perle, with no feeling in her voice. "I remember now. You brought it with you in a box."

This struck a bitter chord in my heart, the bitterest of chords, because that lovely wedding gown I never got to wear was the cruelest of all jokes played on me the Goldenbergs. For all I knew, Madam Perle had sneaked into my room while I was entertaining gentlemen downstairs, tried on that very wedding gown for her own, and discounted it. Perhaps she had taken it in her head to steal it, had plans to sell it to the flea market people in San Telmo. Worse still, she might have offered it to another Varsovian to use as bait for some other young woman just my size. Yes, just my size.

And now here was Madam Perle Goldenberg, twice my age, about to run off and get married, and of course she had no need for my meager homemade dress. She was to have the very best of wedding gowns, made of the very best lace. And what a happy irony that her shopping trip would open the door to my freedom. What a happy irony, indeed.

As a test to the future, Madam Perle left her brother in charge of the house on Talcahuano Street and went off on her mysterious errand. He'd still not been told of his impending ownership, but Tutsik Goldenberg behaved exactly as we expected.

As brother of the boss, Tutsik Goldenberg was obnoxious enough, but as boss of the brothel he was impossible. He ordered us around as if we were maids as well as *nafkehs,* and then we weren't just *nafkehs,* we were his *nafkehs.* He believed he was at liberty to make us do anything that suited his fancy. More than ever I wanted to kill him.

Tutsik Goldenberg and his boys loved you, Hankus, not only as a potential meal ticket, but like a little brother and a son. They all felt bad for you.

"Poor little man." Mordechai Dorfman became teary one afternoon over coffee. "He's a virgin still, at twenty."

"We really ought to show him some fun," said Dov Hirsh, slapping Dr. Dorfman on the back.

"He works so hard, day and night, on those tricks of his." Tutsik Goldenberg placed a slim cigar into his greedy mouth. "He's got one now, you can tie him up any way you want—with your own rope even, you can bring it yourself, tie his hands, his feet, in two minutes, he's free. Hang him upside down when he does it, all right it takes him maybe five minutes, but face facts, the boy is a genius. When his show opens at the Broken Heart—"

"If it ever opens," slipped in Rachel.

Goldenberg pointedly ignored her. "He'll be the hit of Jewish Buenos Aires and then, you mark my words, all of South America, then all of North America, and then, the rest of the world. But he needs to relax more."

"We really ought to get him a woman," Mordechai Dorfman sighed as he signaled Marianna to pour him another cup.

"Well," said Dov Hirsh, pinching my ass, "this is certainly the place to get one."

"We've tried," whined Dorfman. "I've offered to pay for one myself, but he shows no interest whatsoever."

"If you ask me, he's *faigeleh*," chimed in Hirsh. "Look at those little wrists."

Tutsik Goldenberg pounded the table, his eyes popping out of his head. "Hankus Lubarsky is no fag! He's a respectable, talented boy with old world ways, and it's our job as elders of the community to teach him how to have a good time." He wrenched my arm and pulled me onto his lap. He ran his eyes over my bare breasts. I wanted to spit in his face. "Sofia will teach him, I think. She's still got some juice in her. I'll insist, a gift of the house. He's too polite to refuse." He pushed me off his lap and stood up.

"You want me to teach that arrogant *putz?*"

I didn't want to seem too eager or they'd give the job to someone else.

"You'll do it and you'll like it." Goldenberg stuck his bowler on his head and made for the door.

"Where are you going?" Mordechai Dorfman asked, shuffling a fresh deck of cards. "I'm all set to give you a run for your money at pinochle!"

"Start without me," Goldenberg said resolutely. "I'm taking a taxi over to Chacabuco Street to get Lubarsky. We'll give him a *Bar Mitzvah* he won't soon forget."

And so they did. Dorfman ordered Marianna to put up a dinner of *klops* and cabbage and left for the *cantina* on the corner to buy one liter of red wine and two of champagne. Dov Hirsh dragged poor sliced-up Sara out of her room and ordered her downstairs to play the beat-up piano. "Some *Yiddisheh* tango," he insisted, "we want a good atmosphere."

"A good sexy atmosphere," Dorfman added. "That boy's got to

come to his senses about women once and for all."

A couple of early customers came before Tutsik Goldenberg returned with you. They wanted to dance with Rachel and Sara, me they wanted to take upstairs. The first one wanted to fuck me with all his clothes on. The second one wanted to chat about the war in Europe. I was done with both of them in less than an hour. I took their tokens and we went downstairs.

By the time I returned, the seduction of Hankus Lubarsky had already begun. You were sitting at a table in the kitchen, a linen napkin tied around your neck, a plate piled high with Marianna's Spanish-Jewish cooking before you. As usual, Goldenberg was sitting almost in your lap.

"Marianna, more wine. This boy has been working so hard on his fancy tricks, he needs a drink—"

"No more," you said, lifting your glass. "Look here, I've barely drunk this—"

"Drink up," ordered Tutsik, "it's all on the house. Dear boy, it's the middle of winter, our most dismal time of year. Drink up, drink up, enjoy!" With that he signaled to Hirsh, who pulled your head back, and Dorfman, who poured the wine down your gullet. You coughed and sputtered, and all the men of the house laughed and laughed.

"*Pisherkeh!*" shouted Goldenberg. "He can juggle seven flaming torches but he still doesn't know how to take a drink!"

Somehow you managed to eat dinner. At every course, Tutsik Goldenberg and Hirsh threatened to pour more wine down your throat until you gave in to their bullying and drank it on your own.

After dinner there was coffee served up by Marianna, Spanish-style, into which Mordechai Dorfman tipped a little schnapps. "Don't refuse me," said a by-now-very-drunk Tutsik Goldenberg. "I'm your host, the father you never had!"

You raised your hand and took the spiked coffee.

"*L'chaim,*" you said weakly.

"*L'chaim,*" answered the men. Then Dov Hirsh took Mordechai Dorfman into his arms and the two of them proceeded to dance the tango, first with each other, then one at a time with you, Lubarsky, squirming as they thrust you into my arms.

You pulled yourself away, horrified, but the men pushed you back to me. "Relax, *Tateh,*" I whispered in your ear. "I know everything."

Ah, Lubarsky, you looked into my eyes so frightened. "You've nothing to worry about, baby," I whispered, "your secret's safe with me."

The men opened up bottles of champagne, poured it over each other's heads, into one another's pants. When you waved the foaming bottle away, Tutsik Goldenberg grabbed you by your tie and slurred, "Don't resist it, *yingeleh*, it's all for you!"

Goldenberg's cronies danced with each other, they danced with us whores, they stood on the tables, and when Marianna begged for them to get down, God forbid they should break them and then what would Madam Perle say on her return?, the men grabbed her in their arms and danced her around the parlor as well.

By the early Argentine hour of twelve-thirty in the morning, Hankus, you were flat on your face drunk. "Marianna," Goldenberg ordered, "bring more coffee!" Dov Hirsh and Mordechai Dorfman heaved you up to standing. Each pulled an arm onto one of their shoulders and hauled you up the stairs. Marianna followed with a tray of coffee things just as the two men dumped you onto my bed. The two of them stood around with their tongues flapping out.

"What are you *shmucks* waiting for?" I snarled.

"He's out cold," Dorfman said. "We gotta revive him."

"I'll take care of that," I said. "It's my job. And I'll give you *shlubs* a full report in the morning." Then I took them by the hand and led them out of my room. When they were gone, I locked the door.

I poured myself a cup of coffee and sipped at it while I watched you sleep your Lubarsky sleep. Passed out, your collar open, your tie askew—you looked womanly, indeed. The light from my lamp fell softly on your white and open throat. I wanted to bury my face in it at once. I took my coffee and sat beside you on the bed. "Hey, you. Lubarsky," I whispered, "take a sip of this for me." You sat up for a minute, opened your eyes, then fell back flat.

I set the cup down and pulled off your lovely men's boots, your socks, got you out of your jacket, slid your trousers down. I slipped off your well-made shirt and unwrapped the binding that held your handsome breasts flat.

Oh, Hankus, you were a beautiful woman! In that moment, I felt myself wanting you, not like I wanted Perle or even Sara. No, my darling, I craved you, as once so long ago, I craved my sweetest Tamar. I wanted to burrow into your body, Hankus Lubarsky, asleep and snoring, awake and full of magic. I draped a blanket over you and kissed you lightly on the forehead. I wanted into you as I wanted to be free.

An hour passed, then two. I lay beside you, sweet sleeping magician, ran my fingers through your darkest hair, brushed my lips over your strong arms, held your splendid fingers in my own. Suddenly, Goldenberg was pounding on the door. You sat up in my bed with a start. "Keep the blanket on you, I'll get rid of him," I whispered.

I pulled my kimono around me and opened the door a crack. Hirsh and Dorfman stood behind Goldenberg, salivating.

"So *nu*," Tutsik Goldenberg slurred, "you got him up here all night already. What's going on?"

"Give him a chance. The kid is new at it, remember? I'm trying to teach it to him slow, not the way you *chazzers* taught me."

"So he's the sensitive type, so *nu*." Dov Hirsh tried to push his way into my room.

"He's the sensitive type and he's shy," I said, pushing Hirsh back.

"Just so long as you show him a good time," Tutsik Goldenberg said, "because after tonight, he'll pay for it like everyone else."

"Sure, sure," I told him. "Now get out of here so I can get back to work."

They all three grumbled as I shut them out. I opened the door again to find them each scrambling for a bit of ear space at the door. "What's with you *alter kuckers?* Can't a girl have some privacy?" Then I slammed the door and turned the key. I kept it in the lock.

You sat up in bed, Lubarsky, and held your head. You fumbled for your jacket, a beautiful black velvet thing, warm enough for our Argentine winters. You fished your cigarette case out of a pocket. "Do you want one?" you asked without looking at me. Ah, at that moment you were miserable.

"The coffee is cold. I'll ring Marianna if you want some hot."

"I detest Marianna's coffee. I detest all coffee." You took a long drag of smoke. "This is catastrophe," you muttered in Polish, and my heart melted. "This is disaster."

"What disaster? So I know you're a woman now. I knew that the minute I saw you."

You looked at me completely alarmed.

"If Rachel and Sara know, they're very discreet. No one has talked about it, anyway not to me. And don't worry about those imbecile men. They see what they want to see. You are their *goldeneh yingeleh*, Lubarsky, the son most of them left in Poland and never met."

You blew a stream of smoke and glanced down at your exquisite breasts. "Yes, well...so much for that."

Now was the time I should have threatened you, Hankus. Now I should have promised exposure if you would not comply with my plans. *Get me out of here*, I wanted to whisper into those tender ears. *Buy me from the Goldenbergs, tell Tutsik you want me for a gift*. But Hankus, when you left your cigarette to smolder on the edge of the marble table at my bedside, I was struck mute. Moved by the sorrow in your brown eyes, the tender curve of your generous lips, I was able only to bend over you, girl magician, bend to your most handsome face and kiss you with the passion of my whole heart.

In the end, Hankus, we cheated those mugs out of their desolate pleasure. We made love together into the earliest morning, and by the time we were through, all of them lay in a drunken heap atop each other in the bordello parlor.

This night was not one of unbelievable fires burning faster and faster, as mine had been with Sara or even with Perle, nor was it the kind of calculated love I made with johns. You were a silent lover. I think you had never kissed anyone before, woman or man, and so it was all in my hands to touch you and hold you, to lick and kiss away the wounds that kept you silent, and you were not withholding. You met my lips with your own and you opened to me as I had opened to Sara, as I would have opened to Tamar. But unlike my many first times, yours was a conscious opening. You knew who I was, you murmured my name between kisses, and I began to think it possible that for all the days and nights of you coming here, you recognized me as I did you—you saw me, perhaps, as not just one of the Talcahuano Street *nafkehs* in Madam Perle's stable, but for myself. It shocked me that you truly knew my name, knew it enough to call me Sofia in bed. Oh Hankus, sweetest Hankus, you recognized me, it was true!

It began with those kisses, which coursed through me in a most remarkable way, starting with the lips as their source, like the Vistula, running slowly from Chelmno to Warsaw, from Ger to Cracow. Oh, those were wonderful kisses. If all we had were those, sweetest Hankus, it would have been enough. But then I placed my jaded hands on your shoulder blades and felt beneath them a sweetness, a profound sadness, and I put my ear to your heart and there was sorrow there as well. And before I was able to do the rest of my work, to put my fingers inside you, to listen with my ears and mouth to the stories you were telling from the part of you that was undeniably female, all we could do was lie in one another's arms and together sob.

Ah, sweetest Hankus, the more I kissed and held you, the more I felt inside me. When I looked carefully I saw, though silent, that you were weeping too.

"What?" I whispered. "What is it my darling?" For at that moment you were no longer the key to my freedom, you were indeed my darling. How sweet and wondrous were those kisses. "What hurts you so, my lovely Hankus? What hurts you so?"

"*Aye, nisht do gedacht!*" you cried. "You shouldn't know what hurts me so—no one should know this."

"But I want it," I murmured, "all your sorry secrets. I want them. For we are lovers now, and I know the deepest secret of them all."

You put one hand to your breast and the other to your cunt. "But how is it you see me?" you asked. "How can it be? For I am invisible and protected. I know this to be so."

It was then you told me your story, darling Hankus. And all gulfs between us, all schemes on my part, all bets and promises to myself to extort you, all saddest deals with dishonest forces, were off off off.

3

SWEETEST HANKUS! How magnificent were those kisses, how new and wondrous! And yet how cursed. For when we kissed, you remembered everything.

Was it the taste of blood on our lips? Our mutual memory of sad hearts and rolling heads? Speared bellies and slit throats? Years and years you had forgotten all but that bundle that you, like I, carried in your hands. Years and years you heard just faintly the screams of your sister, your mother's cries, a bird noise in the back of your brain which, as in Cracow, sent you running to the furthest corners of forgetting. And then, your grandmother, littlest woman on earth, lost to you until that moment when my heart opened so suddenly to yours! For what was done was done to her by Cossacks, and it was so much better to forget. And you had forgotten, until our kisses, until our sweetest Jewish hands soothed each other's grief-stricken brows. How can it be, darling Hankus, that the tenderness of our touching brought that murderous night back to you? That bloody *erev Pesach,* not so many years ago. Come close, my darling. I'll tell it for you now as you told me, although it breaks both our hearts.

It seemed at first like every other *Pesach* you had seen in your thirteen long years. Your Grandma Tsirel, beloved old lady, *oleha ha shalom*, tiny and spry, got up at dawn and caught the last scrawny chicken with her bare hands, then brought it to the *shochet*, who butchered and blessed it. She carried the bird home and plunged it into a kettle of boiling water. She plucked the feathers and cleaned it. Then she set it in a clay pot with carrots and onions to cook in her brick oven all day long to sunset. Little sleeping chicken on a bed full of roots, how peaceful and full of promise it seemed there. How it filled your tiny cottage with wondrous smells. How little that would matter in the end.

Your sweetest sister, Hinde, may her memory be sacred, polished the candlesticks and your mother's few pieces of special Passover silver. It was your job to sweep down the dirt floor until it was smooth and flat. Then together you girls washed the walls and windows until your home, so dingy on most other days, sparkled. Your mother, may she rest in peace, had bent over *matzohs* the whole week before, rolling and poking them, letting them dry in small patches of early spring sun. On this morning, she held them like pages from a holy book and slipped them with greatest care into the linen *matzoh* cover that she herself embroidered as a girl.

Together you chopped more onions, more carrots, more potatoes, and threw them in with the insides of Grandma Tsirel's chicken to make a golden soup. You peeled potatoes and boiled them, mashed them with fried onion and *shmaltz*, rolled them into balls, and set these boiling, too.

Somehow your father, may God watch over him eternally, found an apple and handful of nut meats on his last trip to Cracow. Your mother placed them on the windowsill, and for a week you children stared at them, full of desire. That round red apple (which in truth was covered with bruises and was brown more than red) and chips of walnut. Yes, scraps and shards. Today, at last, your mother brought them to the table with a wooden bowl and cleaver. She chopped them together to your delight—the apple, the nuts—and added in a splash of wine and honey, too. This was your *charosis*, the mortar of our people's holy temple, destroyed and made new again by the *seder,* our holiday feast.

It was well past noon when your mother laid out the lace Passover tablecloth left by her grandmother as part of her trousseau. You girls set out the chipped Passover dishes, the special goblet for the prophet Elijah. Grandmother Tsirel brought forth her pottery *seder* plate, which belonged to her mother and her mother's mother before her. Then all of you placed upon it the sacred foods that always mean *Pesach:* salt water for our people's tears, roasted egg and shank bone, bitter herbs of the earth, and sweet green herbs of spring. In the center of the table your mother placed her grandmother's candlesticks, and in those sticks two holy candles to welcome in the holiday when the sun at last went down.

Your father, let his soul rest forever, came home from the fields early that day. He changed out of his dusty work clothes and went to the baths where he cleansed himself. He came back to you wearing trousers with two holes in them, not half a dozen, and a shirt he could button straight up to his neck. His *tsitsits* hung down over his pants. With his hair clean and combed straight back he looked handsome and ready for the holiday. He kissed your mother good-bye and went with the other men of the village to the synagogue to pray.

By now, Hankus, the sun had almost set. A person could hear the excitement crackle through the entire village as you became ready to welcome spring to your tiny corner of the world. You were still in your everyday clothes—a dirty pinafore, one of your father's old shirts, your big black socks and shoes.

"*Vildeh!,*" your grandma scolded, "your father will be home in no time, and you look like a wild animal!" She wasn't happy because you waited always until the very last minute to get into your stiff holiday clothes—a white dress too tight across your chest and *toches,* buttons that came all the way up the back of your neck and choked you. Poor Hankeleh, you couldn't move in your holiday best. And poor *Bubbe* Tsirel, she hated the everyday clothes you were wearing. In the end, though, it was those very clothes that saved your life. If only they had done the same for her.

"You'll leave Hannah alone, Ma," your mother told her. "It's a good thing someone is still looking like the cat dragged her in. Hannaleh, darling (for that is what she called you then), your father was in such a hurry to be like a man and get to *shul* that he forgot to fetch us water. Go down to the river and bring us two buckets. Otherwise you'll have nothing to drink."

Your grandmother shook her head and clicked her tongue against her teeth. "Hurry up, the sun is practically set!"

But you knew you could take your time. True, God considered it a sin for adults to work after sundown on holy days, and you were, after all, thirteen. But you were a girl. God wasn't looking to punish you, you thought, although later you wondered if that was true. There were too many men and boys to watch out for, not only in your little village but all over the world. You were happy to go down to the river on this *erev Pesach,* to postpone for half an hour the wearing of the holiday clothes that made you look more girlish than you ever felt.

You hauled the empty wooden pails to the river, dropped them into the water one by one, then drew them out, brimming. You hitched them to the yoke you wore upon your neck like an ox. Before you carried those full buckets back home, your last burden before two days of rest, you gazed out across the river. The sun was almost down. A sweet breeze blew through your hair, soft and damp, chill across your face, but in it still a hint of warm days soon to come. For *Pesach* is the holiday that greets the spring in Poland, and how glad you felt to stand by the river with full buckets of water. Yes, you alone to welcome it home.

You bent a little under the weight of the yoke as you trudged back, but you were always strong and, in those days, confident. Soon those pails were balanced and almost light. You came up over the rise onto the main road of your village with great peace in your heart. How lucky were you to be here, alive on this evening, the loveliest evening of the Jewish year.

Then, all at once, there were hoof beats. And these were followed by smashing glass and screams. You looked up and saw—what? Everywhere, white feathers falling, and then through the feathers, big men on horses charging in all directions, yelling in Polish and calling out names.

You stood at the edge of the road with the weight of your water pails against your shoulders and watched, mouth open, while blood flew, fires blazed, men and women shouted and swore. Above all the voices you heard your own mother's rise, calling out your name and Hinde's. You wanted to run to her but your big feet would not move.

The men on horseback flashed sabers and shot guns. They charged toward the synagogue with lit torches while the men of the village stood frozen in their prayer shawls or else threw stones. This did little to stop the thundering wave of horse flesh and fire. In minutes the synagogue was ablaze, and all around it men and women clutched their bellies, held their sides. Throats were ripped open, blood and *kishkes* spilled into the street, children ran in circles as if they, too, like the synagogue, like your house, were on fire.

You stood frozen. You stood invisible. And there, no more than a foot away, so close you could touch her, was your Grandmother Tsirel, she with your sweet sister Hinde's broken body in her arms. And wasn't there a Cossack standing over her, his hands like paws balled at his hips, laughing his ugly head off? Grandma Tsirel pulled herself up to her full height, which was half his size. She held your sister up to him like an offering. "Murderer!" spat your grandmother in Polish. "Must you come and tear us to pieces for pleasure? Have you no sense of what is right and good in the world? To slaughter us like hogs on any day would be horrible enough, but on the *Pesach* of all days! Child killer!" she shouted. "Cannibal!"

That Cossack (I hope he has swallowed a dozen razor blades) bent down as if to tickle your most beloved *Bubbe* Tsirel under her chin. And instead what did he do? He lifted a pitchfork and without a moment's hesitation ran your grandmother through. Yes, ran her through with that pitchfork, lifted her aloft with one hand, while sweetest *Bubbe* Tsirel, most beloved of all grandmothers, wriggled and screamed, this time in Yiddish, "Murderer! *Chazzer!* Rot in your Catholic hell! Rot there!"

And didn't that Cossack toss her then, pitchfork and all, to where your father stood screaming, "Beasts! You beasts!" and your mother howled, "Where are my children? Gone, gone, gone!" And all the time your poor grandmother, good as dead, good as dead, cursed that excuse for a human with her last Jewish breaths.

Suddenly, a new soldier shouted at your parents, "Is this one yours?" He lifted the body of your sister Hinde in both hands, and without thinking twice that she was already dead, smashed her against a stone wall. Then didn't he raise his pistol and shoot your mother square in the heart at the exact moment his cronies on horseback chose to trample your father and God knows how many others into the ground.

What did you do? Not a thing, not a thing, but stand only as you have told me, with your ox yoke of water pressing your neck, and watch while the smoke rose and the Cossacks who had not yet remounted clamored back on their horses and galloped away. You stood until you could stand no more, then dumped the water out of your buckets, dumped it out of your buckets and let it run in all directions mixing with blood in those sad dirt streets.

Everybody wasn't dead at once. Many were sprawled across the village ruins bleeding, cursing. Some lay in sliced-up pieces on the thawing ground. You pulled the pitchfork out of your grandma. She bled, grabbed your hand. She tried to tell you something but couldn't speak, then her eyes rolled back in her head and she died.

How did it happen that the soldiers never saw you? Ignored you while they ripped your people open with sabers and held their own sides while they laughed. No kindly soldier saved you, no man held a knife to your throat, raped you, and left you for dead. The miracle was that you stood among them and no one noticed you. You looked like all the other girls who were running and kicking and spitting in the faces of the monstrous men, except for your mud-caked shoes, your water pails across your shoulders. You were a Jew like every one of your neighbors. Yet you stood untouched while hell danced about you. And when it was over, you were not just the only member of your family left living, but the only person from your tiny *shtetl* who survived.

You found your smashed Hinde among the ruins and carried her to where your grandmother lay. Then you found your mother, who lay clutching her dead heart, and your father, whose bloody body was frozen in shame. Taking one of their hands in each of your own you dragged them to Hinde and Tsirel, and one by one you carried them to the river. Then you sat down beside them and cried.

You went back and searched through the wreckage of your little village and found a spade. In the ashes of your smoldering synagogue you found a charred prayer book. You brought both to the river bank. With the spade you dug four shallow graves and lay each of your people to rest, covered them with muddy earth, picked up the prayer book and found *kaddish*. In another village, with another father, you would have had to invent your prayer. But your father, may he rest in peace, taught you the Hebrew prayers because you were the oldest of two children, both daughters, and someone had to pray for him when he was gone. How could he have known that this is how his life would end? Not in an old-man way in a bed with a wife and two daughters at his side, but cut down by monsters in the prime of his life on the first night of *Pesach*. Woe is him, woe is you!

You stood with that crumbling prayer book in your hands, still warm from the Cossacks' fire, and prayed for your family: *Yiskadal v'yiskadash shmay rabba....* Four times you prayed this, swaying over each of their graves as the smoke blew over you and the moon rose full above your Passover night.

You slept that night on the muddy graves of your family. You woke with the sunrise and remembered both their screaming and your sorrow. Here was your family, recovered and buried, but what about the others? What was your duty to them? You were numb, your arms and legs weak, but you went to survey your horrible legacy. Here was the head of Shmuel the Yeshiva master, the left hand of Simcha his wife. There were the twisted bodies of your pals Tova and Rosa, their brother, serious Chaim. All dead, all clutching some part of themselves, lying in their own blood.

You were thirteen, dear Hankus! What could you do but take care of your own and pray for the rest of them.

Even in the cool morning, the air above your tiny village smelled of smoke and blood. You crawled into what was left of your home. It was a shambles, bloodied feather beds and shredded *Haggadot* everywhere. But there, by one of the pallets, was what you were looking for—a tangle of your father's clothes. Quickly you tore off your filthy dress and put them on. His trousers dragged over your shoes, his shirtsleeves fell past your hands, and all of it stunk of smoke. You rolled the shirtsleeves and pants cuffs up, pinched the waist tight and tied it with a piece of rope. You wrestled your father's work coat from the rubble. In the pocket were an old hat and a pair of gloves. You put all of it on. As for the stench, sad to say you were used to it by now.

You crawled your way out of that ruin, but as you reached what had been the door, there before you were your mother's candlesticks. You held them to your face and wept. Oh, saddest legacy. Oh, womanly sorrow. You wrapped them in your father's scarf, stuffed the bundle under your shirt. Then you pocketed a rusty kitchen knife that lay on the table among the smashed plates. You said good-bye to the ruin that once was your home and went to the river where you'd buried your family. You sat beside them, put the candlesticks atop your mother's grave, and took the knife from your pocket. With the dead as your witnesses, you hacked off your hair.

So doing, you picked up those candlesticks, wrapped your father's coat around you, and headed south toward Cracow, where what would happen to you, only God could say.

This story you told on our first night of loving. Do you remember how, when you were done, the sunlight trickled into my tiny bordello room? I put my fingers to your lips, touched your hair and eyes. You looked away from me, for even such tiny kindness as mine broke your heart. You sighed deeply, as I did, old-country sighs. Then you sobbed as you had not since your first night with Max and Motke, and I sobbed with you, held you as you rocked and shook, but never wailed. No, we never wailed, for those awful men, our benefactors, were downstairs passed out in their own champagne vomit, but for how much longer we did not know.

I held you, Hankus, and kissed you more, then lifted you from the bed, wrapped your bandage around your breasts, pulled your fancy shirt down over your head. Helped you fasten your trousers, pull on your boots, comb back your long black hair. Then I walked you to the window, Hankus, and you didn't jump, you flew.

— 4 —

WHEN MADAM PERLE GOLDENBERG returned from Mendoza three days later, she brought with her more than an exquisite wedding dress. Oh, the dress was extraordinary, make no mistake: tiny pearls in a line up and down both arms; transparent lace across the bodice that showed just enough but was not immodest; remarkable lace gauntlets; and a train as long as the whorehouse staircase. As for the veil, one never saw such a thing—a combination of traditional Spanish styling (the whole thing was secured to the head with a high ivory comb) and Eastern European wedding ritual (it covered Madam's face completely, but let also a hint of her bright and beautiful eyes shine through). The most outrageous actuality of the gown itself was not the detail as much as the fact that it was white.

"I see that mocking look come to your eyes," she scolded, as she modeled the dress for us *nafkehs* on the night of her return. "As the bride-to-be of a most holy man, I am entitled to wear my gown white. It is written in the Gemara. The exact page escapes me, but I know it is so."

"All your life you've wanted it this way," Sara mumbled, but Madam Perle chose to ignore her.

The rest of us, yes even I, admired the beauty of the lace, the luster of the tiny pearls. We were aflutter about Perle Goldenberg until her brother Tutsik walked in, you by his side. You nodded to me politely, then walked away. We had agreed in my chamber that feigned indifference was our quickest road to togetherness. I watched your amusement at Madam Perle's outrageous get-up, but then I noticed Tutsik and looked about me for a safe place to hide.

"What's this? What's this?" he shouted, incredulous. "What on earth do you do in this dress? Is that some way to get more money out of customers, to wear this in bed for them? It is a known fact, Hankus, that even Jews are not above this type of perversion."

You said nothing, only shrugged and smiled. I tried to catch your eye but you looked away.

At this remark by Tutsik, Perle became indignant. "Is that what you think I do in this?" she spat. "This is not for some mackerel to get his cock hard. This is what I will wear when I get married."

Tutsik took off his hat and coat and sat down in a chair. "Get married?" he guffawed. "Who on earth would marry you?" He knocked you in the arm. "Who would marry her?"

"Why, probably many men," you answered, removing your own hat and coat. "For it is my understanding that this is a solid business. Madam Perle would make an excellent catch."

"Yes, but catch what?" Tutsik laughed. He laughed and laughed more, and this laughter was his downfall, and ours as well. In his hilarity he gave his sister Perle the perfect opportunity to spill her beans, to tell everything to her arrogant brother Tutsik at once, all he wanted to hear and all that he did not.

"Oh, you idiot!" snapped Perle. "You fool! I am being married to a man who makes you look exactly like the simpleton you are. In just one week the most brilliant teacher in all of Europe will come collect me from this hellhole, and through his love and devotion, salvation will be mine!"

"What an imagination," burst the male Goldenberg. "What an incredible ability for self delusion you have, Perle. Has she been dipping into our opium, Sara? Or perhaps you are reading too many books. My sister fancies herself a scholar, Hankus. Did you know this?"

You sat on the piano bench and jostled your walking stick nervously between your knees. "I am aware, Tutsik, that Perle likes a good book now and then." You nodded toward Perle.

"Oh, spare me," Sara spat, and I felt a chill run through me.

Tutsik went to the sideboard and poured himself a schnapps. "What on earth, Perle, makes you think that any man with a sense of human decency, let alone a *rabbi*"—and this word he said with a voice full of venom—"would even *think* about marrying you?"

At which point Madam Perle pulled back her lace gauntlet and held up the middle finger of her left hand. All of us saw for the first time the diamond, the proof that drove her to Mendoza to do her secret errand, a diamond that took up the entire length of her finger to the knuckle. How magnificently it sparkled! Even Sara gasped when she saw it.

"Well," chuckled Tutsik Goldenberg, "well, well, well." He sat himself down in his favorite stuffed chair and became very serious. "And is this lucky rabbi one of our humble Argentine Jews? One of the many men who stumble in here on Saturday night to rid themselves of their heavenly frustrations?"

"No, indeed." There was genuine pride in Perle's voice. "He is from the old country, and we go there together in order to marry."

Tutsik considered this for a moment. He took a long sip of his drink and smoothed his vest. He looked at each of us *nafkehs*, and each of us *nafkehs* looked away. "And who will mind the store for you then, Perle? Who do you intend to mind the store?"

Perle looked her brother dead in the eye. "Perhaps you will, Tutsik."

"Not I," he said, and pulled himself out of his chair and into the dining room. "Where is dinner, Marianna? I am starving!"

There was an uncomfortable silence. Without a look back toward me, Hankus, you followed him.

Perle removed her veil and we *nafkehs* folded her train. She pulled off her gauntlets and slipped out of that gorgeous gown. She snapped her fingers; young Magda handed her a robe. On the dining room table, Marianna had laid out a platter of steaks. You sat at table with your hands neatly folded. But before we had Madam Perle's ensemble safely stowed away, Tutsik Goldenberg had already begun to devour his.

"I beg you, Tutsik, to consider my offer," said Perle when she was seated across from him.

"No, no," he said, taking another enormous bite of steak, "no need. For I have my own property to manage, my own set of business affairs." He beamed at you like the proudest father. You, on the other hand, distinctly squirmed in your seat. "Our magic show is scheduled to open at the Broken Heart Theatre at the end of July," continued Tutsik. "We've secured the date! And Hankus has been working day and night on his magic tricks, haven't you, boy?"

You put a steak in the center of your plate and just slightly, I saw it, loosened your tie. "Yes, day and night, day and night."

"From dark of night to light of sun, a *magiker's* work is never done, eh Hankus," Rachel said flatly.

"Precisely," you said, and reached for the salt.

Perle signaled to Marianna who dutifully brought her bowl full of groats. "My simple-minded brother," she brought the subject back to her own business, "the time has come at last to tell you the truth about your investment in Hankus Lubarsky, and your secret partner."

You continued to eat with the utmost concentration. I studied you, a forkful of steak frozen halfway to my mouth. Was it possible you had known the truth about who really owned your ass all along? Those of us assembled at the table held our collective breath.

"Hankus knows who is paying his bills, Perle. I have no secret partner, only a silent one." He put a firm hand on your shoulder. You sank, just slightly, under its weight. "We've all had it up to here with your smart business, Perle. You go off and marry your rabbi," Tutsik sneered. "By the time you get back, this place will be a shambles, but Hankus Lubarsky and I, we will have made each other rich."

"He isn't yours to make you rich, Tutsik." Madam Perle stared at her brother. Hankus, you shifted in your seat but you did not look in the least surprised. "Tell him why not, Sofia."

An arrow shot through me. "I?"

"Yes, you, my darling." Perle's eyes were blank and glinting all at once. "Tell him why not."

"There's no need for Sofia to tell, Madam Perle." Your voice was strong and clear across the dinner table. "My dear Tutsik, Marek Fishbein owns all of my assets. I have known it for some time."

Tutsik Goldenberg's fork fell with such force that we were shocked when Madam Perle's fancy imported china did not shatter. "Of all the

unmitigated gall!" he said, pushing away from the table, leaving behind the remains of his favorite of all dishes—thick steak, butter soft,
almost still-bleeding. He stood and shook over us, wringing his hands
in such a way as to prevent himself from strangling Perle on the spot.
"You have sold my interest in Hankus Lubarsky to Fishbein?" He
banged his fist down on the table. All the dishes jumped. "Hankus
Lubarsky was never yours to sell! Never yours! He banged again. "Unbelievable," he muttered, "not to be believed!"

You cleared your throat and said, "My dear Goldenberg—I was
never anyone's to sell in the first place."

Sara and Rachel burst out laughing, while Magda looked about,
bewildered, and I felt ready to throw myself out a window and under
the first taxi.

Madam Perle ignored us all. She brushed invisible lint from her
silk robe and looked her furious brother in the eye. "It was my understanding, Tutsik, that I was doing you a favor." She adjusted her fabulous ring. "No one in his right mind deals with Fishbein unless he has
enough money to dazzle him into a stupor or he's under gunpoint.
You, as others have led me to understand, were under gunpoint."

"But that was months ago! Who could have told you such a thing?"
Goldenberg swung his body in my direction. I picked up my steak
knife and held it before me. "You!" he shouted. "Taking advantage of
my drunken state for blackmail purposes! I should have known you
couldn't keep my secrets. And *you!*" Tutsik Goldenberg lunged toward you, Hankus, with murder in his eyes. Rachel and Sara grabbed
him by the shoulders and he fell back into his chair. "Most beloved
yingeleh! Betrayed by *you!*"

"Oh, no one has betrayed you, Tutsik." Perle stood, her knuckles
pressed to the table. "You think Marek Fishbein didn't threaten this
boy with instant death if he gave his secret away? And do I bother
these girls with our petty family problems? Fishbein came to me himself and offered to buy your share of Lubarsky in order to settle your
debt. I, of course, agreed because I hate to see you made a fool of."

Tutsik glared at his sister and said nothing.

"Don't you yet understand how that *nishgutnik* operates? You would
have done all the work of getting Lubarsky on the stage, put up all the
money which you would have borrowed from him, and then when
the profits came rolling in, you'd put out your hand for your cut and

he'd fill it with a pile of shit. That's what you'd be left with—*bupkes.*"

"Yes," Goldenberg's forefinger almost touched Madam Perle's nose, "I would have *bupkes,* but at least it'd be *my bupkes.* Once again, for all to see, you have made me into the village idiot, the financial failure of not just Warsaw but now Buenos Aires, too."

Tutsik shook his head sadly. I thought he might cry. "I saw it all so clearly in my mind's eye." He was plaintive as he talked. "Not a *yentzer* or a pimp any longer, but a respectable businessman. An impresario. And like that," he snapped his fingers over the table, "without a word of consultation about what I might want, you have taken it all from me. Like *that,* my sister," he snapped again, "I've nothing of my own."

"And what do you call this brothel? Which I have worked day and night to make into the most successful of its kind in all of Argentina? I am giving this brothel to you, Tutsik Goldenberg, lock, stock, and barrel. This is a sure thing—financial security for the rest of your life! You call this nothing?"

I looked around the table. Rachel placed her fork down on her plate and sat back in her chair; Magda took a tiny bite of steak; Sara covered a laugh with her hand and swallowed her wine with one gulp. You, Hankus, you looked completely blank. You pushed your plate away.

Tutsik Goldenberg guzzled wine straight from the decanter, then wiped his mouth with the back of his hand and slapped the table. "So I'm to be the boss now, eh?" He directed his furious gaze at me, then another full of daggers at you, Hankus Lubarsky. "Happy circumstances have arranged themselves so that I have lost the one thing I have ever had all to myself. You get to wear that fancy-shmanz dress and get married to a famous rabbi, and I get nothing but this shithole whorehouse. And who gets to have this beautiful Hankus Lubarsky?" You squirmed in your chair as he took your face in his hand. "Who gets to *kvel* from his wondrous magic, his marvelous tricks, and then collect the profits besides? Why, none other than that lover of high art, that appreciator of all things beautiful, that *meshugener mamzer,* Marek Fishbein."

Tutsik Goldenberg hit himself laughing, stopped, and picked the remains of his steak up with his bare hands. He took an enormous bite. Red juice trickled down his chin as he chewed. We watched him carefully as he laid what was left of his steak almost tenderly on his plate. "I have lost the Escape Artist." He looked from me to Rachel to Sara to Magda with such venom in his eye that I felt compelled to duck. "I have lost the Escape Artist and inherited the four of you *zoinehs* in the bargain. My, my. My, my, my, my." He sighed and licked the juice off his fingers. He pointed his steak knife straight at me. "What a sad twist fate has dealt me. What a sad twisted life I lead."

In the days that followed, a terrible silence fell between the betrothed Perle Goldenberg and her dejected brother Tutsik. Business between us whores and our regular customers went on as usual, although for me there was an added heaviness in my heart. For soon after Tutsik Goldenberg left the table that evening you left our house. No words passed between us—I was certain I had lost you forever.

Rumors about Madam Perle's imminent departure flew through the cobbled streets of the Jewish barrio, and before we could settle down to the unpleasant work at hand, our customers made it clear that revealing facts had become an addendum to our usual contracts. Rachel began asking for a few *pesos* extra and then told her clients fabulous stories in return: Madam Perle had become a Catholic and was going to Italy to live in a convent; she was going to Montana in the United States in order to form a new synagogue for women like ourselves on the western plains. Sara started a rumor that Madam had inherited an olive grove in Palestine, was planning to sell it, and with the profits open a brothel just outside the walled city of Jerusalem.

For herself, Madam Perle spent her time putting the affairs of the *bordel* in order and preparing for her long journey. Her evenings were now entirely devoted to the packing of her holy books. The conditions of Tutsik's ownership of the business were conveyed to him in long notes delivered to his room, or at the dining room table by either Marianna or, and how I dreaded this, myself. Tutsik delivered his responses by shattering china and smashing glasses, or else by the hand of Mordechai Dorfman. He could be heard knocking on Madam's locked door and pleading with her to please respond, for there was a small negotiation needed around the exact amount of Marianna's pay raises over the next five years (you will note that there was no mention of a pay raise for any of us whores); or the specific terms of Perle's arrangement (yes, even after all these years) with Red

Ruthie; and other similar orders of business.

Madam Perle opened her boudoir door and took the papers from Dorfman, closed her door, then opened it again a few minutes later and presented the hapless messenger with corrections. On a good day, that was the end of the transaction. But on a day when either the brother or the sister was feeling bitter or brutal, poor Dr. Dorfman could be seen going up and down the stairs a dozen times, each ascent marked by his increasing dishevelment and nervousness, his tie becoming looser, his shirt wrinkled, his brow more furrowed and full of sweat.

Day after day, newly packed trunks and valises appeared at the top of those same stairs. Day after day, Marianna, who was not a young woman, gritted her teeth and dragged each one single-handedly down to the storeroom behind the pantry. Little bundles of Madam's most provocative underwear began to appear outside each of our doors, and for myself, I wondered how she planned to entertain Rabbi Eleazar of Chelmno on her long journey from here to Rosario, from Rosario to Poland, if we each had her fanciest lingerie and I was to keep her books.

Marianna was to have the china, even if she were to leave the *shandhoiz* forever.

"It's tainted now. I can't bring such things into my new home," Perle told us in our last shared breakfast. She ate from a new white porcelain bowl and sipped from a new white porcelain cup, to be touched by no other hands but hers, although I believe Marianna was allowed to fill them, clear them, and wash them. She ate her customary boiled groats, not sweet rolls like the rest of us, but I noticed she took a great deal of cream in her tea.

Tutsik Goldenberg surprised us that morning by taking his usual seat, even though his sister was among us. "Madam Perle must not have tainted plates nor tainted food," he muttered as he opened his newspaper, "but she thinks such things are good enough for me."

Everyone shifted a bit, but no one said a word as Perle stirred her groats and sipped her tea. "You may yet get to purchase new china, Tutsik. Marianna, in her great wisdom, might decide to quit this establishment forever and take the dishes with her."

"At which point," Tutsik rumpled his paper and threw it down, "I'll buy four dog bowls and set them before the ladies of the house with great ceremony." Then he stood, got his coat from the hallway, and slammed out the door.

Madam finished her breakfast and rose with great ceremony. She left her bowl but carried her cup away from the table. "I'll take a fresh pot of tea in half an hour, Marianna."

Marianna nodded and sighed heavily. Before Madam was halfway up the stairs there was a great banging on the door. Rachel ran to open it. In bounded Mordechai Dorfman, covering his face with his hat. "Look out the window!" he shouted in a panic, and of course, for lack of anything better to do, we did.

There in the middle of Talcahuano Street stood five Jewish men with long beards, black felt hats, and caftans, strolling back and forth in front of our door. Each held a placard which read in Yiddish: LORD BURY THESE FALLEN WOMEN! and NO HARLOTS IN HEAVEN! and PERLE GOLDENBERG HAS NO PLACE IN THE PROMISED LAND!

"Come look, Madam!" I shouted, for it was more excitement than we had seen from the outside world in a very long time, and it was aimed directly at us.

Perle poked her head out the window and pointed her finger. "So," she said loudly, "it's the same jokers who come in on Saturday and want to paw the merchandise on credit because it's *Shabbes* and they carry no cash." She leaned all the way out the window and hollered down. "Liars! What you call *traif* on a weekday, you want to lay all over on Friday night and call a *mitzvah!*"

The men looked up at her and shook their fists. Some pointed their fingers. Together they called out, "*Shandeh! Filth! Chazzerei!*"

Madam threw her new cup at them. The men scattered, and the cup shattered on the spot. Perle stood with her hands on her hips, her head thrown back. Her breasts heaved grandly. "In two days we'll see what you think about the likes of me! You with your signs and sidelocks. You can go shit in the ocean, you overzealous farts!" She slammed the wooden blind down with one pull, then turned with great dignity and walked up the stairs. "Who cares what that lot thinks about Perle Goldenberg? Who cares what that lot thinks? Not me."

But as I've said, as you had seen yourself, Hankus, Madam Perle cared a great deal what that lot thought. She made fun of them, she did imitations of them bobbing up and down in their gabardines, but she was terribly hurt by their contempt. Her arranged marriage to Rabbi Eleazar was a most remarkable coup, her greatest revenge. While we *nafkehs* thought that no woman could become more pious than Madam Perle, she herself sought at all moments to become closer to God. Even while packing, she studied longer and prayed harder than the most zealous zealots. Where a *frum* Jewish woman might go to the *mikveh* once a month, Madam Perle found her way to the purifying waters every afternoon. While two white candles were called for to sanctify the *Shabbes,* Madam Perle lit eighteen every common evening in her bedroom. Most scandalous of all, it was said (and I saw this with my own eyes so I know it to be so) that Madam Perle, discontent with the meager role of women in the keeping of Jewish ways, wrapped around her shoulders not only a man's *tallis* and wore on her head that blue satin *yarmulke,* but by now also bound her left arm in leather *tefillin* and wore fringed *tsitsits* close to her body, like a man.

Perhaps because of her impending marriage to the renowned Chelmno rabbi, who would surely demand that she eschew these male accouterments as soon as he came to collect her, Madam took to wearing these items during her remaining week among us at all times.

Perle washed her hands of all bordello social obligations. In this, her last week among the sinful, Perle Goldenberg saw no men, not even her tutors. She found her way to God's ear in the solitary confinement of her own room, confidently and behind closed doors.

No one ever knew for certain how the arrangement between Madam Perle and *Rebbe* Eleazar had been made. Some thought that in one of the rabbi's visits to his brother in Rosario he might have stopped at the brothel, met Madam Perle, and genuinely fallen in love. But neither Sara, nor Rachel, nor even Red Ruthie remembers having met him, and I am certain that unless he came in disguise, I never laid eyes on him before he arrived to get his bride. Others believed that Madam Perle placed an advertisement in the personal sections of all the Yiddish papers worldwide in hopes that, in spite of her dubious business dealings, her dowry and fine self-education would make her a worthy match. Still others wondered whether Perle had not simply written a letter to this rabbi, known far and wide for his reputation at healing incorrigible sinners, and so touched was he by Madam's humility, her brilliance, and her earnest desire to repent, that he decided to marry her at once.

It doesn't matter how the trap was laid. Not two days after the demonstration outside our Talcahuano Street bordello, Rabbi Eleazar ben Yaakov ben Yahuda of Chelmno arrived. He stood in our parlor decked in a sable *streimel*, a new gabardine, and high black boots, his black beard combed and tied at the end with not just a blue ribbon, but a tiny diamond *and* a sapphire. Not a *pais* hair was out of place.

The most revered Chelmno rabbi was careful to avert his eyes from the women of the house, although given the hour, it was a difficult task. Rachel and I were stretched across the two fainting couches, she filing her nails, me reading one of Madam Perle's discarded French novels (in Yiddish, of course), trying to rid my brain of sorry thoughts of you, who I had found after so long and then lost forever. Sara sat limp and dreamy in the red velvet overstuffed chair, and little Magda practiced her scales upon the piano.

We thought he was a customer at first and so didn't pay him much mind. The only man in the parlor at the moment was Dov Hirsh, who was copiously studying a Palermo racing form.

"Are you the brother?" the *rebbe* asked.

Hirsh looked up at him, annoyed. "I'm somebody's brother, but if you mean Perlie's, that cursed fool is down at the corner bar drinking away his troubles."

"I have come to collect Perle Goldenberg and remove her from this *shandhoiz* forthwith."

"Ah, Perle's rabbi..." Dov Hirsh looked the holy man up and down. "You know what you're getting yourself into, do you?"

"You will be so kind as to bring her to me."

"I?" Hirsh guffawed. "Marianna!" he sneered and snapped his fingers. She came out of the kitchen and glared first at Hirsh, then at the rabbi. "Tell your mistress to get her ass down here. Her holy *yentzer* is here to collect her."

The rabbi shifted uneasily for the first time. Marianna flicked her thumb against her teeth at Hirsh before she sauntered up the stairs for Perle. Rachel and I stretched languorously on the fainting couches into some of our more provocative poses. But if the Chelmno *rebbe* was aroused by us, one couldn't tell by looking. He stood at military attention, moving only his head back and forth, back and forth, as if listening to a private music or prayer.

Marianna came downstairs. In a most matter-of-fact way she asked the gentleman if he would have a cup of tea. He shook his head slightly and otherwise acted as if he'd not heard a word she said.

Hirsh folded up his racing form. He offered his seat to the rabbi, who looked him in the eye with no curiosity and declined. He remained standing even after Hirsh left him alone with us, but he never paced or gazed impatiently at a pocket watch. Rachel and I whispered and giggled but the man was unflappable.

After what seemed an eternity, Madam Perle came waltzing down the stairs. She wore a new, quite conservative dress of black taffeta with a small matching hat whose veil was pulled down to her chin. In one hand she carried a carpetbag that was stuffed full, in the other a dainty black umbrella. She put down her bag and presented her free hand to the rabbi. At that exact moment, the wonder rabbi from Chelmno turned and looked the other way.

Before anyone knew what to make of it, Madam Perle Goldenberg, queen of the Varsovia Society, whore princess of Buenos Aires, lord and master of Talcahuano Street 154, was on her knees before the miracle worker, weeping like a little girl.

Madam Perle left within minutes of greeting Rabbi Eleazar. He bowed in her direction, and with a grand gesture of his left hand (of course, without looking at her), beckoned her stand. Marianna wrung her hands together and sucked on her teeth, I think to stop herself from showing her disrespect for this man who stood shaking his head now at his fiancée, her beloved Madam Perle. With a burst of emotion, Perle Goldenberg turned to each of us. She took Rachel's plump hands in her own and kissed them, then swept to Sara, who closed her eyes and held her arms at her sides while Madam hugged her. She pinched Magda on the cheek. I pulled my robe close and held my breath when she came to me. "Sofia," she whispered, "my greatest hope, my dearest dear." And before I knew it, she took my face in her hands and kissed me full on the mouth. In an instant, she was gone.

We leaned out the window and watched as *Rebbe* Eleazar's coachman hoisted Madam Perle into the finest carriage we had ever seen: polished cherry wood and bronze trim, velvet curtains on the windows. Rachel guessed that if this rabbi was so insistent on not laying eyes on Madam, it was likely that there was also a curtain in the carriage itself, dividing the front seats from the back so that the holy man would not need to gaze upon our lovely and most hated Madam as they traveled to Rosario.

Drawing the carriage were a pair of yellow horses, each with blinkers, each with manes and tails braided and capped at the end with ribbons and tiny jewels. Their bridles were fine black leather and their coachman, who was not a Jew (and consequently able to look at Madam closely enough to get a good eyeful), was dressed in evening clothes, the likes of which our fanciest patrons wore when they came to see us after the theatre or a ball.

Behind the coach and horses were two small covered wagons, such as the gypsies used to travel through Poland. They were brand new, not at all shabby, each with a small white horse hitched to its front. Three Jewish men dressed exactly like the *rebbe,* but with many fewer jewels, came into the bordello parlor, made for the pantry, and carried out Madam Perle's many trunks and boxes. These they loaded into the covered wagons. It took them five trips up and down the stairs before they were done.

By this time, Tutsik Goldenberg had come back to the *shandhoiz* on the arm of Dov Hirsh. It was two in the afternoon and he was weaving from side to side as he stood on the sidewalk, clearly drunk. "Good luck to you, *Rebbe Yentzer.* She'll steal your life as she stole mine."

The rabbi, who stood outside the carriage supervising the placement of Perle's belongings, ignored Tutsik as he had us women. Goldenberg banged on the coach window, and Perle pulled back her velvet curtain. "Dear sister!" he shouted when the last trunk was loaded and the little Jewish men were settled in behind their horses.

"What is it?" Perle asked from the coach. We whores wondered if he would ask her forgiveness and blessing. We leaned our heads far out the window to hear what he would say.

The rabbi climbed in and tapped the roof of the carriage with his walking stick. The coachman raised his whip to the yellow horses.

"Good-bye to you and good riddance," Tutsik Goldenberg sneered at his sister. The yellow horses whinnied and they galloped away. "Good riddance!" shouted our new owner, Tutsik Goldenberg, as the covered wagons sped past him and away from us forever. "Good riddance and good-bye!"

5

AND SO WE WERE TUTSIK GOLDENBERG'S NOW, all of us whores: Rachel, Sara, Magda, and me. But Hankus, not you. As Tutsik finally learned the hard facts of his life, didn't you sit beside him at table, sheepish and not the least bit remorseful? And didn't he in turn show his back to you, the son he never had, and declare you from that day forward his sworn enemy? Yes, from that minute forward, Hankus Lubarsky, you were banished from the walls of our Talcahuano Street prison for the rest of Tutsik Goldenberg's mortal life and your own.

You spent the week between Perle Goldenberg's wedding dress return and her departure for Poland in exile, locked away from Talcahuano Street in your little room on Chacabuco, snapping your fingers, making objects disappear. You paced the floor of that tiny room as you had seen orangutans and tigers do. You smoked cigarettes and drank your coffee black. You wondered all the while would you ever see me again? Why hadn't you planned for the moment when the beans would be spilled? You knew about Tutsik Goldenberg's vast anger, but you never guessed he might direct it toward you.

And who told you the truth in the first place? It was Fishbein himself, who made you beautiful promises of a Broken Heart Theatre full of Jews stomping their appreciation. He came to call on you in your Chacabuco Street digs just an hour after he'd made his deal with Madam Perle. It startled you, but you were fully dressed and so you let him in. He sat down upon your little bed, filthy suit and all, and looked you up and down. "Let me lay it out for you, *yingeleh*. Tutsik Goldenberg is talking like he's the guy going to make you famous. Let him talk." Fishbein blew a puff of sticky smoke over your head. "But as of about sixty minutes ago, I'm the one who will crown you magic prince of Jewish Buenos Aires and then magical emperor of the rest of the world." He gave you a *shockle* on the cheek and then stuck a twenty *peso* note into your vest pocket, just like rich uncles did for their *bar mitzvah bocher* nephews. "There's one catch only: keep your mouth shut about this—to the entire Jewish universe, but most important of all, to that *shlemiel* Tutsik Goldenberg. Just play him along like he's the big boss, my boy, and you'll never have to juggle a steak at Casa de Yale Levine again."

You stood before him with your mouth wide open. This was a man who could do what Tutsik Goldenberg could only scheme about. It was your dream come true in nightmare form. "I'll do my best, *Pan* Fishbein," and you meant it, Hankus, too.

"More than your best, *yingeleh*. You will do exactly as I say."

"Exactly as you say, *Pan* Fishbein."

He made as if to leave, patted you again on your smooth baby cheek. "Just one more thing, *bocher* mine. From this minute forward, you will call me *Tateh*."

"*Tateh?*" You could barely find your own voice.

"And I will call you *son*."

You swallowed hard and looked at your self-proclaimed father. He was the exact opposite of the man you saw beheaded and run through not so many years before. Still, Fishbein was offering something you wanted more and more. You swallowed down your anger and managed an actor smile. "*Tateh* it is."

"My boy, my boy, my son, my life." He threw his grubby arms around you. "You won't regret this, not for one minute. Oh, this I promise on my own father's grave."

Fishbein left then and you were quiet. The horrible smell of his dead cigar in the air reminded you of other smoke that burned up another family. The whole incident made you sick to your stomach, and yet...from that moment on wasn't your rent paid as if by magic every month? And didn't little gifts—a diamond tie tack, a set of mother-of-pearl cufflinks, a simple gold pinkie ring—appear mysteriously on your chest of drawers at Chacabuco Street every few weeks, with wrinkled notes attached? *Practice* mein *zun, and make yourself ready* and *Almost time now, heart of my heart, don't despair.* The message was clear: as long as you kept your mouth shut, Marek Fishbein would make life very pretty for you. The only tricky part was that Tutsik still thought it was his show—after all, Fishbein had adopted you without your consent.

Yet how could you complain? As the holidays sailed into common days, you found yourself with plenty of money and lovely gifts. Best of all, the promise of escape artist infamy. Still you were nervous. For no one, neither Fishbein nor Goldenberg nor any lackey in between, said one word about a rehearsal hall, or an opening date at the Broken Heart Theatre. You'd not laid eyes on a contract, you'd seen not one poster with your name on it. When you saw Fishbein in passing and tried to meet his eyes he shook his head at you (and none too discreetly), or he'd say out loud to his shyster brother-in-law, "Ah, the young escape artist, Hankus Lubarsky! Give him five *pesos,* Moritz, toward his career." He'd wink at you and pinch you on the cheek and whisper, "It won't be long now, *kaddishel,* mark my words."

Then one day, in the week that Madam Perle was preparing to leave our *shandhoiz* hell, a note covered with filthy fingerprints arrived at your rooms. It was attached to a badly wrapped package. *Practice every day and be ready,* mein *zun. The time is nearly come. Your loving* Tateh, *MF.* Slowly you unwrapped the package. You laughed and cried when you saw what Fishbein sent you: handcuffs, Hankus, made of gold.

Ah, and what about me? It devastated me that Tutsik Goldenberg had turned you out of the brothel forever, had banished you before I could ask you did you love me, would you get me out? I know how you held me in your heart, maybe not so much before our night of love together in the Talcahuano Street bordello, but every moment after that, oh, every moment, yes I know. But to show your face on Talcahuano

Street was to face that madman Goldenberg and his considerable wrath. Ah, my love, knowing nothing of your fate as magician or lover, I pined for you. I hoped you could find your way back to me, and help me out the door.

At last, on the very day that Madam Perle was to quit Buenos Aires forever, the great king pimp of the Jewish barrio sent his brother-in-law Moritz Shatz to get you, his heart, his son. You were naked, dreaming, I like to think, of that one night we shared, our morning in my Talcahuano Street bed. How quickly you learned about kissing, Hankus, what a pleasure and a surprise! Even as I found the saddest part of you, you longed for more. And in your dream that morning, there *was* more, my hands about you, and under you, my mouth found all of you in that marvelous dream.

Then came a hard knock on your Chacabuco Street door. You sat up with a start to find yourself alone in a sagging bed. You touched your head, rubbed your eyes. And you remembered the circumstances of your life: the love we made that drunken night; the dead faces of your family in their home burned to the ground; and Marek Fishbein who had promised to love you in a most horrifying way. What a deep burning all this made inside you, how it shot through your heart and stabbed your *peeric*. You sat up fully awake while the knocking continued.

You pulled a silk dressing gown around you, pushed your wondrous black hair off your face. "Who's there?" you called. To your dismay, your voice wouldn't find its mannish bottom. At that minute, to your own ear, you sounded just like a girl.

"You'll beg my pardon, *Señor* Lubarsky. It's Moritz Shatz, Marek Fishbein's attorney."

You moved to the door and kept a hand on the doorknob, then breathed deep to make your voice low. "Have I business with Marek Fishbein?"

"Oh, absolutely, *Señor* Lubarsky. Your entire life is wrapped up in *Pan* Fishbein's business. Today what has been official for sometime becomes public at last."

You opened the door a crack. "Could you come back in an hour?"

Shatz pushed the door open a hair further with the flat of his hand. "I'm sorry, young man, but I cannot. *Pan* Fishbein is extremely busy and must keep his appointments as scheduled."

You placed one foot against the door and began to wrap your breasts. "But I know of no appointment with *Pan* Fishbein."

"Of course not, *Señor* Lubarsky. No one has bothered to tell you. But if you would be so kind as to dress and come with me to Maipú Street, I assure you all questions will be answered completely to your satisfaction." He pushed on the door again. "May I come in?"

You shoved the door closed in Moritz's face. "Absolutely not." You ran your fingers through your hair and tried to come to your senses. Moritz knocked again. "I'll be out in one minute—five minutes!" you shouted, wondering how long it would take to leap out the window and run away forever. Instead, you jumped into a pair of trousers and a wrinkled shirt, pulled on your boots and a jacket, and felt at last ready to open the door. It wasn't the way you liked to greet business associates. You prided yourself on your neat comportment, but on this morning you had no time to be meticulous. You opened the door and *voilà*, there you were, the escape artist before the world.

"*Señor* Lubarsky?" Moritz Shatz held out his hand. "It's a pleasure to see the renowned magician again at last. Come, I've a taxi waiting."

You followed him down the stairs, a little more relaxed now. You calmed yourself by admiring the cut of his brown suit, the jaunty angle of his fedora. "You like this suit?" Shatz asked as you climbed into the motor car. "Young man, every day is an occasion for a nice suit. Fishbein likes to see his people looking good day and night. Why, you notice even that *yentzer* Tutsik Goldenberg dresses well for his station. Now that everything is out in the open, we'll get you some respectable clothes. I'll see to you myself."

You took a deep breath and watched the daily life of Buenos Aires through the taxi window. In fifteen minutes, the cab pulled up in front of a brick building on Maipú Street.

Shatz ushered you up the rickety flight of stairs and past the garish-looking man who sat guarding the door with a knife in his hand. When the goon recognized the attorney he greeted you both with a nod of the head, then tossed his knife straight up in the air. You caught it by the handle and passed it back to him without a word. He snatched it from you and began at once to clean his nails.

Fishbein's office was dingy and full of foul smoke. You could just barely make him out in the gloom as he sat behind his desk, feet up, a fat cigar between his teeth. He jumped up and danced around the desk to where you stood the minute he saw you. "It's him!" Fishbein shouted, "truly him, truly him! Ah, *mein kaddishel zun!*" He grabbed you by the shoulders and pulled you up to his face. You flinched at the stench of his cigar. "Look at him. The boy magician of Jewish Buenos Aires!" He took that ragged top hat off his head and offered it to you like a soup bowl. "Pull out a rabbit, *yingeleh.* Pull out a rabbit, I beg you!"

You stared into his filthy hat. *"Pan* Fishbein—"

"Papa—"

You took a deep breath. "Papa...forgive me. I've only just woken up."

"Ah! How foolish of me, how rude! I forget you artists lead ungodly lives!" He hit himself on the head. "Moritz, run down to the *confiteria* and bring us back a coffee. Unless, young man, you prefer that horrible Argentine tea."

You looked at Marek Fishbein and could think nothing but what a baboon he seemed. "I will take coffee, *Señor."*

"Con leche?" Fishbein asked with great authority.

"No, *Señor, sin."* It was obvious it took Fishbein a minute to understand that this meant you wanted your coffee with no milk, but Shatz got the message immediately.

"I'll take care of it, *Pan* Fishbein," the lawyer said, and within seconds he was out the door.

You were alone now with your benefactor, your ersatz father, your boss, Marek Fishbein.

He leaned in to you as if he would kiss you. "At last, my boy, we can bring our spectacular partnership out of hiding. Soon all the world will know that you belong not to Tutsik Goldenberg but to me alone. Oh, how it broke my heart to be silent! For who wouldn't want the world to know he owned 100 percent interest in such a wonder boy as you? But in my arrangement with Perle Goldenberg, I promised to keep the agreement secret until such time as she was safely out of harm's way, and so you had to do the same. Today is the very day her betrothed, some nincompoop rabbi from the old country, comes to collect her. We'll miss little Perlie, but at least now I get to say what's mine." Fishbein pinched your cheek. *"Beardless.* Still beardless! Ah, talented, talented youth! You may now tell the world that I am yours as well!"

And so it was. You were now, in the eyes of the world, the property of Marek Fishbein, gangster and kingpin of the Buenos Aires flesh trade. You could not find one word to say.

"Now then, dear boy, the coffee is on the way. Black, as you like it. For your new boss, do us a favor." He pushed his gaping hat into your face. "Please, *yingeleh*, *zun* of my sons, pull a rabbit out of this, my dear departed father's favorite hat."

Disagreeable as the whole thing was, you left the gangster headquarters on Calle Maipú with something you had wanted your entire escape artist's life. Yes, it was only a piece of paper, but what a piece of paper it was! For there, neatly typed by Moritz Shatz, were the exact terms of an agreement which stated not only that you were to be the star of a magic show all your own, but also exactly how it was to be publicized, where it was to take place, the date, the time, et cetera and so forth. True, there was no mention of actual money. There was one clause Shatz pointed out to you, however, that made signing your only option: you were to have a long run at the Broken Heart Theatre and would get some as yet undetermined percentage of the gate. There was a clause about a new apartment into which you could move immediately. Yes, that very afternoon. Fishbein's thugs would do all the work, you had not to lift a finger. And it said in print that Fishbein would pay for any new costumes or props, that he would pay for all necessary renovations to the Broken Heart stage.

What had you to do in return? The most difficult task was to endure Marek Fishbein's imaginary adoption. The rest was easy. You were required only to provide the most amazing magic show that anyone in the country of Argentina had ever seen. You knew this would not be difficult, because although Buenos Aires was full of fabulous actors and musicians, although for years it had been the home of the famous English clown Frank Brown, it had yet to house a magician of your caliber. Ah, there were fire-eaters, and sword-swallowers; and, of course, your acrobat pals in San Telmo were the most excellent in the City of Good Airs. But never before had there been a magician such as you, Hankus Lubarsky. Marek Fishbein, for all his slovenly oafishness, was no fool as a businessman. Oh, he was no fool at all.

"Listen," he had his arm around your neck by this time, "you have been inside the Broken Heart Theatre? It was built by us, by the Varsovia Society, in the same manner as the Thieves' Shul, as a bribe to our people. You know all about the fine craftsmanship of its five balconies that ascend as if to heaven. You know about the plush velvet seats and the up-to-date gas lighting. For we may be hated by the common Jews of Buenos Aires, but we do not sell them cheap. Know this, little Hankus Lubarsky, most favorite son, love of my life. When you are done with your magic act, the Broken Heart Theatre on Libertad Street in Buenos Aires, Argentina, will be known far and wide as your home. Yes, the home of the Escape Artist, Hankus Lubarsky. And who, my son, can resist this?"

Oh, you were the luckiest magician alive! You were luckier even than the North American Houdini, for Houdini had lean times even when performing for the crowned heads of Europe. But you, Hankus, your lean times were about to be over forever, your dreams come true. You could hardly contain your pleasure as you walked down those rickety steps past the man with the knife in his hand and the racy magazine in his lap, out the doors into the chill Buenos Aires sunshine, and straight over to Talcahuano Street and all of us. Most especially you were coming to bid Perle Goldenberg a fond good-bye, for it was due to her business acumen that you had a decent benefactor at all. More than that, you hoped against hope that you would be able to sneak by Tutsik Goldenberg and make your way into the *shandhoiz* to me.

All the way down those gangster stairs and over the cobblestones into the chilly spring air, all the way to our little bordello, you were giggling, Lubarsky, shouting to the open windows and cigarette-smoking street-sweepers, "I'm rich! I'm rich! I'm rich!" They looked at you as if you were an idiot, and, perhaps, for those few moments you were.

You walked up the street to Talcahuano 154 and the first thing you saw was Madam Perle Goldenberg in her traveling best being swept off by a strange-looking rabbi with the beadiest eyes. Oh, Eleazar looked at you all right, he sized you up in your wrinkled shirt, your marvelous boots. *Yentzer,* he thought, ordinary man. How wrong he was, how horribly wrong.

You stood with your mouth open and witnessed with the rest of us the whisking away of Perle Goldenberg, veiled face and all, tucked into a fabulous carriage. Like something out of a fairy tale it was, complete with her evil prince of a brother, my disgusting boss, Tutsik Goldenberg, spitting at her as she flew down the street toward the road to Rosario. Tutsik looked you in the eye in that vile way of his, that way he reserved for us women, and for the first time in many years you feared for your life. For a minute, Hankus, I feared for you too. For Tutsik Goldenberg grabbed you then, as I had never seen him grab you or even look to grab you, he grabbed you by your shirt collar and he pushed you against the building. "Traitor!" he screamed into your face. "No better than a woman!" he shouted, and he wound back his fist to deck you. At that moment Mordechai Dorfman, who had by now joined the farewell party, grabbed Tutsik by his swinging arm and pulled him away from you.

Poor Dr. Dorfman! Tutsik landed his punch upside his soft face. Mordechai's nose bled, but he saved you from a beating. You nodded to him and waved to all of us, straightened your shirt and yelled up to me, "I'll come for you—I'm rich!"

"You'll do nothing of the sort," Goldenberg hissed. "You'll be lucky if you stand on the ground outside her window. For you are a traitor, a filthy traitor, and I will never let you show that handsome face inside the walls of my house again!"

"It was your sister sold me over to Fishbein to save your ass!"

Goldenberg lunged toward you again but you somersaulted backward and out of his reach.

"I'll come back for you, Sofia!" you shouted again.

"Try it, Hankus," spat Tutsik Goldenberg, "and I'll rip both your hearts out with my bare hands!"

6

IT MIGHT HAVE SEEMED AN EASY MATTER to escape the clutches of Tutsik Goldenberg, to make one's way from inside the walls of the Talcahuano Street bordello once the infamous Madam Perle had made her ceremonious exit. In fact, just the opposite was true.

Instead of becoming relaxed and secure with the knowledge that the *shandhoiz* was his and his alone, Tutsik Goldenberg became more anxious and foul-mouthed than ever before. Worse, that horrifying control he had that allowed him to threaten women in public but never actually harm them (except for the one time he took after poor Sara with his sharpest knife) gave way to a loose-fistedness that enabled him to lash out at any of us with no warning. It became clear within twenty-four hours of Madam Perle's departure that Tutsik Goldenberg not only loved the feel of a woman's face under his angry palms, but with Perle gone, he felt freer than ever to give a *frassk* across the face or a *zetz* in the belly whenever the desire overcame him. Yes, with his sister on her way to a sumptuous wedding, there was no one to stand between the thick gold rings on Tutsik Goldenberg's well-manicured fingers and the once-smooth skin of our sad, wan faces, no one to stop him from shoving us against a wall or holding us out a window by our wrists.

The old regulars, Dov Hirsh and Mordechai Dorfman, came by as always, but they weren't as glamorous as they once were in the eyes of Tutsik Goldenberg, who had grown a pencil-thin moustache and had taken to wearing a silk smoking jacket and red fez around the flat. There were new thugs who hung around, of higher value to Tutsik because they were close to the ear of the chief of police, and Tutsik used them to weasel in tight with the muckamucks of gentile Buenos Aires society. While Madam Perle had taken it upon herself to keep out the razor-carrying roughnecks and blackjack-bearing *shtarkers*, those very roughnecks now counted themselves among Tutsik Goldenberg's closest friends.

In private, we *zoinehs* made no bones about insulting Tutsik Goldenberg, once or twice even told him to his face he looked ridiculous in his smoking jacket, his ascot, his mustache and fez. But Tutsik Goldenberg's newfound friends fingered his satin lapels with respect and chucked him under the chin. Of course, us they wrinkled their noses at with utter contempt, acted like they were doing us some big favor to fuck us and beat us up, to humiliate us in ways we had thus far not experienced.

At first, stupid me, I imagined this a good thing, that the new clientele would hate us so much that Tutsik Goldenberg would be forced to throw us all out on our ears and replace us with a newer, more glamorous batch. Alas, things became much worse. Tutsik wrote a notebook of new laws, put into place severe rules and regulations that limited our movement in obscene ways. There was no more lingering of whores around *maté*, no more playing of twenty-one after late lunch. We were let out of our cages to eat, and then Tutsik ordered us up to our rooms again until five o'clock in the evening when we were expected to sit around the parlor practically naked and entertain customers. If a john came before five, the new policy under Tutsik Goldenberg's supreme dictatorship was to have Marianna show him up, unlock our doors, and allow him to jump on us without ceremony. As I mentioned, Goldenberg could care less how those customers treated us. All of Perle's rules were suspended, all her bets called off. If a mackerel wanted to hold a razor blade under our chin—or worse—while he leaped all over us, that was what he got to do. Dr. Dorfman and Dov Hirsh were supposed to see to our safety, but this was a practical joke.

None of us *nafkehs* was allowed to leave the *shandhoiz* at any time, for any reason—not for a new pair of silk stockings nor for a packet of cigarettes. Instead, Marianna was instructed to make all of our purchases for us, with the money coming directly out of each of our nightly takes. None of us, from that point forward, was to hold so much as a paper *peso* in our hands.

Worse for me, Hankus, I had no word from you. Our insane boss, to spare himself the embarrassment of telling his cronies he was sold out by his madam sister, had banished you from our establishment forever. The old mangoes asked for you though, and when they did, Hankus, Tutsik Goldenberg met their inquiries with chilly silence. More likely than not, he never spoke to those customers again.

Twice you tried to come in the door of Talcahuano Street 154, and each time you were met by a cruel-eyed Dov Hirsh who made no bones about shoving a wickedly sharp dagger to the base of your throat and telling you to be on your way. I called after you the second time, and Goldenberg held me by the throat against the banister and slapped me until Mordechai Dorfman struggled to pull him away.

I took some pleasure imagining what your life was like. Red Ruthie told me that Fishbein had provided you with a flat up in Once, but she didn't know exactly where. How I loved to picture you in your new flat, getting in and out of knots, holding your breath under water, and juggling everything within reach. How liberating it was to see you in my mind's eye, hanging upside down, freeing yourself from those fine gold handcuffs, entering magical chambers before the eyes of hundreds only to mysteriously and with great panache absolutely disappear.

I tried very hard to believe that if it was within your power, you would come to my room as you had begun to come to my dreams, since that very first night I held you in my sorry *nafkeh* arms.

I became every day more fearful that, in his current condition, Tutsik Goldenberg would kill Sara, Rachel, Magda, and me just to be rid of us. Yes, that he would murder us simply because it was within his right as owner of the whorehouse. His new best friends now included half the Buenos Aires police department, who were happy as could be to look the other way if some stupid *prostituta* was sliced to ribbons by an anonymous razor or, for that matter, simply disappeared. Although it must also be said that should a woman take it into her head to jump out a window or walk out the Talcahuano Street door to freedom, those selfsame police would more than happily find her, beat her up, and bring her back exactly where they thought she belonged—to Tutsik Goldenberg's evil arms.

As far as jumping from the window went, mine looked out onto Talcahuano Street and was three flights up. Not so bad, I think, for jumping. You did it yourself that first night we spent together. Back in the old days, when cutting up *nafkehs* was not allowed in our little bordello, I watched a *shadchen* from La Plata exit from that very window after he brandished a razor and held it to my throat. He bounded over me when I called Madam Perle for help and leapt onto the balustrade and out that window like a swashbuckler. Then he hobbled away on a broken ankle. I've no doubt that any one of us *nafkehs,* in the best of times, could get out of here with just that damage. But to be honest, we had been treated like a herd of veal calves for years, and now it was even worse because Tutsik never allowed us out of our darkened rooms in daylight for five minutes. We never got a supervised walk outside anymore, let alone the chance to run freely away. We were still fattened up daily on Marianna's cooking, although these days Tutsik Goldenberg, in the name of what budget I'll never know, took it upon himself to supervise Marianna's menus as if he were the manager of some failing hotel. Our portions became daily smaller. We were faced with more potatoes and less meat, the bread became coarser, the coffee weak. We were starved and puffy all at once, except for Sara, who was thinner and thinner still.

But even if we had been in the best of health, the strongest physical condition, escape would have been impossible. For among Tutsik Goldenberg's new practices was one that was common among other Varsovia houses, but never before in Madam Perle's: he began to shave our wages. Because he no longer let us out the door, and Marianna, as I said, was sent to buy underwear and stockings (although once in a while, for a little treat, I think Tutsik sent Hirsh or he went by himself), and because these stockings and underwear he took out of our wages, he was able to double what he charged us for everything. At the end of an evening, when the *pesos* were divided up, his pile was the biggest. Ours kept getting smaller and smaller as the days and weeks went by, until it was clear that in due time, there would be no money coming to any of us at all. Even if we could escape out the window with no broken bones, we would have nothing in our pockets, no way to get anywhere, and we'd be back in the *shandhoiz* before long. It was all that we knew.

Since we had only the street clothes we came with to our new home, none of us had much to speak of. What did I have but a joke of a wedding dress so small it looked fit for a doll now, and a couple of shawls left me by Madam Perle. I wanted out of the whorehouse on Talcahuano Street, I wanted my life, I wanted my life now with you, Hankus, an earnest and honest life. As long as I believed we were both alive, then I held hope I would have it. But to jump down three stories practically naked into the rainy Argentine winter, to be picked up and found by those awful police and then dragged back here—no, I didn't want that.

I was more desolate than ever. For before you were my lover I could dream about you as my golden key to freedom. Now you were so much more than that—you were my heart, my very breasts and soul. I had lost, in the instant Tutsik Goldenberg banished you, more than I even knew I had.

And so it went. For weeks and weeks I had no word of you. No, none at all, which was a new and crueler form of torture. This alone would have been bad enough, dear Hankus, without my constant fear that to settle his score once and for all, Tutsik Goldenberg was going to have you killed. I had no doubt that this was something Goldenberg was entirely capable of doing, but if, God forbid, he *did* do it, I would never hear about it now. For eventually, dear Hankus, along with you, Red Ruthie was also forbidden to come to our whorehouse—she had remained loyal to Madam Perle until the last. And to make our *nafkeh* isolation complete, Tutsik also forbade us the Yiddish paper against which to check the facts of our fading imaginations. Yes, Hankus, I was terrified that Tutsik Goldenberg would take it upon himself to murder you with his own well-manicured and rageful hands, and that no one would be the wiser.

When I thought about this for very long, I became completely heartsick. But one morning, as I opened my unhappy eyes, I gathered strange hope. If Tutsik Goldenberg took it upon himself to end your escape artist's life, Fishbein and his cronies would be upon him in a flash. This house and all of us in it would be burned to the ground. Even Tutsik Goldenberg at his most possessed was not able, I was certain, to forget the wrath of Marek Fishbein, and now that you were *his goldeneh yingeleh,* ah, perhaps you would be safe. Yes, because I believed that in his very guts Goldenberg was at best a coward, I fervently hoped that not very far from us, in your new Once flat or somewhere other, you, Hankus Lubarsky, were safe and sound.

Still, how I longed to hear from you. If you sent me notes, I never saw them; it certainly wasn't beyond Tutsik Goldenberg to tear up our mail. I wrote you letters every day, letters begging you to save me, letters pouring out my love to you and all my desire. These I burned as soon as they left my pen, burned them and crushed the ashes into powder, then blew the powder out my window to be taken by the winter wind wherever it might find you. It was here in these letters that my love for you was told, and also our deepest secrets—our deepest secrets of two women loving. I knew that for this crime itself, in spite of Fishbein and his mad fury, Goldenberg would kill us. He would kill me *and* you, Hankus, with no fear of Fishbein, only with rage. We had doubly betrayed him: we loved each other and not him, and we were women together.

The idea to escape as Sara had escaped with an opium pipe seemed more and more appealing. I gazed out the window and wondered how much worse a life with two broken legs would be than the one I had now. When customers came to my room, I prayed to God that one of them would have a razor tucked away and would take his deepest pleasure from slashing my throat. I prayed that Marianna would go insane, put arsenic in the food and poison us. I begged God for some maniac to push his way into the whorehouse brandishing his pistols and murder us all on the spot.

I was in this very state of despondency when one evening a caller arrived, a stranger to Talcahuano Street 154, well-appointed and dressed as European gentlemen here in Buenos Aires often were, in a grey suit and grey gloves, with a grey top hat, a vest and cravat. He carried with him a black walking stick topped with a ball of gold.

Around his shoes he wore spats. He was short and also portly, with a gold watch chain stretched across his belly. He was a bearded Jew, though in the modern way, his goatee and moustache neatly trimmed. His eyebrows were thick, and in his right eye he wore a monocle. He spoke with a husky whisper of a voice in Yiddish, though his accent appeared above all to be Italian. He stepped into the parlor of our *shandhoiz,* nodded to Tutsik Goldenberg who sat lazily with Magda in his lap, and directly addressed Dov Hirsh. I, who sat by the piano, put the book I was reading aside, for there was something compelling about this visitor. Yet just what it was I couldn't say.

"I am told in Bologna that for the best girls in Argentina, this house is the one to come to." He patted his big belly and looked straight away at me. I felt an odd shyness. I couldn't help myself, I lowered my eyes.

"I am wondering," continued the stranger, "if it is possible to engage the services of one Madam Perle?"

With this, Goldenberg, in his ridiculous fez, pushed Magda off his lap and burst out laughing. "You can engage them all right, but you'll have to go back to Europe to do it. The good Madam, I am afraid, has left us for the Carpathian Mountains. We'll see her again I think not 'til hell."

The man looked disgruntled. "But I am told she is the most extraordinary courtesan in all the world!"

Goldenberg soured and went up to the gentleman. He brushed off his dressing gown lapels. "Well, she isn't here. Now I've got other girls here, younger than Perle, and less stuck-up. And I dare say a little cheaper, too."

The man shook his head for a moment, then patted his belly. "I'd my heart set...I'd my heart set on Perle Goldenberg." He looked at me and then at Magda. He glanced at Sara, who was half-asleep, and at Rachel, who glanced back. Immediately he averted his eyes. "You see, I've more than a few gold *pesos* to spend, I'd like to get my money's worth." For the first time during my life on Talcahuano Street I wanted a man to choose me. There was something about him, oh, something familiar, yet I couldn't say for certain what it was. So many men came through this way, or passed by on the street below. Usually, when a new customer walked in, my heart was full of dread. I didn't want to be chosen, for I was tired then and sick to death of everything. But when this man stepped over to me, tipped my chin with his gloved fingers, I felt inside me the tiniest ray of warmth. "How much for her?" he asked.

"Depends on what you want," said Tutsik.

"The works," said the little man.

"Tell you what...you take her upstairs and do what you will, we'll charge you by the hour. Special introductory offer because you came in search of Perle and all we have is her leftovers."

"You'll keep a tab?"

"The clock starts now."

"Excellent," said the man. He touched his fingers together and hopped up and down on the balls of his feet. "Come along," he said smiling, a glint in his eye. Did I know that glint? I knew no men from Italy.

"Her name?"

"That's Sofia," Dr. Dorfman chimed in. "Very nice goods."

"Sofia," repeated the little man, then patted my rump. "Lead on, Sofia."

And up the stairs we went.

When we got to my room, the man became urgent. "Lock the door," he whispered. "Please lock the door!"

"If you insist," I said. I acted bothered, but if truth be told, I wanted to be locked away with this strange little man.

"I do," said the man. "I insist, I insist."

I turned the key and he touched my hand. "Leave it there. Let it block the hole."

Some men are so peculiar. They come into a brothel, they make all their wishes known in public, and then they want to do it in secret. I wondered what strange tastes he was going to show me. Read him the Bible while I rode on top of him? Have me recite some lines of Shakespeare in Yiddish? Suck his *shlang* and call him by a baby name?

"Leave the key in the lock, Sofia. Leave the key and come over here." Something stopped me then, something about the earnestness in the man's voice, the warmth and power of it. I stood before him and watched.

The man took off his hat and then his gloves. And then his coat and then his vest and then his shirt. And when he took off his shirt, next he took his belly, which was no more than a flattened pillow tied around his front. And with the pillow gone, there stood before me, in a false beard and not a stitch more, no one but you, beloved Hankus Lubarsky, who held out your arms to me and whispered, "*Voilà*."

The new john, who told us his name was Dr. Katterfelto, came to call on me now three times a week. He arrived promptly at 7:30 on Tuesday, Thursday, and Saturday evenings, wore exactly the same grey clothes, down to the gloves and walking stick, and stayed with me until 10:00. At such time he would leave, head down, barely saying good-bye. For my part, I made it seem always as if the ecstasy I shared with the good doctor was a terrible chore. For if Tutsik Goldenberg were to learn our sweet secret, Hankus, were he to know that for those two and one-half hours we looked with love into one another's eyes, that three times a week you told me your new tricks and escapes, ah Hankus, we would be far too dead for me to tell this tale.

But we kept our voices low between our kisses as I implored, "When will you save me? How much longer?" And you answered, "Soon, my darling Sofia, soon."

For these stolen pleasures, Tutsik Goldenberg charged you twenty gold *pesos,* which your Dr. Katterfelto always had. I soon found out they were the same twenty *pesos* used over and over again because, unknown to Tutsik Goldenberg, Dr. Katterfelto was not only an impostor but a pickpocket as well. No sooner had our alcohol-soaken owner put those *pesos* into the breast pocket of his smoking jacket than Dr. Katterfelto pulled them out again.

I loved to see you, Hankus. Oh, to see you any way at all was a blessing in those terrible times. But I began to fear that our love was destined to be stuck forever in that horrible little room which I shared with so many bad memories. I was just about to give up ever calling another place my home, when Dr. Katterfelto arrived one evening, not alone but with a friend.

This friend was a slightly taller man, an Argentine who dressed formally in the Argentine way. Instead of a top hat he wore a straw boater. He wore a bow tie and a winter suit. Like our Dr. Katterfelto, he carried a walking stick. Unlike his companion, he carried also a small valise. His demeanor was distinctly not European—he was stiff, but there was movement in his hips. Goldenberg left a pinochle game with a sergeant of the Buenos Aires vice police to see to the two gentlemen himself.

"Ah, our friend the good doctor. What sinful pleasures can I offer you tonight?" Tutsik lifted his head and gestured to Sara, who sat staring blankly, and Rachel, who to all appearances was knitting a scarf. Magda was poking out a sorrowful tune on the piano, while I lay on the fainting couch and pretended to have no interest in our two guests at all. "Perhaps you and your friend would like to sample other tasty morsels from our menu? Rachel, for example, has often trained two roosters at once, if you catch my drift."

Rachel sniffed loudly and began to count her knitted rows.

Dr. Katterfelto chuckled audibly. "My good man, my dear Tutsik Goldenberg, please, dear fellow, I am a man of few appetites. Sofia suits me just fine. If chicken tastes delicious, why eat beef? Here is my first wife's brother, Maishe. He visits this week all the way from Moisesville. We were chatting over luncheon this afternoon and we thought it might be interesting to uh..." He looked nervously over at the sergeant, who smiled slyly, then stared once again at his pinochle hand. Dr. Katterfelto leaned in to Tutsik and whispered nonetheless.

Goldenberg's eyebrows shot up and his chin stuck out. He pushed his fez back on his head as Dr. Katterfelto continued to talk, this time pointing at Mashie's suitcase. Tutsik Goldenberg let out a little "Whoaho."

The doctor whispered for a few seconds more. At one point, Tutsik reached down through his dressing gown pockets to his own crotch. Beads of sweat popped up on his pink forehead. At last the doctor leaned away from Tutsik's ear and said, so that all could hear, "What do you think?"

"I wish I could join you myself," answered Goldenberg, who gave himself another little squeeze.

The doctor stepped back for a moment as if he might leave.

"I'm joking, Doctor, it's a joke, just a joke. You two go up there with Sofia and have yourself a ball. We'll get her to tell us the details later."

The doctor stepped back again.

"I'm kidding, Doctor, really. What happens behind closed doors— it's between the three of you."

The doctor seemed to consider this for a minute, to mull this over, to decide whether he believed Tutsik Goldenberg or not.

"It's a holy trust, Doctor. Just like those Catholics at confession. What goes on between you two fine fellows and Sofia stays right behind that door. Cross my heart."

At this the sergeant burst out laughing. Tutsik readjusted his fez and went back to business. "Now because there are two of you, I'll have to charge double. And for keeping my mouth shut—another fifteen."

"You drive a hard bargain," said Dr. Katterfelto, this time paying his gold *pesos* in advance.

"My work is my life," Goldenberg said humbly. "Sofia!" he shouted, and I came when he called.

Up in my room we worked quickly. You undressed, Hankus, and I put on Dr. Katterfelto's clothes. The portly belly we stashed in Maishe's mysterious suitcase, out of which came another goatee and a set of eyebrows, which you gently glued to my face with spirit gum. While this was drying, you pulled a set of your own clothes out of Maishe's bag and dressed quickly. "Look," you said urgently, "what do you want to take with you, within reason, that will fit in this bag?"

I dug under my mattress and pulled out the one relic of Madam Perle's ruined library that I knew to be truly mine. It was the Yiddish translation of Shakespeare my father sold Tutsik Goldenberg along with my soul those many years ago. With great remorse I stuffed the leather-bound volume into the suitcase, along with my forsaken wedding dress and my one pair of real shoes. And just for remembrance, a pair of Madam Perle's silky panties.

On the bed we laid out my Chinese silk wrapper and placed inside it a camisole and two silk stockings, as if they were me without my body. My mules we laid at the foot of the bed. You looked nervously at your watch. "Lock the window behind me, the door behind you. We must hurry. If we go over time he'll ask for more money and the game is up. Sofia, bow as you go, look a little sheepish. He's used to Katterfelto leaving without much of a good-bye. Maishe will make the biggest splash, he'll be your cover. You must walk out of here, Dr. Katterfelto, bravely, a bit embarrassed at your pleasure, and nonchalant. Ready?"

Maishe shook his head, pointed to his eye. You hit yourself on the head. "*Signore* Doctor K., you've forgotten your monocle." You took it from my breast pocket and helped me fit it to my eye. Then you kissed me on the cheek, but lightly. "Handsome," you whispered. I could only gaze back at you with a swiftly beating heart.

Maishe picked up the suitcase then, loosened his tie, pushed his hat back on his head, and put a silly-as-anything grin on his face. We barely breathed. You, Hankus, opened my bedroom door. There was no one in the hallway, but it was my job to back out of the room and wave. In your best Dr. Katterfelto voice you said, "Ah, my dear Sofia, a million thank-yous. We will see you again in a few days, I think." Then you winked at me and jumped out the window, over the balustrade, and landed three flights down like a cat on your feet. Maishe locked the window after you. He closed the door, and with a skeleton key he kept in his pocket, locked it.

I strode down the stairs as I'd seen the men do it, sated and shame-faced all in one. The policeman was gone now, and Tutsik was at the card table drinking schnapps with his pal, Dr. Dorfman. He turned to us and burst out laughing. "It's the other good doctor and his Moisesville *shvoger*. What's the rush, Doctor? Tell me and your brother physician here all about it."

I became scared now, not nervous, and fought all impulses to pick up my pace. Instead I walked slower and managed a low chuckle. But Maishe, Maishe God bless him, giggled out loud, giggled out loud and shook his head. "No, no no," he shrieked, and then he laughed again.

"Too much fun for you?" asked Tutsik Goldenberg, getting up to see us out.

I kept walking toward the door, shrugged my shoulders, nodded my head, while Maishe, that Maishe became hysterical. "Yes, yes, very much fun—I, oh my...," and behind me I could feel him all chortling arms and legs.

Dorfman looked at Goldenberg quizzically.

Goldenberg put a finger to his lips and shook his head.

I stiffened up just as I'd seen you, Hankus, do it, and headed faster for the door. My only hope was that Tutsik wouldn't get there first and stop me in an effort to embarrass the good doctor even more. But I had little to fear because Maishe took over again. "No no no no no," he shrieked, "she must never tell, never! If she tells I'll send my cousin here with a big gun and he'll shoot all your heads off!"

"Calm down, calm down, you *yold*. She won't tell me anything. That's why you paid me so good. To shut her up."

I got the door open. Maishe raised his fist and waved it in front of Tutsik's pasty face. He pushed it away and rolled his eyes.

"Will we see you again, Dr. K.?" he shouted.

"Absolutely," I mumbled.

Maishe turned on Tutsik as we walked down the stairs. "My cousin in Moisesville has a very big gun!" he shouted.

"Yes, I'm sure he does, Maishe." Tutsik opened his smoking jacket. "So, you *trombenik*, do I."

My first free breath of Argentine air was taken in hurried gulps as rain pelted everywhere. Even on the street we heard the men laughing, while Tutsik told Dorfman his side of the story, but when they called up to my room, "Sofia!," Maishe and I ran. We flew down Talcahuano Street to Córdoba Avenue, where you were waiting in a horse-drawn cab. We jumped in.

"To Maza Street, in a hurry!" you shouted.

And in a flash we were off.

The sights were plentiful and new to me as we rushed along the cobbled Buenos Aires streets, but I saw little of them from my carriage window. I was too terrified to look at any sights but those in my mind's eye. At first it amused me to think of the surprise we'd laid out for Tutsik Goldenberg. I had known him for so long, had watched him through so many rages, that although I wasn't there in body I've not a doubt as to what was happening on Talcahuano Street 154 at the very minute we sped our way to freedom. Oh, it was easy to imagine.

"Sofia!" Tutsik called, swallowing his cruel laugh and hollering up the stairs. "Tell us all about your fun with the Italian and his buddy! Come down here and tell us what he did to you! *Sofia!*" He grew impatient and smacked his schnapps glass down on the table, and because he was too lazy to do it himself, he told his buddy Dorfman, "Go up and get her." Tutsik slapped himself on the cheek. "I hope they didn't kill her!" Both of them burst out laughing.

"No," Dorfman stifled a chortle, "she likely would have screamed."

"Not if they gagged her!" And the two men fell all over themselves laughing again at their big and sorry joke.

"I better go up and check," Mordechai said then, "she might be in need of a doctor."

Goldenberg poured himself another drink. He held the bottle over Dorfman's glass, but Dorfman, moved by the small amount of sympathy inside of him, waved it away. "Poor Sofia," he sighed.

Not Goldenberg. No, he knocked his drink back and slammed that empty shot glass down once more. "Poor Sofia? Poor Tutsik!" He pointed to himself. "I had aspirations, you know, Dorfman. Unlike you, I wanted to be a person some day. I had my eye on a future—a big future. And what do I get instead? I get to be king of this shithouse." He poured another drink. "You have a sister, Mordechai?"

Dorfman shook his head. "Not that I know of."

"Then you're a lucky man. Because a sister—even a whore of a sister like mine—always makes out, and we the brothers, we get stuck with *drek*."

Dorfman took a good look into his own empty shot glass. "You know," he ventured, "some men wouldn't think of this place as *drek* at all. Some men would look at this little *nafkeh bais* and think, what a cozy set up. Women to *shtup* anytime you want to. Lots of fellows coming over to visit. Good schnapps, good coffee. A cook in the kitchen. Listen, Tutsik, some men might envy you."

Tutsik Goldenberg speared a chunk of hard salami with his knife. "Then some men are fools," he said. "The women are tired, the men bore me. The schnapps and coffee I could get down the street. And the cook in the kitchen costs me fifty gold *pesos* a month." He ripped the salami from the tip of the knife with his teeth and chewed it carefully. "I'd rather be a chicken plucker than do this for the rest of my life."

The two men sat in silence for a minute. Mordechai Dorfman shuffled the cards. He cut them once.

"Well, let's go up and release the spitfire."

"Yes," answered Dorfman, and they walked up the stairs.

I could see them laughing again when they got to my room. Tutsik pulled himself together and knocked. "Sofia—hey." He knocked again, and tried the handle. "It's locked." He shook the handle harder. Suddenly, I bet, he was completely sober. "Sofia! Hey you, Sofia! Open up!" Then I bet he pounded on the door and Dorfman pounded too.

"*Tahkeh,* maybe they really *did* kill her."

Goldenberg smacked the door then with his open hand. "That's all I need, a corpse in the house." He smacked the door again.

By now Rachel and the police sergeant were standing in the hallway, he with a towel wrapped around him. Even dead-eyed Sara was in her doorway, wearing her ratty old robe. The guy she was with busily buttoned his pants, while Magda only poked her head out of her room just the littlest bit.

"For God's sake, Tutsik, use your key!" Rachel told him.

Tutsik felt in his robe pockets and pounded on the door all at once. "If she's not dead already, I'll kill her myself."

Rachel took matters into her own hands. She ran downstairs. In a minute she was back with Marianna, who was talking to herself as she fumbled with her huge ring of keys. Tutsik was still banging on the door when Marianna placed a skeleton key in the lock and turned it once. The door flew open. Oh, what I wouldn't have given to see the look on Goldenberg's face.

There was no Sofia tied to a chair with her throat cut as he had imagined, no little Polish whore chained to the bed or hanging from the ceiling. There was no Sofia Teitelbaum for him to see at all, for I was gone from there. Gone gone gone.

Tutsik tried the windows. Locked. He threw open the armoire and pushed the few clothes in it to the side. Nothing. He pulled the top of the cedar chest at the foot of my bed open—full of books, but no other trace of me. As a last resort he looked under the bed. No, I wasn't there either.

All that was left of me was my kimono and my stockings and those ridiculous, useless mules. Discovering me disappeared thus, Tutsik Goldenberg turned back to the little crowd huddled silently in the doorway.

"What are you staring at?" He pushed at the locked window. "She's gone, all that's left of her are these stupid shoes." He picked up my sorry mules and threw them at the bed.

"Where could she go?" Rachel asked. "Everything was locked from inside."

"Maybe those Italian Jews cut her up in little pieces and stashed her in that valise," Dorfman suggested. "There was a case like that in England not long ago—"

At that, Tutsik smacked Dorfman right across the head.

But here is what frightened me, as I sat back in that rescuing cab and sped toward Once: the moment that came, as I knew it must, when suddenly, every ounce of worry left Tutsik Goldenberg's face and his lips curled into a sneer. "I see," I knew he would say. "I see. Light begins to dawn." The others hung back then, as I would have done if I had still been there instead of driving with you, Hankus, for they became more afraid as Tutsik became eerily calm. "Lubarsky is responsible for this." He pointed a finger first at the bed, then at the window. "I don't know how he did it, but mark my words: this is the work of that *pisher* magician or I'm the Baron de Hirsh."

"At least Sofia's not dead then," Dorfman clucked.

The other whores, my sisters, met him with a sigh of relief.

"Not yet," Tutsik Goldenberg sneered. "But I'll strangle them both by the end of next week."

PART FOUR

*Two Brides Escape
(1916)*

I

OUR ACTUAL TAXI ESCAPE from Talcahuano Street to the Maza Street flat where Fishbein kept you like a lover is no more than a blur in my memory. I remember Maishe waved us good-bye from the street. "My cousin in Rosario has a very big gun!" he shouted after us, and you, Hankus, you burst into laughter. But me, my heart cracked open then, and by the time you opened your arms to the narrow brass bed that was to be our harbor, yes, by that time I was sobbing. All life as I had known it for five years was over, and I was relieved, my love, but also I was bereft.

We looked like two brothers coming up those narrow steps to your flat, me still in my Katterfelto beard and hat, you in a grey suit that matched mine exactly. You locked the door behind us and threw yourself down on that cradle of squeaking springs and horse hair. "Our marriage bed," you whispered in my ear, but I could only look at you, in desperation and gratitude. You pulled me down beside you, gently knocked the hat back off my head. You fingered the threads of my false beard, then carefully pulled off the fake eyebrows, one, then the other, smoothed my true brow, kissed it with a tenderness that broke my frozen heart in two. Then you gently peeled back the beard you yourself had pasted to my chin only an hour before and rubbed the spirit gum from my face with your thumbs. "Our marriage bed," you said again, reaching up to open my shirt. But I stopped you then, held your wrists down on the pillow, ripped your shirt open with my teeth, pulled the binding back from your breasts with my bare hands, and took you there, Hankus, in desperation, in gratitude, I've no idea, took you with my tongue and hands, and you succumbed, and in the end together how we wept ourselves to sleep.

It was in that grief-stricken sleep that I had my first true dream since I had been in Argentina. In it, the whorehouse was empty of men. It was, instead, full of women who I knew and did not know from all the places in my small world. Sara was at the piano, and my beloved lost Tamar played upon the violin. Tamar wore a diaphanous dress. Sara was in her ratty kimono, but on this night she was not dead. Indeed, she was radiant. Her hair was down off her head and flowed as Tamar's did, long and red and wild. In our usual places the rest of us whores sat: me in my underwear on the fainting couch, Rachel on a wooden bench close to the piano, Magda upon her lap. Red Ruthie and her girls lounged about, and even Madam Perle sat among us. She was regal on the velvet-stuffed chair, once again wearing her green silk wrapper that made such an impression the first time I met her. But there were more women in that dream Talcahuano Street parlor than even these, women who in a million years would die before they set foot in a *shandhoiz* in waking life. Yet in my sleepiness, there they were: my mother, Tamar's mother and sister, and also my teachers from gymnasium. In a corner, holding a bouquet of red roses, you stood, Hankus, in your manly garb, watching us all.

At Madam Perle's signal Tamar and Sara started to play, not a tango as you might expect in a whorehouse parlor in Buenos Aires, no, not a tango but a waltz. The saddest waltz I ever heard, in this country or the old one. At first there was nothing to do but listen. Then Red Ruthie took Rachel up in her arms and danced her around the parlor slowly. There was no laughter as sometimes happened on Talcahuano Street in real life. No, just a dreamy smile on both of their faces. Red Ruthie's bright crimson slip stretched lusciously across her soft, freckled breasts, Rachel's steady brown hand rested sweetly on Ruthie's lovely behind. It was unmistakable, the pleasure they found in one another's arms.

One by one, all the other women began to dance—the whores, the mothers, all. Sara left the piano, which miraculously played on. She gathered Madam Perle into her arms as my mother bowed to Tamar's mother, and they took each other up and danced. Then, one by one, each of the women assembled took her turn with me. Yes, one by one, how I sailed with them across the wooden parlor floor: first Red Ruthie, then Rachel; then Sara, with whom I lingered, but only for a second. Next I swayed in the arms of my mother, who looked at me with the tiniest sweetness. In seconds she passed me on to Madam Perle, who I am taller than. For some reason, in this dream I bent down and kissed Perle's forehead. I was gentle to her when I did this, and although if she were to walk into my life again tomorrow I would murder her on the spot, in this dream I felt toward Madam Perle, for one little minute, nothing but love.

At last it was my turn to dance with Tamar, who left her violin by the piano and spun to me with most open arms. We swung together on our high toes through space, just as we did when we were girls. She held me in her arms and twirled me about, and I lay back into those strong arms of hers and let her dip and sway me, let myself look into those eyes, those Tamar eyes that I have missed all these long years. That was when the tears began in my dream, dear Hankus, and that was when Tamar passed me gently into your arms.

We looked into one another's brown eyes. I saw you, dear Hankus, but also there, oh, I saw myself. Then, only, did the parlor walls and all their trappings fall away, until together, in the middle of nowhere, we two stood alone.

I do not know how many days and nights passed between us in that narrow bed, as it sang and moaned beneath us. I was cruel to you as you were generous, played you all the sad tricks I had learned at Talcahuano Street from Sara and Perle: held you down and let you beg; coaxed deepest sighs and howls from you; but cruelest trick of all, when you reached to give me pleasure I turned my back. How could it be, I wondered, as I held your newly discovered nipple between my freshly sharpened teeth, that our first Talcahuano Street tryst had been so delicious, so liberating, and now that I was free I repaid you like this. But we didn't stop. When I turned my back to you, it was you who became cruel and fearless, pulled me close to you, whispered all desires into me, all burning flesh and sorrow in a language not quite human. It was you who held my hands above my head and dove into me and dove again, fevered, belligerent. There was love between us in that narrow Maza Street bed, but it was a ruthless love, relentless, and after days and days we were neither of us sated. As our first tryst on Talcahuano Street had made us whole, had joined us through our sorrow, so had this, our first voyage into each other outside those cursed walls, rendered us ravenous. Yes, starving, and thirsting for each other's very blood.

When one drifted to sleep, the other woke her. When one became hungry, the other fed her some part of herself. I feasted on your fingers, your buttocks, the palms of your hands; you sucked my entrails out through my navel, my asshole, my *peeric,* my teeth. We licked our chops and then began again until the bed screamed its pleasure with ours. I do not know how long, how many days and nights passed before there was a loud, insistent knocking on the door. We froze.

"Tutsik!" My terrified whisper was hoarse.

"Maishe?" you mumbled. The knocking continued, steady and dangerous. Together we climbed into each other, burrowed deep into the bed.

"My boy!" a voice boomed from the hallway, and then, most horrible, there was the jangle of keys in the door. "My boy, it's Marek Fishbein, adopted father of your heart and soul!"

We held each other, hardly breathing, as if this would save us from discovery. In a minute we heard the door push open. I sniffed his foul cigar as the floor creaked under his heavy feet. "My darling *petseleh,* please tell me you are here!" he shouted, and step by step we heard him creep toward our tiny haven. "Remarkable boy of my heart and soul," he was practically crooning, until he finally found us and peeked through the crack in the bedroom door. "My boy, there you are!" he boomed, and firmly pushed the door open. Then he held his face between those filthy mitts of his. "God in heaven, the whore's here, too! My God, forgive me! What Goldenberg told me is true!"

I didn't even think about it. As much as it offended me to give that *shmendrick* of the head pimps a show, I had no choice. I leapt out of our bed, naked, full of our sex. "You've caught us!" I said, and led him by the tip of his greasy beard out of the bedroom, closing the door.

Fishbein tried to shove past me. "That idiot Goldenberg has been telling the whole city that you were stolen by my darling Hankus, but you put him up to this, didn't you, filthy whore!"

"Who cares how it happened, Daddy Fishbein. The fact of the matter is, here I am." I pulled Fishbein by his rotten tie over to the sofa, pushed him down, and although it nearly killed me, sat naked on his lap. I made as if to kiss him, but he pulled away. "Pheh!" he spit. "You've corrupted my heart and soul and got me in so deep with your old employer I might have to strangle you for revenge."

I played my fingers against his cracked lips. "Go ahead, strangle me," I whispered, then reached down. I almost had my hand on his horrible *shlang* when, thank God, you emerged from the bedroom, wrapped suavely in a satin robe. With that Fishbein threw me from his lap and practically rushed into your arms.

"My boy, tell me that she put you up to this! Tell me that her whore's heart played terrible tricks on your good and honorable judgment! Swear to me that this was all her doing!"

"*Pan* Fishbein—"

"Papa," he corrected.

"Papa," you whispered through gritted teeth, "I'm sorry, I cannot."

The two of you sat facing each other in your magic room, Fishbein taking up most of the sofa, you on a wooden chair. I boiled some water and made Fishbein a glass of tea. He took a grimy sugar cube from his vest pocket and held it between his teeth. "In the old country, we drink tea thus, and in our new homeland, also. I don't care for those gourds, do you?"

You said nothing, Hankus, only drew me to you. I took your hand from my naked arm and pulled away.

"Cover yourself," spat Fishbein.

I thought for a minute about not doing as he ordered. I wondered why I'd served him his tea and not thrown the boiling water over him instead. But I didn't have to cook your adopted father in order to contain him. My nakedness was enough to render him powerless. It was a well-known fact amongst the *nafkehs* of Jewish Buenos Aires that while Marek Fishbein loved the profits they brought to him, he despised the sight of our *kurveh* bodies. According to Red Ruthie, this was true because he hated to be naked himself; he made it a point never to be without his clothes, not only in the presence of women, but even among other men. On the rare occasion when he thought it prudent to go to the *mikveh* (the last reported incident being after he strangled the La Plata rabbi with a piece of piano wire), Fishbein paid the matron huge numbers of gold *pesos* to shut the place down so that he could bathe alone and cleanse himself of his heinous sins in private.

This was why Marek Fishbein preferred a big suit with a high-collared shirt and a nice tight tie, even in summer. Madam Perle whispered to me once that Fishbein kept his long underwear on when he was alone with any woman except, of course, his wife. When he made love to her (which he did only one Friday night a month, and this merely to keep his religious obligations in order) he did it the old-fashioned way—a sheet with a hole between them so she could gain no pleasure from the sight of him while he was doing his *Shabbes* duty.

Some naked women he liked to look at. He told Perle he liked to watch us frolic about in the *shandhoiz* like deer in the woods. He even liked to *shtup* us once in a while if he kept his shirt on. There was one time I was cursed with this dubious pleasure. He lay on top of me and jiggled around with no finesse or fun, then slapped me on the behind and sang, "Sofia, ah! Well done."

But now I was your lover, Hankus, the son he never had's very own beloved. To look upon me was to look upon his daughter naked, and this he could not bear. "Cover yourself!" He spat it again, and this time we heard the click of his tiny revolver. I went into the bed-room and wrapped myself in a kimono. You lit a cigarette and offered one to Fishbein.

"I'm a cigar man, my boy. About me you should know at least that."

"Of course," you said. You ran your fingers through your lovely black hair and pointed to Fishbein. "You've your tea now, and Sofia is covered. To what do we owe this pleasure?"

I was amazed at how brazen you were in that moment.

"You've humiliated Tutsik Goldenberg." Fishbein smacked his lips at the hotness of his tea. "And as much a weasel as that man is, as much as he deserves all the maligning and bad wishes that the uni-verse has seen fit to provide, you must remember, dear boy, that he is a business associate of mine. It is I who do the humiliating when there is humiliating to be done, do I make myself clear?"

"Quite clear, *Pan* Fishbein—"

There was the loud slam of Fishbein's tea glass on top of the table before him. *"Tateh!"*

You pulled your robe belt tightly around you. *"Tateh..."*

Fishbein softened slightly. "Much better."

"But what is to be done after the fact?"

Fishbein sipped his tea and smacked his lips. He put a cigar in his mouth and signaled you to light it. You snapped your fingers; it was done. "A genius," he said, shaking his head with pleasure, in spite of his obvious anger. He took a long pull on his cigar. "Sofia is to be returned to Goldenberg immediately," Fishbein said flatly.

You looked at your adoptive father and then at me.

I stood by the window and felt more naked now than before. Fishbein looked at me with disgust and shuddered. "Moritz is waiting in a taxi downstairs. He shall return her to Goldenberg with a bank note for the week's lost profits. After that, Tutsik Goldenberg can do with her what he will."

Your window was higher even than my own at Talcahuano Street. If I jumped now I would surely end up a pile of dead bones, which would be entirely better than going back to Tutsik Goldenberg's house of shame. Ever so slightly I fingered the window latch.

"I'm afraid," you said, puffing yourself up very big, "that is impossible."

I pulled my fingers from the latch.

Fishbein chewed on his cigar. He pushed his stovepipe hat back on his head with a greasy thumb. Then he pulled on his earlobe and whispered, "Excuse me? Do I hear correctly? I am giving you an order and you are telling me no?"

"That is so, Papa."

He wiggled that same grimy thumb at me over his shoulder. "All because of that filthy *nekaiveh?* Listen to me, Hankeleh—if you want to *shtup* cows go to Moisesville. That's where all the Jewish cow-*shtuppers* go."

You walked to me, Hankus, and stood with your arm about me. It was everything I could do to keep from exploding into tears. "*Tateh* Fishbein," you said, your arm not moving, "do I tell you how to do your job?"

Fishbein turned to us both. His face was beet red. He kept pulling his beard down with the palm of his hand. "If ever you should try it, dear boy, despite all familial bonds, that would be the end of you in an instant."

"And so I must ask you not to tell me how to do mine."

Fishbein opened his hands in an offering of hurt feelings. "Never once—"

"*Pan* Fishbein—*Tateh*—father of my heart and soul," you rolled your eyes just slightly, "this woman is more than a lover to me. She is my lovely assistant, she knows all of my magician secrets. To send her back to Goldenberg would be very bad business, for as sure as I am standing here a man before you," you cleared your throat just the tiniest bit, "Tutsik Goldenberg will do everything in his power to wrest those secrets from Sofia and that will be the end of the best magician in all of Jewish Buenos Aires."

Marek Fishbein looked from one to the other of us. "You have told her all of your secrets, but to me, who would be your own father, you have told nothing?"

"Alas, Papa Fishbein, you are not the woman I love. Besides which fact, if she is to be my lovely assistant she must know all my tricks. Why, who is the North American wonder Harry Houdini's assistant? None other than his wife, his darling Bess. And since our show opens so soon, that presents another small problem should you return our lovely Sofia to that weasel Goldenberg's den. I have taught Sofia the theory behind my magic tricks, but in order to assist me we must practice—a feat we cannot accomplish if she is locked away and disabused on the other side of town."

Marek Fishbein adjusted his grubby hat upon his head. He moved his cigar from one side of his mouth to the other with a curl of his tongue. He slapped himself on the cheek and shook a filthy finger at us. "You youngsters have me over a barrel. But mind you, this is not solved for me yet. I am a man who is not above cutting a throat or shooting a person's brains out, no matter who they are to me or what."

"I'm well aware of that, *Tateh,*" you said too sweetly.

In spite of himself, Fishbein looked at me; there was no one else to tell. "He's a *kaddishel,* a sweetie pie. How I *kvel* from this boy!"

"I know what you mean," I said, opening my robe just enough to give him a peek at my *tsitskehs.* I don't know why—I couldn't help it.

"I'm not done with you yet," said Fishbein, and he walked out the door.

Not ten minutes later—his cigar butt was still warm in the ashtray—there came a fresh pounding at our door followed by the jangling of keys and the second uninvited entrance into your Maza Street flat by your adopted *tateh*. He was accompanied this time by his lawyer brother-in-law, that *trombenik* Moritz Shatz.

"All right, it's settled. If you must live with this *tinef tsatskehleh*, it will not be in sin."

I looked at Marek Fishbein and bit my lip against asking who he could possibly know in his big Varsovia Society who did not live in sin.

"I'm not sure I get your meaning," you said.

"You get my meaning, *pisk-malocheh*. Moritz!" Fishbein signaled to his brother-in-law with the top of his head.

"It's very simple, really." Shatz opened his leather case and procured a piece of paper and a fountain pen. "If you must live together in this little apartment which Marek Fishbein has so generously provided for you, then you must live by his rules. Since you refuse to do otherwise, he wishes you wed."

And that is how, for the second time in my short life, I found myself the object of a sham marriage arranged by thieves.

_—.·— 2 —·.—_

MY LOVELY ASSISTANTSHIP was a relatively easy task to accomplish. We simply changed the type of calisthenics we performed from your tight little bed to the big open Broken Heart stage. Though I would learn no fancy backflips, and was by now too old to start walking on my hands, the fact was I had turned a somersault or two during my Warsaw childhood, and cartwheels were a specialty Tamar and I developed especially for birthdays. Yes, on those days, we would flip across the marketplace head over heels, head over heels, one cartwheel for each year of our short happy lives. With your help, Hankus, and Maishe's too, I resurrected my body's knowledge of these skills despite my veal-atrophied muscles. Roughly at first, little by little I managed to tumble across the floor, and while I couldn't fly through the air as you did with fabulous ease, you assured me that under the right light, in the proper costume, I would be the perfect diversion while the real trickery was performed.

In six weeks' time we would dazzle the audience of the Broken Heart Theatre with our opening night performance. As with its sister, the Thieves' Shul, the Broken Heart Theatre was a performer's dream come true: the stage was wide and deep, the sound warm and electric. It was possible to hear a stage whisper all the way up to the highest balcony, and a clever person could make the best use of smoke and light to make even an elephant vanish from those well-varnished boards. Maishe and his acrobats built a false floor on top of the actual one, in secret, early in the morning before most *porteños* had sipped their first coffee of the day. Into the false floor the acrobats installed trapdoors, the exits which you needed, Hankus, in order to walk through brick walls, and even to disappear.

Maishe himself had a part in the show. Indeed, from the moment Fishbein moved you to Maza Street, Maishe was essential to your reputation. For how else was it possible that you were one minute crossing a tightwire stretched high across Rividavia Street, and at that exact same moment seen dangling upside down from a winch in the middle of the Plaza de Mayo? How else could you escape from handcuffs while hanging from the prow of a steamer in the harbor at La Boca, and at just that minute predict the winning horses at the Palermo racetrack for visiting royalty from Bialystok? It was true that whenever the Jewish hoi polloi saw you manifesting yourself in two places at once, it was always you doing the escaping and Maishe posing as you, the mind reader and acrobat on the other side of town. He was your double, your twin brother, as well as your cousin from Rosario who rescued me and brought me home.

For the purposes of our show at the Broken Heart, Maishe would appear in a different capacity entirely. He would wear a dark suit jacket and tie and comport himself like a butler. For myself, I was to wear a bustier and silk pantaloons with fancy slippers that curved up at the toe. Although I found the costume silly, it was more clothes than I had worn in public in a long time.

My job, for the most part, was to walk in front of the audience and wiggle my ass in order to distract them from your tricky hands. If this were all I had to do, I should never have endured it. But along with somersaults you taught me easy juggling, and this exhilarated me. I learned quickly, and it thrilled me to toss vases back and forth between us, to keep torches and even sabers in the air, spinning and dancing.

Each time we practiced I was reminded again that I had abilities we Jewish women were assumed not to have. That round women such as myself were believed not to be able to do a cartwheel, to spin a somersault forward through a hoop and wave at the end to the crowd. Hankus, what a thrill it was to learn that my body could do more than lay back on a bed and catch the semen of arrogant men. And better still, it seemed that all these new skills came naturally to me, that I had always known how to catch a plate or a torch midair! Still, it was my job to do these tricks and then bow toward you, who always topped my hard work with a backward flip or a spectacular handspring off the stage and into the audience.

I gave this attention over to you easily, for you had freed me. It put me in mind of that last day of my childhood when Tamar and I watched the magician cut his woman in two. To be the man was to get all the glory, but without the woman, what would he be sawing but an empty box? Ah, Tamar, to be the woman in the box was no shame. It had a kind of power all its own.

Now speaking of women in boxes, if my lovely assistantship was a simple matter, our impending wedding was a more complex one in every aspect, in all of its meanings. To the world you were a man and I a woman, but no ordinary woman, Hankus. No, I was a former whore. And as Marek Fishbein made very clear, what might be at best a scandalous arrangement under normal circumstances became now a public relations emergency. Like Madam Perle, your *Pan Tateh* Fishbein was most concerned with what his conventional Jewish neighbors thought, and clearly, they did not think well of us at all.

In truth, Marek Fishbein wanted to send for the rabbi immediately that morning he barged in on us, yes, just as soon as you signed his little paper. But thank God, Hankus, you figured out a way to buy us time.

"Marek, you're like a father to me and in matters concerning your own business, as I have told you time and again, I trust you implicitly."

The gangster's face was absent of any paternal gentility. "But in this case?" Fishbein snapped his fingers and his shyster brother-in-law procured a silver flask. Then he looked at me, with a new twist of disdain upon his ill-shaved face. "If you're going to live here, make yourself useful. Glasses for everybody!"

I went into the kitchen and found glasses. I spit into Fishbein's, making sure I gave him that one. Then I handed him a glass for me.

"What's this? This is men's business, what makes you think you can drink on it?"

"Pour me a finger, Fishbein, or I might start acting like a woman and never shut up."

He sneered at me and nodded to Moritz, who dribbled a few drops into my glass.

You waited, Hankus, while Fishbein sipped his schnapps, then sat back down in your seat. You watched while Fishbein reached into his pocket and procured two cigars. He offered one to you. You shook your head. "No? My boy, you've no idea how rare these particular tobaccos are." He opened your tiny hand and placed it in your palm. "Roll it between your fingers, see how good it feels."

"Very nice," you said, looking over to me. I said nothing, only stuck my tongue into my shallow glass of schnapps.

Fishbein lit his own cigar and settled back onto the couch. He became all business once more. "You were saying, Hankus?"

"Marek, if you want to call the rabbi and marry us right now, I won't complain—"

My breath caught.

"But frankly, *Pan* Fishbein—*Tateh,* I think it's a serious mistake."

"You're the one who's made a mistake. You, a fine upstanding *haimishista* boy living with this wicked maiden, this former *nafkeh!*"

"Yes, well, she is a *former nafkeh*—"

And what were you if you worked for Fishbein I wanted to ask, but I knew better. I kept my mouth shut.

Fishbein chomped on his cigar. He rubbed his face with his big hands. "But a man and a woman unmarried, living together..." Fishbein's eyes filled and he almost wept. Then just as quickly he stopped crying and looked up. "What mistake do I make?"

"Look here. I am soon to be the master magician of all Buenos Aires. My dream come true, my life to be entirely lived in the public eye." You sipped your drink, snapped your fingers, your schnapps glass disappeared.

"Precisely. The people will soon hate you as they hate me and my Varsovian brethren. Why do you think I set you up on Maza Street and not in some more convenient apartment on Rividavia? You think they'd rent to me on Rividavia? So near their precious *shul?* The *shul* that I helped build? It's a joke. I give half of those *shleps* their fun and games, no one will even sell me a corned beef sandwich! Those *shmucks* hate us—even when we do something nice for them, they can't wait for us to fuck up." He tipped Moritz's empty flask hopelessly into his shot glass. Then he rose without speaking, poked a finger at his lawyer, and said, "Moritz, go down to the corner and get another bottle of schnapps."

You snapped your fingers again, your glass reappeared, half full. "Have mine."

"Very good," said Fishbein, downing your schnapps, "but I'm still thirsty. Shatz," he signaled to his brother-in-law.

"There are still pressing legal matters," Shatz protested, pulling down the sides of his neatly ironed jacket.

"They'll be here when you get back. I'd send the *kurveh* but she has no clothes on. Go."

Moritz gave me a hate-filled look, then placed his well-blocked fedora upon his head and left the flat. Fishbein leaned out the window and called after him, "Ice, too, I'm *shvitzing* like crazy here." He sat back down and looked you in the eye. "Where were we?"

You suppressed a sigh. From your place across from him you studied Marek Fishbein, your benefactor, your pimp. There he sat, on the very sofa he had provided you, this slob who was one of the most powerful men in the Argentine underworld. He had grown men killed regularly for looking at him the wrong way or playing the wrong card in a pinochle game. Now he was looking you dead in the eye. "You know, little Hankeleh, as gangsters go I'm a generous man. You want an apartment in which to live, I find you an apartment. You want a tightrope stretched across Córdoba Avenue at 4:00 on a Tuesday afternoon, I make sure it happens. You want to hang upside down in front of the Libertad Street Synagogue, hang. Do I do this for myself? Is it all for me? Hankeleh, Hankeleh—of course not! I do it for you. Because a good magic trick gives me pleasure, reminds me of the lovely childhood I never had. You're going to do a magic show, Hankeh, so spectacular that even the great Houdini will be green with envy. Envy! Do I ask for one penny in return for all this? Have I asked for one *groschen*? Dear boy, no—no, no, no. And I never will. There is but one thing I want from you and yet you deny me the pleasure!"

You stared down at your gift cigar which by now had become soggy in your hand. "I deny you nothing, Papa Fishbein. I only suggest that for publicity purposes it would be so much better to wait—" The gangster jumped up again toward you, and you signaled him down. "Because all right, the community doesn't respond to a synagogue, they don't love you for a theatre, but what Jew, on this or any other continent, does not love the man who throws a wedding for his son and invites them all to partake of his pleasure?"

"Am I to understand you want to wait to get married until after your magic show opens?"

"That is precisely what you are to understand."

This interested me, and my own business *kop* began to whir. In spite of myself I chimed in. "We could get married on opening night. Right after the show. That way lots of people would come for the double spectacle."

Fishbein chewed his cigar and scratched his head up under his hat. He gazed out the window, then stomped on the floor with the full force of his muddy boot. "Of course! Why didn't I think of it sooner? We'll have the wedding as a kind of encore on your very opening night!"

I was about to remind that filthy *fresser* Fishbein that it was my idea, that I was the brilliant one, when you caught my eye and just barely shook your head. Fishbein, in the meantime, was slowly pacing the length of the apartment, planning slowly out loud. "I'll pay for everything. As remarkable as your magic show, that's how remarkable this wedding will be. I'll bring in lox from New York City and caviar from the old country!" He sat. "They'll be talking about this wedding all the way to Moscow. I'll take care of all the details, you won't have to do a thing." He stood and smacked you on the back. "You, of course, will be free to practice your magic day and night. I'll have Moritz place a betrothal announcement in the Jewish papers immediately...of course, we'll have to say that he's your uncle. It wouldn't do to have you so closely associated with me at this time. Later, when you're a really big name, you can make a public declaration, tell about my goodness to all who will listen. But for now, I will forgo that pleasure. Moritz, that idiot, will be your uncle—which, given that he is my brother-in-law, is practically true." He tapped his lip with the end of his cigar. "Now what do we tell them about Sofia—"

"*Tateh* Fishbein," you said, wishing that your newly declared Uncle

Moritz would please arrive with that bottle of schnapps. But Fishbein was uninterruptible. His eyes were glazed over with the glory of a time to come.

"We'll worry about her later...oh, can't you see it my boy? A midnight wedding! All of Jewish Buenos Aires invited! Even that *putz,* Goldenberg, just to show him I'm a sport and hold no hard feelings. Yes, just like the old country, all the peasants will come, we'll have music, we'll give them to eat, and Hankeh, Hankeh, they'll dance until dawn!"

You sighed, but you knew from the serene look covering Fishbein's face that we'd best go along. "Opening night will be marvelous, *Tateh!*"

"Yes, opening night. We'll see you both married on opening night!"

"Well," you said, gingerly lighting your cigar, "that takes care of that."

Not two days later our betrothal was announced in the Jewish papers, conveniently located in a column right next to an article about your spectacular new magic show opening five Saturday nights hence at the Broken Heart Theatre. Two days after that the papers featured an open letter from your ersatz uncle, Moritz Shatz, Esquire, inviting all Jews of Buenos Aires, young and old, to his nephew's nuptials, following "what will be the biggest, most breathtaking demonstration of prestidigitation and escape artistry on five continents."

My name, in all of this ink, was hardly mentioned, although once I was identified as a retired chanteuse (name withheld), and another time I was alluded to as Miss S. Teitelbaum, late of Warsaw, Poland. Your uncle, interviewed on the society page the following week, was quick to quash any rumors about my erstwhile odious livelihood: "If Miss Teitelbaum ever had a blemished past, I'm sure our Hankus never knew it. For he is a good boy, the very son of Cracow, and we remain ever and ever proud of him."

I was horrified and insulted by it all, but I was not surprised. You begged my forgiveness a thousand times. "Sofia, please understand. To have a show on the scale of this one...if there were any other way..."

I shrugged my shoulders. "Look, little man," I said with great irony, "business is business, and this is your way to do it. But here you see again the benefits a person gains by wearing always trousers and a well-cut jacket instead of a flimsy dress. At least we'll get a decent meal for our troubles. Who knows, maybe even a new bed. Finally I have a use for that cursed wedding gown, although God in heaven knows if it will fit me now."

"We'll have more than that, Sofia. For I will be the most respected magic-maker since Houdini. And all the world will know my name."

For how long, Hankus, would this be so?

— 3 —

ONE DAY WHILE I WAS ALONE in the flat, sewing shiny sequins onto my magic pantaloons, I heard a womanly foot upon the stairs followed by a gentle knock at our door. "Who is it?" I called in barely a whisper, because I didn't know if Tutsik Goldenberg had sent an assassin, or perhaps my dear Sara had at last come to her foggy senses and escaped.

"Red Ruthie," came the whispered answer, and in a minute I had thrown down my handiwork and unlocked the door. There she stood before me, to my delight and relief, wearing a broad-brimmed felt hat, white gloves, and a trim black suit. She looked for all the world up here on Maza Street like somebody's maiden aunt, not a whorehouse boss. She glanced over her shoulder and slipped into the apartment. Then she went quickly to the window and looked out onto the street. "Ah, no one has followed me." She took off her gloves and sat almost primly on the sofa. It was shocking to see her completely dressed in what were considered, in this neighborhood of Buenos Aires, respectable clothes. More shocking than this was the fact that all of the merriment seemed gone from her flashing eyes.

She put one hand to her bosom and fanned her face with the other. "I'm getting much too old for this cloak-and-dagger business. In the old days, it gave me great pleasure to give the boys the slip. Nowadays, too much trouble." She looked at me as if for the first time and took my face in her hand. "*Motek,* life away from Talcahuano Street is good to you—you radiate. Or is this merely a fact of love?"

I sat beside her on the couch. "Love, a little, and the freedom to walk around with all my clothes on, I think."

"It can be liberating to wear more than your underwear in certain circumstances," Red Ruthie said, "and I see you've taken to trousers."

It was true. I was wearing a pair of your pants, adjusted to fit my fuller waist.

"You don't go out on the street like that!"

"Red Ruthie, I barely go out on the street at all."

"That's wise, my child. If Tutsik Goldenberg finds out where you live, there's no telling what he will do to you...you've no idea what he's doing to those women, your sisters." She fanned herself with her hand once more. "Quick, *neshomeleh,* get your old aunt Red Ruthie a little tea." I went to the kitchen. "And if you've got it, a *biseleh* something sweet. It's a long way up here from the barrio, especially if a girl is looking over her shoulder all the while."

In a few minutes we were settled on the sofa. Red Ruthie sat with her tea before her, and I managed to find her a hunk of bread and a little jam. "So you are a show girl now, and engaged to be married. *Mazel tov.*"

I shrugged my shoulders in a noncommittal way. "Thank you, Red Ruthie. But you didn't come all the way up here for simple well wishes."

Red Ruthie took a sip of her tea and sighed. "Alas, Sofia, I have not. Things are very bad on Talcahuano Street. When you deserted your sisters, *motek,* you left everyone in a horrible mess."

"I?" I was tempted to take Red Ruthie's tea from her and show her out as quickly as I had let her in. "Life on Talcahuano Street, as I recall, was one horrible mess after another for many years before I left."

Red Ruthie pursed her lips and spit little *tsk* sounds from between them. "Until Perle Goldenberg left for the old country, you girls had it almost soft."

I stared at Red Ruthie, who had no twinkle in those black eyes now. No, those eyes were dull and flat. "With or without Perle Goldenberg, we were a bunch of *kurvehs* and we were treated as such by all concerned," I muttered, "including you."

Red Ruthie raised an eyebrow. The white powder she wore barely covered the wrinkles in her soft skin, and now, in the Maza Street light, I could see that her eye paint was on crooked and her red hair was streaked with mousy grey. "You may say what you like about me, Sofia, but I'll not hear one word against Perle Goldenberg. All I have today I owe to her." She took a sip of tea and smacked her cracked lips. "That brother of hers, on the other hand, is a millstone on all of our necks. A *choleryeh!* When I tell you what he has planned for your pal Sara, you'll see how in the old days you Talcahuano Street *nafkehs* had it better than most."

I shook my head, disgusted.

"I know he was bad before, Sofia, but now Tutsik Goldenberg is worse than ever." Red Ruthie settled back into the sofa and put her feet up. "Most of what I'm going to tell you I got from Marianna, for as your boyfriend Hankus was banned from Madam Perle's house, so was I. From time to time, when Tutsik is out of the house—and, my dear, those times are rare indeed—I sneak up for a visit with the girls. As you will soon see, that is what brings me here today." Red Ruthie sipped her tea. "Very good, Sofia. You've turned into a little *balebosteh*—"

"Get to your point, Red Ruthie. I'm growing impatient."

"Relax, dolly, this story takes a while. The first thing I will tell you is about Goldenberg himself. To see him now, Sofia, you would laugh out loud, for he has become a joke of himself. His trousers are stained in revealing places, and his once beautiful silk robe has tiny holes where hot matchheads fall. That Egyptian fez he wears, which looked absurd in the first place, is dented and frayed, and he can never keep the tassel out of his weasel eyes.

"Also, he wears a moustache, pencil-thin, which he now waxes and twists into two tight points. They jut over his lower lip like upside-down fangs. When Tutsik Goldenberg begins to pull on those fangs, to rub them between his fingers, watch out. It's a sure sign that someone is about to be slapped or punched, or maybe even worse."

Red Ruthie looked around our flat. "You have a view of the street from here?"

"Better than the old view."

"Hmm," she said, and rested her teacup on the table before her. "The long and short of it is that the man sits day and night in his fez and dressing gown in the middle of the parlor and sulks. Some days he smokes opium right out in public, then nods into dreams. His feet and hands twitch like a big sloppy dog. But when he wakes from his dreams, Sofia, Marianna tells me it is your name he calls. And after that, your beloved Hankus'. Then he snortles and spits, 'Oh, woe to them if I see even a hair of their sorry heads.'"

I sighed.

"On days he does not take opium, I am told he chews coca leaves. For he becomes a devil, a junkyard dog, meaner than he was before our dear Perlie left. He files his nails in the middle of the parlor like a Chinese emperor and cleans them with that deadly little blade he at one time kept hidden. And he slaps those girls something awful. It doesn't matter who's sitting there—it could be the mayor of Buenos Aires for all he cares.

"Rachel and Magda have learned to make a wide path around him. But Sara, poor Sara, take it from me, her face is a map of bruises because she is too stupid with opium to get past even Tutsik's slowest punches. And it isn't just the girls he picks on, either. His good friend Dr. Dorfman made the mistake last week of showing him your pre-nuptial announcement in the paper and then, God forbid, said that he wished you both well. In a matter of minutes that depraved Tutsik Goldenberg had him by the ankles and tried to hold him that way out a window. It was only some finger of goodness in Dov Hirsh's heart that stopped Tutsik before the poor doctor landed on his head on the cobblestones of Talcahuano Street." Red Ruthie sat before me shaking her head sadly.

"I'm sorry, Red Ruthie, but I could have guessed all this before you came to tell me. There must be something bigger, more pressing—"

"Oh yes, my dear. I have more to tell. But first, if you don't mind, a little more tea."

I dragged myself to the kitchen. After what seemed an eternity, I presented Red Ruthie a fresh cup.

She blew into it and said, "What is happening, my dear, is that Tutsik Goldenberg plans to sell Sara off to the cribs in La Boca."

I knew all about those cribs, Hankus. In the old days when Madam

Perle took us down to La Boca to make *tashlich,* how we passed them with so much dread and trepidation—both the stables themselves and the women unlucky enough to be caught inside them. Stick-figure women as Sara had become, women who were once *zaftig* and laughing. The thought of Sara stuck there like a starving cow broke my heart. When I answered Red Ruthie, it came out in fury. "Everybody knew that weasel Goldenberg would someday dump Sara there. That's no surprise. The real surprise is that he didn't do it the first chance he could."

Red Ruthie lifted her head haughtily. "You say that now, Sofia, because you are bitter. But I say it is a blessing on all of us that Perle Goldenberg has not seen what we have become."

And then Red Ruthie told me how it had transpired, and in my mind's eye I saw it all.

One cold afternoon, just before lunch, Sara heard a knock on her bedroom door. Perhaps, she thought, it was Marianna with her coffee. Just her luck, though, it was Dov Hirsh, empty-handed and laughing, it seemed, at nothing.

"Boss wants to see you," was all he said. His upper lip curled in a sickening smile.

"In the throne room?" Sara asked, because she still had it in her to give those *shmucks* a hard time.

Hirsh looked at her as if she were entirely stupid. "In his bedroom."

"Sure." She might have looked like a zombie, but she had not one ounce of submission in her voice. She tied her kimono around her, slipped her feet into her scuffed mules. "I'll go see his majesty at once," she said slowly. Oh, how I wish she had spit in that arrogant ass-licker's face.

It must have been strange to visit Tutsik Goldenberg in what was once Perle's private library. For so many weeks after Perle left, Red Ruthie told me, he never touched those rooms, left the books exactly as they were. "He treated them as though Perle truly left them, Sofia, entirely to you."

But less than a day after I ran for my life and left that hellhole, Tutsik Goldenberg decimated the library. He and Dorfman packed up all the books. Tutsik took them himself to San Telmo, where he sold them to a dealer. He hardly bargained for a price, and he did keep Perle's sex books—all but the one or two Dorfman managed to slip under his coat. "He goes back to San Telmo twice a week now to buy more," Red Ruthie said with a strange satisfaction. "He brags to anyone who'll listen that he is known far and wide as a smut connoisseur." And I could see it, Hankus, dealers absolutely wild to pull Tutsik Goldenberg over and show him what they had hidden at the bottom of their carts. "Like Perle, he comes back from the stalls with books wrapped in brown paper, but what different books these are!" Red Ruthie chuckled. "Please, dolly, open a window just a touch."

By now, as Red Ruthie told it, Tutsik Goldenberg had filled the shelves of Madam Perle's once sacred library with exotic pictures of all kinds of depravity: men and women, women and women, men and men, men and beasts of all kinds, engaged in acts that even the likes of Sara would find unspeakable. It didn't matter that he had live women around to look at and abuse. In fact, he hardly looked at Magda or Rachel or Sara at all. The picture books consumed him as his drugs did. He spent hours fingering the pictures in provocative ways, and if a person came to talk with him and he was this way engaged, that bag of scum never even bothered to look up—except if it meant money or a big fight.

When that *toches licher* Dov Hirsh summoned Sara to him, Tutsik Goldenberg was busy studying a picture book full of naked women. The perfect joke on Perle, he lay the profane book upon what was once her holiest study desk and examined it with a gigantic magnifying glass. Sara knew she was doomed, for as soon as she crawled into his study, Tutsik played the ends of that stupid moustache between his fingers.

"Your pet rat, Hirsh, said you wanted to see me."

Goldenberg glared and put the magnifier down. He drummed the table with his fingertips. "This is how you talk about our little Dovy now? The two of you used to be so close. Like brother and sister." He shut his book with a *thump*. Without a word of warning he slapped Sara hard across the face. She grabbed her mouth and fell backward. Then, she couldn't help it, she started to laugh.

Tutsik played his moustache ends between his fingers. "I'm so glad you find this funny, Sara." His arm shot out and he slapped her again. This time she tumbled onto the floor. He crossed his arms and stood over her. She stopped laughing, but the ends of her mouth curled up just a bit into a smile.

That snake Goldenberg sat down and pushed a gummy ball of opium into a clay pipe. Sara's eyes got big then, and Tutsik, just to torture her, waved the bowl of the unlit pipe under her nose. "You think this is for you? It isn't for you."

"Too bad." She rubbed her throbbing cheek.

"When you carried your weight around here, it might have been. I never minded treating you to my private stock once in a while. To show my appreciation." He set the pipe on top of the picture book. "But as it stands now, Sara—" oh, he spat her name—"not only don't you pull your weight, you're dragging the rest of us down with you. We're all sinking into the same quicksand as you."

She stared at her tormentor. A new laugh formed in her swollen mouth, but she pushed it back into her throat and swallowed it whole. She found a cigarette in her kimono pocket and lit it. She smoothed the frayed toe of her satin mule. Then she eyed the clay pipe once again. "What is it you want?"

Goldenberg's eyes became wide. He held up his picture book and pointed to a page. "Women are supposed to be beautiful. See here? Classical beauty. Rachel has it. Little Magda will acquire it. Even that sow, Sofia Teitelbaum, may her soul roast in hell, she has it too." He held her face between two fingers. "Men pay a great deal of money for the privilege of touching classical beauty like this, sticking their *shvontzes* into it, coming all over it." He dropped her face and began to twist his moustache again. "But they have to see it as real beauty or they don't want it." Quite suddenly he threw his book across the room. "You were beautiful once, *Tante* Sara, but now you are just a corpse. Yes, a living corpse."

Sara dragged on her cigarette and eyed Tutsik's pipe once more. She looked into his rheumy eyes. "So you don't like my looks any longer, big deal. What's your point?"

Tutsik took his knife out and pointed it straight at her throat. "I can't afford to keep you and you can't afford to buy your way out. Dov Hirsh, God bless him, had the good sense to recommend the cribs in La Boca months ago, but I dragged my feet because I thought perhaps you might see the error of your ways and come back to us. But *meineh Tante* Sara, just the opposite has happened. You become thinner and thinner and more and more vacant. You are not worth your weight even in copper *pesetas*. You are a drain on me in all ways, pathetic Sara, and so I've authorized Dov Hirsh to bring you at last down to La Boca and get what he can for you. At least those sailors will get their money's worth."

It took almost a full minute for Sara to understand those horrible words. She thought, Did he say *cribs?* and answered herself, Yes, cribs. Then a terrible shudder ran through her.

"It's really a shame," Goldenberg continued, as if he were chatting about a polo match, "because here we are in the middle of winter. In your current condition it's unlikely you'll make it past the holy days."

Sara looked hard at Tutsik Goldenberg and then at her stubby whore hands. She wondered if she might not have the strength to strangle him on the spot. She decided to act as if he didn't mean a word he said. "Stop trying to scare me, Goldenberg. Even you couldn't possibly betray me. After all, this is Sara Koblentz, your sweet *Tante* Sara." It disgusted her to do so, but she put an arm around his shoulders and gave him a little squeeze. She ruffled the tassel of his fez. "How many women did I lull to sleep for you on those long trips across the ocean?"

But Tutsik Goldenberg brushed Sara off him like a handful of rice at a wedding. He adjusted the lapels of his foolish dressing gown and straightened his hat. "Sentiment is boring, Sara, especially from the likes of you." He looked down at his fingernails. Instead of cleaning them with his tiny knife, he simply bit them. "We'll take some time to fatten you up, if such a thing is possible. Then Hirsh will accompany you to La Boca, where he will find that water rat, LaMarc. A pitifully small cash exchange will occur, and you will be gone from this house forever. Alas, you'll miss the social event of the season."

"Oh?" Sara asked, trying to keep the tears out of her voice, "and what is that?"

Goldenberg walked over and picked up his book. He flipped to the back, retrieved a copy of the Jewish paper, and handed it to her. "It doesn't say her name here, but your honeybunch Sofia and her prestidigitator boyfriend are having a wedding. The whole family's invited. Says so right there." He tossed Sara the paper. She read it and her heart stopped.

"But this cannot be!" she shrieked.

"Take that paper, Auntie Sara, and get out of my sight. I've work to do. Can't you see what a busy man I am?"

Sara clutched the newspaper to her breast. "You're too kind," she spat.

"No, Sara. If I were truly kind, I'd choke you to death."

"Why Tutsik Goldenberg, I was just thinking to do the same to you."

She stumbled back to her room and a minute later heard the door lock behind her. Tutsik and Hirsh mumbled something to each other in the hallway, but she didn't care. She sat with the wrinkled Jewish paper stretched across her lap and read with disbelief the notice of our betrothal over again. She thought to herself, Impossible! She thought to herself, How brazen and full of *chutzpeh* can two people be? So stunned was she by this news that she memorized the article. *Escape Artist to Wed Polish Chanteuse* it said. It made her blood run cold.

Half an hour later, Dov Hirsh unlocked Sara's door and presented her with that familiar silver tray on which lay Tutsik Goldenberg's own beautiful clay pipe, a vial of opium, and a box of wooden matches. "Compliments of your boss," he said, smiling.

She looked at the tray. For one second only, she thought she might turn away from it so that her brain could have the clarity to think. But when Dov Hirsh touched that vial of opium and made as if to put it in his jacket pocket, Sara forgot all reason and grabbed the whole business out of his hands.

"For ten years of loyal service," Dov Hirsh sneered.

Get out of my sight was what she wished she could say. But she was too busy filling that cursed clay pipe.

In the days that followed, even through her sticky haze, Sara mulled over the facts of our engagement. Each time she could not believe that she remembered it right, that it wasn't just a smoky dream. And so she unfolded the newspaper and read the item again and again. She wanted some kind of reprisal, revenge, and the bitter taste in her mouth surprised her. She had heard revenge was sweet, but perhaps it was the act of it they meant—the pulling of the trigger, the twisting of the knife, the practical joke that ended with a look of supreme mortification on the face of the victim. That was what Sara craved, the taste of blood on her lips, but for once not her own. It was someone else's blood she longed for, and God forgive her, in her insanity, her jealousy, you know who it was she chose.

Now Hankus, I myself know what it's like to live a life like Sara's. Didn't I often hunger for revenge myself? Didn't I want, all these years, to fix Madam Perle for the bruised arms and split lips, those daily indignities of overzealous mackerels and bloody underwear?

But me, I aimed my bilious fury at Tutsik Goldenberg, who did the lip-splitting on behalf of his missing sister Perle. If all of us whores ever thought about it, we might actually plot to assassinate Marek Fishbein or set a bomb in the Varsovia Society's Buenos Aires headquarters. Better still, we'd set fire to the Cossacks and Jew-haters who drove us to Argentina in the first place and were, after all, the true source of our troubles.

In circumstances like Sara's, however, the *nafkeh* is not the clearest thinker.

She saw the fist in her face all right, and she even saw that it was Tutsik Goldenberg who planted it there and Perle Goldenberg who left him to plant it. But what hurt Sara more than the slaps and the punches was the fact that I had gone and left her, that I had escaped with you, my darling magician, and poor Sara was left to endure her indignities alone.

Red Ruthie looked anxiously around our little flat. "Listen, *motek*, things have gotten very serious." She reached into the bosom of her dress and pulled out a thick, scented envelope, unsealed, with my name scrawled upon it. "Here, *motek*. You may read for yourself the rest."

> Meineh teier shvester *Sofia*,
>
> *Why have you forsaken me? I have never in my life felt so alone. Each day, I hope against hope that you will come for me. I study the faces of each new customer, regard their build carefully, for perhaps it is you or Hankus in disguise. Perhaps Dr. Katterfelto will come one more time to save another Talcahuano Street* kurveh, *but, alas, it is never so.*
>
> *It is now many weeks since you abandoned me here. I waste into a bag of bones. My hair hangs thin and greasy about my face like bits of string. Basherter! Basherter! I am old, old, old.*

Our tormentor, Goldenberg, has horrible plans for me. In a very short time he will send me to the cribs in La Boca. As if this were not torture enough, he has chosen to torment me further with the terrible news that you and your Hankus are to be wed. But how can this be? Even if you were nothing to me, Sofia, and my heart were not shattered at the news, a wedding between you and Hankus is against all laws, yes all laws, even those in our shabby moral universe!

It makes me laugh, Sofia, and it makes me cry!

I do not tell you until now, Sofia, but since your arrival in our Talcahuano Street hellhole—no, since I first saw you in the dim light of your hotel room in Plock, and then in our shared bed aboard the ship Viktorius—*I never said, I know, but I felt for once that my nightmare life might at last become bearable. Something about you, Sofia, so touched my heart that I allowed myself for the first time a dream of the future, though I also let my cursed opium pipe wash those dreams away.*

When you and Hankus fell in love I was left utterly alone. You think I did not know what went on between you? That I did not notice how you two spoke a secret language? You two were like those cheap mind-reading acts one saw all the time on the streets of Moscow in summer. You know the ones—they must have had them in Warsaw—the magiker *cries, "You, young lady, think of a number, now write it down," and all the time the lovely assistant is looking over that girl's shoulder so that with a wink of the eye and a secret code of gestures, she can pass the magician that private number. You and Hankus spoke to each other in Madam Perle's parlor with that same semaphore language of eye blinks and coughs, secret finger signs and smiles meant only for the two of you. How I hated you for it! I knew that sooner or later you would leave me to my own sorry fate.*

Oh, you may say, Sara, what a foolish little twit you are! You are not alone. What of Rachel and Marianna? What of silly young Magda?

But Rachel is a simpleton, smiling all the time, laughing at everybody's jokes no matter how they diminish her. She endures her lot like Job. For all these years she sits across from me at dinner, for all the johns I have heard banging into her in the next room, do I even know her? I bring out the fear in Rachel of what she might become. She sees my despair, my seeming hollowness of heart, and doesn't she worry that one day she will be like me? This despair has not killed me, yet Rachel worries that surely one day it will reach in and murder her.

Marianna believes herself to be in a higher station than we whores, and she is right. She has mothered me in strange, cold ways, but she has never been my friend. In time, wait and see, she will leave this house, too.

As to little Magda, she is young, younger even than you were when first I lay with you, and you know as well as I that for weeks and weeks after Hirsh delivered her to our door she did nothing but weep. She has a sweetness but she lacks your intelligence, Sofia. She has not one inch of the smartness you carry in your body, both in bed and in the parlor, or seated at table. I have not the pleasure of that smartness now. That smartness belongs to Hankus. Oh, I could kill you both, but I will not. I could kill you, but then you could not rescue me. And Sofia, rescue me you must. Who else is there to do it?

You have become respectable at the very minute that I, Sara, am to meet my demise. You are to marry, in a huge and dignified wedding, to which all of Jewish Buenos Aires will come and dance. And your groom-to-be is that cursed magician who is no man at all. No, Hankus Lubarsky isn't even a man, she is a woman like me! And this fact, my beloved, is the gun I will use to save my own life.

Neshomeleh, *darling Sofia, it is only a matter of days before LaMarc returns and Dov Hirsh will carry me off to the* nafkeh *garbage heap in La Boca. I have written this down to you in hopes that Red Ruthie, who burrows into our house from time to time, will deliver it to you before it is too late. Tutsik Goldenberg may not know where the Escape Artist keeps you, but Red Ruthie has her ways, and I know she can discover you.*

Come to me, Sofia! Free me from my horrible fate! Else I have no recourse but to tell all I know.

I remain yours,
Sara Koblentz, with love

I folded the pages of Sara's tight script and stuffed them back into the envelope. Red Ruthie sat on the sofa, her tea glass empty in her hand. "Have you read this?" I asked her, but I knew the answer.

"Of course, every word. But I knew the secret before it was written. Take my advice, love, and get out of town."

SWEET HANKUS, the very next Sunday we were to open! How could we look this threat our Sara was offering right between the eyes? Darling Hankus, how could we not?

We still had so much work to do: there were winches to check and mirrors to place, handcuffs to oil and locks to spring. Every two hours, it seemed, either Marek Fishbein, or Sholem Big Sam, or that shyster lawyer Moritz Shatz arrived at the theatre to beleaguer us with wedding details and wedding questions. There was caviar coming, for example, in a shipment from Odessa. How did you feel about having it molded into the shape of handcuffs? There were cases of sangria coming on a steamer from Spain. Would you object, Hankus, if it flowed from a fountain mixed with champagne? Faced with these decisions which, presented as they were by Marek Fishbein, seemed a matter to him of life and death, and our own rehearsal, we had barely a moment to ourselves.

Then two evenings later, yes, two nights before our very opening, as you were preparing to wiggle out of your ropes, and I to assist you, it seemed, my love, we were saved.

On that very night, a tall thin man with jet black hair and a handle-bar moustache to match presented himself at the door of the Talcahuano Street bordello. He wore a broad-brimmed black hat, a cheap sharkskin suit, and extraordinarily pointy black shoes. "Constantin LaMarc to see Tutsik Goldenberg," he told Marianna in a thick French accent.

Marianna reluctantly called Goldenberg down from his smut-filled library and the man, in the meantime, poured himself a drink. He stood with uncommon ease in the whorehouse parlor, an elbow draped over the mantle, and sipped his schnapps slowly as he took in the sights, which at this moment consisted of Rachel, sitting in a blue satin lounging robe filing her fingernails, and Magda, in a nearly trans-parent camisole playing pinochle with a seemingly ancient gentle-man in very fine formal evening attire.

Dov Hirsh was at the card table, cheating himself at solitaire. Dr. Dorfman sat in the big stuffed chair puffing on a second-rate cigar and reading the Jewish paper.

Goldenberg made his way downstairs at last, sporting his ratty smoking jacket, his dented fez, and his newest affectation, a gold-rimmed monocle, stuck against his right eye. The man in the cheap suit put down his drink and met Goldenberg halfway across the room. He extended a hand and said in French, "Tutsik Goldenberg, I pre-sume?"

Goldenberg put his face practically into that of his visitor. "You are not the French pimp, LaMarc. I have met LaMarc, and you are not he."

"I am not the man *you* know as LaMarc," the visitor said in broken Yiddish, "for I have been in Buenos Aires less than twenty-four hours. I am *Constantin* LaMarc, brother of the LaMarc you know. We ar-rived just yesterday on the steamer from Nice. When we arrived at my brother's flat there was a note from your man Hirsh explaining that you had a woman here for him. Ah, we thought, what better way to acquaint myself with Jean Pierre's business associates than to come and get the baggage myself."

Tutsik Goldenberg looked at the man through his monocle and examined him from head to toe. Quite suddenly he pulled on the man's moustache. LaMarc grabbed at his upper lip and called out in pain. *"Monsieur,* I don't understand what it is you do!"

Goldenberg suppressed a chuckle and shrugged. "So sorry, *Señor,* but just weeks ago I had some trouble with a bearded man who was not at all what he seemed." Goldenberg studied the face of this LaMarc once more carefully. He came nose to nose with him and peered into his eyes. No, there was not one familiar aspect about him. He was neither you, Hankus, nor your partner in crime, Maishe. He moved close to Constantin LaMarc one final time just to be certain. No, neither was the man in question me.

"I was told that you Jews had strange customs of commerce, but I had no idea it was this." Constantin LaMarc rubbed his upper lip again with the tips of his fingers and cleared his throat.

"No, I suppose not," said Goldenberg, "but a man in my position is better to be safe than sorry."

"Perhaps this is so, *Monsieur,* but you have little to fear from me." He shook his head, then pointed first to Rachel and then to Magda. "Which of these ladies is the bundle in question?"

Tutsik Goldenberg breathed a sigh of relief. How easy it had all become for him now. The burden of Sara could be got rid of immediately. He would waste not one minute more. "Neither of these is the package you've come for," said Tutsik Goldenberg. "That parcel, sir, is waiting upstairs."

There was a huge commotion at that moment coming from Sara's room, a great clattering of objects and smashing of glass.

"Ah, Sara is awake now, I see."

Rachel looked up from her nail filing as LaMarc ascended the stairs. "She's cut back on her opium and won't go quietly."

Goldenberg sat back on the fainting couch. "Those LaMarcs are quite used to this. He'll have her wrestled to the ground and out of here in no time." Goldenberg fingered the twenty gold *pesos* LaMarc had handed him for Sara's ass, sight unseen. It wasn't much, but Tutsik didn't haggle when LaMarc offered it. Sara was like a cow with hoof-and-mouth disease. As far as he was concerned, he was lucky to get even twenty *pesetas.*

There was a crash from the top of the stairs. Magda's elderly card-playing opponent cleared his throat and drew out his pocket watch just as something large and unwieldy thumped against Sara's bedroom door. He pushed a small pile of coins near the youngest *nafkeh* at Talcahuano Street, leaned over, and kissed her on the cheek. "Good-bye, my dear," he said in gruff Russian Yiddish. "It's getting a little rowdy in here for an old man like me."

"You can't leave now," Dov Hirsh laughed, "the fun's just begin-ning."

"My wife is meeting me at the opera."

"Too bad," said Dov Hirsh, "this here's a good show."

"Yes, but my old ticker can't take too much excitement." All the men laughed and the old man made as if to leave. Just as he shuffled toward the front door, Sara's voice tore down the stairs. "I ain't going anywhere!" she shrieked. "I'll not be sold to you or any other flesh peddler just to die like some sick she-ass in a cold, sorry stable!"

There was another thump against the floor above all of their heads. Constantin LaMarc let out a muffled "Ouch!"

"I know something!" they all heard Sara shout out. "I know some-thing about Hankus Lubarsky! Tell Goldenberg!"

There was more scuffling and another shriek from Sara. "Tell Goldenberg I know something about Lubarsky, and when I tell him, he will set me free."

With that, Rachel sat up tall. Even Marianna came out of the kitchen, holding a dishrag in her hands.

"Perhaps you should go up there and see what she's talking about," Mordechai Dorfman offered.

"Don't bother, Tutsik. A girl will say anything when she's at the end of her rope." Dov Hirsh grinned horribly. "Besides, the sound effects are best down here."

Tutsik Goldenberg adjusted his monocle and walked toward the foot of the stairs. "You don't think I should hear her out?"

"You got your twenty gold *pesos*," said Rachel calmly. She gazed over to Marianna who only stood and shook her head. "What could she possibly tell you about Hankus Lubarsky that you don't already know?"

"Really," Hirsh chuckled. "She's probably going to announce that Lubarsky's engaged to be married."

Tutsik tapped his pink finger against his chin. "Maybe so, maybe so," he murmured. "But perhaps it is better to be safe than sorry..."

He moved tentatively toward the stairs just as Sara shouted again,

"I tell you, I *know* something!" There was one final crash, after which the whole *shandhoiz* became eerie and silent.

All assembled in the parlor, including the old john who had moved back from the door as the fireworks increased, looked at each other with wide eyes.

"Has he killed her?" the man asked.

"Not if he's already paid for her," answered Rachel flatly.

Magda's pale eyes filled with tears.

After what seemed like an eternity, Sara's door creaked open, and all eyes, however blurry, were trained on the top of the stairs. Constantin LaMarc appeared with Sara, completely limp, draped over his shoulders like a *tallis*. In one hand he carried a small carpetbag into which he'd stuffed a few of Sara's belongings. In the other he held, wrapped in a handkerchief, what appeared to be a hypodermic needle. This he stuffed into his suit jacket pocket. He looked down at all gathered at the foot of the stairs. "She was a little difficult to manage," he said in broken Yiddish, "so I was forced to inject her with laudanum."

"Laudanum?" Dorfman was incredulous. "Where does a man like you acquire laudanum?"

"That's a stupid enough question," muttered Rachel. "He gets it from quack doctors like you." She took one last look at her sister prisoner and went up the stairs in disgust.

LaMarc followed her with his eyes. He adjusted Sara's body in order to cradle it in his lanky arms. The old man watched in horror.

"So there's still a little life in her, eh?" Tutsik sheepishly followed LaMarc to the door.

"I should say." LaMarc nodded with his head to the scratches on his neck and his ripped shirt collar.

"She didn't say more about what she wished to tell me?" Goldenberg held his fingers for a moment on the doorknob before turning it for the French pimp.

"After the injection, *Monsieur*, what more was there to say?"

"When she comes to, LaMarc, if she should happen to have a message for me, you will have someone fetch me down to La Boca so I can talk to her, won't you?"

LaMarc shifted uncomfortably under Sara's dead weight. He looked nervously over to Magda who, with each passing second, was becoming more visibly upset, and to the old man, who had his fingers tangled in the hairs of his beard. "I'm afraid, *Monsieur* Goldenberg, that this will be impossible. Your *Mademoiselle* Sara's services are needed on a freighter full of mercenary soldiers bound in just two hours for Germany."

All, including Tutsik Goldenberg—even Dov Hirsh—were genuinely shocked at this news. "By the time she wakes up," continued LaMarc, "this woman will be in the middle of the South Atlantic Ocean and no one will give a fig about the news she has to share."

"Oh my God!" shrieked Magda, and she ran into the kitchen.

The old man said nothing, merely walked toward the door with his head hung sadly. He left with LaMarc and his charge.

Twice did this story come to us, Hankus, both times on our opening night. Each time it was horrible music to our ears.

The first to tell was Red Ruthie, who was at the Broken Heart Theatre to fix my hair and help me dress. Since she knew our biggest secret, we reasoned, she might as well be trusted with them all. She's like a bridesmaid, we told Marek Fishbein, and he agreed to let her do this job because he could think of no other woman himself.

"It's a lucky thing for you they took Sara away," she said, *tsk-tsking* and whisking the hair from in front of my eyes.

"A lucky thing indeed," you said, oiling your gold handcuffs and checking the mechanisms one more time. You looked at me with that magician poker face and whipped the handcuffs quickly about your own wrists.

"But how lucky for Sara?" asked I.

Red Ruthie *tsk-tsked* once again, her mouth full of hairpins. "On a freighter full of mercenaries...well, maybe fortune has smiled on her and she's dead by now. I can't imagine a crueler fate."

You said nothing, only flicked your wrists as the cuffs flipped open. You spun them into your pocket and stood straight away on your hands.

A half hour later, as Red Ruthie was helping me into my bustier, there was a knock on the dressing room door. "There's no modest women in here," called Red Ruthie.

"Come in, Hankus," I said, "the door isn't locked."

Oh God in heaven, I wish it had been. In a minute, there in our dressing room doorway stood Dr. Mordechai Dorfman. I felt cold as ice, and more naked than I had during many of my years on Talcahuano Street. The doctor stood with a small bouquet of yellow roses in one hand, a dripping umbrella in the other. True, he was the least of my chief tormentors, but the sight of him here, in my most joyful and private life, sent a chill through me. I knew he wasn't coming to wish me well.

Red Ruthie quickly stood between us and handed me a wrapper. "*Reb* Dr. Dorfman," she said, "you're breaking all your master's rules."

"Quite correct, Red Ruthie. This visit is strictly against policy," he mumbled. "It is plain to see, however, where *your* loyalties lie."

"I have always been in favor of the girls, Dr. Dorfman, make no mistake about that. Lucky for you I'm not speaking to Goldenberg. If he should find out that you've come to the enemy camp, and bearing gifts, too, there's no telling what piece of you would pop up first in Buenos Aires harbor."

The doctor shuffled his feet and stared into his roses. "I suppose it would be too much to ask to see Sofia alone?"

Red Ruthie opened her hands to me. I felt terrified that he was sent to take my life, and so I put on a tough face. "You can leave me alone with the good doctor for five minutes," I told her, "and you might tell Hankus we have a guest."

Dr. Dorfman came to attention like a little dog. "I've no business with Lubarsky," he said. The short hairs at the back of his neck stood up.

"I'll tell him you're here anyway," said Red Ruthie. "He'll be happy to know this, provided he isn't hanging upside down from the rafters like a bat."

With that she left us, but the door stayed open.

Mordechai Dorfman took the opportunity to look me up and down in a way I never noticed at Talcahuano Street. "The magician's life agrees with you, Sofia. You're looking very well." He offered the roses. I took them, although I would rather have spit in his face. "Raining is it?" I asked him.

He inched closer to me and bowed his head sadly. "Like cats and dogs." I backed away. "But I have come not to talk about the weather. I have, unfortunately, some terrible news."

I knew what he was going to tell me and the roses felt suddenly heavy in my hand.

"A French pimp came and paid twenty gold *pesos* for Sara the other day. We thought he was taking her to his brother's cribs in La Boca. Instead she was taken to a ship full of soldiers and made to sail for Germany."

"And none of you cared to stop him since Goldenberg got his money."

Dorfman stood and looked at his muddied shoes. "Unfortunately, that is true." He sighed heavily. "I knew her since she was a very young woman, just past from being a little girl." He reached out to touch my face. I turned quickly away.

"You watched her grow up the same way you watched me, eh Mordechai?" I threw the flowers onto my dressing table. "With your mouth shut and a lock on the door."

Dr. Dorfman shrugged. Then he took my hand into his own and kissed it. To my surprise it was a rather sweet kiss. Nonetheless, I tore my hand away. Dorfman sniffed and laughed just the tiniest bit. "It is my truest regret, Sofia Teitelbaum, that I did not gather the courage to steal you away from Talcahuano Street and marry you myself."

"Dorfman, you are joking." A laugh escaped me.

Dorfman looked stricken. "*Señorita* Teitelbaum, I have never been more serious in my entire life." He reached for my hand once again, and who knows what else he would have grabbed for if at just that moment, Martín, one of Maishe's acrobats, hadn't stood in the door. Martín, a normally calm man, tall, dark, incredibly good-looking as men go, jumped back a bit when he saw Dorfman. He pointed to his pocket watch. "We open the house in half an hour, Miss Sofia," he said in Spanish.

At the sound of Martín's voice, Mordechai Dorfman became startled and turned around to get a better look.

"Forty minutes to show time."

"Oh my, is it after seven already?" Dorfman looked quickly at his own watch. "I must run," he huffed. "I'm to meet Goldenberg and Hirsh at the *shandhoiz*. Then we will attend the festivities together."

"How nice to know you'll all three be here," I said, not one shred of sincerity in my voice.

Mordechai Dorfman looked around for Martín, but the acrobat was gone.

"I must fly," said the doctor, and without another word, he ran down the hallway and out the stage door.

Here is what I think happened next:

There was something in Martín's voice, something in his easy stance in the dressing room doorway that Mordechai Dorfman recognized at once. As he made his way down the backstage hall and out into the pouring rain, Dr. Dorfman pictured our friend Martín in a bad suit and a handlebar moustache speaking broken Yiddish in a phony French accent on the night of Sara's departure. The doctor also remembered back to Magda's ancient card player on that same night. He thought about the old coot's height, his beard, about the way his suit hung on his shoulders. Dr. Dorfman recalled, as he walked quickly but in a kind of daze through the heavy drops as they fell about him, another gentleman who came calling at the Talcahuano Street whorehouse not three months before. A doctor like himself, he thought, with the same shoulders and a similar stance who wore just the sort of beard the older gent wore, only that fellow's was grey and the old man's was snow white. And as Mordechai Dorfman slogged his way through ankle-deep puddles and muddy rivulets, never thinking even to open his umbrella, he did a kind of arithmetic that was dangerous to the likes of you and me.

"They've done it again!" he slapped himself as his shoes filled with water. "They've duped Goldenberg out of another *nafkeh*. But why would they save that used-up trull, Sara? What was it, what was it that bitch claimed to know?"

Mordechai Dorfman stood on the corner of Paraguay and Maipú streets while the rain ran down his hat brim and into his collar. He used what was left of his faded physician's intelligence to unfold the mystery of what someone as wasted as Sara could have on you. He imagined you, Hankus, from head to toe: your sparkling eyes, your serious mouth, your Dr. Katterfelto shoulders, your tiny hands—

"The hands!" Dorfman shouted out loud into the teeming downpour. "Hankus Lubarsky has tiny, delicate hands like a woman! *A woman!* Lubarsky is a woman, and Sara knew all along!"

Now under normal circumstances, Mordechai Dorfman might have kept this information to himself. He was not an ingratiating man like Dov Hirsh and, realistically speaking, there was nothing he could gain from winning Tutsik Goldenberg's favor at this point in the game.

But I had, just fifteen minutes before, thrown aside Dorfman's roses. He had opened up his heart to me after all these years, and I laughed in his pitiful face. Limp as his backbone was in the face of rotten men like Tutsik Goldenberg and Dov Hirsh, Mordechai Dorfman still had it in him to be insulted by a common whore. He was a man, after all, and not only had I tossed him over, I had tossed him over for the likes of you. And you, Hankus, were no man at all.

As if for the first time Mordechai Dorfman noticed he was soaking wet. He opened his umbrella and ran as fast as his drenched feet would take him to the Talcahuano Street *shandhoiz*. "I must tell, I must tell. I must tell what I know."

5

BUT LET US NOW IMAGINE OTHER THUGS on that same momentous evening, as they likely found themselves just hours before our show was to begin.

Marek Fishbein's proudest night, and for this reason he must arrive at the Broken Heart Theatre at the top of gangster style. He steps from his hot and fragrant bath, dresses with the help of his lawyer brother-in-law, Moritz Shatz, who adjusts Fishbein's cufflinks and straightens his cravat, only to watch them slip and pop in a matter of minutes into typical Fishbein disarray.

Sholem Big Sam Horowitz, sent to collect Marek Fishbein's motor car, slides in behind the wheel and starts the engine. It was he who always drove the big yellow-and-black Packard, shipped all the way from England and used exclusively to transport Fishbein from his villa on the Tigre River to his daily business in the City of Good Airs. Moritz Shatz, on the other hand, was assigned not only the thankless task of trying to keep Fishbein well-groomed, cigar hole and gravy stain-free, but also to carry the gangster prince's briefcase, and today, as on all rainy days, to hold an umbrella over his damp brother-in-law to prevent him from getting wetter than he already was.

By the time Fishbein got out of his mansion and into the car, even in those three short minutes, the biggest pimp in Buenos Aires, a completely nervous wreck and wearing his second clean shirt in an hour, was already soaked again with sweat. Although the gangster had combed his hair and beard only moments before, curls and cowlicks were springing up everywhere under the brim of his top hat and throughout his beard. Moritz sighed heavily and did his best to keep Fishbein under the giant bumbershoot. But the gangster was a tall man and Moritz came up just to his shoulder, so while Fishbein was protected from the plunging raindrops, the lawyer was as soaked as his illustrious brother-in-law by the time they got into the car.

"You think people will come out in this rain, Big Sam?" Fishbein dug into his vest pocket for a cigar.

"Oh sure, Boss. Big party like this one? Of course they will."

To Moritz, Fishbein said, "I'm *shvitzing* like a pig in here, open a window."

"Marek, I'd love to, but if I do it'll rain all over you."

"I'm *shvitzing*, I tell you. Either way I get wet."

All the way into Buenos Aires proper, Fishbein *kvetshed* and *krechtsed* about the rain, about the wedding, about the lavish and complex arrangements, spewing cigar smoke while he talked. Nonetheless, in spite of himself he found he was completely pleased when they drove into Once. For even in this torrential downpour, Jews were flocking toward the Broken Heart Theatre three and four abreast. "Look at this." He was positively cheerful. "They come out in the pouring rain to watch our little magician, to attend our wedding! They wade through water up to their assholes, do they care? Look at this!"

"It's good, Marek," Moritz said.

"Better than good!" Fishbein growled at his brother-in-law. "A magic show with a pretty girl and fabulous tricks, this is one thing. But a magic show with a pretty girl and fabulous tricks followed by a Jewish wedding and feast guaranteed to last three days and nights—ah!" He breathed out a long stream of sticky smoke. "I'd call that a work of genius!"

Moritz couldn't resist. He had to shine his fingernails for one minute on his own soggy lapel. "Well, the *magiker yingeleh* is my ersatz nephew after all."

Fishbein felt his breath leave him. How dare that upstart of a lawyer take credit for any part of this, the greatest moment in Varsovia Society community relations. When word of this coup got back to Odessa, why Fishbein wouldn't be surprised if the brotherhood voted him king, and not just of Buenos Aires, but of Constantinople and Johannesburg besides. "And whose big idea was it that you even act like Hankeleh Lubarsky's uncle? Who assigned you that role?" Fishbein reached over and held his brother-in-law by the throat. "Tell me that, *Señor* Mouthpiece. Who thought it up?"

"Well actually," said the red-faced attorney, "I think it was Big Sam's idea."

There was a little thud as Fishbein pushed the lawyer into the side of the car. "Sholem, was it your idea?"

Big Sam looked at his boss through the rearview mirror. "You know, Boss, I don't think it was." He scratched his head and then his clean-shaven cheek. "I think it was yours."

Moritz gulped down a mouthful of bile. "Why yes," Moritz purred as Fishbein eased his grip, "it was your idea, Marek. It comes back to me now."

"That's good," said Fishbein, "that's very good." He removed his hand and put two fingers around his cigar. "Because I would hate for Big Sam to have to clean a bloody car up half an hour before the proudest moment of my gangster life."

Meanwhile, on Talcahuano Street, Dov Hirsh and Tutsik Goldenberg waited none too calmly for Mordechai Dorfman to arrive. Goldenberg was dressed in a full suit of clothes for the first time since his sister left for the old country, and while there was nothing actually wrong with the way he looked, compared to Marek Fishbein for example, his old snappiness, his shine, had all but disappeared.

"My, my," said Dov Hirsh, as he peered out the window and into the soggy night, "this weather don't bode well for Marek Fishbein's blessed events."

Goldenberg glared at Dov Hirsh as he took an ivory toothpick from his vest pocket. "What I mean is," the mackerel leaned back into his chair, "what self-respecting Jew likes to go out in the rain? Sure, those wonder Jews, the *Hassids,* they sometimes find pleasure dancing their little circles in the snow. But I never met one Jew, religious or otherwise, who likes to get covered from head to toe by pelting rain. That's one thing I don't like much about Argentina. A man is always up to his *pipek* in muck and mud."

Goldenberg picked at a piece of lint on his jacket. "No Jew likes it," he said. "Reminds us too much of the old country. Why do you think so many of those Zionists come running back to the city from places like Moisesville?"

"Not enough cobblestone under the feet," answered Hirsh, poking the toothpick into his gum. "Why leave the *shtetl* just to live in the *shtetl?*" Dov Hirsh winked at Tutsik Goldenberg and pointed to his own head. "No, the Jew wants city life. Indoor plumbing, nice suits, and, if he can afford it, a motor car."

"Well then," said Goldenberg peevishly, as he tried in vain to pare back his once impeccably manicured fingernails, "the Jews have come to the wrong place. It won't stop raining again until Yom Kippur. I begin to envy little Sara and her seafaring jaunt to Germany."

"I don't know about that." Dov Hirsh sucked the end of his toothpick, then popped it back into his pocket. "But I do wonder what Jew is going to want to come to a big fancy wedding in their best clothes in the middle of a downpour. Think of all them muddy hems and high-button shoes. The cobblestones were already slippery when I came over an hour ago. What Jew will come watch that *goldeneh yingeleh* today?"

"We'll be there," said Goldenberg flatly. "That is, if that idiot Dorfman ever arrives."

Hirsh picked up a deck of cards and shuffled them flamboyantly. He flipped them over into neat solitaire piles. "Yes, I wonder what's holding him up. Perhaps he misunderstood and is waiting for us at the theatre." He stopped for a minute and cocked his head. "Kind of quiet around here. What did you do with the ladies?"

"The ladies are entertaining themselves this evening." Goldenberg held out a key. "I've taken the liberty of locking them in."

"Like lap dogs," snorted Dov Hirsh.

"Get the umbrellas," Tutsik Goldenberg said suddenly. "I'll not wait for that *shmendrick* Dorfman one minute more."

By the time Tutsik Goldenberg and his crony Hirsh were out on the sidewalk, torrents of water were swirling through the cobblestone streets. Normally, Hirsh might dash out into the rain, umbrella in hand, and walk up to Once, but his pal Goldenberg had barely been out of the flat except for trips to the dirty bookstalls in San Telmo, and he moved like an old man. Goldenberg looked shrunken in his street clothes, and hard-eyed. There was no light within him, and here on the street, in the midst of this downpour, Tutsik Goldenberg seemed not to exist at all. He stood paralyzed in the *shandhoiz* doorway and stared. "I've seen nothing like this rain in all my days," he said dreamily. "Perhaps it is a sign from God."

"Look, Tutsik," Hirsh said, because he had known him since the old days in Warsaw, and in spite of his own hard heart felt somewhat responsible for Goldenberg, "it's hell out here. No one's going to notice if we don't show up at the theatre. Besides, why should we? We wish all of them ill. Come back upstairs, Tutsik. Marianna will fix us both a brandy, I'll fill you a pipe. Mordechai Dorfman will tell us about everything we missed." Hirsh could hardly believe he was saying this because he himself had looked forward for weeks to these events, never mind for once, since he got to Argentina, to having a decent corned beef sandwich.

"I'll see it with my own eyes or not at all," said Goldenberg.

"Well then," Dov Hirsh answered, "I'll find us a taxi."

They peered together through the rain for signs of life. Indeed, contrary to Dov Hirsh's prediction, there were many. Jews appeared under umbrellas, walking in droves toward Once as if on their way to *shul.* They moved in groups of three or four, men mostly, and many young women, who walked under parasols and held their skirts tight around them, fairly skipping through the sheets of rain.

"Well, I'll be damned!" said Dov Hirsh.

"No, they will," said a man's voice, a voice that came from a water rat in a three-piece suit with a silk umbrella held over his head. A familiar voice that emanated from a body plastered head to toe with mud.

The rain at last began to stop. Hirsh none too gently bundled Dorfman into a blanket and squeezed him between Goldenberg and himself in the back of a taxi. Because even he, the cruelest of Tutsik Goldenberg's cronies, could see the value of keeping Dorfman warm, he gave him a swallow of brandy from his hip flask. Goldenberg leaned toward

Dorfman and looked into his eyes with no tenderness. "All right, you charlatan—just exactly what do you know? How will you slander my beloved Hankus Lubarsky?"

The doctor took another suck off Dov Hirsh's flask. "Oh, Goldenberg, not only Lubarsky, but Sofia Teitelbaum as well. The two of them and who knows how many others have duped you in a dozen ways!"

"Name one," Goldenberg demanded, "besides the obvious kidnapping of Sofia Teitelbaum from my business establishment."

"That was just the tip of it, Tutsik." Dr. Dorfman wiped his face with a soaking-wet hankie. "Hankus Lubarsky came and took Sara out of your whorehouse the other night as well."

Goldenberg made as if to punch Dorfman right in the nose, but the quarters in the taxi were tight and he was weak from the already exciting events of the day, so his swing had no power. Dorfman stared at Tutsik and didn't shrink back. "That French pimp was a practical joke and I'll bet you a thousand *pesos* that the old geezer playing cards with Magda was Lubarsky in the flesh."

"Why would they steal that broken-down piece of ass?" Dov Hirsh was incredulous.

"It was all an elaborate ruse to keep Lubarsky's secret safe," said Dorfman with conviction. "They knew what Sara planned to tell and so they stole her away."

"Dear God," Goldenberg let out, and then he was laughing. "Dr. Dorfman, you water rat, you are lying through your teeth. Sara is at this very minute on a freighter being reamed through by dozens of mercenary soldiers, if they haven't already tossed her over the side."

"I am willing to bet you an additional thousand *pesos*, Tutsik Goldenberg, that she is not."

Goldenberg stared at Mordechai Dorfman, whom he had known for many years, his first business associate in Buenos Aires. "Did you see Sara with your own eyes?"

The physician downed the rest of Dov Hirsh's brandy and handed him the empty flask. "Indeed sir, I did not."

Goldenberg waved his hand in front of his own face. "Well, if you didn't see her, then how do you know she isn't on that boat full of gorillas?"

"Because I saw the man who calls himself Constantin LaMarc this evening. And Monsieur LaMarc the second is no LaMarc at all, he's a stagehand for Hankus Lubarsky."

They were all three silent in the taxi as it made its way to the Broken Heart Theatre. At last Goldenberg said, "All right, then. Even if every word you say is true—and I am not convinced by any stretch that it is—what kind of secret could Hankus Lubarsky possibly need to protect so badly that he'd go to these great lengths?"

Dorfman took a deep breath. He was relieved that they were all sitting down and that he was a little *farshnoshket* besides. "Hankus Lubarsky is a woman," he hissed, still barely believing it himself.

"Impossible!" shouted Goldenberg.

"Oh, Tutsik," Mordechai Dorfman shook his head sadly, "only think about those dainty little hands."

They were all three silent for a minute. Suddenly Tutsik Goldenberg lunged at Mordechai Dorfman and grabbed him by his waterlogged lapels. "Did my slut of a sister Perle know this? Was this part of her plan to supremely humiliate me?"

Dorfman pushed Goldenberg away and whispered, "Who knows, Tutsik? These women tell us none of their secrets, but foolishly we tell them all of ours."

Goldenberg stared with absolute hatred at Dr. Mordechai Dorfman. He would have tossed him out of the taxi if he could have.

Finally Dov Hirsh chirped, "Now that we know it, couldn't you tell? Couldn't you see it from the way Hankus held himself and held himself back?"

Goldenberg stared out the window. His voice was cold and lifeless. "In retrospect, I might have known it the night we set him up with Sofia. But it really doesn't matter who knew it when. Because we all know it now. All but that buffoon in a monkey suit, Fishbein. Yes, my friends, divine justice is operating swiftly." Tutsik's eyes became clear and cold. "Tonight I will bring Marek Fishbein so profoundly to his knees that no man will ever fear him again. Yes, yes. Lubarsky and that whore Sofia will do their magic act. Before the world, a man will be tied up in knots and untie himself, juggle an entire kitchen of pots and pans, tumble and somersault through space. Before the world, a man will bow and be hailed as the greatest magician the Jews of Buenos Aires have ever known. And before God, a man who has been living in sin with a sinful woman will marry her and make her pure.

"And I, the keeper of the secret, will bide my time and hold my tongue. I will hold my tongue until the happy couple has promised themselves to each other unconditionally, for all eternity, 'til each has said their final 'I do.'

"I'll wait until that Hankus Lubarsky stomps upon the wedding glass and all those gathered, faithful and profane, gangster and goody two-shoes alike, have shouted out their *mazel tovs*. And then, in front of everyone, I'll rise and tell it, from the very farthest reaches of that cursed Broken Heart Theatre. 'Marek Fishbein's precious *goldeneh magiker* is a woman! His prodigal son a girl!'"

6

AT LAST, HANKUS, our opening night.

Do you remember it? It was to be the beginning of your dearest wish come true, and what an auspicious start: Every plush seat in the Broken Heart Theatre full! People standing on tiptoe in the back and crowding all the way down the aisles! At the door, a cigar stuck in his mouth, in his too-tight tuxedo and his soiled white shirt, a diamond stickpin jabbed into his spotted cravat, didn't our cursed benefactor Marek Fishbein look like the proudest papa? Wasn't he the very picture of the father of the bride? Master of all ceremony, there he stood, gloating for the world to see.

He was flanked on either side by his idiot brother-in-law and Sholem Big Sam Horowitz, each dressed in a navy blue suit and tie. They wore *yarmulkes* and looked as if they were waiting for their nephew's *Bar Mitzvah* to begin. Which in a way, it was.

It was difficult to say which was more exciting to the assembled crowd—the prospect of our magic show, or the prospect of our horrible wedding. People paid their money and made their way to the best seats. All the boxes and balconies of the Broken Heart Theatre were full for the first time since the Varsovians built it. Ushers in red jackets and white gloves, their pillbox caps tilted to one side, showed people to their places with surly pride. Skinny women in tutus walked up and down the aisles hawking chocolates and cigarettes. Fishbein wandered through the crowd and waved, kept himself busy shaking hands with gangsters and rabbis alike. "Welcome friend, welcome!" he told each. "You'll stay for the wedding I hope? Food all the way from the old country. Scotch whiskey, too, and vodka from my home-town of Odessa. Yes, you must stay and partake, *Señor!* Enjoy, enjoy, enjoy!"

For ourselves, Hankus, we were treated to a huge bouquet of gladi-olas and roses, irises and lilies. Was it for a funeral or for congratula-tions? It was hard to tell the difference. There was a note in the flow-ers. You recognized Sholem Big Sam's businesslike handwriting, al-though the message was clearly from his boss: *To my talented twosome, for all the joy you bring me, Love, your Papa in Spirit, Marek Fishbein.* This made me not only uneasy but sick to my stomach as well. But not you, Hankus. No, you were busy breathing. Like one of your gangster benefactors preparing for a heist, you played the whole act out in your head. Each tumble and spin, each trance and escape, you were doing it all without lifting a finger, for this was to be the best night of your life.

When at last all the audience was seated, when Fishbein and his cro-nies had taken their places in their special box, Martín walked into our dressing room and gave us a nod. The lights dimmed. A hush of anticipation swept through the audience. The footlights came up, and with a bang the band began to spill wild Jewish music into the theatre. The audience, filled with the promise of what was to come, stomped their feet in time, until at last the curtains parted.

All at once, there you were. Hankus Lubarsky—somersaulting for-ward from the back of the stage toward the audience, flying through the air, head over heels, head over heels, until you stood before them in your fine, slightly baggy tuxedo, your red bow tie, your lips curved into that warm and generous smile.

You bowed to the right, and Maishe appeared in his well-fitting tie and tails. You bowed to the left, and I appeared in my sequined bustier.

The men in the crowd hooted and cat-called when they saw me, but once we began our sorcery, their mouths froze open in silent awe.

I handed you a walking stick. You turned it into a violet scarf, and then a bouquet of marvelous roses. Maishe revealed a table of vases. You changed the water inside each from clear to crimson to emerald green, then back to diamond clear. You called for volunteers from the audience, and two of Maishe's troupe, dressed like sailors from La Boca, came onto the stage and tied you upside down. In a matter of minutes you were free of your bonds, which earned you a roar of applause from the crowd.

You pulled a small peacock from inside my ear. You somersaulted backward and stood on two hands, then one hand, then for a minute you seemed to stand on no hands at all. You looked for all the world to be suspended in thin air.

You flipped to your feet and clapped your hands.

Now I came forth with five Indian clubs which I juggled, Lubarsky, one by one to you. We juggled together until at last it was you kept all of them up in the air. For minute after minute they spun through space until Maishe entered with three lit torches, which he juggled to me and I juggled to you. You mixed them in the air with the clubs, then juggled the clubs back to me until you had all lit torches aloft, and me, I juggled the clubs.

While you kept those torches high above your head, Maishe arrived bearing a butcher knife, a cleaver, and a pitchfork. The knife he juggled to me, the cleaver to you. I passed you my knife, you passed me one torch, then another, and suddenly, there I was, juggling three, while you, Hankus, you flashed the sharp kitchen tools around and around through the air. I made the torches disappear and Maishe threw you the pitchfork, which joined the cutlery as it circled in front of you, behind you, under your legs and over your head.

At last there was a drumroll and all became quiet. You balanced the pitchfork on your nose, then flipped it into the stage so that you yourself were balanced on its handle. Then upside down, atop that pitchfork, you juggled knives and cleaver, and out of nowhere you were juggling lit torches and the Indian clubs, too.

With each addition to your circle of motion, the audience gasped. When, as if by magic, there you were, standing upright, the knives and clubs in one hand, the lit torches in the other, the crowd was on their feet, stamping and screaming. My darling, they went wild. For they had seen jugglers before, they had seen acrobats, some even remembered watching you spin the holy Torah on the balls of your feet. But never had they seen you, their most beloved Hankus, doing everything at once.

You bowed a humble bow, clapped your hands, and the music became mysterious and slow. I entered next in a silk top hat and velvet cape. With great ceremony, I placed that hat upon your Lubarsky head. My Hankus, you lifted the cape off from my shoulders and swept it up onto your own.

You snapped your fingers and on their tips a dove appeared, then another and another. You clapped your hands and these doves flew into the air. You took off your top hat, reached in, then in a flash brought forth nine fabulous scarves, each one longer than the next and the next. You stuffed them all back into the top hat and reached in again, this time producing one luxurious scarf of all the colors, which you pulled out of that top hat for what seemed forever.

Then it was Maishe and I wrapped you up in that brilliant, luxurious scarf. We tied you in knots, covered you over, head to toe, until the music stopped. It was I clapped my hands this time, and the scarf fell to the ground. Maishe took it up and searched within its folds, but Hankus, you were gone. The audience gasped as Maishe and I held the beautiful cloth up to prove to all that you, our beloved magician, were absolutely disappeared.

The music started up again. Maishe rolled out a lacquered box as big as a person. He opened the doors and folded them flat into a remarkable lacquered wall. We spun the wall around to show everyone there were no hidden panels, there was no hidden Escape Artist. We folded the wall back into a box, and draped the huge scarf over the top. Then we spun that box around and around before the audience's very eyes until suddenly, didn't that scarf begin to disappear into the box? When the scarf was completely gone, I stood aside and opened my hands to the audience. Maishe did the same.

All at once the box burst open, and there you were, our Hankus, your hands locked in your golden cuffs, and didn't the crowd explode!

Suddenly there was green smoke. When it cleared, it was I stood with my hands in cuffs and you, Hankus, were once more disappeared.

Then hand over hand from the back of the Broken Heart Theatre you somersaulted onto the stage. You spun down the aisle in a blur. You bounded forward and landed with ease at the edge of the stage on the tips of your toes.

You bowed and you smiled. You unlocked my cuffs. I bowed with you as well. The audience rose to their feet and clapped their hands to the music, they stomped their feet and they cheered. There was a drumroll. You somersaulted off the stage, Hankus, and I followed. Then all of your acrobat stagehands, led by Maishe, tumbled off the stage behind us. The crowd whistled and howled and shouted *Encore!* until Fishbein and his idiot lawyer appeared.

"Ladies and Gentlemen," Fishbein said (someone in the audience started to boo), "as a special treat to you, our most beloved members of the Jewish community in this, our exile home, sweet Buenos Aires—"

Somebody shouted, "Pimp!"

Fishbein reached for his pistol, but Moritz grabbed his hand before it made it all the way out of his pocket. The gangster narrowed his beady eyes into the audience and began again. "As a special treat to you, our most cherished brethren and sisters in the City of Good Airs, I, Marek Fishbein, and my associate, uncle of the Escape Artist, *Señor* Moritz Shatz—"

"Shyster!" someone shouted.

Fishbein merely shrugged. "Perhaps. Nonetheless, he is the uncle of our own Escape Artist, Hankus Lubarsky—"

The applause was deafening for a full minute, until Fishbein could stand it no longer and this time did bring his pistol out and shoot it into the ceiling. Now the crowd became quiet, although by no means compliant.

"Listen to me, Jews! In just a few minutes, the Escape Artist and his lovely assistant, Sofia Teitelbaum—"

"Whore!"

Fishbein overlooked this completely and went right on talking.

"—will be married right here on the stage of the Broken Heart Theatre. We want you to join us, each and every one. The ceremony will be short and sweet, and then afterward," there was some heckling but Fishbein spoke right over it, "I will provide for you the most spectacular old world meal you have ever seen in your life. It would make your grandmother, *olehe v'shalom*, weep, so sweet and delicious it will be."

As he spoke, Martín and two other acrobats assembled a wedding canopy behind Fishbein, full of spectacular flowers. When the acrobats stepped away, the audience became hushed again, they *oohed* and *aahed*, so lovely was the *chupeh* before their eyes.

"So stay right where you are, and be our guests at the wedding they will talk about in this city and cities the world over for the next thirty years!" Fishbein looked behind him and saw that the *chupeh* was completed. He clapped his hands once and a man dressed as a rabbi walked onto the stage. Then he waved his cigar at the band. "Maestro, a wedding march, please!"

How the band played! What music! It almost made me want to get married.

I was elated not just by the band or our splendid performance. There was a score I was about to settle. For I would not shame my mother one minute longer. That foolish wedding dress of mine was about to be put to excellent use. This made me extremely happy, giddy even. It pleased me, but not more than the fabulous way I had spun and flown through the air that night! I had passed you lit torches and helped with all your vanishing. And now we were about to perform our greatest trick, our lives as we know them were about to begin. I only regret, darling Hankus, it would cost us your beautiful dream.

The crowd clapped in time to the music and Fishbein could not be contained by the Broken Heart stage. Merrily tapping his feet he leapt down into the audience. He grabbed old friends by the shoulders and shook them with pleasure.

So full of music and excitement was the Broken Heart Theatre, so stuffed to the gills with people ready and willing to dance down its beautiful aisles, that no one saw those three vermin—Dov Hirsh, Tutsik Goldenberg, and that traitor to us all, Mordechai Dorfman—hidden away in the back of the theatre, yes, hidden away and ready to pounce.

Fishbein, Shatz, and Sholem Big Sam Horowitz didn't see them, nor Red Ruthie and the women of her house, nor even Rachel or Magda or Marianna, who had released her wards and joined them in a kind of joyful disguise. Nor Sara—wait, was she truly there? Maybe yes, maybe no. Who can say.

There was no drumroll, only the sweet wedding music of our *klezmer* band. Fishbein's rabbi stood on the stage in his holiday best. At once all eyes were trained on the theatre's center aisle where four veiled women carried me aloft in a chair and four men carried you. I, the bride, was draped head to toe in white lace. A linen *tallis* draped you, Hankus, the groom.

The Jews of Buenos Aires watched as, like two Torahs, we were carried aloft and loved by the crowd. The grand music made old people and Marek Fishbein weep because it brought them back again to the lands of their childhood. When at last we, the happy couple, were brought up to the stage and set down under the *chupeh,* and the rabbi began the earnest work of joining us as one in the name of God, a reverent hush fell over the crowd.

"Bride and groom," commanded the rabbi, "take one another's hand!" All witnessed as he spread the *tallis* from your shoulders over both our heads. He charged you with loving me in my good health and bad, with riches or in poverty, to all eternity we were to love each other well. Me he charged with being your helpmate, your footstool, your truest love. When he asked would we do this, all gathered held their breath as I nodded my head, and you, Hankus, said, "I do."

The crowd gasped in pleasure as first he gave us wine to drink from a silver cup, and then he put his hands on both our heads and blessed us forever in the eyes of God almighty and all those gathered in the Broken Heart Theatre on that night. And just as the rabbi laid the marriage glass down at your feet, just as Tutsik Goldenberg, that weasel, was getting ready to leap onto the *bima* and condemn us to a certain death, three acrobats appeared with your long and magnificent scarf. On a signal from Martín, the band leader nodded to his players. Before those congregated knew it, the theatre was full of mystical music and your huge and wild scarf flashed. A puff of purple smoke filled the stage. When it cleared, the space beneath the *chupeh* was empty. We were vanished! Poof, we had disappeared!

A hush of anticipation fell over all assembled. Fishbein, the rabbi, and Moritz Shatz looked out into the congregation as if the bride and groom would at any second come tumbling back down the middle aisle. When after a few minutes it became clear that we would not, all turned their attention to the empty *chupeh,* and up above it to the rafters. Nothing. No one. All that remained of the wedding was that lovely piece of silk and our unbroken wedding glass.

Then the hush turned into pandemonium.

Fishbein madly felt his way through your glorious silk scarf until, satisfied that no one was hidden within its folds, he shot it full of holes. Moritz Shatz, silver-plated pistol in hand, made a methodical search of the velvet curtains, while Sholem Big Sam shook down the acrobats, assuring them he didn't want to hurt anybody, but where, where, where was the little magician and his bride? But as much as Big Sam shook the acrobats, limp as noodles they became, or they slid over backward and pretended not to understand the gangster's terrible Spanish.

The audience, our wedding guests, were delighted. Not since the days when the English clown Frank Brown blessed their Buenos Aires stages had they seen such expert physical humor.

"Play something!" the rabbi shouted to the *klezmorim*. They did, a bouncy little tune to which the wedding guests, those lively Jews of the City of Good Airs, began to dance. And while they were dancing, and Big Sam was shaking, while Moritz searched the battens and trapdoors, and Fishbein held his sorry pistol in the air, Tutsik Goldenberg leapt onto the stage from his hiding place in the shadows.

With the little strength he had, he grabbed Moritz Shatz's silver-plated pistol out from the solicitor's slippery hands and aimed it at Marek Fishbein. Like Rumpelstiltskin, he stomped up and down until he nearly made a hole in the floorboards. Everyone was quiet. There he stood, Tutsik Goldenberg, shaking and quaking, prepared to retrieve his ruined moment. He twisted the ends of his moustache and looked out over the dumbfounded congregation. Before any other Jewish *porteño,* sacred or profane, could utter another peep, Tutsik Goldenberg, bedraggled and brandishing Moritz Shatz's shiny little gun, puffed himself up. "Be happy, Marek Fishbein, that your wedding was not consummated! Be grateful that this wedding glass remains whole! For your pride and joy, your little Hankus Lubarsky, is no man at all."

The crowd gulped.

Tutsik continued. "Thank God they have eluded you! For their sin would have become your own. Your betrothed sweethearts are two girls, not one girl and one boy!"

Marek Fishbein stood on the stage of the Broken Heart Theatre, his own pistol still in hand, and looked at all assembled. "Liar!" he shouted, and pointed his pistol at Tutsik Goldenberg, who did not move. Fishbein pointed the pistol at himself. The crowd gasped. He pointed it at the rabbi, who ducked. He aimed that gun out into the congregation, which hid itself under their seats.

Then, without warning, and in spite of the huge number of witnesses, Marek Fishbein once again turned his pistol on Tutsik Goldenberg, and shot him on the spot.

EPILOGUE

El Escape Maravilloso Final

HOW MANY SAW THE TWO YOUNG women dressed up in bonnets and bustles with gloved hands and unopened umbrellas walk out of the Broken Heart Theatre and down Rividavia Avenue that rain-streaked Saturday night? Who saw them board the train for Rosario at ten minutes past midnight? They had between them one trunk only, and the conductor who saw them to their first-class seats wondered if they were sisters. You said nothing, only wiped a tear from your sad brown eyes. "Yes, sisters," I told him, "off to the pampas."

"To family?" the conductor asked in that juicy Argentine Spanish.

"In a way. Our new home."

It was a long ride, and tiring. We ate from the food basket Maishe and Red Ruthie packed for us. You polished off the red wine almost single-handed, then fell asleep. The night felt endless, lonely, but at dawn there it was, the Rosario station. We hired a wagon and I drove the horses the rest of the miles to Moisesville, our colony home.

We arrived late in the day and went straight to the People's Housing Authority. We gave our names as Sofia Teitelbaum and Hannah

Lubarsky. The woman behind the table stared at us. Was she remembering another Lubarsky due here once long ago?

They found us a room for the night. In a week's time we were given a little plot of land all our own. With the help of the other colonists and the money Maishe lifted from the box office for us, in a year's time we had a tiny ranch and a dozen sheep to tend. I learned to ride and to rope.

You were made endlessly sad then, for your glorious life as Hankus Lubarsky was once and for all converted. But it was Max and Motke's dream come true, and you held it with their memory in your broken heart. Indeed, we saved our lives.

You are the village locksmith. For the children and for old time's sake, sometimes you pull *pesetas* out of ears. Once or twice, when neighbors sit at our table for *Shabbes* dinner, you take out the scrapbook that tells your story. Yes, here was the great Hankus Lubarsky, Escape Artist, whose finest hour was his opening night. *Your brother?* the neighbors ask. *Me*, you say, in a clear strong voice, *the Escape Artist was me*. They look at you now, your black hair piled atop your head, wearing a long skirt and those marvelous leather boots, and they don't know whether or not to believe you. You snap your fingers, and when a vase of roses suddenly appears on our table, they nod and shrug and say, *Maybe so*.

Most days, on the edges of Moisesville, out on the pampas, a *zaftig* woman rides a white horse. That woman, who swings her lariat high into the air, can capture lost sheep and cattle with one sweep of the rope. That woman on a white horse is me. Not bareback in a circus dress, nor on my head; not riding with some john on my lap, nor I on his. No, I wear proper gaucho clothes: a broad-brimmed hat, wide pants, a jacket made of wool.

Sometimes with the tight leather reins in my teeth, I think about *tefillin*. I think about a life where I might ride this horse, you atop its head, juggling flaming torches, flipping them forward and back like the old days, a spectacle of fire and dazzle, white doves and rubies springing from your marvelous lips.

In the end, one trick:

I stand barefoot on our steed's sturdy back. I lift you high in one hand, you in your fine linen shirt, your black trousers, your bare pink feet. A drum rolls, the horse's hooves beat steadily across the pampas grass. Before us, a huge and burning hoop. All is silent as we barrel through, together, tumbling and landing so surely on that horse's back, hand in hand, as hooves pound.

Now at last we are free.